TREE OF GOLD

Books by Rosalind Laker

TREE OF GOLD

ROSALIND LAKER

DOUBLEDAY & COMPANY
GARDEN CITY, NEW YORK
1986

Library of Congress Cataloging-in-Publication Data

Laker, Rosalind.
Tree of gold.
I. Title.
PR6065.E9T7   1986   823'.914   85–31210
ISBN 0-385-23193-8

TO SUSAN AND IAIN

My grateful acknowledgements for kind help and advice to Karen de Lewandowicz and Brian Kilcoyne of the Macclesfield Heritage Centre and Silk Museum, and Robert Goodden and Colin Mayes of Worldwide Butterflies Ltd. and Lullingstone Silk Farm, Sherborne, Dorset.

TREE OF GOLD

Nobody could have foreseen the danger. Least of all Gabrielle Roche, who was being driven to her wedding through the narrow medieval streets of La Croix Rousse, the silk weavers' district of Lyons. It was the first day of spring, 1804. The sky was a clear morning blue with a few harmless white clouds drifting light as dandelion down. The sunshine slanted down the stone walls of the ancient buildings, leaving in shadow the deep-set, black-timbered doorways, and gleamed across the worn slabs of dark alleyways leading to inner courtyards.

The windows on the street-level floor of every house were wide and high, allowing plenty of light to enter the weaving workshops and loom-rooms, the square panes reflecting back the day's brilliance with prism colours through which the wedding carriage passed. In its wake it left the scent of the garlands, tied with love-knots of satin ribbon, which bobbed on the horses' harness and swayed in loops around the domed roof.

Gabrielle, outwardly the traditional bride, young, composed and ethereal, put aside on the seat her bouquet in its starched white frill. "We'll see our weavers soon now," she remarked eagerly to her elder brother, who was escorting her to the ceremony. "I must be ready to wave to them."

Henri Roche sat squarely opposite her. At thirty-six he was fifteen years her senior, an overweight, abrasive man, and at her words his mouth compressed to a line of irritability in his florid face. The weavers were of no interest to him except when at their looms. His only concern at the moment was to get his sister to her venue with the least possible delay. He disliked the fact that she had asked for a moderate pace to be kept throughout this district in order that she might make her farewells without haste to a part of her life that was at an end. In his opinion she should never have been allowed to visit the weavers' homes from childhood and take instruction like a common apprentice. Yet the truth was she had been born late in their parents' marriage and, left motherless from birth, she had become an outcast with nobody in the family to really care about her or supervise her, a wild young girl with a mind of her own. Discipline had been introduced far too late.

"I hope this won't take long," he commented uncompromisingly.

"You need have no fear of that," she replied confidently. "Time is too valuable to these hard-working people. You should know that after all your years in the silk trade."

Word of her approach was going before her. Children of the community, posted as look-outs, were scampering across the cobbles to wave a bright rag of silk to the next in line. Sighting them, Gabrielle sprang up to call from the open window, knowing each one by name. Then the monotonous noise of the looms was stilled briefly as those who served Maison Roche, alerted by the signals, came clustering out of their homes to give her a cheer and a wave as she went by. Silk was in her blood as it was in theirs, and they respected her for it.

"Oh, thank you so much!" Gabrielle caught the nosegays, mostly of wild flowers, that were thrown to her, petals scattering over the carriage floor. Henri took his gold fob watch into the curve of his soft palm and noted the time impatiently.

"We're going to be late," he informed her.

Unconcerned, Gabrielle continued to stand waving back to the family group at each doorstep. The craft of weaving involved the whole household from the grandparents down to the youngest child, their lives revolving around the loom that occupied a large section of their living space, and she appreciated these joint demonstrations of goodwill. Weavers were a stubborn, independent breed of people, many of them owners of their own looms as well as of others rented to neighbours, and they lived by their own rules and guarded their traditions jealously. For that reason she considered herself fortunate to have been accepted into their community during her weaving days.

She gave a final wave as the carriage left the last street inhabited by those she knew and resumed her seat in a rustle of oyster silk. The Chantilly lace of her wedding cap wafting light as a cobweb. Her smile hid the pang the partings had given her.

"We can proceed now at a faster rate."

Henri grunted. "Let's hope for no further delays of any kind." He gave the ceiling of the carriage a sharp rap with his gold-headed cane to remind the coachman of earlier instructions to make up for lost time when the moment came. The order was promptly obeyed with a burst of speed that made Gabrielle clutch at the seat to steady herself.

Although Henri was unable to view her in any other light than as his sister and an objectionable nuisance whom he wanted out of the family home as much for his wife's sake as his own, he accepted that her looks, particularly on this day in her wedding garments, were above average, a marketable asset that should have ensured a far better marriage of convenience than the one on which she was about to enter, if only she could have been persuaded otherwise. Now she was about to wed a solemn intellectual, the owner of a silk farm with almost no conversation in company and no liking for the social pleasures of city life which she had enjoyed. As far as Henri was concerned, she was getting exactly the bargain she deserved after the trouble she had been to everyone. Consulting his watch once more, he gave another rap of his cane as a spur to still greater speed.

Neither he nor Gabrielle heard the warning shout to the coachman from a bystander who was able to see beyond a Renaissance archway through which the carriage was about to pass at full pelt.

"Look out, citizen!"

It was too late. Seconds later Gabrielle was tossed from her seat as the wheels of the carriage collided and locked with those of another that had emerged ponderously from a side street. In the crunching impact Henri was thrown back in the corner, holding his breath, his eyes tightly closed, as the carriage teetered precariously. It hung suspended at a sharp angle for timeless moments until the terrified horses, straining to bolt, jerked it free. As it crashed down again onto its wheels, he fell across Gabrielle, half crushing her with his weight. Managing to get back onto his knees, he pulled her forward into a sitting position.

"Are you harmed?" he demanded, hoarse with anxiety. If the collision had not been such a sobering one she might have allowed amusement to come through. It did happen occasionally that brides being given into marriages of convenience made last-minute bids for freedom if any chance presented itself, and he had been on tenterhooks ever since they left the house. He had no need to worry. She had no intention at this late hour of rescinding the decision she had made after many hours of deliberation.

"I'm perfectly all right," she answered breathlessly, touching her lace cap to check that it had not been disarranged. "Make sure nobody else is hurt."

"It's the horses I'm worried about." He helped her back onto the seat. She accepted his support thankfully, more shaken than she had at first realised, and in looking out of the window she saw what he had already seen. Her spine stiffened and she sat as though frozen, taking automatically with nerveless fingers the bruised nosegay that he had rescued from the floor. Their carriage had collided with a cortège hung with funereal drapery, its black horses plunging their plumed heads in snorting agitation and alarm, nostrils dilated and eyes rolling, hooves stamping the cobbles. It was a bleak sight; one to strike a chill on such a day. The mourners had broken rank from the procession in the rear to swarm forward and view the situation, a midnight crowd in their sober clothes, some red-eyed from grief momentarily forgotten in current outrage at what had occurred. As Henri prepared to alight, she put a white-gloved hand hastily on his arm.

"Do apologise to the bereaved family," she urged, knowing his obdurate nature. "It must have been our coachman's fault."

To her astonishment, he glowered back over his shoulder at her from the open door, his face congested with temper. "Indeed I shall not! I've just realised whose funeral this is. I had heard that Louis Devaux was being brought home from Paris by his only son for burial today."

She shivered convulsively. If ever there was a bad omen for her marriage, this was it. As if it were not enough that the shadow of death had fallen across her wedding day, the fact that the cortège should be that of her family's most bitter enemy struck home even to her normally quite unsuperstitious nature. In a city as large as Lyons, with its hundreds of silk merchants and thousands of weavers, it would have been expected that the Roche and Devaux families could have produced their own silk for ready markets without falling foul of each other. But that had not been the case. Now, on this day of all days, the feud had reached out a macabre hand to touch her in her wedding finery.

In the midst of the mourners Nicolas Devaux had sought to quieten the most frightened of the four cortège horses. It had been grazed in the collision and was still in pain. He had rushed forward to lend his aid at the first impact and his attempts to soothe the rearing animal were not helped by the shouts of advice being given by the occupants of the ancient houses on either side, who had flung back their shutters at the commotion in the street below. Others had come from alleyways and inner courtyards to gape and get in the way as always happened with any public disturbance.

"That's it. Quiet now. There's nothing to be afraid of." His tone was calm and reassuring as he clapped the sweating neck, hanging on to the bridle with all his strength. He had lost his high-crowned hat almost in the first instant of the struggle for control, yet he still gave the appearance of being in deep mourning from head to foot, for his crisp hair was as black as his clothes. "No more now, boy. It's all over."

The horse finally paid heed. Trembling, it settled, hooves still restless, and gave one last sweep of the head. As the sweeping mane fell back like a closing fan Nicolas saw the occupant of the wedding carriage for the first time. He believed he caught his breath; he could not be sure. Young, oval-faced, she sat leaning towards the open door, her violet-blue eyes deep with fear of him, lips moist and slightly parted, and a crowning mass of dark chestnut hair drawn back smoothly under a bridal cap. A violent and irrational surge of desire, emotional and physical, pounded through him, eliminating his surroundings and erasing the reason why he was there.

Gabrielle drew back a little under the searing intensity of his stare, having seen how his glittering grey irises had seemed to break at the sight of her, and her heightened fear increased, accompanied by a rise of inexplicable excitement. She knew him. She had seen him once before, although he had not seen her. Then he had been a youth in a scarlet Phrygian cap of the Revolution, cockade at the side, yelling his defiance of the Roche family and all it represented of the old France. That had been in 1793 when Lyons had been besieged and then half demolished during Robespierre's Reign of Terror; the time when the Devaux had closed their mill and fled to join the extremists, those opposed to the moderates of the city of silk.

Eleven years had gone by since then and yet there was no mistaking the gaunt-boned sculptured face, the bold straight nose, the big well-shaped mouth and the strong jaw, all of which had made him with the passing of time into a man of arresting appearance: the wild revolutionary tempered, not to handsomeness, but to a virile and forceful presence.

Her pulse raced. He had moved to the front of the horses as if about to come across to her. Then Henri, stalking forward after examining his own horses, shattered whatever might have been said or done in the next few minutes by grabbing Nicolas Devaux by the sleeve and, catching him unawares, hauled him about to bellow wrathfully in his face, a shower of saliva twinkling in the sun.

"You Devaux always caused trouble in this city! I'm a Roche with every right to order you out of it! Living or dead, anyone bearing your detestable name is not wanted here! Do you see what damage your hearse has done to this wedding carriage?"

The injustice of the accusation and the virulence of the insults delivered by her brother filled Gabrielle with embarrassment. It had a different effect on Nicolas Devaux. Furiously he threw off Henri's clasp, his black brows drawing together ominously.

"It seems the Roches have learned neither manners nor tolerance since I was last in Lyons! The ability to lay false charges is still with you!"

"Do you dare to slander my family name?" Further enraged, Henri made a bullying gesture with a clenched fist. "Damnation to you! Your late father is already ensured of that!" Turning his back offensively, he began to retrace his steps to the carriage.

An eager ripple ran through the crowd that had gathered as people watched to see what would happen next. Those who knew of the old feud, revived this day, were passing word of it to others. Gabrielle felt sick with shame on her brother's behalf. She regarded him with cold distaste as he re-entered the carriage, his weight causing it to dip, and let himself drop heavily onto the seat, his face beaded with the sweat of ill temper and exertion. He drew out a handkerchief and began to mop his brow.

"I told that Devaux a thing or two," he growled with satisfaction. "He'll be out of this city when the funeral is over even quicker than he and his parents scampered out last time." His tone changed to total exasperation. "Why hasn't that fool of a coachman closed the door? I told him to get on the way again."

From where she sat Gabrielle glanced out of the window and saw what had happened. The coachman had been stopped by an authorative signal from Nicolas Devaux, who had retrieved his hat, put it on and was advancing formally on the carriage, clasping a glove in readiness for the time-honoured challenge of demanding satisfaction.

"Oh, no," she breathed fearfully. Henri had never been in the least athletic and was as poor with a rapier as he was with a pistol.

"What's the matter now?" he rasped, throwing up his hands to show he was completely at the end of his tether.

She had no need to answer him. Nicolas loomed in the doorway. Acting totally on a protective impulse towards her brother, she snatched the glove from his hand and threw it to the floor, stamping her satined foot down on it. At her action, Nicolas shot her a look of astonishment before throwing up an arm defensively as Henri, who had snatched up his cane, lunged at him, striking wildly.

"Get out of my carriage!"

The cane was grabbed from his grip and snapped in two. Nicolas threw himself forward, seized Henri by the revers of his coat and hurled him down onto the edge of the seat like an oversized puppet.

"No man shall insult my father's memory as you did a few minutes ago!" His voice was quiet and steely, far more alarming to Henri than if he had raised it. "You'll give me satisfaction and not with a paltry cane."

Gabrielle cried out in protest: "No, please," she implored frantically. "The fault of the collision was entirely ours. We were to blame with our speed. Words have been said in too much haste."

Nicolas's grip merely tightened inexorably on his thoroughly frightened captive, who emitted further choking sounds of abject distress. He answered her without as much as glancing in her direction, his attention riveted on Henri. "You would be well advised to leave this carriage while you have the chance to escape the marriage lying ahead of you, mademoiselle. You'll find no happiness in wedlock with this bumptious fellow."

"He's not my bridegroom!" she exclaimed, seeing how he would have drawn that conclusion. "He's my elder brother and my escort. I'm Gabrielle Roche and I apologise fully on his behalf." Her voice rang with appeal. "Surely on this day of days, sad for you and joyful for me, amends can be made."

To her overwhelming relief he did then release her brother, throwing him back in the corner seat. While Henri coughed and gasped for breath, Nicolas turned towards her again, resting an arm across one knee, one foot being in the carriage, the other on the step. The look he gave her was clear and penetrating, awakening the same response in her of mingled pleasure and trepidation as it had done earlier. He inclined his head in a nod.

"I accept your apology on your brother's behalf, Mademoiselle Roche. Allow me to repeat the advice I gave you about the marriage ahead of you today. Wait awhile. Mistakes are made all too easily."

Her one thought was to get Henri away while the going was good. "I know you mean well. I shall do what is best. Don't let us delay you any longer. I'm thankful that all this has been resolved peacefully."

He picked up his glove from the carriage floor and stepped down to the cobbles, still looking at her with that extraordinary demanding stare. The very air seemed charged between them. He raised a questioning eyebrow. "Has it? I hope you are right. Remember what I said."

"Goodbye, Monsieur Devaux," she heard herself say.

He bowed to her and turned away, pulling on his glove. The carriage door was shut. As the wheels rolled forward, Henri finally appeared to regain his breath and exploded with rage, secure in the knowledge that he was saved from further onslaught.

"What infernal impudence! Devaux would have dared to call me out over such a trifling matter! Bad blood! That's what that family has always had. I hope you saw how he backed down when I maintained a dignified silence, ignoring whatever he said. Your babbling was uncalled for and unnecessary. I know the Devauxs. No backbone. He and his father ran like hares from Lyons at the time of the siege."

She did not listen. Through the window she watched Nicolas returning to his position at the rear of the cortège, heading the procession of mourners, all of whom were regrouping. He turned his head and his mesmerising gaze held hers once more as the wheels began to increase pace across the cobbles. Then her face, which was framed for him like a lovely portrait in the carriage window, pearl drops swinging from her pretty ears, was abruptly, and with a sudden burst of speed, swept from his sight.

Gabrielle sank back against the velvet upholstery, dazed and stimulated, almost as though laughter and tears were high in her, brought about by a meeting and a parting that could have no bearing on her life. Opposite her, Henri had almost succeeded in smoothing out the creases in his coat, which was evidence of the quality of the cloth, for he had a taste for luxury and always had the best of everything. The bow of his neckcloth had also been disarranged and he set it to rights, the high points of his collar fashionably level with his fleshy cheekbones. Peering across at her, he splayed his hands across his heavy thighs, which strained the burgundy doeskin of his pantaloons.

"You're looking pale." He knew she was not the fainting type, but bridal nerves did unpredictable things to women, and both of them had just come through a most disturbing incident. He attempted to soften the blunt manner he usually used towards her. "Try to forget that little contretemps that took place. It mustn't spoil your wedding day. Remember that Émile is waiting for you."

She gave a little nod without speaking, turning her head to look unseeingly at the passing wineshops and small cafés, the high buildings, the endless flights of steps that led from one cobbled street to another, and always the accompanying rattle of looms like a continuous heartbeat that was silent only when times were bad. Henri's advice was not easy to follow. It had been a strangely emotional encounter with the representative of a past that had not only aroused Henri's ire today but was still spoken about in Roche gatherings in the same hostile tones that several generations of a family can retain over an old grievance, unconsciously echoing the wrath expressed in the original quarrel.

Yet Nicolas, although Henri had offended him deeply, had had no enmity in his eyes for her. In fact, the look he had given her was not what a bride should receive or return on the day of her wedding to another man. What was more, she did not regret it in the least. It was like a last fling, both sweet and bitter-sweet. Now she must forget the whole incident, wipe it from her memory as if it had never been. She would concentrate on other things. There was a lot to think about as the last quarter of an hour of her single state drew towards its close.

Since she was sixteen there had been plenty of men wanting to marry her, but she had always been determined to make her own choice when the time came. The battles to retain her independence had been hard. Henri and his wife, Yvonne, who was entirely self-centred, had ranged themselves with her father against her. Her only allies had been her other brother, Jules, and his sweet-natured wife, Hélène. Unfortunately, Jules was in the army and rarely at home. As for Hélène, although she was the one who waited most upon the cantankerous Dominique Roche, she had no influence with her father-in-law on his daughter's behalf.

Gabrielle's hope had always been that she might take some official part in the manufacture of Roche silk, and to this end she had applied herself to learning every stage of the procedure. It was not surprising that she should want to look beyond docile domesticity, for at the most impressionable time of her life she had experienced the full turmoil of the Revolution. The cry for liberty had been an echo of her own demands for the right to decide her own future, setting the course of her choice for the years ahead.

Lyons had suffered more than most cities in the Revolution, and none deserved it less. Since medieval times it had been a great international trading centre in cloth, although it was not until the introduction of silkworms into France in the fifteenth century that silk weaving took hold and flourished, bringing a new prosperity to the Lyonnais.

With these long traditions of supplying the rich and the noble, they had been less inclined to follow the new rules laid down by the Revolutionary regime and had revolted against the Convention and its murderous excesses. Gabrielle had witnessed her city's agony. Government forces had moved against Lyons, bombarding the city when the gates were found to be closed and barricaded. A siege began which brought starvation to the city; after holding out for two months the white flag of surrender was raised in the hope of mercy.

It was not forthcoming. As a punishment to the inhabitants, Lyons was condemned to demolition, a terrible and ignominious fate for a city that had been the very birthplace of France as a nation and which had once come close to being the nation's capital. Even its name was taken from it. Gabrielle had stood with her brothers to read the inscription that had been nailed to a pillar: LYONS MADE WAR ON LIBERTY. LYONS IS NO MORE.

Every day after that pronouncement, smoke and dust from fires and explosions had drifted in dark clouds across the peninsula on which the city stood in its uniquely advantageous position at the confluence of the Saône and the Rhône rivers. Flanked by quays, it was linked by many bridges to the old quarter of Vaise and the hill of Fourvière on the west bank, some of it Roman in origin, most of it an untouched spread of Renaissance properties, and to the newer districts on the east bank. Cradling the city to the north was the weavers' hillside quarter of La Croix Rousse, through which Gabrielle's wedding carriage had passed; no area had escaped the butchering of Frenchmen by Frenchmen as gunpowder and grapeshot were used to lay the city low.

In the Place des Terreaux in front of the magnificent Hôtel de Ville the guillotine had been put to work again, taking the heads of local civil leaders and other Lyonnais until it proved too slow for the impatient Revolutionary tribunal and firing squads took the place of the blade. For two months of horror the destruction and the slaughter went on, taking over two thousand lives, until in Paris the tyrant Robespierre fell from power and the Reign of Terror came to an end.

By then there were no Devaux of the silk world left in Lyons, for during the early days of the siege Dominique Roche had seized the chance to rid himself of his old enemy once and for all by denouncing Louis Devaux as an extremist in league with the government forces outside the walls. It was this which had brought about Nicolas' revolutionary display of defiance. Louis Devaux had had to flee for his life, leaving the city secretly and taking his wife and Nicolas with him. The Lyonnais had long memories. No Devaux had returned until this day, when Nicolas had come home on his mission, and after the brush with Henri he was undoubtedly as full of hatred for the name of Roche as he had ever been, no matter that he had been courteous towards the daughter of the house. Gabrielle hoped he would leave Lyons after the funeral as speedily as he had left last time. It would be best for her never to see him again. He was too disturbing, too disruptive a personality.

"We're here," Henri said, breaking into her thoughts. Straightening up, she saw that they had stopped by the stone steps of their destination, one of the many churches that had been turned into a public assembly hall since the Revolution, when the atheistic government in Paris had annexed all ecclesiastical property.

Gabrielle smoothed the gathers of her gown carefully into place. For all its delicate appearance silk was ever a hardy fabric and it had suffered no harm through her fall to the carriage floor. The current fashion of the skirt flowing from a high waistline under her full breasts suited her well. On the steps Henri offered her his arm. Passers-by paused to watch her as she ascended the wide flight, a graceful girl, tallish and possessed of a provocatively beautiful figure, her hand resting lightly on his wrist, and disappeared into the entrance.

Inside it seemed to her that the scent of incense and wax candles still lingered amid stone walls, which were surely infused by centuries of worship that all the flags and national paraphernalia in place of the altar could not dispel. An orchestra was playing in what had once been a side chapel. All marriage ceremonies were civil ones now, although government moves were afoot to restore certain rights to the church.

There was a stir of movement among those present at the bride's arrival. Among the familiar faces gathered there she caught an affectionate grin from her brother Jules. Sandy-haired and freckled, still retaining his boyish looks in spite of extensive service on foreign battlefields, his narrow eyes a twinkling brown, he was unassailably jaunty and at ease, tall and dashing in his grey and red uniform of a regiment of the Hussars, his plumed fur hat held military fashion in the crook of his arm. By his side, Hélène was smiling at her, dimples playing, happy in the occasion and in having her husband home again, however short his sojourn was to be. Her tranquil disposition was such that people were quick to turn to her in trouble, sensing the kindness in her, and she always seemed to have a lame duck under her wing. Today, in festive mood, she wore a fashionable turban of amber gauze, which echoed the colour of her eyes and set off her shining black hair.

Gabrielle was heartened by the warmth of the expressions of these two who meant most to her. Others were nodding and smiling too, but she looked beyond them to the head of the aisle, where Émile awaited her. His dark brown hair was winged with grey and shining in the sun's rays that poured down on him through a stained glass window that had escaped the blasts of demolition. Behind him the draped Tricolore flamed blue, white and red, adding its own brilliance to the setting.

She returned his steady, serious gaze as she advanced step by gliding step towards him, her gown whispering about her. From the first he had pleased her with his meditative grey eyes in a lean, sensitive face, his deep attractive voice and his quiet demeanour. She felt that with this restful, intelligent older man she would be able to forget once and for all the swift, sweet love affair she had shared with Philippe, a weaver's son, when she was seventeen. It had been crushed as much by Philippe's side of the family as by hers. Both fathers had been in agreement that he should be sent away from Lyons, Dominique threatening in his attitude and the weaver himself fearful of being deprived of work for the family loom. She would have gone with him if she had not been kept under lock and key. It had taken her a long time to recover from her youthful anguish at knowing she would never see Philippe again. His name still held a last echo of music in her ears.

It was her belief that Émile would prove to be as much friend as lover, a firm foundation on which to build their lives together. She wanted their marriage to be a good one. Love, as she had once expected to find it, did not come into this union any more than it did in most marriages of convenience. Practically, she did not expect this lack to detract from the value of their relationship. Although divorce had become commonplace since the sweeping changes wrought by the Revolution, she was resolved that there should be no broken vows for her, and she knew Émile was of the same mind. Now he was coming forward to meet her.

"My dear Gabrielle." He seized her hand and kissed it ardently, his eyes absorbing her. Then he linked his fingers with hers as they turned together to face the magistrate.

"Citizen Émile Valmont and Citizeness Gabrielle Roche, you have come before the law of France to be joined in wedlock."

It was a bleak ceremony that involved the reading of sections of the law appertaining to marriage and properties acquired through marriage. There was nothing to uplift the spirit. Yet all went well until she removed her glove for the giving of the ring, a custom from the past that had been revived on this occasion at her request. As Émile made to slip the gold band onto her finger she jerked her hand back involuntarily. Aghast at her own action, a tremor went through her whole frame. A fleeting look of surprise passed across Émile's face, but he remained in control, simply tightening his hold on her fingers. Nobody else, except the magistrate, was aware of that instinctive last bid she had made for freedom.

Keeping a tight clasp on her beringed hand, Émile bent his head to kiss her lips with reassurance and promise. Her absurd sense of panic ebbed away as if it had never been.

Well-wishers immediately surrounded them. Her first kiss on the cheek was from Hélène. "May you always be happy, dearest Gabrielle."

"I echo my wife's sentiments, little sister." Jules embraced Gabrielle affectionately. With an age gap of only four years between them, they had always been close, and he had been the one person on whom she could rely for support at all times. The only real difference of opinion between them had been about silk, for he had never had the least interest in the family business and she would have given anything to take on one of the appointments available to a son but not to a daughter.

"How I wish your leave could have begun sooner," she said to him.

Until his arrival home the previous day, neither she nor Hélène had seen him for many months. "I've hardly had a chance to talk to you."

"I'll bring Hélène out to the Valmont silk farm to visit you before I go again," he promised. "I'd like to see where you'll be living now."

That cheered her immensely. Then she turned to receive the kisses and embraces from the rest of her family and friends. Yvonne, Henri's wife, came from congratulating the bridegroom to beam at the bride, showing the small, pearly teeth of which she was proud. As usual she was the height of elegance, her dress yellow-striped silk with a large diamond brooch at her plump throat, her hat ornamented with tall plumes that wafted romantically. Full-bosomed and wide-hipped, she exuded a strong perfume blended of powdered flesh, frizzed hair and expensive rose-water as she leaned forward to kiss the bride on both cheeks.

"My good wishes. Your bridal gown is certainly charming." Her glance at it was uncertain. "Oyster is not a shade that is easy to wear. It doesn't suit many complexions, although I could get away with it."

Gabrielle hid a smile of amusement, not taking offence, for she knew her sister-in-law well. Even on another's wedding day, Yvonne could not cease to be completely self-absorbed. Then more people came forward to wish the bride well and it took a little while before she and Émile were able to leave the assembly hall and go out into the sunshine together. Observing the old custom that the bridal couple must make a grand entrance at the wedding feast, they were to be driven by a longer route to her father's house, giving everyone else the chance to arrive first.

After waving to those gathered on the steps of the assembly hall, Gabrielle turned her head to look at her bridegroom where he sat at her side. He was gazing composedly out of the window at the passing scene and not at her, his fine profile etched almost coin-like against the sun. She would have liked to talk, but guessed he was thankful for this quiet respite before he had to face the feasting and chatter that lay ahead. There would be plenty of opportunity to converse and discuss and even argue points of view with him in the future, particularly whenever she should praise the Life Consul for all he and Madame Josephine had done to stimulate the Lyonese silk trade by refurbishing the palaces of France. Émile had no enthusiasm for Napoleon Bonaparte, yet he was always ready to listen to her opinions and was interested in whatever she had to say. In that way he was like Jules, in spite of being as serious as her brother was merry. It was the reason why over past months Émile had gradually won her trust and respect. There were still depths in him that she had to plumb, for they had had almost no time on their own, Hélène having always been present as chaperone. Only on the evening when he had proposed to her had they been alone together.

She glanced at him again. His attention was still diverted. Not for the first time she wondered just how much he did care for her. There had been moments, such as her arrival at his side in the assembly rooms, when she thought she glimpsed a deep passion. Yet never once had he mentioned the word "love." She would have liked him to hold her hand on this short drive as he had done during the marriage ceremony. To encourage him she placed her hand with its new gold band palm downwards on the seat between them. He did not appear to notice.

They soon came to her father's house in the Rue Clémont. It was a spacious residence not far from the Place des Terreaux, and it was as much a show-piece as a home, since business associates and buyers were received there. Two offices used by Dominique and Henri respectively, as well as design and checking-rooms, were situated to the rear of the house, with independent access. Every one of the main salons and upper rooms was hung with panels of Roche silk; the designs varied from the spectacular in the Grand Salon to modest moss roses and lilacs against an azure background in one of the smaller salons, which had been her mother's favourite and where the furnishings had been left unchanged.

During the time of the demolitions, Gabrielle and her father and brothers had had to leave the house and go into hiding. They had taken refuge in the medieval quarter of Traboules, which was full of secret cellars and a maze of passageways that had given the place its name. Fortunately their home had escaped damage, except for a few broken windows, which were soon repaired. Shortly after their return Henri had married Yvonne and brought her to live there. Since then Hélène had been another bride to take up residence in her father-in-law's house, for with Jules away on active service most of the time there was no chance as yet for them to build a home together.

In the Grand Salon Dominique Roche had received his guests and was awaiting the arrival of the bride and groom. The walls of the handsome room blazed with the rich hues of golden peacocks with tails in full spread enclosed in lozenges within compartments of interlaced foliage and flowers on a crimson damask ground. The drapes at the tall windows, the door drapes and the seat covers of the sofas and chairs held variations of the pattern, giving a jewel-like quality to the whole salon that dazzled and beguiled the eye, making it one of the most spectacular salons in the whole of Lyons.

Dominique, in spite of being long accustomed to it, still felt pride every time he entertained there. It showed all comers that Maison Roche could match and outweave its rivals. From the looms under his control, as from others in Lyons, there came the most sumptuous fabrics to be found anywhere in the world. Damask, moires that shimmered like rippling water, velvets soft as a cat's fur, satins, *gros de Tours*, lampas, silk *brochés*, the most magnificent of which were those of gold and silver, and all of them proof that it was Lyons silk that made France superior to all other lands in the manufacture of exquisite fabrics.

Dominique sat in his great carved chair with its seat and back of peacock brocade, which had been specially made for his enormous bulk. Since a fall three years before, when he had damaged his hip, lack of exercise and his gourmet appetite had increased his already considerable weight. He chose to dull the persistent pain with good wines, a glass and decanter always within reach. Yet his brain remained as keen as ever, honed to a new sharpness by his suffering. In spite of being confined to his chair most of the time, he missed nothing that went on in his house or in his business domain. Where once he had seen for himself how things were going, he now employed spies, not trusting Henri to give him the blunt facts as he would wish to receive them. What he hated most about his handicap was that it put him at a tremendous disadvantage, and he had to use his wits as never before to ensure that his elder son, impatient for full control, did not take over on the pretext that he was in his dotage. His temper, always short, was quicker than it had ever been, as a result.

"Émile and Gabrielle have arrived." Hélène's smiling face lowered towards his.

"Good girl." He nodded, closing his hand paternally over hers, where it rested for a moment on the chair arm. He could always rely upon her to keep him notified of any social development beyond his range of hearing. Being the wife of his favourite son had endeared her to him as much as it was possible for him to extend affection beyond his own flesh and blood. His other daughter-in-law was jealous of Hélène's position in his regard. It gave him wicked amusement to aggravate that state of affairs whenever possible by taunting Yvonne on any pretext. She would have hated him more, and slept less well in her marriage bed, if she had had the slightest idea that his spies kept him informed of her amorous activities beyond its realm.

Dominique looked across at his elder son, who had inherited his heavy features, thick brows and breadth of cheekbone and jaw, as well as a tendency to put on weight before the age of forty. Henri in his splendidly tailored clothes, his high white stock allowing just a glimmer of cambric shirt frill as decreed by the First Consul for formal attire, was every inch a pillar of respectability as he stood considerately at his wife's side, looking expectantly with everyone else in the room towards the open double doors through which the bride and groom would soon make their appearance.

Dominique smiled grimly to himself. It was a fact that Henri had never known how to enjoy life as he himself understood enjoyment. Henri gained his satisfaction from long hours of work, which Dominique thought a poor substitute for carnal pleasures, and his relaxation from gaming hard with male companions. He left his voluptuous wife too much to her own devices. Now and again Henri had a mistress for a few months at a time, but his urges appeared to be moderate. Dominique thought him a commendably industrious businessman and a thoroughly dull fellow. In addition, Henri was excessively lenient towards Yvonne; a spender himself, he gave in to her extravagant whims far too often, and yet she had never borne him the sons he wanted. In ten years of marriage she had had several miscarriages. If ever she should go her full time, Dominique was resolved he would know her whereabouts at the time of conception before acknowledging the offspring as his legitimate grandchild.

With relief he turned his head to look towards Jules. There had been four other children between the births of his two sons, but they had not survived. Was it any wonder that Jules should have come to mean so much to him? Unlike Henri, Jules had followed closely in his own footsteps as far as women were concerned, until marriage settled him down. Again, differing from Henri and himself, Jules never bore malice and had his late mother's light-hearted temperament as well as her charm. Yet there was steel behind the twinkling eyes that came from the Roche side of the family, and it had shown itself in full force on the day he had announced his intention to go into the army and not into the silk business. For Dominique it had been a bitter disappointment, and for once in his life he had tried stern persuasion instead of threats to get his own way. When it proved of no avail, he accepted his son's decision, wanting no barriers to come between them, and made his own secret plan to bring Jules into Maison Roche when his soldiering days were done.

"Monsieur and Madame Valmont." The bridal couple had been announced. No citizen and citizeness nonsense within this house. As they came through the doorway from the Blue Salon beyond, applause broke out, rippling around the walls of silk peacocks, and striking tinkling echoes from the waterfall glitter of the central chandelier.

Dominique watched the couple approach him, the guests drawing back on either side to clear a way for them. He supposed he must look like an old lion wedged in his wide chair, particularly as he was finding it difficult not to let a belligerent expression take over his loose-jowled face. It was one of the occasions when he felt the old hatred of his daughter rise up in him for no other reason than that she was alive and his beloved Marguerite was long since gone, because of her. On the day of her birth he had not so much as glanced in the cradle, and at his instruction she had been fostered out immediately with a peasant couple in the country, who had her baptised and chose her name. When Gabrielle had just reached her second natal day, pestilence laid low the village, killing her foster parents.

In spite of the risk to himself, he had gone to fetch her out of the centre of infection, for after all she was his own flesh and blood. Any chance of full reconciliation on his part was lost from his first sight of her, for fate had intervened savagely again, giving her a likeness to her mother that was destined to keep raw the embittering sense of loss in him that had destroyed whatever little compassion he had ever harboured for others. Always a womaniser, for such was his lusty nature until old age played its own cruel trick on him, he had never found another to take his wife's place.

Today his daughter was unwittingly twisting the knife in the wound again, as she had done so often before. As through a veil of memory, he could glimpse again the only woman he had ever loved in Gabrielle's dramatic beauty, her chestnut helmet of curls, her movements and her grace. As she curtsied to him while her husband bowed, he wanted to strike her, an impulse he controlled by addressing Émile and ignoring her.

"So now you are my son-in-law," he declared heartily. "May good fortune go with you and your bride in the years ahead."

Émile bowed again. "I thank you for your kind words."

Dominique, shifting his bulk in the chair, signalled that he was ready to rise from it. Then he would let no one but Jules help him walk the tortuous distance into the adjoining dining salon, where the wedding breakfast was set out on the long table in silver, crystal and damask. Sweat bathed his forehead at the excruciating pain as he set a slow pace, leaning heavily on his stick and with the support of Jules's arm.

Gabrielle followed with Émile, the rest of the company falling in behind. Her father's deliberate slight had struck deep, even though there was no reason why he should have been prepared to change his pattern of behaviour towards her on this day more than any other. Only when she displeased him, which had been often enough in the past years, had she received the full force of his angry attention. The fact that she had a will to match his meant that he had never broken her. He was a tyrant in his dealings with all except Jules, and she was thankful that the younger of her brothers had always escaped persecution.

As for herself, Gabrielle wondered sometimes if her passion for silk had its origins in a childhood yearning to break through Dominique's hostility by showing that her interests were the same as his. If that had been its beginnings, the reason no longer applied, for now she loved silk for its own sake as the most beautiful fabric in existence. Her wedding gown gleamed lustrously as she took her place beside Émile at the long table. She had woven its silk herself, and it was her last link with the Roche looms. At least through her marriage she would continue to be involved in silk, although by another channel, for her life in future would be spent at the Valmont silk farm, a long-established and successful business situated around a charming old house in the country outside Lyons. Émile, restrained in the jovial atmosphere, raised his first glass to her. He thought she appeared perfectly collected, if a trifle pale.

The feasting with the speeches and toasts lasted several hours. It was early evening when Gabrielle finally went upstairs with Hélène, who helped her change out of her bridal attire into a lilac travelling dress and high-waisted coat, tiny silk flowers framing her face within the brim of her narrow bonnet. The journey to her new home should take no more than an hour.

"Here are your gloves." Hélène was holding them out to her.

Gabrielle took them and then caught her sister-in-law's hands in a tight clasp. "I shall miss you so much. You've been such a friend to me."

Hélène tried to speak cheerily. "We'll be seeing each other again very soon when Jules brings me to visit you."

Gabrielle's urgent expression did not change. "I'm thinking of afterwards, when Jules's leave is over. Please visit me often. It will be lonely without your company."

"You're forgetting," Hélène reminded her gently. "You'll have Émile now."

A shuttered look came down over Gabrielle's face. She withdrew her hands and began to put on her gloves. "Yes, I have."

"He's a good man."

"I have no doubt of that." Gabrielle picked up a hand-glass for a final check on her appearance, her movements brisk and her voice controlled. "Or else I should not have married him."

Hélène watched her. It was almost possible to believe that Gabrielle was experiencing qualms, which was in total contrast to her self-assurance that morning while dressing for the ceremony. It was not that Gabrielle was ignorant of what marriage involved. Through working alongside the weavers she had heard and seen much of life. Hélène herself had been totally innocent on her wedding night but, loving Jules as she did, everything had been a joyful revelation. She hoped with all her heart, for Émile's sake as well as Gabrielle's, that their marriage would prove to be a happy one. There was no knowing how far passionate first love had taken Gabrielle in the affair that had been so ruthlessly crushed.

The trouble now was that there was a cruel imbalance in this new partnership, with too much love on Émile's side and none on Gabrielle's, something a caring outsider could observe. At first he might be afraid to touch her, for he was a refined and sensitive man with feelings that ran deep. Hélène had recognised traits of herself in him, which gave her a special understanding. Now it seemed to her that something had happened between her sister-in-law's leaving the house that morning and returning afterwards; in fact, in searching her memory, it was almost as though there had been a change in Gabrielle when she entered the assembly room on Henri's arm for the marriage. Perhaps that unfortunate accident with the hearse, which Henri had been talking about until silenced abruptly by his wife, had upset Gabrielle far more than anyone realised.

"Are you ready?" she prompted the bride gently. "It's time for you to go."

Gabrielle put down the hand-glass. Wordlessly she embraced Hélène as if not trusting herself to speak any more at the moment. With a smile arranged on her lips, she swept ahead out of the room and down the stairs to the hall where Émile waited for her. All had gathered to send them on their way. Even Dominique was there, leaning on his stick with Jules at his side. He actually encouraged her to kiss his cheek in farewell; she guessed it was because she had pleased him for the first time in her life by leaving his house for a home of her own. She and Émile departed in the usual noisy excitement that accompanies the going away of newly-weds. Hélène was the last to re-enter the house after the barouche was lost to sight in the fading daylight.

In another part of the city, Nicolas Devaux was setting out for an address he had not seen since he and his father had gone from it in flight. It was in the Croix Rousse quarter, where earlier that day the Roche carriage had halted the cortège like a last throw against his father's memory, made worse by the verbal abuse of Henri Roche.

He ascended one steep flight of steps to reach a narrow cobbled street and followed its winding slope upwards. From the windows of the high stone houses, which stood in an unbroken line on either side, there wafted the mixed aromas of garlic and soup and wine as people sat at supper, lamplight appearing as darkness fell.

It was all familiar to him. He had spent his boyhood in these streets, taken his first girl in one of the tiny walled courtyards and learned his trade as a silk merchant's son the hard way, put to the looms at any time he was free from schooling and his books. Unlike the Roche family, who a couple of generations before had moved in their prosperity from the crowded heights to a more elegant district, the Devaux had remained at the heart of the industry, the black façade of an ancient house hiding a treasure trove of silks within.

His old home came into sight. The timbered entrance, which opened directly into the building from the street above two front steps, had an iron knocker in the shape of a hand and was clearly illuminated by one of the street lamps suspended on a chain strung between opposite walls. Reaching into his coat pocket, Nicolas took out the key that was about to take him back into the past. Before admitting himself into the house he stood back briefly to gaze up at the four storeys, where all the windows were closely shuttered, those of the ground floor with curling grilles for protection. What would he find inside after all these years? He knew the place had been searched after he and his father fled. Maybe he would find it ransacked and thick with mould. Preparing himself for the worst, he turned the key, exerting pressure to counteract a certain stiffness of the lock through long disuse, and let the door swing wide.

The lamplight from the street showed him the chequered marble floor and the dark shadow of the staircase rising beyond. He stepped inside and closed the door behind him. It smelt musty and neglected as houses always did when left to stand uninhabited over a length of time. A lamp stood on a side table and he lit it, brushing aside cobwebs. Holding it high, he looked around him. Paintings still hung on the walls and none of the hall chairs was overturned. No sign of disorder yet. He pressed down the handle of one of the double doors leading to the main salon and entered.

The damage was worse than anything he had envisaged. The silk panels that lined the walls hung in frayed and dusty tatters where they had been slashed to pieces. Gilded chairs lay in splinters, the stuffing pulled out of the ripped silk brocade, and one had apparently been hurled at a looking-glass above the marble fireplace, for it lay in front of the grate in a mess of jagged shards. He was appalled by the wanton destruction. Selections of the finest silk ever produced by the Devaux looms had gone into the ornamentation of this room, where special clients had been received.

Stepping over some of the debris, he went to another pair of doors that led into a long narrow room that had been known as the gallery, all its many portraits and pictures woven in silk. As soon as he entered he saw that not one had escaped. Not all had fallen to the floor, some still hung at drunken angles. It was as though somebody had run the length of the gallery bludgeoning each one with a spiked instrument.

Nicolas bent down to pick up one of the fallen pictures, brushing away pieces of broken frame. It showed the Three Graces awaiting the judgement of Paris, intricately woven in white on a soft green background, now damaged beyond repair, with many of the delicate threads snagged and torn. It dated with others in the collection from the early part of the previous century, when the Devaux looms had begun to specialise in silk pictures. Later there had been a commission from Louis XVI for a portrait of himself in silk, and the royal head, destined to be severed from its neck, had been captured in an accurate likeness and encircled, somewhat prophetically, by forget-me-nots. It had been hung in Versailles, where it aroused such admiration that there had been a flood of silk portrait commissions from the royal circle that had continued until the Revolution. One had still been on the looms at the time of the flare-up, and it had never been finished.

The gallery opened into his father's office, and this had been left untouched. So was the adjoining design room, with its brushes and paints and coloured inks ranged neatly in rows, half-finished cartoons of designs on the sloping desk boards bearing evidence of work that had been in progress on the day in 1793 when life in the house and the mill came to a standstill. Upstairs also proved to be free of damage anywhere.

Downstairs again, he went out into an inner courtyard, where he unlocked a door that led to the mill. Holding the lamp high, he sent the glow over sixty looms which stood dark and skeletal in four rows. He saw at once that the vandals had been operating here, probably before entering the house. Axes had been used on the sturdy looms, which bore raw gashes like wounds in the time-weathered wood, the warps slashed and half-woven lengths knifed through. It was from these looms, together with work drawn in from independent weavers, that the silks of Maison Devaux had flowed out to all parts of the world.

He moved slowly down one of the aisles between the looms, remembering how he had been put to every task in this place, for his father had been determined that there should be no gaps in his practical knowledge of weaving. The worst time of all had been in early boyhood when he had to take his turn stooped all day under a loom retying the threads as they broke, a gruelling and exhausting task that was allotted to children in every mill and weaving household. Fingers became sore and limbs cramped, and it was not unusual to see children weeping as they worked. In the Devaux mill rest periods had been allotted, one child taking over from another, but since this involved additional labour many mills disdained this practice and the children suffered. The *maître ouvrier*, subject in turn to the orders of the mill-owners, deducted pay every time a loom stopped, making the weavers as keen as their masters that there should be no delay in the thread-tying. Even when the children were their own offspring, they sometimes added the toe of a boot to keep young fingers at the arduous task. There were always those at home who had to be fed.

He completed his tour of the workshop, sometimes stepping accidentally on one of the hundreds of silk bobbins and the shuttles that had held them, which had been thrown across the floor. All but one of the bobbin winders, which were like spinning-wheels in appearance, had been smashed. He righted it and touched the emerald thread that gleamed amid the cobweb strands in the lamplight. Young girls had had the task of bobbin-winding, and he had always thought them a pretty sight in their frilled caps and aprons, particularly in summer when the sun through the ceiling-high windows shone down on the flower colours of their cotton dresses where they sat together at one end of the workshop.

Locking up again, he returned to the house. No sooner had he sat down at his father's desk to look over what was there than a knocking sounded on the front door, echoing through the quiet house. He frowned at the unwanted interruption, pushed back his chair and went out into the hallway where earlier he had lit the sconces on the walls.

Opening the door, he was met by the sight of a short, grizzled old man in the weaver's garb of belted loose tunic and trousers, the cap peaked with a full, soft crown. With a guffaw of pleasure, the visitor seized Nicolas's hand in a gnarled clasp to pump it heartily.

"It is you, then, Citizen Devaux. It's good to see you back, although it was a sad mission that brought about your return to Lyons. My wife and I were grieved to hear about your father. When a neighbour just told me that a stranger had been seen entering the Devaux house, I was certain it would be you come home to your roots at last."

Nicolas's mouth had widened into a broad grin of recognition. "Jean-Baptiste Rouband! After all these years! Come in, come in. If it hadn't been for your timely warning when my father and I were marked men, I shouldn't be here today." He threw an arm round the old man's shoulder, bringing him into the house, and shut the door on the street. "This calls for a bottle of wine. If there's none left in the cellar, we'll go elsewhere for it."

"Haven't you taken a look?" An anticipatory gleam had leapt into Jean-Baptiste's wily glance.

"There's been no time yet. I've had other things to occupy my mind." Nicolas flung a hand in the direction of the open doors of the salon, his tone bitter. "See the damage that was done here in the name of law and order. The workshop has suffered similar damage."

Jean-Baptiste had a light tread, being wiry and quick in spite of his years, and he took a few paces into the salon, where he stood to view the debris on all sides. Sticking his thumbs in his broad belt, he spoke phlegmatically. "It's bad, but nothing that can't be put right. I dare say it's the same with the looms. In any case, the law didn't do it."

"Then who did?"

The old man turned, taking satisfaction in giving the information. "It was Dominique Roche's men. They broke in after it was learned that you and your father had escaped, prepared to destroy everything. They would have done more damage if some of your weavers hadn't moved in with clubs and staves to drive them out."

Nicolas had turned white about the mouth, the skin taut across the bones of his face. For the second time that day he experienced an almost uncontrollable fury against the name of Roche. "I should have guessed. It wasn't enough to put our lives in jeopardy. He had to see our home and mill destroyed."

"How did your mother stand up to the escape?"

"Not at all, I'm sad to say. It was too hard on her physical strength. As you may remember, she had been sick previously for several weeks. Having to leave her home in those circumstances hastened her death, there is no doubt about that." Nicolas moved restlessly, pacing to and fro. "I tell you, I have a heavy score against the Roches, and today more has been added to it."

Jean-Baptiste gave him a sideways look that was sharp with curiosity. His fellow workers had defended the Devaux property as much for their own sakes as for any other reason. They had wanted Louis Devaux to return one day. One silk merchant less in the city meant loss of work for the weaving community. "If you wouldn't be offended, citizen," he ventured warily, "I'd like to ask what chance there would have been of Roche's charge of Devaux collaboration with the Terror being upheld against you and your father if it had taken you both into the Lyons courts."

"Plenty!" Nicolas did not attempt to hedge. "Feelings were running high at the time and I didn't help with a personal demonstration against the accusations outside the Roche residence. It would have been hard to find an unbiased judge in such a turmoil of events. You know as well as I do that opportunists on both the extremist and moderate sides took advantage of the twists and turns of the Revolution to rid themselves of enemies." He stopped his pacing. "That's enough gloomy talk for today. Seeing you again calls for a celebration."

He led the way down to the cellar and was in for a pleasant discovery. Roche's men had been thrown out before they had reached that part of the house and nothing had been looted. There was plenty of Beaujolais, a natural choice since Lyons bordered on the vineyards of La Beaujolais, and a number of other good wines, the choice wide. Nicolas, more discerning than his companion, made the selection. Armed with bottles and glasses, the two men settled themselves in what had been the family salon. Because of his mood, the deeper Nicolas drank the more serious and thoughtful he became. In contrast, Jean-Baptiste was thoroughly jovial, although the reason did not emerge until they were well into the remaining half of the second bottle.

"When shall you be starting up the looms again, then, Citizen Devaux?" There seemed to be no doubt in the old man's mind as to why Nicolas had chosen to open the house for inspection.

Nicolas, reclining in a comfortable chair, his long legs stretched out before him and crossed at the ankle, regarded the weaver over the rim of his glass. "What makes you think I should want to live here again? After serving four years in the army, I left to rejoin my father in Paris, where we went into silk negotiating together. Now I control a number of looms in the outskirts of the city. I also reside in Paris, which suits me very well."

Jean-Baptiste respected the work of silk-negotiators. These were the merchants who drew in orders and commissions from home and abroad, going far afield.

"So you have your looms again." Jean-Baptiste had no patience with any location beyond the borders of his own city and showed it in his expression. "Silk isn't silk if it isn't woven in Lyons. It's all to do with the water and the air and, above all, the unique skills of the Lyonnais. Parisian silk? Bah!" His contempt needed the leavening of a refill of his glass; he took a gulp and then gestured with it. "Don't you be afeared the mud slung at your good name would still stick. Times have changed."

"If I decide to come back to Lyons," Nicolas said lazily, "it would be to re-establish myself as a member of *La Grande Fabrique* in my own right."

Jean-Baptiste wagged a finger. "But you can't deny that the goodwill of the banks in Lyons would not go amiss."

"I already have a bank in Paris on my side. As for Parisian silk, which you so despise, I recently fulfilled a commission for silk for the Tuileries in its refurbishing."

The old man grunted impatiently. "You'd still do better in your own city. There's never been such competition as there is in Lyons these days to capture the orders for all the work that needs to be done to the great houses and palaces of France." Cunningly he added an inducement of his own. "Maison Roche is certain to secure good commissions before long."

Nicolas narrowed his eyes. "So the Roches are in the running, are they? Maybe it is time, after all, for Maison Devaux to open once again."

"Well said!" In triumph, Jean-Baptiste slapped his knee exuberantly. "You mean it. I can see that! It's the best news I've heard in a long while." Putting his glass aside, he seized a bottle by its neck to swallow its contents jubilantly, the wine spilling down his chin. He remembered little after that and had no recollection of Nicolas helping him home.

Returning to the hotel where he was staying overnight, Nicolas guessed that Jean-Baptiste would always boast of being instrumental in restoring the making of Devaux silk to the city. The truth was, it had been in his mind all the way back to Lyons in the wake of the funeral cortège. The silk trade was recovering at last from the Revolution and he found himself wanting to return to the heart of it, where his father and grandfather and his forebears before them had produced the best of Lyons silk.

In his hotel room he removed his coat with a hiss of silken lining and arranged it on the back of a chair to keep its shape. In his shirt-sleeves, he glanced at his gold fob watch as he unfastened it to place it on a chest of drawers. Midnight. His thoughts went to the bride he had met that day. The truth was, she had lurked hauntingly at the back of his mind throughout all that had been happening, ready to rush in with the same tantalising effect the moment he was ready to accept her image again. In the aftermath of that clash of locking wheels, he had looked at her and wanted her and thought himself demented that at the height of his father's funeral he should be seized by desire. Never in his life before had he been so enthralled on sight by any woman. He had sensed the response in her. It had emanated from her, richly and sensually, making the rapport between them complete.

He was not foolish enough to suppose she had not gone ahead with her marriage that day. At the funeral reception, a local mourner had been able to give him valuable information about her, including the name and occupation of the bridegroom she had been on her way to marry. Nicolas intended to see her again if ever the chance presented itself. He considered how curious it was that he should have become violently attracted to the daughter of the man who had tried to send his father and himself to the guillotine. Whatever happened, it would be hard to forget her. Particularly on this night.

By candlelight, Gabrielle prepared for bed. Supper with Émile had been a pleasant meal, their conversation as general as on any other occasion, and afterwards he had escorted her to the foot of the stairs. She was being assisted in her undressing by the maid he had employed to wait on her. She had never had a personal servant before, for Dominique had always been parsimonious in household staff and affairs, and it was a novelty to have someone put away her clothes and brush her hair. It did seem that Émile was giving thought to everything for her comfort, even to ordering books by her favourite authors for his library shelves.

She had made only one visit to the house prior to her marriage and had liked it at first sight. Built of mellow stone, sun-baked to a golden hue, it dated back a hundred years or more and had well-proportioned rooms and a welcoming atmosphere. She had been accompanied by Henri, who had been acting as their father's representative in seeing whether Émile's house came up to the standards required for her before the marriage settlement was signed. It would not have been delicate to show her the bedchambers, and so she had only viewed the downstairs. It had been his grandfather's home, and she was pleased that Émile had not thrown out the furniture that belonged to royalist days, as so many had done, for the charm of rococo was above politics.

Now that she was upstairs, she could tell that extensive redecoration had been done for her benefit, for the white paintwork of the bed-chamber smelt new and the wallpaper was patterned prettily with mimosa blossom, a tree she had once mentioned as being her favourite. The bed was new and had probably replaced a four-poster. Sleigh-like, in the latest style, it was set sideways against the wall, with a circular canopy suspended centrally above and filmy draperies looping down over both the head and the foot, creating a tent-like look that was far removed from any military campaign.

She liked everything about her new home. Somehow she felt safe in it, although safety was a quality she had not thought about before, and she did not know why it should seem important now. It had never been her policy to seek security in anything; quite the reverse, in fact. Maybe it was that she had not fully recovered from the extraordinary incident in La Croix Rousse. She could not dismiss the impression that her life had been marked by it as if everything that had ever happened to her had been building up to that moment when Nicolas Devaux turned his head and looked deep into her eyes.

"Is there anything more, madame?" the maid asked her.

She shook her head as much to clear away her uneasy thoughts as to indicate the maid's tasks were at an end. "No, Marie. You may go."

Left on her own, Gabrielle crossed to the window, the candlelight shimmering her body into silhouette through the fine lawn and lace of her nightgown, and looked out.

The moon was bright and she could see beyond the formal flower gardens to the copse of trees that hid the silk farm beyond. A path led to it from the house, and on the day she visited Émile had shown her the white stone buildings with terra-cotta tiles known as the silk sheds. There had been nothing to see then, except the thousands of eggs being stored in a cold cellar until the time of hatching. It was a procedure that would soon be taking place, and the whole cycle of sericulture would begin again.

As a child, her favourite story had been that of the origins of silk:

how when the Chinese Empress Hsi Ling Shi had been taking tea in her garden in 2640 B.C. she had found a dropped cocoon floating in her cup. Noticing a fine thread loosened from it, she pulled it gently and, surprised to find it continuous, began to reel it onto a twig. Then, as now, it proved to be over three miles in length. Realising its potential, the Empress introduced sericulture on a serious scale, and for hundreds of years China kept the secret of its glorious silks, a fabric unknown to the rest of the world. For Gabrielle it had always been easy to feel akin to the Empress in a love of silk, particularly when she was at a loom and sending the shuttle through from one hand to the other while the pattern spread, rich in colour and in texture, growing steadily before her.

By holding back the curtain and looking westward, she could just see the mulberry plantation where it spread out under the stars like a dark blanket covering many undulating acres, the trees kept to size as bushes, as much to assure a lush crop as to aid the pickers. Since silkworms were entirely dependent on mulberry leaves, taking nothing else for their sustenance, it was no wonder that the mulberry had become known world-wide as the "Tree of Gold," a magical name that appealed to her.

On the landing, Émile passed the bedchamber door to go into his dressing-room. As he made ready for bed, he was clear in his mind as to how it should be between Gabrielle and himself on their wedding night. He accepted that she did not love him. Not once during their courtship had she made any pretence about her feelings, and he, reserved by nature and not one to wear his heart on his sleeve at any time, had made it appear that his were on the same level. If he had needed further proof about biding his time, he had had it during the marriage ceremony when she would have snatched her hand from his ring and he had seen how close he was to losing her forever. He was thankful that he had kept control of the situation at that moment of crisis, but the hurt of it had been like a dagger thrust and the pain had not ebbed, made worse by the desire for her that was high in him.

He planned to win her love gradually. He would rush nothing, for, loving her as he did, it was his dread that submissive resignation on her part would emasculate him temporarily, a humiliation his pride could not endure.

She was in bed when he entered the room, her hair copper-bright in the candlelight as she lay on the wide lace-trimmed pillows. Taking the silver candle-snuffer, he put out the flame before removing his dressing-robe. As the moonlight fell softly into the room, he turned back the bedcovers and got in beside her. Trembling with restraint, he leaned over to cup her face with his hand and kiss her gently.

"Good night, my dear Gabrielle. You must be tired after this long day." His voice was thick with strain. "Sleep well." Then, when he would have withdrawn in his own private physical torment to the far side of the bed, she flung her arms around his neck, pressing herself to him, her firm young flesh warm through the gossamer-thin nightgown.

"What's wrong?" she cried in bewilderment. "I'm glad to be your wife."

He uttered a groan of joy, taking her mouth in passion. She was left in no doubt that there was nothing wrong between them as far as he was concerned. He found her generous and responsive and he believed he had awakened a need of him in her that boded well for their married life together. If she lay awake after he slept, he did not know it.

2

Ten days went by before Jules and Hélène made their promised visit. Gabrielle, sighting their arrival from a window, ran down the steps of the house to meet them, her arms held wide, her muslin gown billowing behind her.

"Welcome! Both of you! I've been watching the road for you since mid-morning."

Jules, alighting first, greeted her exuberantly. "Then here's your reward!" He caught her by the waist to swing her around, she laughing in protest, as if they were still in their nursery days.

Émile, emerging from the house at a more sober pace, creased his brows at this buoyant display of sibling affection. It annoyed him immensely, since it seemed to herald what he might expect from the duration of this visit. The trouble was that he did not feel ready yet to share his lovely young wife with other people, least of all two of her family who would be more demanding of her time than ordinary guests would have been. In all fairness he had to admit the fault was not theirs; it lay in his own newly-wed possessiveness. With the courtesy that was inherent in him, he went forward to receive the company.

"I endorse my wife's welcome to our home," he said to them. "We are privileged that you are prepared to share some of your time together with us."

"They can stay for three days instead of two," Gabrielle informed him happily. Politeness compelled Émile to register pleased surprise.

As the servants carried in the baggage, he took Jules through to the salon to offer him wine after the journey while Gabrielle showed Hélène upstairs to the room that had been prepared for them.

"This is a handsome room," Hélène remarked as she pulled off her gloves, glancing around at the blue and white striped wallpaper and the bed with its gilded mouldings and pair of ornamented pilasters at each end. "We shall be most comfortable here."

Gabrielle took her coat and bonnet from her. "How is Father?"

Hélène's dimples appeared. "Not easy," she admitted forbearingly as if speaking of a child's tantrums. "He doesn't like to lose sight of Jules when he is at home, so it was quite difficult to get away. But Jules insisted."

"I'm glad he was firm about it. Father wants to rule everybody's life." There was an edge to Gabrielle's voice.

Hearing it, Hélène turned from the window, where she had gone to look out at the view of lush green hills with the bright glint of a river and the village in the distance. "I know from what I've heard he has always been a contrary man, but now that he is old and in constant pain we should make allowances."

"Father will never be old," Gabrielle remarked cynically. "He treats you as a daughter, but otherwise he can't keep his hands off women. You know how hard it is to keep maidservants under his roof. That's why you're far more at his beck and call than you have any right to be. Has the new housekeeper arrived to take my place as chatelaine?"

"Her appointment was cancelled. After you left, your father did not want a stranger taking charge."

Gabrielle sighed. "So now you've shouldered the supervision of that big house yourself?"

"It's no burden."

"Not on its own, but you do so many other things. You're companion, nurse and slave to Father. His hold of you gets tighter and tighter. In addition to everything else, you're the one who has the task of calming his irascible temper after he has quarrelled with Henri and shouted at everybody else."

Hélène linked her fingers and twisted them uneasily. "I'm glad you mentioned that. I'm rather worried. Things took a new turn yesterday. Father discovered that Yvonne had run up dressmakers' bills beyond all bounds. How he found out I don't know. He actually told Henri to divorce her, saying she was a useless baggage whose extravagances would pauper him."

"How ever did Henri react to that?"

"Very badly, I'm afraid. I believe if Father could have been on his feet they would have come to blows." Hélène dipped her head in distress. "I wished I hadn't been present. Unfortunately I had no chance to leave. I know Yvonne is foolish and reckless at times and nobody can deny she's a spendthrift, but she's amiable and harmless in herself, easily hurt and quick to cry if anyone speaks harshly to her."

Gabrielle refrained from saying they were crocodile tears, frequently induced to escape trouble. Yvonne was one of the few women able to look pretty when she cried and she used this attribute to full advantage. "I think we've talked long enough about family frictions. You're here to forget them for a while. Let's rejoin the menfolk. They'll be wondering what has happened to us."

Her first act as hostess was to take her two guests to view the silk sheds. Although the silkworm eggs had yet to hatch, Gabrielle thought it would be of interest to them to take a tour of the place, for neither had visited a silk farm before. She linked arms companionably with Jules on one side and Hélène on the other, the three of them laughing and talking together. Émile followed in their wake.

The three days went by all too quickly for Gabrielle. She was careful not to separate her brother and his wife by any social arrangements, knowing how important it was for them to make the most of each other's company. The opportunity for which she had been waiting did not come until the evening before their departure, when Émile invited Hélène to view his collection of rare silk moths from India and the Far East, which he bred for their beauty alone and not for any commercial reasons. At the end of their brief life span they were kept in display cases on his study walls. Gabrielle went with Jules out into the garden room, where plants of every height, some in blossom, created a tropical atmosphere. It was here that those same silk moths, some with wingspans of several inches, were allowed to fly after emerging from their cocoons, mesh doors being fitted across the glass ones to prevent escape. It was a sight she had yet to see and she was looking forward to the hatching.

"At last a chance to talk to you alone," Jules said at once.

"And I to you. I know you've never wanted Hélène to endure the hardships of following you on campaign since she took a fever not long after your marriage when with you during the fighting in Italy. However, now she should go with you or you should buy your own home for her. She really deserves to have time to herself instead of being the mainstay of a house where she is never left in peace. Her duties have doubled since I married Émile."

"That's what I want to discuss with you." He took her by the elbow and led her to a seat for two. "Hélène and I have talked the matter over. She does not want to move into a place where she would have little more to do than worry about me. It does her good to be busy. She also believes that Father needs her presence, and it pleases me that my wife can be a comfort to him." He saw the shadow pass over his sister's face and he gestured apologetically. "I didn't mean to hurt you. I'm probably the only one, with the exception of Hélène, who knows that, in spite of everything, you do care about Father. God knows you would have every right not to."

She gave a little shrug of resignation. "The filial bond is not easily broken. He is an extraordinary man, prepared to die shouting at us all. I admire the power he wields. I should like to have it myself, although I would use it in a different way."

"Henri is the one who will inherit the power one day, which is as it should be, since he has been Father's right-hand man for years." He rested an arm on the back of the seat, leaning towards her, his tone urgent. "That brings me to what I want to talk to you about. I see a change in Father. He has deteriorated in health since I saw him last. We must face the possibility that his life might not last as long as we would wish. When he does go, Hélène must not remain in the house. Yvonne will take over where he will have left off. I've seen all the signs, and Hélène is too kind for her own good, always considering others before herself. I don't want my dear wife to spend the rest of her life in submission to others."

"Why should she?" Gabrielle exclaimed. "These wars will end one day and you'll be home to stay." She broke off, seeing how he was looking at her, the boyish look gone from his face to reveal the grimness of the soldier beneath.

"There's no guarantee that I'll be among those to survive."

She extended a hand defensively, refusing to accept the possibility. "Don't say that," she implored.

"I have to speak of it for Hélène's sake. You see, we are both hoping that she may have conceived a child during this time we have spent together. If it is so, it means she would be more vulnerable than ever to the demands of others, taking advantage of her being left a widow with a baby." He reached out to grip his sister's hand, which had dropped into her lap, and he held it with an almost painful pressure between both of his own. "Will you promise me that you'll get her away from our father's house when he is dead and if I'm no longer able to protect her?"

"You know I will!" The promise burst from her. "I just hope and pray that particular duty never has to come my way."

Some of his usual cheerfulness returned and he smiled broadly. "I'll do my best to ensure it doesn't. In the meantime you've set my mind at rest."

All that had been said filled her thoughts when she stood with Émile to wave farewell to Hélène and Jules the next day. Her brother had hugged her, chucked her chin playfully and made some amusing remark that had set them all laughing. He was departing with the same air of confidence and optimism that he had always maintained at such times, not wanting anyone, Hélène least of all, to know he harboured doubts as to whether he would ever return.

When the carriage was lost from sight, Gabrielle sighed and turned to walk back into the house with Émile, only to find he had not waited for her. During the next few days, when she would have been grateful for a show of tenderness and comfort in her new anxiety about her brother, Émile was cool and withdrawn by day, silent and fierce in his love-making by night. She realised with dismay that he had resented sharing her with two people whom she loved and had felt neglected. He was the last person she would ever have suspected of jealousy, and it was as if layers of his character were beginning to peel away, leaving her with the knowledge that her husband was a complex man with dark emotions that warred with the more benevolent side of his nature. It was a relief to her when he recovered from his moodiness by the end of the week and everything appeared to be between them as it had been before. Unfortunately the moment had passed when she would have confided in him, and some of the hope that they would be true companions in their life together faded from her.

Spring gave way to the summer of 1804. During these weeks their marriage followed a smooth path, which made a sudden and unexpected confrontation between them something of a shock to her. It occurred not long after the thousands of silkworms had hatched out, bringing a bustle of activity throughout the silk farm and on the plantation where the mulberry trees, their new growth coinciding with the hatching, were being plucked by pickers from morning until night, the leaves being shredded afterwards for the larvae.

Émile came into one of the smaller silk sheds, where she was spreading a fresh supply of mulberry leaves over netting that had been fastened across each tray of larvae. The silkworms would crawl through

to reach the new food and the waste matter left below was easily removed. Hygiene was important during the rearing. It was an almost
continuous task throughout the farm, for the silkworms were voracious
eaters and it took a ton of leaves to feed those from only an ounce of
eggs. That same ounce produced enough silk thread from the spinnerets
in each tail-end, when the time came, to encompass the earth five times,
which she thought quite wondrous.

"You are spending far too much time in these buildings and not
enough in domestic duties," he informed her crisply, an indication that
he had been harbouring irritation over the matter and was annoyed it
had come about in the first place. "I want my home properly run and
not left to unsupervised servants."

"That's an unjust accusation!" she protested indignantly.

"I disagree."

She put down the emptied basket she had collected earlier from one
of the leaf-pickers, facing him in the aisle between the tray-shelves, the
bright sunlight diffused by the shade of slatted shutters. "I don't understand you, Émile. I should have thought that you would be pleased that
I'm taking such an interest in our means of livelihood."

"I am, but it's not fitting that my wife should be working in the
sheds like a hired hand."

"That's a ridiculous attitude. The workers know that my share of
the chores is done for pleasure and is not on the same footing as theirs."

He was unmoved, folding his arms grimly. "I hear that you actually
went into the plantation this morning and helped with the picking."

So that was it! She sighed, remembering she had been in full view of
the road, and neighbours had passed in their carriages. Tattling tongues
had been quick to voice disapproval and had naturally caused him embarrassment. "The pickers had been held up by that early morning
storm. It seemed only sensible to join them for a while."

If the heat of the day had not returned with full force after the
storm, every leaf would have had to be dried by hand, but instead the air
had been filled with the aromatic scent of the newly sun-dried leaves and
she had enjoyed the picking session, a wide-brimmed straw hat shading
her eyes. The pickers and other workers on the silk farm never became
familiar when she worked side by side with them. It had been the same
with the weaving community, for she was business-like at any task she
did and had an authoritative attitude at such times. As a child she had
been extremely precocious, which had had the same effect.

Émile was shaking his head. "All this has to stop." Seeing her indignation was mounting, he held up his hands placatingly to calm her
outrage. "By all means visit the sheds now and again to see what is

developing. That is a different matter altogether. I want you to see it all. It won't be long before the larvae begin to spin their cocoons."

"I know." She was extremely angry with him, her voice controlled and defiant. "I've done my own collecting of dried grass and twigs and straw for anchorage when the time comes. You see, I've read all about it. I know what signs to look for when the silkworms are ready."

His face tightened. As far as he knew, she had not opened one of the books he had ordered specially for her. Instead she was forever browsing through his tomes on sericulture, studying the causes of disease among silkworms or the reasons for blights that affected the mulberry on rare and disastrous occasions that no owner of a silk farm cared to contemplate. In addition she sat for hours with her head in the dusty old ledgers and ancient business correspondence, which were kept in the library cupboard, studying records and writing figures and facts in a notebook of her own. At first he had thought it a simple absorbing of information previously unknown to her in order that she might talk intelligently to him about his work, although he soon had to make plain to her that when the day was at an end he wanted to put the routine of the silk farm from his mind and not have it as a main topic at the dinner table. She had admitted to her enthusiasm running away with her and they had made a little joke of it.

After that she did not discuss her reading with him and he had thought she would soon tire of such dull study. Then gradually it had become apparent that she intended to have more than a passive interest in the silk farm. Although he had been patient with her, not wanting trouble between them, she had ignored his tactful hints. This morning had broken all bounds by her lowering herself and her position as his wife in doing field hands' work. She deserved severe correction.

"Then, since you know all the signs, you can wait now until that stage is reached. Nothing of any real consequence happens in between to compel your presence here."

She coloured sharply. He was forbidding her access to the rearing silk sheds! Her eyes flashed dangerously. "Are you condemning me to boredom?"

He kept his patience. Occasions when he lost his temper were mercifully rare, for, as with most equable people, when it did happen it was an explosive experience and he felt drained and depressed for days afterwards. He had been prepared for difficulties in his marriage, having been aware from his first meeting with her that she was quick and intelligent, with a mind of her own and independent to a degree that would have daunted lesser men. Yet, if anything, he was more in love with her than ever. In spite of that, he had to make a stand on the present issue for her sake as well as his own.

"You can find plenty to do. It's high time we returned some of the invitations we have accepted over the past weeks. We've had no one to the house since Jules and Hélène were here."

She was reminded painfully of the jealousy he had shown. It had been different at the social events they had attended in the weeks since then. For all had been strangers to her and there had been no one to talk of the days before she was married to him. She had also been careful to keep flirtations at bay.

"I can arrange a supper party," she said stiffly, "with a hired orchestra, and there could be dancing on the lawn."

"A capital idea!" he declared with more enthusiasm than the suggestion warranted. Then he took her by the shoulders, choosing to ignore her rigid stance, and his voice softened in tone. "Do you think I don't know why you've been directing your energies towards the silk sheds? It has been to assuage your homesickness for Lyons and city life, which is why I've said nothing until now. However, the time has come for you to fulfil your rightful role in life."

Her face became bleak with disappointment. Nothing she had said had had any effect. Even her willingness to meet him half-way had been to no avail. Jerking away from him, she flung up her hands in exasperation.

"I can't remember a time when men have not tried to thwart my interest in silk. Everything I have ever learned has been through my own efforts. As a child I bribed instruction from the weavers with my shawls and scarves and shoes, any piece of jewellery given to me on my natal days, and more often than not with food from the kitchen. When I was older and my skills matched theirs, they were glad of a respite while I worked a loom for them. My reward was always in the mastery of an intricate pattern and it was my dream that one day my father would relent and let me take my place with Henri in the business."

"That would have been impossible."

"Why?" She whirled about to face him. "It's not too much to ask. I know my grandmother used to sit at a desk to list the presented bolts of silk that the weavers brought to the house then as they do now. It was she who paid out the monies due to them for each piece of work. I would have been grateful for that task, but my father refused me, preferring to leave it all to Henri and a clerk, along with everything else."

"Would you have been content with so simple a chore?"

She looked at him almost in surprise that he should have asked such a question with its obvious answer. "Of course not. I should have made it a bridge to more important things. I have an instinct for selecting patterns and defining good design. That came out under tuition with an art master when Father decided I should receive some formal education."

"Go on. I'm interested."

She became calmer, seeing that, as always, he was sincere, and she was pleased to tell what he wanted to know. "I learned the ins and outs of commerce, but because of my sex I realised I should never be allowed to discuss finance with bankers or negotiate for orders and so I was resigned to not asking for the moon. What I did want was a position in an advisory capacity. If only my father had not been so biased and shortsighted, he would have seen that I had talent to match my brother's. I could have put new life into the business."

"Did you have the same aims towards the Valmont silk farm when you decided to marry me?"

Completely unabashed, she regarded him frankly, her eyes so clear he could see the shading of the irises from deep blue to darkest violet, almost as if they were illumined from within. "Surely you guessed that? You had shown me that you were an enlightened man ready to accept that the Revolution had given women like me a new freedom of spirit."

His gaze was cool. "Is that the only reason why you married me?"

"No!" Her forceful answer rang with truth. "I visualised a true partnership, my role a dual one of wife and business aide." Her expression relaxed and she came forward to rest her hands against his chest, looking up into his face. "More than that, I respected and admired you. I would never want any difference of opinion to come between us."

It was said without guile, for it was not her way to use wiles and pretence. She had truly believed that, by showing her genuine interest in his work during their courtship, he had comprehended her wish to be actively involved in it. His serious, considering gaze showed how much it distressed him to be at loggerheads with her, stirring her compassion. When he put an arm about her waist she did not draw away and willingly laid her head in the hollow of his shoulder. She wanted no bitterness to come between them.

In his opinion she was too emancipated for her own good. The Revolution had opened doors for women in many ways, and their throwing aside of corsetry and lacing in the new, soft and unrestricted fashions symbolised the mood of liberation that had originated at that time and still prevailed. With so many of the old formalities gone by the board, they were able to speak and act with an openness in public and private life as never before, and, on the whole, men had accepted these changes. Yet certain male-imposed restrictions remained unshaken. A man was still head of his own household, wives were expected to be obedient, and daughters, unless extremely self-willed, could be given by their fathers into marriages of convenience. Most satisfactory was the

fact that no woman could get one of the new and speedy divorces introduced by the Directoire and upheld by the succeeding government of
the Consulate unless her husband was of a like mind.

Cupping her chin in the palm of his hand, he tipped her face up to
his. "Accept my ruling, my dear. It is for the best. I love you and I don't
want to share you with anyone or anything that might distract you from
what I want above all else, which is that you should become completely
mine as I am yours."

Uneasily she turned away from him. She had come into marriage
looking for friendship from him and she had not expected to discover
that his sole aim was to compel love from her. If it had been possible to
wish herself in love with him she would have done it, for he was a good
man with much kindness in him, but so far fondness and loyalty were
all she could offer and she had looked for no more from him. Automatically she took down from a nail in the wall the straw hat which she had
worn on the plantation that morning, picked up some cotton gloves she
kept there for some of the work involved, and said in a quiet voice: "I'll
go and draw up that guest-list."

When she reached the house she went upstairs to put her hat away.
As she closed the bedchamber door behind her, she fell back against the
panels as reaction took over. Convulsively she clenched the hat-brim,
buckling it in her hands. All her will power had been needed to stop her
screaming at Émile. Perhaps it would have been better if she had, except
that there was a deep reluctance in her to hurt him in any way. He had
married her in good faith. It was no fault of his that she found it impossible to fall into a conventional role. Suddenly she felt like one of the
exotic Indian silk moths that he bred as a hobby. They had the power of
flight and the illusion of freedom but were hemmed in by the mesh
walls that kept them from the outside world.

In the days that followed she went ahead with preliminary arrangements for the party and, her disappointments set aside, began to look
forward to it. She loved to dance and enjoyed jovial company. The invitations went out, and she was sorry when Hélène declined for the reason that her pregnancy was becoming noticeable. It mattered less when
Henri and Yvonne were also unable to accept, having a previous engage-
ment. As for Dominique, he never attended any social function outside
his own home. The numbers still came to over a hundred, for Gabrielle
had friends in Lyons whom she wanted to welcome to her home, and
Émile had included some business acquaintances and their wives among
others whom he had known for a long time.

When Émile's ban on the rearing silk sheds ran out, Gabrielle was
able to see for herself that the silkworms had stopped eating and were
beginning to wander, something they never did until this final stage.

They raised themselves, waving their heads about in what was a curious sight, showing they were almost ready to spin.

The spinning itself began three days before the eve of the party when she could not have been busier, for carpenters were erecting a dais on the terrace for the orchestra, the gardener was sorting potted plants for her approval, and in the kitchen the first baking was in progress. She managed to snatch a few minutes now and again to view the delicate process, the silk from the silkworms' tail-end spinnerets hardening when it came in contact with the air and enveloping them in misty veils that gradually thickened. By the day of the party the majority of the silkworms were already encased in small golden-yellow cocoons of silk, beautifully rounded at each end and feather-light.

"I remember how surprised I was years ago when I first learned that it is the silkworms' gum that makes the cocoons all shades from white through yellow to orange," she said to Émile, who had accompanied her to the rearing silk sheds in the last moments she was able to spare on that busy day.

"As you know, it depends on the type of *Bombyx mori* being bred." He picked up one of the cocoons with its curiously fuzzy appearance and put it into her palm, where it lay like an opaque gem. "When the cocoons are boiled in preparation for reeling, some sericin does disperse, but the colour finally goes when the silk is actually degummed in the process, just before it is woven."

She cupped the cocoon carefully. That morning Émile had called her into the garden room to watch an Indian moon moth emerge from its rough-looking brown cocoon. These exotic silk moths were hatching earlier, not being dependent on mulberry leaves in the caterpillar stage, like their less attractive counterparts. The moon moth was a marvellous sight once its wings had dried out, being a translucent ice-green with delicate markings. Yet her affections were lodged with the humbler silk moth that would come from the cocoon she held. No longer able to survive in the wild, totally dependent upon man, it gave in its turn the means to create the queen of fabrics that was beautiful, waftingly light, warm and strong.

Touching the cocoon with an explorative finger tip, she discovered it was completely hard. Émile smiled at the absorbed expression on her face.

"Inside, the pupa is already forming," he said. "I'm sure of a good season this year, and at the end of it you shall have a gown of Valmont silk."

She flashed him a look of delighted surprise. "I'll weave it myself on the loom I brought with me from home." Swiftly she implanted a kiss on his mouth. Always moved by any spontaneous gesture of affection from her, he clasped her to him. Afterwards her ribs ached from the pressure of his embrace.

The evening was warm and mild, the velvet sky full of stars. Paper lanterns had been hung in the trees, twinkling rainbow lights between the branches. People arrived in open carriages, the women wearing diaphanous gowns in all the pastel colours, their jewellery vying with the illuminations. Some had adopted the high-fashion fad of dampening their undershifts to reveal their figures as if they were naked, which indeed they were underneath. Turbans were much in vogue, ornamented with jewels or a single upright plume. Otherwise hair was entwined with pearls, ribbons or flowers. Gabrielle's gown was cream lace over peach silk and wafted gently against her body, a gold fillet in her curls. Émile had picked her a perfect cream rose, and she wore it at her cleavage, fastened by a pearl brooch amid the lace.

They stood side by side to receive their guests within the hallway. When the dancing began, some chose the wide terrace to be near the orchestra, while the rest spread out across the lawn, where the little lanterns created multi-coloured shadows that crossed and recrossed in the pattern of the dancers. After partnering each other in the first quadrille, Émile and Gabrielle parted company to dance with their guests. He did not care for dancing and it was a tedious duty for him; he hated parties, even his own, but he believed in fulfilling social obligations, particularly now that he had a young wife. Shortly before supper he reclaimed her attention, coming across the lawn to where she stood talking in the pastel glimmer of the lanterns to several young people from Lyons who were old friends of hers. Their conversation was merry by the sound of it, punctuated by bursts of laughter.

"Gabrielle, my dear, I should like to present a guest who was unavoidably delayed in getting here. Here he is—Monsieur Devaux."

For a second or two she did not move. Then abruptly she turned her head and looked fully, with dilating pupils, at Nicolas where he stood at her husband's side. The sight of him brought delicious shockwaves to her heart, and she saw a muscle clench involuntarily in his jaw as if seeing her again had been the same for him. He was even taller than she remembered, seeming to fill her whole vision.

"We have already met, have we not, Monsieur Devaux?" She felt weak, engulfed by pleasure. And dread. Out of the corner of her eye she caught Émile's glance of surprise.

"You know each other?"

"Only slightly." She let a smile creep along her mouth, for Nicolas had a smile for her as he bowed over her hand.

"It was the briefest of meetings," he said, "in somewhat unusual circumstances."

She recalled how there had been no smiles between them on that strangely dramatic day when her life had entered a new phase. With that previous gaunt and serious expression lifted from his face, it was as though another side of him was being revealed to her, enabling her to see that he could prove to be an even greater threat to her peace of mind by having qualities of humour, compassion, sincerity and steadfastness such as she had not previously suspected or thought about. A likeable attractive man held far more power to devastate than one who was wholly looks and ego. As if a chord of warning had been struck in her, she adopted a bland tone, every inch the hostess welcoming her husband's guest.

"I know I echo Émile's wishes in hoping that you have a pleasant evening at our home."

"I thank you. You are most kind."

She thought the conventional phrases they were exchanging were almost laughable, except that she did not feel in the least like laughing. Fortunately Émile was taking charge of him again and presenting him to those in the group she was with, afterwards leading him away to meet more people.

As soon as it was possible she slipped away herself on a pretext and went into the house, needing to adjust to the impact of this unexpected reunion. In her bedchamber she sank down sideways onto a chair, resting her elbow across the back of it, and reviewed the situation. She blamed herself for not having asked Émile the name of his new business acquaintance whom he had chosen to invite at the last minute after a chance meeting in Lyons when he happened to be there for the day. Then she would have been prepared. Or would she have suspected ahead of time the effect that seeing Nicolas again was going to have on her? She understood now that she had kept and suppressed their impassioned encounter, locking it away somewhere deep inside of her, not knowing that it would erupt with volcanic proportions at the moment she saw him again. When Émile had mentioned there was one more name to be added to the guest-list, she had been busy at the time, checking items that had been delivered in readiness for the party. Barely paying attention, she had said there would be more than enough food for a score of last-minute guests, and later had simply pencilled in a tick on the guest-list.

What was happening to her? If she had been less realistic, less practical and level-headed, she would have imagined herself to have fallen disastrously in love. The thought was so alarming, threatening the whole of her newly established and orderly existence, that she pressed a hand across her eyes as if to blot out the entire concept of it. But what she was feeling in her heart was all too familiar. She had known it before when she was seventeen. Now it had returned a thousandfold, eclipsing even the memory of the youth she had loved with adolescent fervour. This was mature and forceful, stirring her mind and her body towards a path that was full of danger. It would take every bit of her strength of character to withstand the attraction of a man who was, to all intents and purposes, an enemy of hers and her family.

"Are you not well, madame?"

She let her hand drop from her eyes and raised her head to see that her maid had come into the room. With effort she tried to make her smile convincing. "Yes, I am perfectly well. Just a little tired after all the preparations, I suppose. I shall return to my guests now before I'm missed."

As she braced herself to face the rest of the evening she wondered why Émile should have invited Nicolas in the first place. He must have heard of the feud between the Roches and the Devaux, for it was legend in Lyons. Possibly he had forgotten and he was certainly unaware of the crisis he had caused by letting Nicolas come to their home.

Émile met her as she came out onto the terrace. "I've been looking for you. Is anything the matter?"

She assumed a bright expression. "Nothing that can't be amended. We'll talk later when the evening is over. I think it's time for supper now."

There was a rising buzz of chatter as people strolled leisurely into the long salon where the buffet awaited them. Warily she watched for Nicolas. Being of such a good height, he was quick to detect in a throng and she soon saw that he was in company with the group of her friends with whom she had been talking when Émile brought him to her. At least he was being well entertained, for the men were good conversationalists and the women pretty. Yet the attention he appeared to be paying them did not ease her conviction that, even though she was presently out of his sight, he was as conscious of her presence in the room as she was of his. The tingling of her nerves confirmed it. She half believed that if she released her mind she would receive his thoughts, a frightening and unnerving possibility that she thrust from her.

Resolutely smiling and gracious, she moved among her guests, making sure that all plates were full and glasses being replenished. Deliberately she avoided the corner where Nicolas and her friends had seated themselves, certain that she would find his eyes waiting for hers. Eventually she reached Émile, who was about to have some supper himself. It pleased him to fill a plate for her, selecting what he knew she liked best. She realised as she took it that she had come instinctively to him for protection. Food had been the last thing on her mind.

After supper, at Émile's suggestion she took several interested guests into the garden room to see his exotic silk moths, many of which had now hatched out, seemingly light-years away from their less colourful relatives in the rearing silk sheds. Their marvellous wings gave brilliance to the flowers and a stained-glass effect to the windows where they rested, the pale green of the Indian moon moths contrasting with plum and gold and ochre and purple of the giant Atlas moth, with its twelve-inch wing-span, and the Chinese oak moth, fluttering wings of shaded apricot.

"Do they give silk?" someone asked.

"Their cocoons are either unreelable or too coarse to be a commercial proposition. Émile says their beauty is reward enough for him, and I feel the same way."

By the time she had answered further questions and led everyone back to the party, the dancing again in full swing, the weather had changed with the threat of a storm. The air had become turbulent, and a curiously warm wind had come up to send clouds scudding across the sky and make the glowing lanterns bounce on the branches. It was having an exhilarating effect on the company, more potent than champagne, swirling the skirts of the women and buffeting them in closer contact with their partners than the steps of the dances warranted. The orchestra, caught up in the same spell, had switched to playing their liveliest tunes. When the music struck up for a *contredanse*, everybody joined in, Gabrielle among them. She was equally affected by the wind's wild game. A large circle was formed with linked hands across the lawn and changed shape as it wound in and out of the trees of the copse where the shadows were dark and secret. A roll of thunder, beating like drums over the hills, served to heighten the excitement. When the chain broke at every twelfth step for people to catch hands with a new partner and twirl around together, many seized the chance to kiss and fondle flirtatiously. Although the stars could no longer be seen, the rain continued to hold off as if kept at bay by the exuberant festivities.

Then, just as another rumble of thunder gathered the clouds still closer together, Gabrielle whirled forward to find herself facing Nicolas as her new partner. The planes of his face were highlighted by the swinging lanterns and showed him her sparkling expression as his outstretched hands seized hers. She almost cried out in released excitement at this physical contact, and if electric currents had leapt up her arms from their joined clasp she would not have been in the least surprised. He laughed under his breath, totally triumphant, his eyes crinkling at the corners.

"I've been waiting all the evening for this moment!"

She laughed with him, feeling completely reckless, knowing now that it had been the same for her. Happiness gushed through her as he swept her into the steps of the dance. The thunder had caused several couples in their region to hesitate, looking skywards uncertainly, and in breaking the chain they left her free to dance on with him. "I must confess that I didn't know you were coming this evening. You were quite the last person I had expected to see again."

He was thoroughly amused. "I suppose it was a shock."

"Not at all an unpleasant one."

There was no need for her to have told him, for he had seen in her expression what it had meant to her. "In any case, you must have known that sooner or later we should meet again."

She looked down and away from him, sensing danger. In her present exhilarated mood it would have been easy not to care. In fact, did she care? It was a long time since she had felt so buoyant and light-hearted, although perhaps light-headed was a more apt description. "I might have expected to sight you in Lyons, even though it's a large city. Not in my own home out in the country."

"Should I not have come?"

"Oh, yes. Why not?" She tilted her head back challengingly, her eyes full of mischief, her wind-blown skirt whirling about and clinging to his legs. "Except that I can't help wondering if it crossed your mind as to whether my brother Henri would be here."

He regarded her sportively. "He wouldn't have kept me away. The proverbial wild horses couldn't have done that." Then he raised his eyebrows in mock inquiry. "He isn't, is he?"

Laughing, she shook her head. "No, I'm thankful to say."

"I knew this was going to be a splendid party."

She could have completed his words for him. "Because there's nobody else to come between us this time." There! She was reading his thoughts. What could he read of hers?

He had slowed the pace of their dancing to a leisurely drifting in and out of the trees, for it was no longer possible to catch more than an occasional snatch of music from the terrace in the rustling of leaves and the creaking of the tossing branches overhead. Inevitably they came to a standstill, she to lean back against a tree, he to stand facing her, resting one hand on the bark beside her. The rumbling of the thunder was nearer.

"Have you been living in Lyons since the day we met?" she asked him.

"No, I returned to Paris the following morning. That's where I have my silk looms. I'm back in Lyons now on a few days' visit to see about the redecoration and repair of the family house in La Croix Rousse." The wind was whipping at his hair and the ties of his neckcloth. "It's going to take months to put it in order again."

"Why is that? It's not so many years since you and your parents left there."

He could see that her query was without guile. She did not have the least idea what damage had been perpetrated at her father's instigation. "Damp and dust are hard on silk. New panels and drapes and chair and sofa coverings are needed throughout. There's some other damage, too."

She did not question him about that, being interested in the silks. "Will the weaving be done in Paris?"

"Yes, it will."

Around them other dancing couples had spread out, disorganised by the dispersing of the chain and the lost music to linger by themselves. For Gabrielle the erotic atmosphere created by the approaching storm was spiced by an awareness of stolen kisses and embraces out in the heavy darkness, and she did not doubt that Nicolas was tuned to it too. Suddenly she felt she had to keep talking at all costs. A silence between them might lead to anything.

"Do you plan to return often to Lyons when your house is habitable again?"

"That is my intention. More than that, I hope eventually to settle there permanently."

She both welcomed and feared that piece of news. "Don't you consider yourself to be a Parisian now?"

"Nobody born in Lyons ever feels really at home anywhere else."

That completed her feeling of being fully in harmony with him. "Would you like to know my most favourite part of Lyons?"

He could not take his eyes from her. A flickering lantern nearby, resisting the wind's attempt to extinguish it, gave enough radiance for him to see the eagerness of her expression, the pale gleam of her throat and shoulders, the alluring swell of her breasts above the rim of her gown. "Tell me," he urged.

"It's on the slopes of Fourvière. I should like to build a house there. It would be away from all the houses and streets and the mills, and yet, through the view from there, would be more a part of the city than being at the heart of it in my childhood home in the Rue Clémont."

"Have you picked the exact site?"

She smiled reminiscently. "Once. Long ago. My brother Jules and I were children and went on a picnic there by ourselves. We found some pieces of Roman pottery. I marked a special spot with it. That was where I thought one day my house would be. Then he wanted to take the pottery home with him, and so I left one piece there. It will be covered over with grass and leaves and earth by now, and yet I still know where it is."

"I should like to see it." He was serious. The mood between them had changed to a deeper, more intimate level. She realised too late what she had done and attempted to rise out of it on a teasing note.

"Then you must search for it yourself. It is my secret."

It did not work. His gaze remained steadily fixed on her. "So you feel cut off from Lyons out here in the country?"

"I do sometimes." It was on the tip of her tongue to admit that her existence had become dull since her activities on the silk farm had been curtailed, but she stopped herself in time. That was separate from her appreciation of the countryside itself. "This is a lovely district. There are tranquil views from every window." She saw that he raised an eyebrow and she collapsed into smiles. "Very well. I might as well say it. I do miss being at the centre of everything in the silk trade."

He smiled at her in return. The levity they had shared earlier was gone. These were the smiles of the understanding of each other that was between them. "Not many women would have given such a reason. They would have said they missed the social round, the card-parties, the gossip, the access to milliners and dressmakers and all the rest. But then you are not like any other woman I have ever met, Gabrielle."

At his first use of her Christian name she rolled her head slightly away from him, looking back towards the lights of the house that showed distantly between the trees. The silhouettes of those dancing on the lawn and terrace were passing to and fro. There were fewer lanterns glowing now, many blown out by the wind, including the one on a branch close by, which had just left them in almost complete darkness. Tendrils of her hair, tugged from the gold fillet, danced about her face with a life of their own.

"Am I not?" Her voice was barely audible.

"If time could be turned back to the day we met, I wouldn't stand aside again and let you go."

She did not protest that he should not say such things to her, because she loathed all forms of coyness and he had spoken truthfully. "Nothing could have been changed. I had given my promise to Émile that I would be his wife. Never think that anything you could have said or done would have made any difference."

"Then I wish I had come home weeks before that day, when there was still a chance."

Slowly she turned her head to look at him again. Whatever she might have allowed herself to feel for him had no past and no future. The rich pleasure she was experiencing in being with him had to be confined to the short time left to them and then must be eliminated from her life. "I'm happy that we met again this evening," she confessed gently, "even though that is an end to it. I shall try to ensure that our paths don't cross in the future."

He moved close, looking down into her eyes. "Do you fear what is between us so much?"

"There is nothing of any real consequence between us. I only know that you and I have lives of our own to lead."

"I came here this evening only to see you. You know that."

"Then let us both be content with having had the chance to finish any wondering about what can never be."

A great stream of forked lightning suddenly split the sky. In the fleeting bluish glow each saw the other's face nakedly revealed, sweeping aside any last doubts about the magnetism that had first drawn them together. As a tremendous clap of thunder followed directly overhead, making the earth shake beneath their feet, he wrapped her into his arms and covered her mouth with his in a devouring kiss of such unleashed passion that she could only cling to him in frenzied response. It was as though they would eat each other alive. She knew then that she had been made for this moment and this man alone.

With the thunder came the rain, slashing down in great heavy drops that made the wood come alive with its pattering, dousing the last of the lantern lights. They defied the downpour, scarcely aware of it, moulded together in the darkness as if they were already one, unnoticed by those scurrying for shelter under the thickest branches of the tallest trees. It was only when someone charged past quite near them that they finally broke apart breathlessly, she searingly aware that if he had borne her down onto the ground she would have clawed him to her. Yet the feeling they had ignited in each other was more than desire, and he was as stunned by it as she. They stood heedless of the rain that was glueing his hair down in fronds and bringing all the contours of her body into sharp relief through the half-soaked fabric of her gown.

"Come away with me!" he urged tautly, flinging out a desperate hand to her. The leaping lightning showed the wrenched passion of his face. "Now! This minute!"

Her whole being yearned to take flight with him. Because the temptation was such that she hardly knew how to resist him, she took refuge in an explosion of temper as if throwing herself back from a cliff's edge. "No! You must be mad!" she shrieked, making herself heard as the thunder boomed like a cannonade, her arms pressed to her sides defensively as if she might yet take his waiting hand.

"It's a second chance! Don't you see?"

"There's no such thing!" She drew back sharply as if she almost expected him to grab her wrist and pull her forcibly away with him from everything to which she was committed and had ever known.

"We belong together!"

"Never! I'm not yours! I never will be!" She was almost beside herself with panic. "Go away! Go out of my life!"

She swung about and ran from him. It was as though she were running away from herself, some shadowy phantom of her own form remaining with him, full of smiles and willing and melting as if a thousand obligations and promises did not exist to keep her severed from him.

He shouted after her on a new note of command. "Keep away from those tall trees! They're dangerous in this storm."

Thunder almost drowned his voice and she only just heard him. She stumbled to a halt and looked back over her shoulder. Blinking through the rain, she could see that he had run to round up those clustered under the trees, persuading them to move, the light-coloured gowns of the women showing him where they were. Her head cleared of panic, she saw, as he had done, that in such a storm any one of those trees might be struck by lightning. She darted across to him, tripping several times over gnarled roots, although she managed to get near without falling down.

"There's the orangery close by," she called out. "I'll lead the way."

He nodded to show he had heard her. As everyone crowded after her, he dropped behind to search out more people. Lightning showed the way, and when she opened the door of the orangery an aromatic scent wafted out to drift around those following her inside. There the women began exclaiming about their hair and their appearance, shivering in their dampened gowns, for the temperature had dropped sharply with the coming of the rain.

Each flash of lightning showed the activity going on outside. Gabrielle, standing by the windows, was able to see through a clearing in the trees to the lawn. Émile had organised his servants as well as the guests' coachmen into holding up tarpaulins and leather coach-covers into canopies under which guests from other directions in the copse were hurried towards the house in clusters of threes and fours.

Eventually he came to the orangery with the canopy bearers. Cold air swept in with him. He was as soaked through as if he had come out of a river. "This way, my friends."

They all left the orangery together, Gabrielle with the women under the canopies, the men preferring to make a dash across the lawn into the house. Indoors the atmosphere was quite hilarious, nobody's spirits depressed by the experience, but the party had drawn automatically to a close. Gabrielle, upstairs with some of the women still chatting before departure, did not see Nicolas leave.

When the last carriage had gone Émile went to pour himself a large cognac. He was chilled through and shivering. He followed the first quickly by a second, taking it in gulps, and then poured a third, all in the space of a few minutes. Gabrielle came to rejoin him.

"I think we can congratulate ourselves on a successful party," he said to her, "even though it did end in such inclement weather."

"I agree. However, there's just one thing."

"Yes? What's that?"

Her throat tightened. She felt choked on what she had to say. "Monsieur Devaux must never be asked to this house again."

"Why not?" His lids came almost together on a hard glance. "Did he attempt a liberty?" When she shook her head, knowing she bore an equal share of responsibility for what happened, he gave a nod. "I thought not. You didn't have a single dance with him that I saw. What is your reason, then?"

It showed her the extent of his watching her whenever they were in company, even to the point of noting her dancing partners. This time the trees and darkness had hidden her away with Nicolas and he had not been with her in the orangery. No wonder Émile was not prepared to hear ill of him. Her answer, which she had prepared, came readily.

"I should have thought it was unnecessary for you to ask. He is a Devaux." It was the only defence she could offer out of which the truth could not be probed.

"Well?"

"Surely you have heard of the old enmity between his family and mine?"

He was unperturbed, swallowing a gulp of cognac. "I knew of it."

She was mystified. "Yet you invited him here, knowing that his great-grandfather killed mine in a duel and there have been unsettled scores on both sides ever since. At our wedding reception, didn't you hear Henri ranting about the traffic collision that had occurred? That was how I met Nicolas Devaux."

"I never listen much to what Henri says at any time, least of all on that day." He put his head on one side, regarding her quizzically. "This evening I must admit I thought you were not yourself. You seemed strained."

"Did you deliberately withhold the name of Devaux from the guest-list in case I should raise an objection?"

He answered her phlegmatically. "You should let bygones be bygones. No good comes of keeping up old hatreds." Although he was tired, chilled to the bone and slightly drunk, he was determined to settle this matter before they went to bed. "How can you be sure there were not faults on both sides at the time of the original quarrel that caused the famous—or should I say infamous—feud? The men in your family are quick enough to bandy about the words 'murder' and 'treason' with regard to the Devaux, but if your great-grandfather was killed in an honourable duel it wasn't murder. As for treason, that was simply a matter of which side one supported in those bloodthirsty Revolutionary days that are best forgotten."

"You needn't think I haven't considered all that in my time."

"I'm not surprised. You've too much intelligence to have done otherwise. Dominique is a man who harbours totally unbalanced grudges. You've told me how he never pardoned you for causing the death of your mother. Maybe he let a grudge run away with him when he denounced two fellow Lyonnais, one of them little more than a boy. Have you wondered who wrecked their mill after they left?" He gestured towards her with his glass. "Maybe you should ask Dominique about it sometime. He could probably enlighten you if what I've heard is correct."

"You're turning this whole argument away from my simple request."

"Only because I'm trying to remove the reason for it." He weighed his words carefully, aware himself that the cognac was causing his voice to become blurred. "Devaux strikes me as a man who will do much for the silk industry. He is ambitious and far-sighted. I intend to do business with him."

"No!"

Émile thought this outburst on his wife's part confirmed how right he had been not to grant her a foothold in his business. Women always allowed their emotions to come between them and the real issue at stake, which in this case was a new customer with the prospect of many good deals. "He's in Lyons on some business of his own at the present time. We had a preliminary talk about the amount of raw silk he requires for his Paris looms, and when he places an order I shall fill it."

She took several paces towards him, her hands clasped in agitation. "Believe me, I feel no hatred towards him. None at all." Inwardly she cried out that it was entirely the reverse. "I just think it best there should be no further contact in order to avoid any possible trouble in the future."

Wearily Émile pulled loose his rain-dampened cravat and ran a finger around the high collar, which was sticking uncomfortably to his neck. "Be logical, my dear. This man has done you no personal harm and I can't turn aside good trade. He aims to open the Devaux mill again in the Croix Rousse district at some future date. If and when this takes place, he is going to be in the market for still more raw silk. I'm going to be the one to supply it."

She was filled with foreboding. It was as if the ground were falling away beneath her feet and there was nothing to stop her hurtling towards Nicolas, no matter how hard she fought against it. Desperately she made a final appeal. "Do business with him if you must, but I beg you to excuse me from meeting him socially until I feel myself ready to accept his presence."

He'd had enough of the whole argument. "Very well," he conceded. "But you must remember that our paths are likely to cross Devaux's again once he has re-established himself in Lyons, because the silk world is a small one in many ways." Something he saw in her eyes disturbed him, for it revealed an inner torment that was totally out of proportion to the situation. Intending to reassure her, he touched her beloved face with his finger tips, meaning to stroke her cheek, but involuntarily she jerked away at his ice-cold hand and caught it within her own, her expression changing, her voice ringing with anxiety.

"You're frozen through! Dear God! I had no idea. Go and get out of those wet clothes at once." She gave him a gentle push towards the stairs. He went without protest, draining the last of the cognac from the glass and hearing his teeth chatter against the rim. Hastily she summoned two servants who were clearing up, telling them to take hot bath water upstairs without delay.

In the morning the good weather returned as if the storm had never been. Keeping tiredness and a headache to himself, wearing a heavier coat than he would normally have worn on a warm day, Émile announced to Gabrielle at the breakfast table that he had suffered no ill effects from the downpour of the night before. Pouring his coffee, she was unsure. His complexion looked patchy and his eyes red-rimmed. She hoped it was only due to a surfeit of cognac.

By midday her worst fears were confirmed. Émile returned to the house barely able to walk and in a state of high fever. His doctor was summoned at once while she helped him to bed. He collapsed thankfully against the pillows, only to attempt to get up again when he remembered he had left some letters on his desk.

"I will see they are sent with the post-chaise," she reassured him. "Just rest now."

It did not take Dr. Jaunet long to arrive. A cheerful, rotund man of middle age, he sat with knees well apart to accommodate his large stomach as he leaned forward to put an ear to Émile's chest and then to his back. His face gave nothing away, but outside the door he spoke seriously to Gabrielle as she went downstairs with him.

"Your husband must be nursed with great care, Madame Valmont. The danger of a fever like this is that it can cause permanent damage to the lungs, resulting in consumption. The trouble is that he suffered a similar fever in the winter about three years ago after rescuing a child from the river."

"I never knew that."

"Well, he came through the fever that time and there's no reason why he should not again, except that this will probably be a harder fight."

"I'll do everything I can."

It proved to be a fight for Émile's life that lasted many crucial days. Hélène, hearing how ill he was, earned Dominique's displeasure by leaving him in the charge of his personal manservant and arriving to help Gabrielle with the nursing. She was blooming in her pregnancy, her health radiant. It was a challenge to her that she should help get Émile well again, although she did accept Gabrielle's decree that for the sake of her baby there must be no night duties or physical lifting of the patient. To compensate, she made a point of rising early in order to relieve Gabrielle from the bedside at dawn. After a few hours of fitful sleep in an adjoining room, Gabrielle would return to her vigil.

It was inevitable that, with Émile indisposed, those working in the silk sheds should come to ask his wife's decision as to what should be done over certain matters that occurred and that correspondence should mount up on his office desk. He was still in a state of crisis when the *maître ouvrier* consulted her over the most important issue to date.

"I regret having to trouble you, madame. It's time now to bake the cocoons to kill the pupae. Could you tell me the approximate amount that Monsieur Valmont intended to set aside this year for breeding purposes?"

If Émile had mentioned it to her she would have remembered, for there was nothing she did not take note of in connection with silk. "I don't know and my husband is too ill to be asked."

"He may have written it down in his office."

"I shall go at the first opportunity to try to find it."

For another few days she did not think of the cocoons. Émile was delirious and the doctor's potions had no effect. There was nothing left but to keep sponging him down with cool water to combat the high fever, and she became so exhausted that Hélène feared she would collapse. No amount of persuasion would make her surrender the task that Hélène shared with her for some of the time, neither would she allow a reliable woman from the village, Madame Barale, called in by Dr. Jaunet, to take over the nursing from her, delegating only the unimportant tasks.

When finally the fever broke and Émile slipped into a peaceful sleep, she gave way, covering her face with her hands and sobbing helplessly like a child in her relief. Hélène signalled to Madame Barale to take the chair by the bedside while she put an arm around Gabrielle and led her away.

Refreshed by a sound sleep, bathed and revived, Gabrielle returned to the sick-room to hear that Émile had woken, taken a few sips of egg-wine and slept again. Leaving Madame Barale in charge, she went out of the house for the first time since Émile had fallen ill. It seemed like months since she had felt sunshine on her face. She stood for a few moments on the steps of the front entrance with her eyes closed, basking in its warmth. A step on the gravelled drive caused her to shade her eyes against the brightness to see Hélène in bonnet and silken stole coming from the direction of the gates.

"Where have you been?" She went down the steps to meet her.

Hélène smiled, untying her bonnet ribbons. "I've despatched two letters. One to Father to let him know that his son-in-law is well on the way to recovery, although not to expect me home for a while. The second was to Jules, recounting all that has been happening."

"Does he always get the letters you send? Sometimes when I receive one from him I can tell that mine haven't reached him."

"Letters do go astray when his regiment is on the move, and it's particularly bad when they're on campaign. Are you on your way somewhere now?"

"I'm going to Émile's office in the hope that I'll find some information that the *maître ouvrier* needs."

In the small outer office the clerk greeted her. "I heard the good news that Monsieur Valmont is better. How soon before he can get back to work?"

"That will be a long time yet, I'm afraid."

The clerk shook his head in concern. "I have a pile of letters I can't send without his authorisation."

"Let me have them. I'm here to go through some of my husband's papers."

At Émile's desk she unlocked a drawer with a key he kept in a pocket. There was a purse of gold coins, a number of official-looking documents and private letters. She knew the clerk had searched the ledgers in vain for any entry about the cocoons that Émile might have made and the contents of the drawer were a last chance. Opening an almanac, she glanced through, and there, entered only a few days before his illness, was the information she had been seeking. Relocking the drawer, she went to the *maître ouvrier*, who was relieved to be able to go ahead.

For a little while she watched the division of the cocoons being made. Those left to hatch meant that the silk moth, after shedding its pupa shell, would break through the cocoon, which then could not be reeled.

Returning to the office, she sat down again at Émile's desk with the correspondence the clerk had put there. She had acquired a great deal of knowledge about the business, and there was nothing so complicated as to necessitate her putting it aside to await Émile's own scrutiny at a later date. Some unanswered letters needed her attention and the orders in them she passed on to the clerk to be entered in the appropriate ledger. Then suddenly she came to one that had been sent from Paris. She felt her heart stop. It was from Nicolas. A confirmation in writing of the amount of raw silk that he had previously discussed with Émile at a time before he was sure of the amount he would require. The sight of his name aroused without warning the memory of the kiss they had shared on the night of the storm. She tried never to let it come to the surface, and now in a moment of unguarded weakness she could remember vividly the touch, sight and clean male scent of him, the wildness of his mouth, the pressure of his body, the marvellous closeness of his embrace.

Her elbows were on the desk in front of her and she let her head tip into her hands. The yearning in her was as fierce now as it had been then, making it impossible to believe that the risk of meeting him again at any time had been diminished.

With a sigh she straightened up. This letter called for a reply penned by herself. Without hesitation she drew a fresh piece of writing paper towards her and wrote that the Valmont silk farm would not be able to supply the Devaux mill with raw silk now or at any time in the future. She signed it, dusted the wet ink with sand, shook it off and then folded the letter and sealed it with red wax.

She was convinced she had done the right thing in the circumstances, for once one business deal had gone through others would follow. There would be serious trouble when Émile found out about it. That was a risk she had to take. All that mattered was that by this letter she had eliminated any chance of Nicolas's coming to the house, or to the office, of his own accord, and with Émile not in business with him the chance of meeting socially was lessened.

She went through the rest of the letters. Two or three needed consultations with the clerk, and the rest were queries she was able to deal with herself. When the clerk brought her a fresh supply of quill pens that he had cut in readiness for her, it showed her that he was as certain as she was that between them they could keep the business running smoothly until such time as Émile was well enough to take over his desk again. By then she would have established proof that she was able to combine the roles of wife, housekeeper and manager without detriment to any of them. Whether Émile chose to accept that proof depended on many things, not least of all on her termination of the Devaux order.

Whatever the outcome, she felt herself to be a whole person again, independent in her own right once more.

Leaving the office, she strolled back to the house. On the way she picked fresh flowers for the sickroom.

3

Émile's recovery was slow. As soon as he was able, he asked about the business. Hélène, who happened to be on her own with him at the time, told him soothingly that he had no cause to worry about anything. "Gabrielle is looking after everything," she said with the best of intentions, "and you have nothing to worry about."

To her surprise, he uttered a tortured groan, turning restlessly on his pillows before dropping into a sleep of exhaustion again. Gabrielle, forewarned by this reaction, which was clear enough to her, sent the *maître ouvrier* and the office clerk to his bedside in turn as soon as the doctor permitted it, allowing them to tell him of the work in hand. By emphasising that he must not be worried by anything, she ensured that they kept their reports brief and reassuring. He was left with the impression that his wife was only a temporary figurehead, while the business continued to run according to his rules. Satisfied that his authority was not being undermined, he was somewhat easier in his mind, although his physical condition still gave cause for anxiety.

"This is as crucial a time as when he was in fever," Dr. Jaunet told Gabrielle after one of his daily visits. "Nothing must be hastened or you'll find yourself with a permanent invalid on your hands."

She found the atmosphere of the sickroom stultifying and was convinced it was having the same effect on the patient, for the doctor had warned against too much fresh air and insisted on the windows being kept shuttered. When she expressed her anxiety about Émile's slow progress, Hélène, more used to nursing, reminded her that he had been bled twice by the doctor in an effort to bring down his fever and that source of energy took time to replenish. She assured Gabrielle that his convalescence was following a normal path. When Dominique sent an irate message demanding to know how much longer his son's wife intended to absent herself from his home, Hélène replied with unusual spirit by saying that she must stay where she was most needed.

If it had not been for Hélène's extending her goodwill sojourn, Gabrielle would have found it almost impossible to leave Émile's bedside. As he began to recover he wanted her with him all the time and was as irritable and difficult in his gradual convalescence as any other normally healthy man going through the aftermath of a more serious illness than he had ever experienced before. Only Hélène was able to calm his moods, and a rapport grew up between them, so that eventually he began to tolerate Gabrielle's absences. She did not think he would have done so if he had suspected that whenever she left him she went straight to his office to deal with letters and orders, and to receive customers. Yet all was going smoothly. Both the *maître ouvrier* and the clerk worked well under her direction. When Émile, propped up against pillows, began to issue orders, each one was endorsed by Gabrielle. His favourite reading became the letters she had had the clerk prepare for his signature, and he was well pleased when the *maître ouvrier* brought him the good news that the crop from the cocoons, which were being reeled after boiling to remove the gum, a process differing little from the days of the Empress Hsi Lung Shi, had never been better. Émile passed the news on to her in his turn when she brought her embroidery to his bedside, and she smiled as if she had not already rejoiced over it in the silk sheds.

There had been only one woman among those she had seen in the office. Madame Hoinville was a stout-hearted widow of middle age who owned four looms and chose to buy her raw silk direct, afterwards selling her woven silk on the open market instead of being tied to one negotiator.

"It's good to do business with you, Madame Valmont," the woman said when the price had been settled and a date for delivery arranged. "I'm sorry your husband is ill, but you are living proof that we women are not slow to learn the ropes when the need arises."

"I should like to see your mill for myself one day when I'm in Lyons."

"You would be more than welcome. I employ only women like myself who have been left on their own through death, deceit or desertion."

From her Gabrielle learned much of what it meant to compete in a man's world. They talked each other's language and there were none of the irritating attitudes she had had to contend with from male customers. Flattery, condescension, bullying, crooked tactics and sexual advances had all come her way, some from men she already knew as her own father's business associates, but it had not taken long for each of them to realise that they could not get the better of her.

It was a month from the day of the party when the cocoons put aside for breeding purposes began to show signs of life. Gabrielle was in the rearing silk shed to see the first of the silk moths emerge. Dark and damp-looking, they would soon be white in colour, stubby in shape, with creamy threaded wings that would flutter ceaselessly as if the yearning to fly was still in them. Hélène, coming to find Gabrielle, was met with a triumphant glance.

"Everything is going as it should. They'll pair as soon as their wings are dry."

"Won't they fly away then?" Hélène looked uncertainly at the wide-spaced wooden slats of the shutters at the open window. "Those beautiful moths in the garden room are flying about all over the place there."

Gabrielle shook her head. "Centuries of domesticity have deprived these little silk moths of the power of flight."

When the reeling started in the filature shed, she took Hélène along to watch. The atmosphere there was hot and steamy. Women were carrying out this work, some seated at deep metal trays set into brickwork, which were filled with water kept boiling by fires beneath that were stoked up by boys. The cocoons, tipped into the steaming water, began to unravel slightly as one had once done in an Empress' teacup. These ends, ever without a twist, were skilfully picked out with small sticks, each filament then drawn over a suspended rod to be wound through the hot air onto creels being slowly turned, enabling the thread to dry en route. It gave the whole room the look of being canopied in white.

"Basically this is the same method used from the first days of sericulture," Gabrielle said, "and it can never be changed." She led Hélène across to one of the creels to watch the skeins being taken from it, checked carefully, and then twisted into hanks. Although the raw silk felt coarse to the touch, a further stage of degumming during manufacture would soften it, and it would take on its full sheen.

In the chatter of the women at work, the screeching of the creels and the bubbling of the boiling water, neither of them had heard the clerk from the office enter the filature shed. Suddenly he was at Gabrielle's elbow.

"You have a gentleman waiting to see you, madame."

"Who is it?" she asked, already on her way to the door.

"I think he's a new customer. I hadn't heard his name before. Monsieur Devaux."

Hélène, following after her, saw how she blanched upon hearing the name, checking her pace and telling the clerk to go ahead of her. "What is wrong?"

"Don't you realise the significance of the name of Devaux?" Gabrielle replied abstractedly, pushing a strand of hair back from her eyes. "The old enmities between the Devaux family and ours were revived by that accident on the day of the wedding."

"I remember, but surely you don't share Henri's bigoted views?"

"No, but I dread meeting Nicolas Devaux again. Believe me, I have cause."

"What cause could you possibly have?"

It would have been a relief to blurt out the truth and dispel the bewilderment in Hélène's innocent face. Gabrielle wondered how her disclosure would sound if spoken outright. Would it be any help to admit to feeling such a powerful love-attraction for Nicolas that she doubted her strength of will if she should be alone with him again for any length of time? Her first sight of him on her wedding day had been enough for her to attempt to draw back at the very moment that Émile had slid the ring onto her finger, although it was not until after she and Nicolas had kissed that understanding of her action had come to her. The feud was her only defence. She despised it and felt sullied by having to use it as a weapon, but she had no other outlet. No, she could not disclose her secret to Hélène. To give voice to it might release its force and only destruction could follow in its wake.

"I can't talk any more now," she parried. "I must see him and send him away."

She hurried down the path that led to the office. Hélène continued at a more thoughtful pace back through the woods to the house. She was convinced something was seriously wrong; Gabrielle did not take fright easily, and her agitation was obvious. Slowly she went towards the terrace where Émile sat with a book in a shady corner. He was just able to walk that far each day now.

Gabrielle entered the office by a side door and took her place at Émile's desk. After waiting a few moments to get her breath back, she picked up the little handbell and rang it. The clerk responded by opening the door from the outer office and showing Nicolas into the room. She saw at once that it was going to be a difficult interview. His expression and his whole stance boded trouble. Alert and watchful, he scrutinised her at the desk. She reminded herself that her rejection of him in the storm must have left him raw and smarting, and it was natural that he should be hostile.

"Good day to you, Gabrielle. So you are in charge here for the time being."

"I am," she replied evenly, sitting straight-backed. Unhappily she was aware that his presence was making the same powerful pull on her senses; it was as if his return had filled a void in her life. "Please be seated."

He glanced about at the orderliness of the office as he put his hat and cane aside before taking the chair in front of her desk. His clothes were as well tailored as before, his linen immaculate, his neckcloth tied high. He was a man at ease in good clothes and, as always, thoroughly in charge of himself.

"I hope Monsieur Valmont is well on the way to recovery," he said genuinely enough. "Your letter reached me in Paris. It was a puzzle to me until I returned to Lyons yesterday to learn that he had been seriously ill."

"Émile is making good progress, I'm thankful to say." Her voice tightened defensively. "Why should my letter have puzzled you? It was perfectly clear."

"To you, perhaps, but not to me. Your husband agreed to sell me raw silk and I can't believe he would have changed his mind unless—?"

She gave an abrupt shake of her head. "No, I didn't tell him of what passed between us. Why should you want to buy from the Valmont silk farm?" Before he could answer she continued ruthlessly, "I think it is in questionable taste to want both a man's wares *and* his wife."

He became rigid with anger, the bones standing out on his face, and he moved sharply forward in his chair. "It would be if the incident between us had not ended as it did. Valmont wrote to me the morning after the party, probably before he fell ill, I don't know. In it he made it plain that he would be setting aside the amount of raw silk he thought I would require, and I will remind you that I'm honour-bound to keep that agreement."

"I have rescinded whatever agreement existed on my husband's behalf and take full responsibility for it. I have every right to take this action. You are a Devaux and I am a Roche. Our families have never done business together."

"You *were* a Roche," he emphasised crisply. "As a Valmont, you are in another category altogether."

"I'm still a Roche at heart. I say again as I said in my letter, your custom is not wanted here."

Unexpectedly he jerked himself up out of the chair to slam both hands flat on the desk in front of her as he brought his furious face within a few inches of hers. "Don't imagine I should ever place a second order. That was not my intention in coming here. I wish to God I had never agreed about the present one, because it was on the strength of that discussion that your husband invited me to his house. I have to overcome old prejudices against Maison Devaux in Lyons if I am to re-enter *La Grande Fabrique* there, and I won't have the ground cut from under me at the first step by it becoming known that I wasn't considered to be a reliable customer by the highly respected Valmont silk farm!"

She remained outwardly inflexible, staring at him unflinchingly. "The matter is closed."

He grabbed her by the wrists, pulling her to her feet on the opposite side of the desk. "This business of raw silk buying has nothing to do with what is between us! Whatever you do, you can't change that!"

She wrenched herself away, drawing back by her chair. "There is nothing between us! Neither will anything you say persuade me to let you have any supplies from this silk farm. Your order is cancelled!"

In the heat of the moment, neither had heard the handle of the door turn. Émile spoke from the doorway. "I must ask you to leave, Monsieur Devaux. I uphold the decision my wife has made."

They both swung round towards him, equally startled, their faces torn by the conflict between themselves. He stood leaning for support against the doorjamb, his face ashen from the effort it had cost him to reach the office from the terrace, Hélène holding him by one arm. Gabrielle gave a cry of concern.

"You should never have come this far! It's too soon." She rushed to seize a chair by the wall and push it towards him. "Sit down or you may fall."

He ignored her and the chair, continuing to address Nicolas. "I believe you heard what I said. Nothing was fully settled or signed between us, which I consider sets us both free of whatever order you would have placed. You have my word that this will remain a private matter within these four walls."

"Then I'll not dispute your decision." Nicolas's face was still dark with anger, his tone rasping under control. He took up his hat and cane. "I'll take up no more of Madame Valmont's time or yours." He bowed formally to each of them, Gabrielle receiving a last hard and glittering glance that pierced her through, and then he left the office at a stride and went from the building.

Émile sagged weakly and both women helped him immediately into the chair. Gabrielle snatched a shawl from a peg to put around his shoulders, terrified he might suffer a full relapse. "What made you come?"

Hélène answered for her. "It was my fault. I told Émile that someone called Devaux was here and you were upset about seeing him."

Gabrielle crouched down to look up into his exhausted face. "How did you know I had refused Monsieur Devaux's order?"

He was breathless with exertion and answered haltingly. "I didn't know until I heard what you were saying as I opened the door."

She saw with foreboding that there was a curious intensity in his gaze. "You are angry with me?"

Hélène intervened anxiously. "Please don't be, Émile. Gabrielle has worked hard with only your good and the good of the silk farm at heart. Dr. Jaunet insisted that you be spared all worries, particularly business ones."

Émile replied drily, not taking his eyes from his wife: "Turning away a new customer and a source of new orders is hardly likely to aid my peace of mind, or my pocket. Leave us, Hélène. Send two of the servants to give me a bandy-chair back to the house. I doubt if my legs can carry me that far for a second time today."

As the door closed behind Hélène, leaving them on their own, Gabrielle did not move from where she was. "Have you known all along I was working here?"

"Not at first. I suppose I was too ill to reason rationally. Gradually it became apparent."

"I know I went against your wishes and yet I can't pretend that I didn't enjoy every minute of being in charge."

He liked her frank and candid answer. Her natural honesty was something on which he knew he could always rely. "I suppose you considered yourself to be in your element," he conceded with a sigh, "and, in spite of what I said to you on the night of the party, I can't blame you for taking the chance to get rid of Devaux."

She saw his eyes had softened. The indefinable look had not been anger after all. "You are being very understanding."

"If Devaux had been Bonaparte himself, I would never stand with another against my wife."

Impulsively she pressed her cheek fondly against the back of his hand. He had shown her the loyalty that all along she had vowed to give him as her husband and partner in life. Why, then, was the misery of

Nicolas's departure making her scream inside as if she were dying? For she had accomplished exactly that for which she had aimed.

Émile's effort in reaching the office proved to be a turning point in his convalescence, almost as if the smell of ink and silk and ledgers had been a stimulus to him. Hélène felt free to return home to Lyons now that she could see there was no likelihood of any setbacks to his returning health. It happened naturally that, when he began to spend a few hours in his office every day, Gabrielle should be with him. Together they went over the work she had done during his illness and, apart from some minor criticism, which was more to enlighten her than to find fault, he approved everything. She knew it was only a transitional period and when he was fully recovered she would find herself confined to domestic duties once more.

Then one morning he smiled at her across the breakfast table and said what she had been half expecting to hear every day for over a week. "There is no need for you to come to the office today. I'm sure you have plenty to do here, and it's time you made some social calls again."

As if to compensate for her brave nod of acceptance, he brought her a long-promised gift later that day. Some raw silk had come back from the throwsters, workers trained specially to bind the raw silk into double strands in readiness for the looms, and he had filled a muslin-lined wicker basket with hanks that were almost weightless, white and lustrous.

"Here's the Valmont silk for your gown, my dear. Choose a colour that you like and the dyers shall dye it for you."

Her radiant expression was balm to him. He wanted nothing to destroy the new harmony between them, appreciating her stoic relinquishing of the office work more than she realised. It would have wearied him to have a wife who gave way to tantrums and created scenes. In Gabrielle he had entirely the woman he wanted, and he was determined never to lose her. After the first onslaught of his illness he had had plenty of time to consider many things, not least the tortured look he remembered in her eyes at the prospect of meeting Devaux again. If he had needed confirmation of his misgivings it had come when he opened the office door. The very air seemed to vibrate with the atmosphere the two had created between themselves, and the heated words being exchanged had somehow had no bearing on the way they were looking at each other.

Gabrielle chose a soft apricot shade for the silk he had given her. It was a colour that suited her complexion and her hair. On the day it was despatched to the dyers she spotted a notice in the news-sheet, which she brought to Émile's attention.

"It says here that Joseph Jacquard is to demonstrate his new loom in Lyons. It's going to be on view in the Place Sathonay. I should like to see it. Do let's go. At the same time, it will give me a chance to see how Hélène is getting on with my father since her return home."

"I can't leave the business just now, my dear." He smiled at her. "Why don't you spend a few days at your father's house? You've had a hard and tiring time over the past few weeks. It would do you good to visit Lyons again." He thought to himself that if he had not heard that Devaux had returned to Paris he would have been less willing to let her go to the city without him. "Do some shopping. Enjoy yourself."

She left for Lyons two days later. The road was hard and dusty, clouds flying out in the wheels' wake, but it meant that good progress could be made, and the journey took less than the usual hour. They entered Lyons by way of the hilly Fourvière quarter, and she told the coachman to halt for a few minutes at a certain point where the most magnificent view was to be had of the whole city. She alighted to hurry across to what was practically a sheer drop and gazed out over Lyons once again. Shimmering mistily in the heat, it lay spread out below and up the hillside beyond; the Rhône and the Saône threaded through like satin ribbons, the church spires dominating the pale tints of the pink and ochre and green-grey roofs. She felt as though she were breathing in the sights and sounds of it all, and thought it wonderful to be returning to its throbbing life once more. As she returned to her seat, she instructed the coachman not to stop again until they reached her father's house.

Hélène met her at the door and they embraced affectionately. Although it was not long since they had last seen each other, Gabrielle noticed at once that Hélène did not look so well. There were shadows under her eyes and a tired look to her face. "Has your helping me with the nursing taken its toll on you?" she asked anxiously, holding her sister-in-law by the shoulders in order to study her.

Hélène shook her head. "No, no. I did so little. You spared me all the hard chores and Émile's convalescence was as much a rest for me as it was for him."

"Is it Father, then? Is he showing you no consideration?"

Hélène, who never spoke ill of anyone, waved the query aside. "Don't look so worried. I've been feeling the heat since I returned to the city."

"You are welcome to stay with us whenever you wish."

"I know," Hélène said gratefully. There had been times since her return when she longed to leave Dominique and his cantankerous demands and to escape to the tranquillity of the countryside again. Pity for his physical suffering and his innate loneliness continually overwhelmed her own personal wishes. Sometimes she felt as if she were divided between two babies, one still unborn and the other, ancient in years, equally demanding of her and totally unreasonable with it. In all, it was a difficult time for her and she had never been more thankful for Gabrielle's company. "Father wants to see you as soon as you are ready."

Gabrielle was given her old room and she viewed it without the least sentimentality, only relieved to have escaped its four walls, where, in adolescence, she had been locked in, half starved herself in rebellion, and for many nights wept out her heart for a lost love.

Dominique received her in his office. He sat at his large desk, which had belonged to his forebears and was by tradition always handed on to the eldest son, a handsome piece of seventeenth-century craftsmanship. It was here that he still conducted his work and had quarrelsome sessions with Henri over business matters. "You're not with child yet, then?" he greeted her, his stony gaze sweeping her up and down before she seated herself in front of him. "I hear the Valmont silk crop is good this year."

"Yes, it is."

"Did you know it's rumoured that the Devaux silk mill may be opened up again?"

"I had heard that."

He leaned forward in his chair, his expression one of malicious satisfaction. "Hélène told me how you refused the Devaux order and sent the fellow packing. Give me the details."

She had no intention of discussing it with him. "I did what I felt had to be done. Since I was in charge during Émile's illness, the authority was mine and I used it."

He rubbed his chin thoughtfully. He had alarmed Hélène with his great bellow of savage laughter when she related how his daughter had sent Devaux away, disappointed and empty-handed. For the first time he was beginning to see there was much of himself in Gabrielle, a trait that had escaped his notice through the years of living under the same roof with her, when he had merely been aware of her wilfulness and defiance. By her action over the Devaux matter she had shown that she was a Roche through and through, ruthless when the need arose and with the same tenacity as himself, something she had shown often enough in conflict between them when nothing would induce her to enter into the marriages he had wished to arrange for her. In addition, as he had heard from his own spies, she had applied herself well to shouldering the responsibility of her husband's business at a time of emergency. None of this altered in any way his relationship with her, for she was still the thorn in his flesh, the constant reminder of the loss her birth had inflicted upon him, a raw wound that would agonise him until the end of his days. His animosity towards her surged up in him again, familiar as his own heartbeat. "What brings you to Lyons now?"

"I want to see the Jacquard loom demonstrated."

His gaze sharpened between narrowed lids. "Why? You've a loom of your own. It would be of no use to you."

"It would not be for myself. I was thinking of Roche silk. You see, I haven't lost my interest in commercial weaving just because I've left Lyons. Through news-sheets and the business talk I hear from Émile and his associates, I keep abreast of what is going on." Her face reflected her enthusiasm. "It may be that Maison Roche could benefit from changing to the Jacquard loom if it should prove to be all that is claimed for it. Moreover, it will enable weavers to stand upright at their work instead of being turned into hunchbacks by their old age as so many of them are and, best of all, it will abolish the need to have little children forever crouched at thread-tying."

He gave a nod. "That in itself would cut down the cost of production," he said, considering the reduction of child labour in an entirely different way from his daughter. "Not by much, but everything counts. I remember Joseph Jacquard. He was another traitor at the time when Lyons was besieged. It's a sad day for this city when an extremist from the past can make a public demonstration of a loom for which a deal of high-handed claims are being made."

"Maybe he wants to make amends by benefiting the weaving industry as a whole."

He raised his bushy eyebrows cynically. "I have lived too long and seen too much to be swayed by that argument. All Jacquard wants is to line his pockets. There'll be no change of looms for Roche silk unless Henri brings me an extremely convincing report."

Immediately she was affronted by his remark, brought face to face again with the male dominance of every situation. She exclaimed, "Henri has never sought change in his life. This loom is supposed to speed production, apart from its advantages for the weavers themselves."

His tone became sarcastic. "I suppose you would consider your opinion superior to his."

"I've always been ready to listen to new ideas and to judge for myself. I'll go to the demonstration with Henri and give you my own report."

In spite of herself her voice had risen a note and both of them were aware of the old friction stirring up between them. The truce had been short-lived. "Get out," he ordered bluntly. "You're tiring me. Send for Hélène. She's more of a daughter to me than you will ever be."

Outside his door again she paused, resting a hand on an inlaid console table, her troubled face reflected in profile by a tall looking-glass above it. How was it possible for her to go on being hurt by him? He did it deliberately and succeeded every time.

On the day of the demonstration it seemed as if the whole of Lyons was converging on the Place Sathonay. Weavers had left their looms to see the new invention for themselves, and the silk merchants and negotiators had filled the section reserved for them on one side of the platform on which the loom had been erected. It was with difficulty that Henri shouldered a way through to the enclosure for Gabrielle and himself.

At first sight there did not appear to be much difference in the loom, except for a curious rectangular contraption supporting a circle of perforated cards, laced together and mounted on the top, giving great height to the whole structure. She saw immediately, as everyone else should have done, that many of the low-ceilinged workshops and loom-rooms would not be able to accommodate the extra height of the cylinder of the Jacquard mechanism.

Henri, conscious of his own importance in silk circles, made sure that he and his sister came right to the front, where they could view the loom at close quarters. It was as he secured their places that a civil dignatary, representing the Prefect of Lyons, mounted the steps to the platform. In his wake came Joseph Jacquard, a middle-aged man with mild eyes and thinning grey hair that fell straight on either side of his sensitive, gentle-featured face. To Gabrielle's eyes he did not have the look of one who would have betrayed his compatriots, and she recalled Émile's words about rough judgements having been made in those past difficult times.

The civic dignatary cleared his throat. "Citizens of Lyons! A man of our city comes before you today after an absence of some years during which he received a place in the Conservatoire des Arts et Métiers in Paris, personally recommended by the First Consul when still General Bonaparte. Citizen Joseph-Marie Jacquard is a modest man and will tell you nothing of his successful shawl-making machine. Neither will he take claim wholly for the invention here on the platform, giving credit to the late Jacques de Vaucanson, who first captured a combination of all the principles of weaving in a machine of his own, although with no practical results. Citizen Jacquard has taken that combination to completion. I will now ask him to clarify the workings of his new loom."

He left the platform. Jacquard bowed to all four points of the compass before he began to address the crowd. His voice was thin in volume, matching his appearance, but it carried well in the attentive silence that had fallen.

"Fellow Lyonnais! It is my earnest hope that my machine will bring a new prosperity to our city, because it converts the labour of days into a speedy process that brings forth effortlessly the most complicated of figured silks." He went into detail, explaining that each punch-hole in the cards was related to a section of the chosen design. Then he went to stand at the loom and began to weave.

Gabrielle watched carefully. The pressing down of the treadle operated the harness and transformed the information of each punched card into the selection of the correct pattern of warp thread. When the treadle was released the needles sprang back into position in readiness for the next card. The pattern was repeated swiftly along the length of fabric every time the cards completed a full circle. She was deeply impressed. If this mechanism was generally adopted it would increase the production of Lyons silk a thousandfold.

"What do you think of it?" she asked Henri eagerly.

He shrugged non-committally. "Silk would lose by it. There's no substitute for handwork."

"The loom produces the end product in any case. This would merely speed the process and help to bring down the cost of production. More people would be able to afford silk in a widening of the market."

He had always resented her persistent interest in the commercial side of silk, which he considered to be a thoroughly unfeminine trait. "Silk has never belonged to the hoi-polloi. It never will either if I have anything to do with it."

She fell silent. It was useless to discuss anything with Henri. They had never seen eye to eye. Reaction among the other merchants seemed mixed; some in favour, some vehemently against for Henri's own reasons. Silk was their god and nothing must threaten its perfection. The rumble of their voices grew, but it was being outweighed by a louder and more undisciplined outcry of dissent from the weavers in the other part of the crowd.

"Your loom would bring starvation onto us, Jacquard!" "What of work for our children?" "You're a traitor to our trade!" It was a mood of fear that gripped them. They saw their number being diminished by this mechanised loom like a scythe slicing down corn. Never far from hunger, the memory of the barren years after the Revolution uppermost in their minds, they began to shake their fists at their would-be benefactor, who left the loom to stand alone in the centre of the platform, trying to calm them down enough to hear him out.

"My friends, you are mistaken! My mechanism would not decrease your work! It would increase it beyond your wildest dreams. You have it in your power to dress the whole world in Lyons silk. And think of your children! They can grow tall and straight without their present labour that deforms their limbs and ruins their lungs. It was my task as a child and I would have been in better health today if it had not been for that abominable thread-tying for twelve hours a day throughout my growing years. You'll not miss their wages because you'll be earning more! With my loom you'll be less tired at your weaving, which means you'll work harder and your income will rise steadily as people in all walks of life find they are able to afford the lower prices of silk that my loom will bring about!"

Gabrielle was near enough to the platform to catch his words, but no one at any distance could have heard anything above the tumult of shouting and abuse that was fast turning the weavers' crowd into a furious mob. The mention of lower prices had been a last straw. A single cry was taken up.

"Down with him! Throw him into the Rhône!"

Jacquard went pale and he backed a pace or two towards his loom as if seeking its protection. In the rear of the crowd, police in their bicorne hats were beginning to shove a way through to the platform, but it was obvious they would never reach him in time as the first of the mob began to clamber up onto the platform. Henri, fearful that the inventor was about to be torn limb from limb before their eyes, tried to hustle Gabrielle away, but their way was blocked, fellow merchants having been pushed aside as one of their number from the back came thrusting his way through to the platform. Gabrielle, buffeted and crushed, half strangled by Henri's protective arm about her throat, glimpsed Nicolas's set face in profile as he went past and swung himself up onto the platform in time to charge his full weight against the first of the hostile attackers, hurling them back into the midst of those coming up behind.

It was like a signal for bedlam to be let loose. Men swarmed up onto the platform from all sides, even those at the rear of the merchants' section shoving a way through, jostling aside those on whom their livelihoods depended, everything else forgotten in the heat of the moment as they yelled and bawled their murderous abuse. Gabrielle turned cold with horror as the whole crowd howled for Jacquard's blood. It was the same sound that had reached her ears in childhood from the direction of the guillotine on the Place des Terreaux no matter how tightly the windows were closed or the shutters fastened. Before her the platform was filled with fighting, struggling men, Nicolas and the hapless inventor in the midst of them.

"Help those two men!" she cried in appeal to the merchants, but they were all dispersing while there was still time to get out of the mob, not wanting to become involved. Henri was trying to pull her away with him. "Have you gone mad?" he shouted. "We'll be drawn into this mess if we stay any longer!"

As he spoke, Nicolas and Jacquard reappeared out of the scrum, both of them with their clothes half torn from their bodies, to leap down onto the cobbles within a few feet of her. The inventor stumbled and would have fallen if Nicolas had not yanked him upright and charged the exhausted man forward. Pursuers came after them. Gabrielle stuck out her foot and the leader stumbled and fell headlong, causing others to collide behind him. It enforced only the briefest of delays but she hoped that it helped. Henri, aghast at what she had done and fearing the mob's wrath if her action should have been noticed, bore her away with as much force as Nicolas had used on the inventor in their flight. She looked back over her shoulder and saw that those not still in pursuit of their quarries had turned their fury on Jacquard's loom. It was being knocked to pieces with axes and mallets by those who had come prepared to destroy what they had seen as a threat to their livelihood right from the start.

Later she heard that Jacquard had escaped and left Lyons in haste, the second time in his life that he had had cause to fear his own townspeople. Whether Nicolas had gone with him, nobody seemed to know. From the general gossip she learned that the Devaux and Jacquard families had been long acquainted, and the only sons had been close friends until Charles Jacquard's death in battle. To herself, Gabrielle commended Nicolas for going to the rescue of his late friend's father, something she did not voice aloud, for she could no longer be sure that her face, or her tone, would not give her away if she was drawn into talk about him.

Dominique taunted her with the fiasco of the Jacquard demonstration. "A fine waste of time that proved to be. Nothing left of that infamous loom except a heap of debris thrown into the Rhône in place of its inventor, who was lucky to escape a watery grave by all accounts."

She could tell that Henri had given him a full and derogatory report. "I don't think that invention is at an end. If only you could have seen the speed with which that mechanism raced away with an intricate pattern. It selected the coloured threads required row by row until the eye of the spectator was quite dazzled."

"Hmm, dazzled, were you? Henri doesn't endorse that point of view."

"But several others did. I heard their comments." She named two negotiators known to her father, men he held in esteem, but his expression did not change.

"They didn't lift a hand to protect the mechanism, though, did they?"

"They had no chance. Everything happened so suddenly."

"Well, Jacquard won't dare show his face in Lyons again for many a year. I can tell you that."

She feared he was right and was saddened by it.

As promised, she went to visit Madame Hoinville and look over her small mill, which consisted of two looms in each of the two workshops within the widow's own house in the ancient quarter of La Croix Rousse. It was like many another weaving establishment in the district Gabrielle had visited frequently in her years of growing up and young maturity. From street level a couple of stone steps, worn to a bow shape by centuries of tread, led down to a floor lowered at some distant time in the past before being reflagged to accommodate the height of the looms fastened to ceiling beams for steadiness, although not even these rooms would be able to hold the extra height of the Jacquard mechanism if it should ever be put into general use.

In spite of the absence of men, the setting was much like that of any other weaving household. While the looms thwack-thwacked steadily as work progressed, someone was cooking at the range, another was sorting washing still damp from being slapped on rocks at the river's bank and a young girl suckled a baby at her breast. The youngest children played underfoot while two little boys, aged about ten and eleven, crouched under the looms retying threads. Through an open doorway into the second workshop, beyond, Gabrielle could see two little girls similarly engaged. She thought desperately that, if nothing else, Jacquard's loom would have spared these children from their miserable task. In a wooden cage suspended from the ceiling a bird twit-twitted sweetly, for in spite of the thickness of the window panes the expanse of glass bathed the room with light. It was far less pleasant in winter-time, when the stench of lamps was almost overpowering. The talk between the widow and Gabrielle turned inevitably to the Jacquard demonstration.

"It was a pity it was destroyed before I could get a closer look at it," Madame Hoinville said, she having been on the outskirts of the crowd that day. "I should like to see my weavers' burdens lightened, their personal troubles being more than enough for some of them to bear already. Even the strongest of the women tires quickly at these looms, and their poor backs pay the price." She put a hand to her own spine and straightened her shoulders to ease it. "Since I take my turn working with them, I know what a benefit Monsieur Jacquard's invention would be. Not that I could afford to change looms or to find a new place in which to house the extraordinary height of his mechanism."

The work that the Hoinville looms produced was selective and exquisite. Gabrielle thought it no wonder that the enterprising and charitable widow had created her own niche in such a competitive market.

As she left the premises, Gabrielle turned homewards in a direction that would take her past the Devaux property. Her choice was deliberate. When she came level with it on the opposite side of the street, she saw that everything was closed and shuttered.

Hélène's baby was born in December, the same month in which Napoleon Bonaparte became Emperor of France. Dominique did not hide his disgust that his daughter-in-law had given birth to a girl instead of a boy. A grandson would have been a future hope for the business, particularly the offspring of his favourite son, but a granddaughter was totally without importance. In a strange way his attitude towards the infant was much as it had been when Gabrielle was born. He did not wish to see or hear her and Hélène had to make sure that no crying reached his ears. Unfortunately little Juliette, who had been hastily baptised by the midwife when it seemed she might not survive, cried a great deal, was puny and undersized. It was due to Hélène's tireless care that eventually she began to thrive and by the age of three months was a healthy, bonny baby.

By this time Dominique had developed a senile jealousy of the child who had deprived him of Hélène's undivided attention, and his attitude towards his once favoured daughter-in-law changed subtly and decisively. He began to goad her as he had always goaded Yvonne, but in a different way, simply by being displeased with anything she did and finding fault at every opportunity.

The truth was that he felt himself abandoned and deserted in the midst of his own family. He thought it a bitter trick of fate that the only child who was dear to him should always be far away. He knew Gabrielle did not expect to inherit from him and therefore would not be disappointed when his will was read, whereas Henri was in for a fine shock, a joke he would be enjoying from his grave. Jules was the one who, ending his soldiering days in the face of unexpected riches, would accept his full inheritance of Maison Roche and carry on its tradition of high quality and design. Surely by that time Hélène should have borne him a son or two.

In this hope, Dominique made no objection when Hélène told him that she intended to visit Jules, who had been posted to the Channel coast, in preparation for the Emperor's planned invasion of England. "Here, take this to him." He drew a ruby ring from his third finger and held it out to her. "Tell him it is a keepsake from me in case I'm not here when he comes home again after defeating the English."

Having steeled herself for a tirade, Hélène was overwhelmingly relieved to find she was to make the visit with her father-in-law's blessing. She took the ring and cupped it in her hands. Encouraged by the unexpected benevolence of his mood, she dared to voice a request that was dear to her.

"May I bring Juliette to you before I leave with her?"

"I'll see my son's son from you first! Your daughter is of no interest to me."

She flushed crimson. His rejection of her adored child offended her deepest maternal instincts, needling her, as nothing else could have done, to retaliate like a lioness. "Juliette has a right to be acknowledged! She is a Roche and your own grandchild! You're a foolish old man, Dominique Roche. You're treating her as you treated Gabrielle, who cared for you more than any of your sons! Do you know why?" She took a step forward, her attitude so uncharacteristically threatening that Dominique shifted in his chair. "Because, in spite of all your cruelty to her, she has known what you have never had the sense to see. You are two of a kind in your respect for silk. She would have done more for the name of Roche in the silk world than a dozen sons put together, and you have been too biased to see it!"

She flew from the room, banging the door after her. Dominique grunted in delayed surprise. Who would have expected such a display of rage from that mild little creature? He felt quite invigorated by it.

Gabrielle accompanied Hélène and the baby on their journey to Boulogne. They travelled in a Roche carriage attended by two maids and a considerable amount of baggage. Émile was dubious about letting Hélène and his wife make the journey unescorted.

"I ought to be going with you," he had said.

"It's too busy a time on the silk farm," she had replied, for the cycle of sericulture was shortly to begin all over again. "The coachman and the manservant will be armed, so two men to protect us are more than enough."

He had finally withdrawn his objection but not before giving her a lady's pistol to keep in her draw-string velvet purse. There were times when she felt enclosed by him, his possessiveness threatening to suffocate her, and it was for this reason she needed to be away from him for a little while. He seemed unable to grasp that independence of spirit was vital to her; it was almost as if he had half expected marriage to change her in the same way as domesticity had changed the little silkworms into their flightless state. She felt that more and more he was trying to trap her mind and soul, which inevitably created emotional battles between them that frequently resulted in his uncomfortable silences that distressed him as much as they did her. It was difficult to say which of them was left the most racked and drained after these sessions.

On the credit side, proof of how much he sought real harmony between them, he had not banished her entirely from his business world again as she had expected. Instead he had given her the task, previously allotted elsewhere, of selecting the dye colours for the thrown silk, for many buyers wanted the product already dyed when it reached them.

As with weaving, dyeing was very much a craft involving individual households, and she visited the dyers herself to watch the processes, undeterred by the vile stenches that were frequently incurred. Through her encouragement, work was being carried out to obtain several variations of a colour-fast delphinium blue. Many colours tended to fade, blue in particular, and to guarantee long life to any new shade was of immense value. The Emperor himself had stipulated that silken hangings and panels for the palaces must be proof against fading, for he had been keenly disappointed when a newly hung room at Fontainebleau for the Empress Josephine had lost most of its colour through unguarded exposure to the sun. She had high hopes, for the new dye had passed several tests already.

There were times when, across the dinner table, she and Émile would suddenly smile at each other as if they shared an unvoiced joke. Yet it was more an olive branch than a joke. He had given her the dyeing to placate her business interests while at the same time ensuring she had no actual hand in the workings of the silk farm itself; she had accepted the assignment in the full understanding of his reasons. More than once they followed their smiles with raised glasses to each other, and these were the times when they were truly happy together, times when her own private nightmare was tucked away at the back of her mind and no shadow of Nicolas Devaux fell between them. She knew from hearsay that Nicolas's failure to get silk from the Valmont silk farm appeared to have delayed whatever plans he had made to reopen the Devaux mill in Lyons, but that did not mean he had given up the idea. It was not often that she heard his name spoken, but every time she did it made her pulse quicken. She had begun to hope for pregnancy, as she had not done before, feeling the need of this final anchor to her marriage. So far there was no sign of her wish being fulfilled.

The journey to Boulogne went well. As they neared the seaport the road was flanked on either side by large army encampments. The tents of the camp-followers clustered untidily at the edge, strings of washing in between. Here and there goats were tethered and hens clucked in coops, means by which some of the occupants sustained themselves, for there were only half-rations for officially recognised wives and children and none at all for those without a legitimate claim for support. A few young urchins rushed out into the road at the sight of the carriage and ran alongside to beg. Hélène threw them the food left from the supplies for the journey and they fell on it before fighting for the coins she added from her purse.

Jules had posted a lookout and before the carriage reached the gates of Boulogne he came riding at a gallop to meet them, dust billowing out behind him. His reunion with Hélène was joyous, both of them wrapped in an embrace as soon as the carriage stopped. When Juliette was put into his arms she rewarded him with a smile, enchanted by his gleaming buttons and silver frogging, which she tried to catch. He was filled with pride and again he and his wife kissed, the baby half squashed between them. As the journey continued, he rode alongside, talking to Hélène and Gabrielle through the open window.

"I'm afraid the accommodation I found for you is far from luxurious, and yet I was lucky to get it. Every room, loft, stable and outhouse is in demand, not only by the military but by visitors to this area."

He had not exaggerated the congestion of the town. Boulogne had become one vast army camp teeming with soldiers, cannons and wagons and other equipment, horses everywhere. The Grande Armée had gathered its strength into two hundred thousand men for the onslaught across the Channel. Only one barrier was delaying them. As yet the Royal Navy still had mastery of the seas and the French and Spanish fleets had failed so far to redress the balance. There was no point in putting barges of troops out into the Channel for them to be sunk halfway.

The accommodation proved to be in a small inn which left much to be desired in the way of cleanliness and service. Gabrielle and Hélène had to share a room with the baby, and the maids were in a garret with some other female servants, while the coachman and his companion were consigned to the stable loft. It was only when Gabrielle went out that husband and wife were able to be alone together under a roof. As a result she came to know Boulogne almost as well as she knew Lyons, benefiting from an abundance of fresh salt air as she strolled by the seawalls, explored the winding streets and the markets and took refreshment at one of the many coffee shops.

She wrote a number of letters, taking the chance to catch up with correspondence, and did some sketches and water-colours of the oldest part of the town. In a shop in a narrow side-street she found a rare silk moth in a carved box and bought it for Émile, thinking he might like to add it to his collection. When Jules was on duty Hélène accompanied her, but it never troubled her to be on her own and time passed quickly. Many invitations came her way, for the social life of the town was hectic in its present circumstances, and with her brother and his wife she attended card-parties, dances, receptions and banquets, among other events. With her striking looks and self-possessed air, she was greatly in demand, but she turned aside all attempts at assignations before they could be voiced and remained on good terms with those officers who had hoped to take advantage of her husband's absence.

When there appeared to be no sign of the invasion force making any move, Gabrielle began to think about going home again. Naturally Hélène was reluctant to move, for she and Jules had never had so much time together in all their married life and every day that the invasion was postponed was another day for her to be with him.

"There is no reason why you shouldn't stay on," Gabrielle said to her at last. "I can travel home by public stage."

"Wait until the end of the month," Hélène implored. "We shall surely have heard something by then and I'll be so grateful for your company when Jules has left for England."

Gabrielle refrained from saying that Émile's letters had taken on an impatient tone. He had not expected her to be away for such a long time. "Very well," she agreed. That same evening she answered the most recent of Émile's letters and let him know that the date of her return was still undecided.

The end of June came with still no sign of any movement being launched across the Channel. In the good weather Gabrielle had taken to painting most of the time, and one morning she set up her easel and opened her box of water-colours to finish a view of the old ramparts. Not for the first time she was thankful that at least Dominique had not denied her lessons in painting.

When one of Jules's fellow officers paused to look over her shoulder at her artwork and make a comment, she recognised his voice immediately.

"It's good, Madame Valmont. I like it."

"Thank you, Lieutenant Teralle." She was on companionable terms with him. They had danced together at several of the balls and parties. Moreover she respected his opinion, for he was an accomplished artist himself. "I'm uncertain about those shadows."

"Make them slightly deeper in tone." He sat down on the stone wall beside her, a good-humoured, dark-haired man with a full Hussar moustache. Leaning forward, he watched as she carried out his suggestion. "There, that's it. See how it highlights the sunny side of those ramparts now."

"Yes, I do." She sat back to view the result, adding conversationally: "What news of the forthcoming invasion, then?"

"None. It's a wearisome time waiting for action."

"At least the Emperor's retaliatory blockade on land has successfully barred British goods from Europe."

"The enemy still has one outlet left. If this invasion proves to be a stalemate, it will have to be closed with time."

"Where's that?" She took some fresh colour onto her brush for a cloud in the sky.

"Portugal. They say British trading ships are putting into Lisbon and Oporto and everywhere else along that strip of Portuguese coast every day."

Thoughtfully she washed her brush again. "Are you saying that you don't think this invasion of England will take place?"

"How can it when the British still control the Pas de Calais? In any case I've heard talk that our regiment might soon be moving out in an easterly direction. Rumour has it that Austria and Russia are massing forces in readiness for an attack."

The seriousness of his expression showed that he thought it to be more truth than rumour.

When she returned to the inn she told Hélène what she had heard. It prepared her. That same evening another room became vacant and Gabrielle moved into it, enabling Jules and Hélène to spend their nights together. Both of them were grateful for it, because before the week was out an order came through that the Hussars were to leave the coast for another destination. Hélène accepted the imminence of their parting courageously.

"We have had all these weeks to share," she said to Jules as they lay in each other's arms. "One day you'll be home for good and there'll be no more partings."

He groaned out of the depths of his love for her and covered her with kisses.

Two days later she and Gabrielle stood by the sea-wall to watch him ride out of Boulogne with his regiment. With the standard flying and the pipes and drums of the band leading the way, the Hussars made a spectacular sight with their red plumes, fur-lined pelisses and crimson boots. Hélène held Juliette high in her arms to allow Jules a last glimpse of her, and he saluted them both proudly, his smile wide, his gaze absorbing them. When she could no longer see him, Hélène broke down. Gabrielle took the baby from her and helped her back to the inn, where their belongings were packed and already stowed aboard the waiting carriage.

When eventually they reached Lyons, Gabrielle stayed only long enough to greet her father and take a little refreshment before travelling on to reach home with the minimum of delay. As the last few miles were covered, her pleased anticipation of seeing Émile again began to be tempered by an unease as to how he would receive her after such an extended absence. It was a thought she had kept to the back of her mind throughout the last weeks in Boulogne.

The sun-mellowed house looked as if it had been waiting for her return, but Émile did not appear on the steps to meet her. There was the possibility that he was in his office and had not heard her arrival. But that was not the case. Crossing the hall to reach the staircase, she saw through the open door of the library that he was sitting at the table there, reading a large book. She paused, hoping he would look up in pleased surprise, for he must have heard her footsteps on the marble floor. He merely turned a page. Steeling herself, she approached the doorway, entered, and waited.

"How are you, Émile?"

He did not take his eyes from the book. "You've condescended to come home again, have you?"

"I explained the circumstances in my letter."

"You did."

Exasperation overcame her. Tired and weary from the journey, she spoke sharply. "Émile! Look at me! If you're not in the least glad to see me again, I might as well be elsewhere."

He did look up then, not entirely sure that she wouldn't flounce out of the house and drive off somewhere. The sight of her washed over him. Although the effects of travel shadowed her eyes and drew at her face, her beauty held him as it always did. He wished it was in his nature to laugh carelessly, dismiss his rigidness as a pose to cover the joy of her home-coming and take her in his arms again. But he could not do it. Jealous anger had been building up in him to combine with hurt that she should stay so long away. Yet he was craving for her. He wanted above all else to take her straight to bed. Later.

"You're my wife," he replied stiffly. "It goes without saying that I'm always glad to see you. If that were not the case, I shouldn't have been so displeased that you chose to put the wishes of your sister-in-law before mine. I suggest you go and rest now. We shall meet at dinner."

"Oh, Émile." Words failed her. She let her hands rise and fall again. Shaking her head once, she left the library. Why did he have to be so unreasonable? If he could be so jealous over her spending time with two members of her family, she did not have to ask herself what he would do if ever he believed he might be losing her to another man. Unlike Henri, who was nothing more than a cunning bully, Émile was not a coward and, like every other man of his position in life, he knew how to defend his honour. He had once demonstrated his skill with a rapier against an imaginary opponent for her amusement, and she had seen he would be formidable in a duel. As for other weaponry, she knew from the hunting season, when he always bagged a considerable amount of game in the neighbouring forest, that he would not miss his mark with a pistol aimed at an opposing duellist. She shivered as she went up the stairs, able to see in her mind's eye the only possible face of that duellist, determined that it should never be. Nicolas was forever only just below the surface of her thoughts. Was she never to overcome her inner yearning for him?

It was not long after her return home that the Emperor abandoned his plans to invade England and the bulk of the Grande Armée left Boulogne to meet the growing threat of attack in southern Germany. Then, in October, the British fleet scored a tremendous victory at Trafalgar. Fifteen French and Spanish vessels were sunk, while the British lost none themselves. All chance of a French invasion of England in the foreseeable future had been effectively destroyed.

Gabrielle occupied herself with the work she welcomed, of selecting dyes for the new silk crop. In addition, she resumed her visits to the dyers, strengthening her acquaintance with them as once she had done with her father's weavers. Émile was busy all the time. The rift between them had healed and she was able to make him laugh again, always a sign that he was happy, and she was content.

As autumn turned to winter the news-sheets reported with triumph the victories of the Grande Armée at Ulm and Austerlitz, both due to the Emperor's brilliant strategies. Never had France had such a leader. By mid-December the Austrians had surrendered unconditionally and the Tsar's forces had retreated into their own country.

Early in the new year Gabrielle came out of the house as Émile reached the foot of the steps where she was standing. "Have you left your work to come for a walk with me?" she asked light-heartedly, drawing on her gloves. Then she saw the grave expression on his face. A sense of foreboding overcame her. Her question came shakily. "What is it?"

"I have bad news, I'm afraid," he said sadly. "You must prepare yourself, my dear."

"Tell me what has happened. No, it can't be Jules!"

His eyes were full of sympathy. "A messenger from your father's house came to the office a few minutes ago. Word was received in Lyons that Jules died twelve days ago of wounds received on the Austerlitz battlefield."

She swayed, every vestige of colour draining from her face. As Émile darted up the steps to her she almost threw herself into his comforting arms.

4

It was due to the determination and perseverance of a Hussar sergeant that Jules's body was brought home for burial in the family vault. Officers, unless of exceptionally high rank, were buried near the battlefield, as were the men, but Jules had once said, perhaps referring lightheartedly to his old age, that he would like his bones to lie in Lyons. Sergeant Gaston Garcin had heard him and remembered.

Gaston had been through every campaign with his late officer since Jules, newly commissioned, had joined the regiment, and he was resolved to carry out the last wish of a courageous man. He owed his life to Jules's timely intervention in the thick of the battle at Ulm, and this was the least he could do in return. It was only possible to carry out his aim through his being wounded himself in the leg as the same time as Jules had suffered his fatal wounds. As a result, he found himself invalided out of the army, his military days at an end. With his commanding officer's permission, he began the long journey, his left leg still swathed in bandages, with the coffin-wagon out of Austria and across France.

In his mid-thirties, he was a broadly built, hefty man with hair as unruly as tow and a similar nondescript colour. Large ears flanked his rough-hewn face, and his nose, previously his best feature, had been broken in a drunken brawl. Yet his big physical presence and the wicked glint that came and went in his onyx eyes gave him a tom-cat attractiveness to women, with whom he fared better than many men who surpassed him in looks and wealth. Basically an optimist, always ready to take a chance, he had been a good soldier, clear-headed in a crisis and proud to serve his country as a cavalry man. He was going to miss the horses as much as his comrades. In spite of the hardships and the minor wounds he had suffered before grape-shot mangled his leg, he had enjoyed the excitement of campaigning and was going to feel lost without it.

On the journey he was attacked several times by ruffians hoping to find rings on the body, but he was well armed and had no real trouble getting rid of them. In the towns, villages and hamlets, people stood in respect as he drove past, the flag wrapping the coffin becoming more faded and ragged as the miles were covered.

On the outskirts of Lyons he took an overnight halt, camping at the roadside as he had done all the way. In the morning he groomed the horses for their entry into the city. When their appearance satisfied him he turned his attention to the wagon, washing away the mud and dust of travel until it looked as good as new. Lastly he unfolded a fresh Tricolore he had kept for this moment and spread it over the coffin. He saluted it smartly. Then he climbed into the driving seat to flick the whip over the horses' heads and complete the warrior's last home-coming in full splendour.

He was sighted as soon as he turned into the Rue Clémont. By the time he drew up in front of the entrance to the house the family had gathered on the steps. Automatically his eyes went first to the women dressed in black. To the forefront was the widow, whom he recognised at once, for he had seen her in Boulogne with her late husband. She was a pretty little thing, bravely dry-eyed for this last meeting, in his sealed coffin, with the man she had loved. Behind her was an older, full-figured woman with frizzed hair and a wanton mouth, crying copious tears that were no help to anyone. He assumed that the portly, grim-faced man at her side was her husband. Standing a little apart was a young woman whom he also recognised from Boulogne. This was Gabrielle, the late officer's sister. He gained the same impression of her as he had then. What a beauty! Strong-willed with it. The chin gave that away.

Hélène Roche was coming towards him. He clambered down from the driving seat, cramped with pain and awkward with it, much embarrassed by his clumsiness. She did not appear to notice and spoke to him in her gentle voice.

"I thank you with all my heart for bringing my husband home to me, Sergeant Garcin."

To his astonishment she kissed him on both cheeks in her gratitude. As she moved away to touch a corner of the draped flag, Gabrielle came forward. She gave him no such greeting, simply thanking him with all sincerity for his kind action. "When the commanding officer wrote to tell my sister-in-law of what you had undertaken, it brought great comfort to her and to us all."

"It has been an honour to serve Captain Roche in life and in death, madame."

The servants came to shoulder the coffin and bear it into the house. Hélène and the others followed it indoors, she telling him first to go to the servants' quarters, where he would be given food and accommodation.

Later that day Hélène received him on her own in her salon. For over an hour they were closeted together while he told her of Captain Roche's last days and recounted anything he could remember that would be of interest to her, particularly of happier times.

He was giving her more solace than he realised. She had received Jules's personal effects from one of his fellow officers a while ago, and although that man had been his friend she felt closer to her late husband through contact with this tough-looking, good-natured soldier who had obeyed his orders and respected him for his courage. When she gave way to tears he sat patiently until she dried her eyes and was ready to talk again. She noted that it was only having to move with a limp that caused him any kind of embarrassment, and she guessed how hard this disability was to a man previously active and energetic.

After the funeral she sent for him again. "What are your plans now?" she asked him. The day after his arrival he had delivered the horses and wagon to the local barracks, as ordered before he left Austria. As far as she knew he had nothing except a few possessions in an army knapsack and he had already told her that he had no family.

"To find work, madame. I'm strong and good with my hands. My game leg is not going to stop me getting around."

"I think I can help you. I shall speak to my brother-in-law. I'm sure he will be able to provide employment for you."

He was appreciative. Already he had applied for work, only to find his infirmity went against him and each time fully fit men were taken on before him. Unemployment was high in the city, as he knew it to be elsewhere, for war had brought its own financial difficulties to commercial interests.

Henri did not believe in mixing sentiment with business, but he did not refuse Hélène's request to find suitable employment for Gaston. Having no need of an extra hand among his own employees, he sent him with a letter to a civic official of his acquaintance. Gaston found himself in the city's foulest and lowest-paid work, of night-soil removal, clearing the households' cesspits during the hours of darkness. He overcame his pride, for he had to live until such time as his leg was stronger and he could present a more able-bodied appearance to a prospective employer. As he toiled in his reeking clothes, he thought how far he had come from the banners and drums and the bright uniform in which he had marched to war for France. Hélène, having been told by Henri that Gaston was working for the city, pictured him safe and secure, appointed to a post of responsibility through his service to his country.

Seven months later the Roche family gathered for another funeral. Dominique had been stricken by the death of his favourite son and had never recovered. Hélène, who had broken the news to him, had expected they would comfort each other in their terrible grief, but he had merely glared at her with half-crazed eyes and bellowed that he would be left alone. For three days he would allow no one in the family near him, although servants and others for whom he sent were permitted to come and go. Then, on the evening of the third day, he suffered a massive stroke that left him completely paralysed, unable to speak, and only the torment in his eyes showing he was aware of what had happened to him.

Hélène was with him constantly. Her gentleness and soothing presence did its work as it had done with Émile, and it was owing to her that Dominique continued to be treated as head of the house. Henri met the full force of her anger when he chatted by the sickbed as if Dominique were incapable of comprehending anything that was said. She had pulled him outside the room and upbraided him for callousness. "Your father hears and understands all that is going on! In future you will address him, not me. Talk to him as I do. Tell him good news about the business. Tell him anything of interest that you know would please him. Just because he has lost the power of his limbs does not mean he has lost his mind."

When Dominique died the family were all around his bedside and it was Hélène who sat holding his hand. Gabrielle's grief was tearless and the more harrowing for it, for she was filled with sorrow for what had never been between her father and herself, not even at the end. She would not have attended the reading of Dominique's will if the lawyer had not insisted that every member of the family should be present at the gathering in the Grand Salon.

There were some small bequests, which included an income for Hélène until such time as she should marry again. Then came the moment for which Henri and Yvonne had been waiting, and she squeezed his arm in anticipation. The lawyer cleared his throat.

"The rest of my estate, my house and its contents together with Maison Roche, I bequeath to my daughter Gabrielle Valmont to be held in trust for any son or grandson she may have in the future. In the event of her failing to have issue, the estate shall pass to my granddaughter, Juliette Roche, and in turn be held in trust for her son. It is my earnest wish and belief that Gabrielle will bring to the business the initiative and imagination that were mine when I was young, traits that have ebbed in me through the years and will be revived through her and her issue." The lawyer looked up from the document in the stunned silence. "That is all, *mesdames* and *messieurs.*"

Gabrielle sat dazed. Maison Roche was hers! Her dream had come true. The bequest had been cleverly devised by Dominique to bypass the claim that husbands could make on their wives' property, giving her complete freedom. The required endorsement of a lawyer's signature to legalise hers on any business transaction would be a mere formality. At her side Henri had recovered from the initial shock he had received and he leapt from his chair with a great roar.

"Damn him! Damn him to hell! Maison Roche is my birthright! I'll contest the will. I'll prove he was senile when he signed it."

The lawyer shook his head. "It was drawn up two days after he had heard of the death of his son Jules. I did it for him myself and he requested that a doctor be present in order that he be judged to be of sane mind in case of any such query ever arising."

"He changed it *after* Jules's death?" Henri glared, jowls shaking as comprehension dawned. "The old devil never meant me to have the business, did he? He left it to his golden boy until an enemy cannon put paid to that dream. Then, determined to have a final cruel joke against me, he bequeathed everything to Gabrielle instead. A woman! Untrained and useless. The daughter he hated from the day of her birth!"

Émile rose abruptly from the sofa where he had been sitting beside his wife, who was still in a state of complete astonishment. "I will hear no more of these insults that you are directing towards your own sister out of pique, Henri. Gabrielle has come into this inheritance through an apprenticeship she created out of her own determination to learn the silk trade as well as any man. It makes no difference to me that she was her father's second choice. I'm sure I speak for all of us when I say that I wish Jules had lived to receive this munificent inheritance, but since it has come to Gabrielle she deserves the full support of her family. Knowing her as I do, I think none of you need fear for any lack of security through her ownership."

Gabrielle looked up at him gratefully. Among those present he had in all probability received the greatest blow of all through the very nature of the bequest that had come to her, and yet he had leapt to her defence against this family aggression, making himself heard above Yvonne's display of hysterics.

Henri was shaking a fist at him. "Keep out of this! You're only kin by marriage. Whatever has to be discussed will be between one Roche and another." He rounded in exasperation on the noisy sobbing of his wife, further enraged by her. "Be silent, woman! Good God! Haven't I enough to endure without your caterwauling? Maybe if I'd taken my father's sound advice to divorce you for your spendthrift ways I wouldn't have found myself in this ignominious position now!"

She was furious. Tears flew from her huge eyes like crystal drops as she looked up at him, her face flushed high. "Don't try to shift the blame onto me! It was your fault entirely. You shouldn't have quarrelled with him so much. But that's like you! Always thinking you're right in everything!"

He lowered his head, jutting his face belligerently towards her. "It wouldn't have hurt you to be a little more obliging yourself instead of forever keeping out of his range."

She shrieked her outrage. With an exclamation of wrath, he seized her by the arm, wrenching her to her feet, and thrust her before him out of the room. Their quarrelling faded out of earshot.

Hélène, who still sat on one of the scroll-ended sofas, watched the lawyer bow over Gabrielle's hand, offering to be of assistance at any time. Of those who had listened to the will, Hélène had been the least surprised by its contents. Although she had never suspected that Jules had been the original heir to Maison Roche, she had come to understand a little of how Dominique's mind worked, and he had known more about his family individually than they had realised. She recalled how delighted he had been at Gabrielle's rejection of the Devaux order, how interestedly he had listened to how she had managed the silk farm during Émile's illness and how, in spite of his derision, he had noted all she had said about the possibilities of the Jacquard loom, whereas Henri had kept a closed mind. Hélène knew that Dominique had followed up investigations of his own into the Jacquard mechanism and, although it was doubtful whether he had intended to do anything about it in his lifetime, not wanting to be bothered with the labour troubles that would be inevitable, it was possible that he had an eye to the future. All in all, with Jules gone, he must have decided that Gabrielle would do far more for the business than his surviving son. Hélène did not doubt that this was true. There was only one thing that troubled her. How much would this fulfilment of Gabrielle's dream affect her marriage to Émile? But this was no time to anticipate trouble. Getting up from her seat, Hélène went across to Gabrielle to embrace her in her good fortune.

During the night, Émile awoke from sleep to find when he stretched out his arm for Gabrielle that she was not there and that side of the bed was cold. It was not hard to guess where he would find her, knowing how impatient she had been to begin her study of the business records. For a while he did not stir, thinking over the change that had come about in their lives. He could not deny that her inheritance was welcome in one way. This year of 1806 was proving to be one of economic crisis due to the British sea blockade, the general uncertainty of the times with Bonaparte reshaping Europe through conquest and the nervousness of the financiers. Many of his customers had cut down or withdrawn regular orders, not knowing if they would be able to sell their silk once it was woven, with the loss of sales at home and abroad, and there was more unemployment in Lyons than in the aftermath of the Revolution. Without doubt, the Roche fortune that had come to Gabrielle would keep out the cold draughts for a long time to come.

On the debit side was her determination to seize the reins of the business, which she had made clear to him in the discussion they had had on their own together after coming to bed. He had thought it prudent to say nothing of the private talk he had had with Henri in the library. His brother-in-law had calmed down by that time and Émile had found him slumped in a chair with his elbows on his knees and his head in his hands. Although he had looked up bleakly, his face haggard, his expression had changed when he heard the proposition that was put to him and he cheered up considerably.

It was agreed that Gabrielle should be given her head for a few weeks, long enough for her to believe she had everything running her way; then he and Émile himself would both exert pressure to get her to relinquish her responsibilities and become head of Maison Roche in name only. Émile knew it would not be easy to make Gabrielle conform to a sedentary role, but it should be done.

His brow creased in a deep and thoughtful frown as he sat up in the bed and rested his arms across his updrawn knees. He had heard in business circles that Devaux had put his silk interests in Paris up for sale. It probably meant he needed the money to finance whatever he proposed to do with his property in Lyons. Nobody knew exactly what alterations had been carried out. The general assumption was that he had put to rights the damage done during the siege and made the old looms serviceable again.

Émile recalled the unease he had experienced when he had seen his

wife and Devaux alone in his office together. Equally uncomfortable for
him, for he believed himself to be an honourable man, was the fact that
he had checked Gabrielle's mail for weeks afterwards to make sure there
was no correspondence between them. That fear had eventually been
put to rest, and since then he had begun to suspect that his physical
weakness after his illness had played tricks with his mind and imagination. If there had been some spark of mutual attraction, his wife was not
one to be led astray by any would-be seducer. Time and time again he
had observed how neatly she nipped flirtatious advances in the bud,
sparing him the agonies of jealousy that would otherwise have been his,
for he even resented inwardly the convention that allowed other men to
kiss her hand in greeting. No, it was not Devaux he need fear as far as
she was concerned. It was not another man who would ever part them.
Unhappily it was her own good fortune in receiving a rich inheritance
that was likely to drive a wedge between them.

"Damnation to it all!" He flung back the bedclothes, now thoroughly disgruntled, and put his feet to the floor. There was no need to
light a candle, for moonlight through the windows gave enough illumi-
nation for him to find his dressing-robe and slip it over his night-shirt as
he went from the room and down the stairs. As he had expected, a chink
of light showed under the door of his late father-in-law's office, which
Gabrielle had already decided to make her own. He pushed open the
door and stood there. She looked up from a pile of documents that she
was leafing through where she sat at her father's desk, her loosened hair
full of bronze lights in the lamp's glow, her feet showing bare beneath
the hem of her nightgown. Somehow the sight of her seductively clad in
the midst of a dreary business setting of bookshelves and ledgers and
stacks of yellowed records seemed to emphasise the threat that Roche
silk would take her away from him. She should have been curled up in
bed beside him instead of causing him to come down in search of her in
the small hours.

"This is madness!" he pronounced angrily. "I thought we had
talked everything over before we went to bed and I had agreed you
could stay on here for a few days after I go home in the morning.
There's no need to be working at this hour."

She sat back calmly in the chair, her cleavage framed by the low
neckline of the nightgown, the fine white lawn settling against the nipples of her beautiful breasts. "I couldn't sleep and there's so much to be
done. I can't discuss anything with Henri until I'm up to date with
every fact and figure. Tomorrow I'm letting him have this desk of Father's. It's right that it should be his."

"Come to bed!"

If he had not ordered her, if he had simply held out a hand and spoken normally, she would have gone, but she always felt rebellion rise in her whenever he was dictatorial. It often puzzled her that he could be so sensitive and understanding at times while at others he was as unbending as a stone wall. "I think not. I'll read for a while longer."

His temper snapped. He had never laid hands roughly on her before. Now he seized her, wrenching her to her feet. Humiliated at being treated much as Henri had manhandled Yvonne a few hours earlier, she struggled against him, resisting the urge to cry out for fear of waking the household. He overpowered her and snatched her up in his arms to carry her back through the hall. On the stairs he stumbled badly, almost falling with her. In their room he threw her down onto the bed. Then he came at her like a bull, desire unleashed in him in the need to master her completely once and for all, to dominate and subdue and crush out that elusive spark in her that kept her ever just out of his reach, making it impossible for him to feel that he had ever truly possessed her as he would wish, heart, mind and body. He knew he was hurting her and that increased his pleasure to a frantic peak, dark depths erupting in him in the surge for total conquest. If he had been tearing her apart beneath him he could not have stopped what he was doing to her.

She endured it all without a sound, choking back the cries of pain that rose in her throat. When finally he fell away from her, breathless and drenched in sweat, she lay completely still with her forearm across her eyes, her night-gown in tatters, bruised and too much abused to move away from his side. After a few minutes he shifted up onto an elbow, looking down on her. Even in the moonlight he could see the bruises taking colour. Remorse overwhelmed him.

"My dearest," he whispered hoarsely, "what have I done?"

She knew he meant more than his physical violence. He was looking beyond, not knowing how she would be towards him again. Somehow she could not speak or answer him. He, whom she had known only as a tender, considerate lover, skilful enough always to arouse her to a state of pleasure, had vented his lust on her out of an ungovernable rage. She knew why. He could not bear to share her, not even with something as inanimate as Maison Roche.

"Don't cry," he implored desperately, taking hold of her wrist with his finger and thumb to pull her arm gently away from her eyes.

She was dry-eyed, but she rolled her head away from him, resisting his attempts to turn her face back towards him. He flung himself down beside her again and to her dismay she heard him begin to sob—heavy, wrenching sobs that shook the bed. Half raising herself, she looked towards him. He was lying flat on his stomach, face in the pillows, his arms outflung with his hands clenched in despair.

Unable to bear such grief in another human being, she put out her hand to stroke his hair. At her touch he raised his tortured face to look at her. Reading compassion in her eyes, he hesitated only briefly before putting an arm around her waist to draw himself close to her and lower his head against her breasts. She cradled him to her, looking ceiling-wards from her pillows while the terrible shaking of his shoulders slowly eased. Eventually he slept.

It was then that her own silent tears flowed, running in rivulets from the corners of her eyes down either side of her face to soak into the pillow. In anguish she yearned to be able to turn the clock back to her wedding day, not out of anger towards Émile, but in the knowledge that she had done him the greatest possible harm in marrying him. Fate had given her a last-minute chance to change the course of her life and direct it towards another man. For Émile's sake, as well as her own, she should have seized it. Instead she had condemned him and herself to a tor-mented marriage.

Hélène listened attentively when Gabrielle told her of Jules's wish that she should not remain in the house after Dominique's death. It had been settled that Henri and Yvonne should continue to live there, for Gabrielle had no desire to disrupt their lives further in any way.

"But it was different then," Hélène said in reply. "Jules did not know any more than the rest of us that Father would leave everything to you. You are mistress of the family house now. You will be occupying his rooms whenever you are here. You will need someone to be in charge of the housekeeping arrangements."

"I'll appoint a housekeeper. That's what should have been done long ago. You must be free now to make your own home with Juliette. That's what Jules wanted."

"Only because, as you have told me, he was afraid I should be over-burdened by others on my own here. If a housekeeper is appointed, then that danger is removed. I like living here." She glanced about her at the small salon that was hers. It was circular in shape, its damask panels having a pattern of wreaths of fruit and flowers surmounted with a bouquet of myrtle on a sun-yellow ground. "This is a beautiful room, but there's more to it than that. It was in this house that Jules was born and where he grew up. I feel close to him here, now more than ever before." Her eyes were full of appeal. "Don't make me leave yet. I will in time. When I'm ready. It will be the day when I'll have learned to adjust at last to facing the rest of my life without him."

It would have been impossible to refuse such a request. Gabrielle knew she must respect Hélène's wishes in the matter. Her first move was to appoint a housekeeper, a capable woman who took over the keys and wore them on a chatelaine that jingled against her skirt like a continuous pronouncement of her authority. Hélène was able at last to devote time to Juliette and found consolation in being with her.

It did not take Gabrielle long to discover that Henri had been lining his own pockets for years. Quite possibly Dominique had known about it and it was another reason why he had left him no share of the business. Deciding to say nothing about the fraudulence, she introduced a new system of accounting in which nothing could be duplicated or slipped past. This was in the hands of a new clerk of her own choosing, whom she knew she could trust implicitly.

When inspecting a warehouse cellar one day, her attention was attracted by a large number of straw bales especially made for the transport of raw silk. They looked as though they had been there for a considerable time. Opening one, she found the lustrous hanks in perfect condition just as they had been purchased from a silk farm and never taken out. Further investigation into the ledgers showed the entry of the cost of the lengths supposedly made up from this silk, together with the additional expenses of gold thread and other valuable additions used in this imaginary making up. There was an additional entry to say these bolts of silk had been stolen en route and never reached their destination. She wondered how many other such frauds perpetrated by Henri were hidden in the dusty ledgers. Again she said nothing to him and the silk remained untouched in the cellar.

She interviewed several new designers. It was not her intention to change everything, but she was looking for artists with bright new ideas of design. Eventually she engaged a young man named Marcel Donnet, just out of his student days and newly come to Lyons from Paris in the hope of the very chance she was giving him. His work was brilliant. She asked him if he had seen the Jacquard loom in Paris when it was on display at the Conservatoire.

"Yes, madame." His face sharpened with interest. "Have you considered introducing this mechanism? Monsieur Jacquard has had doors slammed in his face ever since his loom was destroyed in Lyons. That was the ultimate condemnation. If Lyons refused it, then nobody else wanted it."

She set her elbows on the desk between them, looping her fingers together. "I'm keeping an open mind. I should have to try weaving on one of those looms myself before I could make a decision, even though I was extremely impressed by the demonstration when I saw it. Do you think the finished product loses by this new mechanism?"

"Not at all." He was enthusiastic. "On the contrary. Many small human errors are eradicated. Why not go to Paris and consult Monsieur Jacquard yourself?"

"I can't possibly leave the business at the present time. Too many changes are under way."

After he had left, she found herself heartened by the enthusiasm he had shown for the Jacquard loom, and she needed heartening at the present time. Getting up from her chair, she went to look out of the window. The trees had lost their leaves and stood etched against the wintry sky. The year was almost gone, a sad year that had brought news of Jules having died of wounds and her father's death too. It had given her no glimpse of Nicolas, making her wonder if Paris had claimed him after all. Although no estrangement had resulted between Émile and her after the night that had brought wretchedness to both of them, she having forgiven him at the time and he appreciative of it, their relationship was considerably strained. It was the result of the time she was devoting to Maison Roche instead of to him. When she had said once how much she would like to have her father's power, she had not suspected what the cost would be.

She decided to do no more work that day. It was late afternoon and Friday. She had promised Émile she would go home to be with him until Monday. It had been impossible to cut down her working days so far, which was what he wished. As for Henri, since his initial outburst at hearing the will he had changed his attitude to become thoroughly obliging and had offered many times to shoulder some of the burdens she had taken upon herself, not knowing that she no longer trusted him. She had the feeling that he was watching her like a hawk, just as if he were waiting for a chance to pounce on her authority and wrest it from her. Several times she had had to stem his encroachment into her field, which was the main reason why she felt it was vital that she should be on the premises every day of the working week until such time as she had nothing more to be wary of as far as he was concerned. When she had explained this to Émile, he had merely shrugged and said it would be much better for her, and for him, if she allowed Henri to be her manager. "Then at least we could start to get our lives back together again," he concluded, returning his attention to the book he was reading. She had noticed that there were times these days when he could not, or would not, meet her eyes.

Before leaving the house she went in search of Hélène and found her embroidering by the fire, Juliette asleep on the sofa beside her. It was Gabrielle's private hope that one day her sister-in-law would marry again. As yet it was too soon for such a possibility to be contemplated.

"I'm going home now," she said to her, "before it gets dusk. I'll see you on Monday."

"Give my fond regards to Émile."

It was bitter cold outside that day. In the carriage she had a muff-warmer filled with hot coals for her hands and she was well wrapped. It was in her mind to invest in some younger, faster horses and buy one of the new calèches built more for speed than the lumbering vehicles that belonged to the Roche stable. In that way she could make the journey between Lyons and the silk farm in less time and perhaps get home for an overnight stay once or twice during the week.

She was moved by pity for the plight of the large number of beggars in the streets. As she had thought earlier that day, the sooner this year of 1806 was gone the better it would be, for it had brought many looms to a standstill, and this had repercussions throughout the city. The thought that in a matter of a few days 1807 would dawn made her truly thankful.

Suddenly her attention was drawn to a beggar slumped against a wall as if he no longer had the strength to stand alone. It was the military colour of his ragged coat that had caught her eye. There were many disbanded soldiers among those drawn into hard times, often on crutches or missing an arm or an eye. This man had not suffered such loss but he was thin as a skeleton, his features stamped by hunger, unshaven and neglected. She recognised him.

"Stop!" she ordered the coachman. Alighting quickly, she ran back to where the beggar was. When he saw her he turned as if he would shuffle away, but she caught his sleeve. "Gaston Garcin! What has happened to you? Why are you like this?"

"Madame Valmont." He was filled with shame at being recognised in such a degraded state and tried to straighten himself up. "I've had a spell of misfortune. It will pass."

"But I heard you were employed by the city."

"I fell ill, madame. A contagion contracted through my work. Since my recovery I have been unable to get anything else."

"Your recovery! You still look far from well to me." She remembered how fine his military bearing had been at Jules's funeral in spite of his wounded leg, just as when she had seen him in Boulogne. Glancing along the street, she saw they were not far from a café. "Come with me. I think you will feel better after you have eaten a good meal."

She ordered meat-broth and bread, thinking it the most suitable food for someone not far from starvation. He tried not to make a spectacle of himself in front of her, but hunger overcame him and he could not devour the food quickly enough. She would have ordered more for him but thought it unwise for him to cram his stomach too soon.

"Now you're coming home with me," she said to him. Her first thought had been to take him back to the Rue Clémont, except that would have meant extra work for Hélène, who would never have allowed the housekeeper to take charge of this man. "I'm going to see that

you get well and strong again. After that, work will no longer be difficult for you to find."

He passed a hand across his eyes, embarrassed by their watering.
"You have saved my life, madame."

She fetched the coachman to help him into the carriage. He fell
asleep almost at once, covered by the rug she had put over him.

It did not take Gaston long to recover his strength. Plenty of good
food, warmth and shelter provided by a spare room in the servants'
quarters, plus an adequate amount of wine, soon brought him to a point
where he was impatient to be in work again. As soon as he was able, he
made himself useful, chopping firewood and sweeping the courtyard
among other such chores. Gabrielle discussed his future with Émile. He
was fully in agreement that employment should be given to Gaston,
whom he had seen to be quick and willing to work, but he disagreed
strongly with the situation she wanted to offer him.

"A new calèche is an unwarranted extravagance and making him
your coachman is totally unnecessary. I can give him work around the
silk farm or you can place him in a warehouse."

Émile's whole tone implied that she would not be making so many
journeys into Lyons in the future anyway. Over the past two or three
weeks he had begun to exert more pressure on her to relinquish a
greater share of her work to Henri, arguing that the way the ledgers
were being kept now would give her brother no chance to defraud the
business, something she had confided to him. Henri had not ceased his
continual offers to take over this task and that, almost as though his
indulgence of her being in charge had worn thin.

"I've made up my mind," she replied firmly. "I've seen a calèche at
a coachbuilder's in the Place des Célestins, which is exactly what I want;
if you care to give me advice about the purchase of the horses, I should
be grateful." There was another reason why she wanted Gaston as her
coachman. Émile did not know yet that there would be times when she
would extend her working day into the late hours in order to get home
to him in midweek and perhaps spend the following day there. She did
not want to travel the night roads without the company of a coachman
who would know how to defend her and himself against robbers. It had
been different when she and Hélène visited Boulogne, for they had travelled only by day, when the danger was much reduced, and in any case
those coach-servants had been Émile's and she wanted her own choice in
this matter.

"Are my wishes no longer of any importance to you?" he enquired
bitterly.

"You know they are," she protested. "This whole idea came about
to allow me to get home quicker to be with you."

He was unimpressed and retreated into one of his quiet, withdrawn moods that she had come to know meant he was full of hurt. Yet, when the time came for her to buy her new horses, he went with her and ensured that she had the best that were available. Gaston was fitted out with new clothes and drove the calèche in a dark blue caped greatcoat while the cold weather lasted, and with the coming of the warmth of spring, he was able to display his striped black and white waistcoat and his lighter blue coat with the brass buttons. Although most coachmen kept to the old-fashioned tricorn hat, or wore the new top hat, he chose to wear a wide-brimmed black hat turned up in the front with a military cockade from his old regiment. He thought it would do no harm to warn any waiting ruffians that they would have to deal with a one-time soldier. It gave him a dashing appearance and brought him plenty of female attention.

Almost from the first day of taking over Maison Roche, Gabrielle had set aside some time to visit her weavers. In many of the loom-rooms there had been reunions with families she had known since childhood. With those on whom she had never called, who held some animosity towards her owing to their having worked for Dominique with long-harboured grudges, she sought to put matters on a new plane.

In her opinion, there had been too much bread-and-butter work done in recent years. This was silk, its quality of high standard, its designs traditional, that was made for retail in the shops of Paris and other cities throughout France and also for dressmakers' establishments and cabinet-makers' upholstery workshops. She did not belittle its importance, for it kept the looms going and she had no intention of discarding it. Nevertheless with her new designer she was aiming for the attention of the Mobilier Impérial. This was the Paris-based committee with the power and authority to restore and decorate and conserve the great palaces of France and to commission beautiful furnishings for them, not least exquisite silks for hangings and drapes and sofa- and chair-coverings, even to the design of footstools and fire-screens. Under its comparatively new title, it was the successor to the royal Garde-Meuble, which had originated in the mid-seventeenth century by command of Louis XIV, who was concerned that the magnificence due to his palaces should be duly maintained. Gabrielle was certain that Marcel's marvellous designs were worthy of a commission from the Mobilier Impérial, and she was having samples woven for presentation. When they were ready, Henri would leave for Paris with them.

It was Henri who gave her the news she had long awaited, not suspecting the effect it would have on her. They were examining some of the finished samples together when he made his announcement. "Devaux is back in Lyons. To stay this time, I hear. He's taking on weavers for his mill in La Croix Rousse and looks set to start up in the near future."

She was holding a glorious piece of brocade in her hands—an all-over pattern of white doves flying against a lapis-blue background, woven with a brocading weft. It seemed to her she would never be able to look at that particular design again without remembering the unbidden leap of her heart. How was it possible for her to have such a reaction to hearing Nicolas's name spoken after such a length of time?

"I thought his silk interests were in Paris," she said levelly, tracing a dove's wing with her finger tip. Each beautiful feather was delicately depicted.

"He has sold them. Held out for a high price, I was told." He indicated the samples on the table before him. "If he's thinking of competing with us, he's in for a surprise. In all my years in silk, I've rarely seen anything better than what we have here."

There were times when his willingness to praise or to agree with everything she said and did made her highly suspicious. Admittedly nobody could have given anything but praise to the marvellous samples spread out on the table before them, but his geniality always held a false note to her ears. It was not in his nature to be so agreeable, especially when she knew she was going against long-held policies in the business. It was possible that he was enjoying a winning streak at the gaming tables, although his attitude towards Yvonne did not appear to be particularly amiable. She truly wished she could accept his show of good nature towards herself at its face value, for she wanted good relations between them. Yet it was impossible to shake off the conviction that he was working out ends of his own.

When all the samples were ready for the Mobilier Impérial, Gabrielle supervised the packing of them herself. There were gold and orange-red brocade with flowers and palmettos, white *gros de Tours broché* with a pattern in gold of laurel leaves and sprays of scarlet poppies, suitable for a grand bedchamber with that flower's association with sleep, *chiné* velvet with rosebuds on a soft green ground and, among several more, a dramatic black velvet on a white satin ground with a lilac *liséré* lozenge design.

On the morning that Henri departed for Paris, Gabrielle went into the design room to tell Marcel that the samples were on their way. He put the brush he was using back in its jar and wiped his hands with a piece of white rag before bringing forward another high stool for her to take a seat. He had smiling eyes and a bright, cheerful face.

"Let's hope Monsieur Roche secures the commissions we're looking for," he said, reseating himself.

"It would be a turning point for Maison Roche. Our designs have been mundane for far too long. Of course it's not easy to show that a new beginning has been made, but I know we stand a good chance with your designs."

He leaned an arm on the sloping surface of his drawing desk. "Speaking of new beginnings, there's something I've heard about the Devaux mill."

"Yes?" She was immediately alert.

"Do you remember that we talked about the possibilities of the new Jacquard mechanism? Well, I was told that the new Jacquard loom has been installed throughout by Monsieur Devaux."

She felt an odd burst of excitement. It was as if Nicolas had stolen a march on her, almost as though it were the opening volley of a battle she had been long awaiting. Ever since she had heard from Henri that Maison Devaux was to be in operation again, she had welcomed the chance to compete with Nicolas in the manufacture of *le tissue lyonnais*, to match her designs against his, to strive against him in the capture of commissions. It gave a new impetus to the old feud, enabling her to struggle against him while fighting to overcome her own feelings. She truly believed it to be the only way to dispel the yearning that had no place in her life.

"Isn't he expecting labour troubles?" she wanted to know. "After what happened at Joseph Jacquard's demonstration, there will be many people raged against letting that loom into Lyons, silk merchants and weavers alike."

"Ah, it's over three years now since that demonstration took place, and last year was the hardest the industry has experienced for a long time. As you know, many weavers had to give up their looms. It was sell or starve for them and their families. Men who are desperate for work are not going to turn down this chance to get into their own trade again. As the word spreads, there may be demonstrations outside the mill, but if Monsieur Devaux has the work force he wants, it is not going to trouble him."

"How I should like to see inside that mill! To watch those looms in action in a rightful setting."

"It's my guess he won't let strangers in. Monsieur Devaux probably has secrets of design that he'll be guarding closely, just as we haven't let slip any information about the samples that have left today."

She smiled to herself. Marcel had no way of guessing that she did not consider herself to be a stranger to Nicolas, but business was business and they were competitors now. The door would be barred to her as much as to anyone else. It was an old rule in the weaving industry that nobody from a silk-negotiator to a child tying threads gossiped about any new design, the success of which was of benefit to everyone concerned. The theft of designs was not unknown. In the old days a watch had been kept at the city gates to ensure that no weaver, spinner, or dyer left Lyons under any pretext, for there was always the danger of their taking the precious secrets of their craft to another city, or even to a foreign country eager to capture the special trade of the Lyonnais.

She proved to be right in her belief that Nicolas would meet strong opposition to his Jacquard looms. The news-sheets brought out a full report of a fiery uprising among other weavers, who had advanced on the Devaux mill with bludgeons and home-made pikes and rocks to throw. It had taken a strong force of police to disperse them and many arrests had been made. Later she heard of Nicolas's carriage being stoned, and missiles through the windows of his property had become almost a daily occurrence.

The idea of seeing inside his mill persisted with her. She could not dismiss it. All was fair in love and war, and there was war now between his industry and hers as far as she was concerned. The feud between his name and hers had taken a new turn, for there was no hatred in this new rivalry on her part, and yet the battle would be unremitting. For that reason she had to do whatever needed to be done.

Late one evening, when she was ready to go home to Émile, intending to spend the following day there, she collected up the amount of work she always took with her. When told that the calèche was at the door, she asked that Gaston be brought to her. As soon as he appeared, she told him to close the door behind him and to sit down opposite her. Briefly she outlined the help she wanted from him in a plan she had made.

He looked at her steadily for a long, unblinking moment. His expression had not altered once during all she had said to him. "What you ask can be done," he said at last, "but there's a better way. Let me go into that mill by night. Just tell me what it is that you want to find out."

She shook her head quickly. "That wouldn't do. You are not a weaver and the technical details would escape you. In any case, I'm not going to let you break the law on my behalf. If there's any punishment to be reaped, it shall be mine. But I don't intend to be caught. There'll be no danger if you do as I've asked. What do you say?"

"Very well, madame. Leave everything to me."

She pulled open the cords of her velvet draw-string purse. "I'll give you the money you'll need now—"

He held up his hand. "Not yet, madame. To be done properly, time is more important in this case than money. That can come later if I should find it necessary."

She let the purse sink back into her lap, her hands resting on it.

"Thank you, Gaston," she said with feeling, her eyes shining with gratitude. "I was certain I could rely on you."

As he drove her out of Lyons he noted to himself that she had not asked him to keep to himself what she had disclosed. She trusted him completely. He knew well enough that there was nobody else she could have asked to carry out the same task for her. It pleased him greatly to be of special service to her.

Henri returned from Paris a week later. He was cautiously optimistic. The committee of the Mobilier Impérial had received him, studied carefully each sample that he presented in turn and eventually told him to wait in the anteroom. When they had summoned him into their presence again, it was to inform him that he would be notified at some time in the near future of any decision they might make.

"Did they look impressed?" she demanded eagerly. "Was any comment made?"

"Only that the samples were up to standard."

"Is that all?" She was indignant. "I should have expected their eyes to pop out."

"That committee does not give praise lightly. Just by saying our silks meet with the high quality set by their standards is something to be proud of. Take heart, Gabrielle. They tossed nothing aside. If luck is with us a commission for at least one might come out of it."

During the days that followed she had to learn patience. Gaston carried out his duties by driving her to and from Lyons, but he made no comment on whatever he was doing to further the plan she had made. When letters came she went through them in haste before opening them, looking for the seal of the Mobilier Impérial, only to be disappointed each time.

One morning when Gaston came to see her in her office, she knew that at least one period of waiting was over. "You want the money for the bribes now?"

"The sum to be paid is almost negligible due to the person concerned not seeing it as a bribe, madame." Something close to amused self-satisfaction passed across his leonine features. "I made it my business to strike up an acquaintance with a young woman named Hortense, who winds for the Devaux mill. That's what took the time, you see. I had to be sure that when I asked a particular favour of her our friendship had reached a point where she would refuse me nothing."

"Indeed?" Gabrielle observed to herself that Gaston had a life of his own that would probably surprise her. "And were you successful?"

He gave his oddly crooked grin. "Entirely, I'm glad to say, madame. The only money that needs to change hands is for Hortense's sister, who is one of her fellow workers and whom she has persuaded to let you take her place for a day. All the girl wants is compensation for loss of pay. Neither is mercenary and they both like me."

"So it appears." Gabrielle pulled open a drawer and took out her purse. "How much does the girl require?"

He told her. It was a modest amount and she added extra money out of appreciation. All that remained was to fix a suitable day for her to become a winder at the Devaux mill and he had already allotted a Thursday, subject to her approval. It happened to be the day of the week when Nicolas was least likely to go into the loom-rooms, a point Gaston had ascertained from his new acquaintance.

When the day came Gabrielle, suitably attired, left the house with him just before dawn. It was quite a long walk to her destination, but he thought it best that she fit into her role from the start. A Roche carriage or her own calèche might be noted and remembered afterwards as being in the early morning streets near the Devaux mill, and they had to cover their tracks. She enjoyed the walk. As the sky turned to rising gold, the whole of Lyons was touched with gilt—spires and roofs and the very cobbles underfoot. With it came all the awakening sounds of shutters opening, dogs barking, the trickle and then the hiss of water being turned on in fountains and other street water supplies, the clatter of buckets and the first sweep of brooms.

The two of them attracted no attention, he in his simple clothes, she in a cotton cap, shawl and plain print dress and stout shoes. He led her down a dank alleyway, where he knocked on an inset door. As it opened, she entered ahead of him and the door was closed after them. They were in a small, low-beamed room that combined living, kitchen and sleeping quarters for the two sisters. Hortense had admitted them. She was a sturdy-looking girl, neither plain nor pretty, but she had fine dark eyes that sent a special velvety glance at Gaston before she addressed Gabrielle in a practical manner.

"*Bon jour*, citizeness. Let it be understood now that my sister and I are doing this favour on Gaston's behalf and not yours. If you're nabbed, you're to swear that neither of us knew anything about you, which is the truth because Gaston has told us nothing. As far as I'm concerned, you're just an out-worker who heard that my sister was sick and asked to take her place." She jerked a thumb in the direction of the wall-bed where her sister lay curled up asleep. "Nicole don't often get a chance to sleep, so I'm not waking her. Do you have a noon-piece?"

Gabrielle patted her apron pocket, where she carried a packet of bread and cheese. "Yes, I have."

"What am I to call you?"

"Ginette."

"Ginette what?"

"Desgranges." It had been her mother's maiden name.

"Come along then, Citizeness Ginette Desgranges, we must be on our way." Hortense looked enquiringly at Gaston, although her tone was demanding. "Shall I see you this evening when all this is over?"

"At the usual time," he replied easily.

She softened visibly and, when the three of them reached the outlet of the alleyway, blew him a kiss from her finger tips as she and Gabrielle turned up the street. It was a romantic gesture that somehow jarred with her whole appearance. Gabrielle had no idea how much Hortense had come to mean to Gaston, but she hoped he realised that beneath the present veneer of charm and sentimental glances there were all the makings of a shrew.

"How do you like working at the Devaux mill?" she asked her as they hurried along.

"It was frightening at first when the mob gathered outside. There's been some minor incidents since then, but Monsieur Devaux was prepared from the first day. He has his own force of law-keepers."

"Do you mean the police?"

"Oh, they came, but they couldn't be expected to give daily protection to his workers, which is what his law-keepers do. They patrol to ensure there's no personal harassment. Without exception they're soldiers who were disbanded or invalided out of the army for some reason or another and in need of employment."

"What about the working conditions for you and the others?"

"Good. Wages are fair and we can earn bonuses. The hours are long but that's the same as everywhere else and Monsieur Devaux has the right to expect his money's worth. Did you know he was born in Lyons?" Hortense did not wait for a reply, her talk flowing on. "He's a handsome man, no doubt about it. If he was like some employers I've known in my time, he could have his pick among any of the female workers and found 'em willing, but that's not his style. There's a woman from Paris, a Madame Marache, staying at his house now. He had a party of people from the capital to celebrate the reopening of the Devaux mill and she stayed on when the rest left. I haven't caught sight of her yet. Those who have say she's quite a beauty, and her clothes are in the latest mode, hardly any bodice at all now, just a cupping of the bosom and the waistline almost level with the armpits." She drew breath. "Here we are. Keep your head down and follow me."

Women workers and men weavers alike entered by the same side entrance. In the hallway there was chatter amongst them as shawls, hats and coats were hung on pegs, the men preferring to work in their comfortable loose and baggy shirt-sleeves. Some were already in the workshops and had set their looms going. To Gabrielle the looms had a new and unfamiliar sound, which she had heard only once before, when Monsieur Jacquard demonstrated his invention. Gone was the *thwack-thwack* of the old hand-loom. This loom had a voice of its own. *Biston-claque-bistonclaque.*

At Hortense's side she went into the loom-room that opened out of the hall. She almost paused to stare in amazement. The *maître ouvrier* was checking numbers as they came through and she did not dare to draw attention to herself. Again with Hortense, she fetched the hanks she needed for the winding wheel; the colour she was given was a rich yellow. Sitting down at her wheel, she began the work of winding the continuous thread of the hank onto the bobbin; in appearance the thread was as fine and glossy as a strand of hair and with no more weight to it, and it also had the characteristic toughness and elasticity that made silk easy to work with in all its stages. When the bobbin was full, it would take its place on a large circular bobbin-stand known as a creel, until needed by the weavers to set into the shuttles. It was quite a few years since she had learned to wind, but the old skill soon came back to her, even though her speed left much to be desired. As she worked she began to take note of her surroundings.

She saw that this loom-room had been of normal height, but the whole of the floor above it had been removed, leaving only the widely spaced giant beams that had given the original support. This meant there was plenty of space for the mechanism at the top of the Jacquard looms while at the same time double amount of light was given by the windows of the upper floor. It gave an airy atmosphere, which was good, for weavers were extraordinarily sensitive about draughts in summer and winter and would never have a window open anywhere. It was as much from fear of smuts blowing in on their delicate work as their own vulnerable joints, which were liable to enough aches and pains from the very nature of their work, particularly on the old type of loom.

Beyond the first loom-room was another, divided off in the same way as the winders' section was enclosed, which was by a wooden partition with a central archway, no higher than a stable stall in order that no light should be lost. Gabrielle was able to see that the ceiling had been lifted there in exactly the same way, and she estimated there were at least seventy looms in operation.

"Watch what you're doing!" Hortense hissed, leaning over from the neighbouring winder to give Gabrielle a prod in the arm. "You're over-winding."

With dismay Gabrielle saw she had put too much silk onto the bobbin, something none of the others would have done, and she had to rewind to the required amount. A snip of the scissors and it was ready for the basket at her feet. Later, when she had done a few, these bobbins would be collected up to replenish the bobbin-creel by one of the few children employed there in similar light tasks. Not for them the arduous thread-tying of the old looms. It was also a splendid sight for her to see the weavers standing straight-backed at their task. Never again would any of the Devaux weavers know the back troubles of the past that sometimes affected the mind as much as the spine.

To her relief, Hortense had answered the other girls' questions about who she was. Talking was discouraged by the *maître ouvrier*, and in any case the noise of the looms made it a vocal strain, but the girls had devised a silent language of mouthing their communications, and often, without a word having been spoken aloud, half-a-dozen of them would burst out laughing simultaneously at a silently mouthed joke that had been made. More than once Gabrielle was certain they were laughing at her, for they had filled three times the amount of bobbins in their baskets when the boy came to gather them up. At first Gabrielle was nervous that this discrepancy would be noticed by the *maître ouvrier*, but he was busy helping a weaver with the threading of a loom harness, a process that needed two people, one "reaching" the thread through the eye and the other "entering" a hook to pull it through. As her confidence grew, her speed on the winding wheel increased, and by the time she and Hortense ate the food they had brought with them during the noon break, she had become quite proficient. As yet she had not had a really close look at one of the looms in operation and she vowed to herself she would do so somehow before the day was at an end.

Luck was with her. In mid-afternoon some trouble developed on one of the looms in the far workroom. Over the partition she could see the *maître ouvrier* up a ladder beside a repairer as the two of them investigated the trouble. It gave her the chance she had been waiting for and had not dared to hope she would get. She had seen the designer's room was adjacent to the store where the hanks were kept. Through a window set into the passage wall she had already glimpsed that he was drafting an artist's design onto squared paper. On the pretext of fetching another hank, she paused by the door, tapped on it and entered quickly, closing it behind her. The designer, a young man, sat on a high stool before his sloping desk on which the work was fastened. He was alone in the room and paused in his work to look over his shoulder at her. "Yes, ma'amselle?"

"I'm sorry to interrupt you, but I'm new here and I want to learn everything. Could you tell me exactly what you are doing?"

He was struck by her well-spoken voice and lovely face. "Come and take a look," he invited good-naturedly. When she came to stand beside his high stool, he explained how he was transferring the sketch, which was of a new pattern shortly to go into production. It was of bees woven in gold on a rich blue ground. "A card-cutter will use my draft to punch holes in the cards, which will then be laced together as you see over there." He indicated some cards already laced and hanging on a lacing frame. "The colours I'm using bear no relation to those used by the artist. These are simply a guide for the card-puncher, who makes the holes that will convey the pattern on the loom. Every time the circle of these punched cards goes around, the pattern is repeated along the length of the fabric."

She asked him a few more questions about the process and then she thanked him and left. He looked after her, impressed by her intelligent appreciation.

Again later she used a chance, when unnoticed, to stand and watch the work being done on the two looms nearest to her. With one eye on the distant figure of the *maître ouvrier*, and ignoring Hortense's frantic beckoning to come back, she watched long enough to know that herein lay the whole future of Lyons silk. She had not been mistaken on the day of the demonstration. The work being turned out was perfection; that in itself was no more and no less than the best of Lyons silk had always been, but truly this new mechanism had brought the unique and exquisite fabric into its own.

"Are you mad?" Hortense demanded aggressively when she resumed her seat at her wheel. "When I let you come here today I didn't expect you to run such risks."

"Don't worry," Gabrielle replied calmly, yellow threads shining as she wound them onto the bobbin. "I've seen all I want to now."

She had also seen more than she had bargained for and it had given her a considerable jolt. The pattern of the golden bees on the designer's desk had told her that Nicolas had a commission from the Mobilier Impérial, for the bee was the symbol that Bonaparte had taken as his imperial emblem. Nobody would weave it except by express demand. Nicolas was much farther ahead of her than she could have been expected to know.

Her speed at the winding wheel continued to increase as the day advanced. It was not far from the end of the working day when events took an unexpected turn. She did not realise Nicolas had entered the far loom-room from the house until Hortense gave her another prod. "The *maître fabricant* has just come in. He's taking a look at that faulty loom."

The information had been mouthed by a winder who was able to see directly down the aisle. Overcome by curiosity, Gabrielle rose cautiously from her seat to get a better view and saw that Nicolas had removed his coat and was on a ladder beside the repairer, the two of them releasing the circle of cards. Then she saw much more than she had anticipated, in the sight of a fashionable woman, tallish with distinctly feline looks, wandering along and glancing at the looms on either side as she came. This was undoubtedly his present companion, Madame Marache, who had come to look at the weaving while waiting until Nicolas rejoined her.

Abruptly Gabrielle sat down again and bent her head industriously over her work. Out of the corner of her eye she saw the woman approach; her long-sleeved gown of carnation velvet was worn with satin shoes to match. At the sight of the winders, Madame Marache raised her eyebrows.

"What is going on here?" Her voice was attractive, her tone half amused. Hortense answered her, explaining the task in hand and its purpose. A beringed forefinger tapped Gabrielle patronisingly on the shoulder. "Let me take your seat, girl. I should like to try this bobbin-winding, and tulip yellow has always been one of my favourite colours."

In furious dismay, Gabrielle gave up her seat. The last thing she wanted was to be standing up conspicuously if Nicolas should decide to come in search of this voluptuous creature. Fortunately Hortense rose to give Madame Marache some instruction and signalled that Gabrielle should take her place.

The woman proved to be surprisingly deft and was well pleased to be getting some speed up on the wheel. Her fault was that of every beginner's, in an uneven winding of the bobbin. "Give me a fresh bobbin," she demanded playfully, seeing the knobbly effect of the one she had finished off. "Let me do one entirely on my own."

What was a game to her was a loss of earnings to Hortense, who glowered as she put a fresh bobbin in place and explained to Madame Marache how to begin. After several false starts, the woman gleefully managed to get going and with a degree less unevenness than before. Gabrielle, glancing across at her, was alarmed to see Nicolas was approaching the winders' section, looking for Madame Marache as he came. Her heart began to hammer against her ribs, and she bent her head still further over her work to avoid any chance of recognition. Worst of all was the bitter-sweetness of being near him again, to experience the tug and pull of his physical presence as if it had been yesterday that she had last seen him instead of many months' interval.

"Is this where you are!" he exclaimed with a chuckle, sighting Madame Marache at the winding wheel.

"Come and look, Nicolas," she coaxed happily, preening with pride. "I'm doing well, am I not?"

The frill of Gabrielle's cotton cap hid his face from her sight, for she did not dare to look up, and she was only able to see up as far as the middle buttons on his cream silk waistcoat. His highly polished, calf-length boots caught a sun-ray from the window as he moved around to stand behind Madame Marache, taking both her shoulders into the curved palms of his hands as he leaned forward to watch the thread twirling around the bobbin. "Splendid! Who would have thought that I'd gain a new winder in my mill today?"

"Maybe I'll try my hand at one of your Jacquard looms tomorrow," she said coquettishly.

"I'm afraid they would defeat you, Suzanne. The speed alone needs a background of weaving experience."

"I suppose so." She was getting bored with winding. It was no longer a novelty, and she released the thread. Only his quick action in halting the wheel saved it from sending a tangled cobweb of yellow silk thread all over the floor. "Have you mended the faulty loom?" she asked, looking up at him.

"It was nothing more than a simple adjustment. Shall we go?"

She stood up, shaking out her skirt gracefully, and slid a hand into the crook of his arm, smiling at him and entirely heedless of the disruption to work she had caused. It was he who thanked Hortense for showing her how to use the winding wheel. As the two of them strolled back along the aisle, he pointing out items of interest to her as they went, Hortense swore savagely over the wasting of her time. Gabrielle, changing places to sit at her own wheel again, stood briefly to look after Nicolas and the woman in his life. She felt an ache within her that awakened a curious kind of anger she could not define. All she knew was that she had a primitive longing to take that expression of smug satisfaction off Suzanne Marache's proud face. And she was angry with Nicolas for being responsible for putting it there.

She saw him pause to have a word with the *maître ouvrier*, Suzanne Marache going ahead of him through the doorway by which they had originally entered. The two men had their heads close together because of the noise of the looms, and the *maître ouvrier* nodded, glancing back towards the winding section. Gabrielle took her seat quickly, out of sight. It seemed as if Nicolas was as fair in his dealings with his workers as she had heard and had mentioned that Hortense was to be compensated for whatever time had been lost.

It was as she had supposed. Not long afterwards, the *maître ouvrier* came to check on the time Hortense had spent with Madame Marache. It was not more than about twenty minutes, but it all counted when transposed into money. Later a boy went past to summon the designer from his room to go into the house. As he went through the winders' section, his glance sought out Gabrielle and they exchanged smiles. She did not have the least doubt that he had it in his mind to talk to her again, but not about work. Unfortunately for him, she would never be at this winding wheel again.

When a handbell rang at six o'clock, the girls all sighed with relief, halting their wheels. None was more thankful than Gabrielle that the time had come to go home. It had been a traumatic day. The looms fell silent and the weavers took brooms to sweep up their own debris of scraps of silk and thread while the boys came with sacks to take it away. Gabrielle took her shawl from its peg and wrapped it around her. She was leaving with Hortense but not going back home with her. Gaston would be waiting with a carriage a short distance away. In the hub of home-going traffic, nobody would pay it any attention.

There was quite a crush in the doorway and Hortense was slightly ahead of her. Gabrielle hoped to be able to thank her for the part she had played when they were outside. As she reached the threshold and felt the cool evening air on her face, a heavy hand fell on her shoulder and gripped her hard.

"Not you! You're not leaving yet."

It was the *maître ouvrier*. At the last minute she had foolishly forgotten to turn her face aside and he had spotted she was a stranger. She reacted swiftly, kicking his shin hard and wrenching round to loosen his hold. He gave a yell of mingled pain and fury as she made a desperate attempt at flight. It was in vain. Departing workers had halted in surprise at the sound of the outraged bellow to watch what was happening while those already outside turned back to crane their necks. There was no way she could get through, and the *maître ouvrier* had seized her with both of his powerful hands this time, yanking her back into the hallway.

"Wait there!" He shoved her into the section where she had been working all day, and she had no choice but to do as he said. She was fuming at her own carelessness, and her only hope was that Hortense had seen what had happened and would inform Gaston. She was certain he would come to her rescue.

This hope faded as the last worker left, hustled out quickly by the *maître ouvrier*, whose face was red with annoyance at the commotion she had caused. After slamming the heavy door shut, he shot the bolts home before turning the key and pocketing it. Alone with him in that empty place, misgivings of a different kind began to fill her and she drew away from him. He must have seen it in her face, for he gave an impatient shake of his head.

"You've no need to fear me. I'm a family man with daughters your age. What you're doing here and why is another matter. That has to be explained."

"It's simple," she protested. "I needed work and one of the winders was sick. I begged to be allowed to take her place. It's nobody's fault but mine."

"I'll do my investigations among the workers tomorrow. For the moment, everything is out of my hands. Monsieur Devaux wants to see you on your own in his study. I'm to take you there."

When he saw she made no attempt to follow him, remaining where she was, the colour draining from her face, her hands clasped nervously, he beckoned impatiently. "It's no good thinking you can persuade me to let you go. It's out of my control. You're a trespasser and therefore you've broken the law. Monsieur Devaux is not easy on law-breakers, so I'm giving you good warning. Don't try any tricks on him as you did on me back in the doorway or you'll only bring more trouble on yourself. Now come along."

He led the way through both loom-rooms to the door that led into a small inner courtyard dividing the mill from the house. There he opened a side door and stood aside for her to enter first, not out of courtesy but to ensure she did not balk at the last minute. His words had told her that Nicolas himself had identified her, and it was no slip of hers at the end of the day that had given her away. She would face up to whatever awaited her.

As she crossed the threshold into Nicolas's home, there was a strong contrast to the atmosphere of the mill, with its mixed odours of oil and new silk and the sweat of those who had worked there that day. Here was the scent of beeswax and fine furniture and a hint of Suzanne Marache's fragrant perfume.

Nicolas stood by an open doorway leading off the hallway with lamplight behind him. "This way, Gabrielle," he said in a hard voice. It told her she could expect no mercy. She lifted her chin, summoning up her courage. Even if she no longer meant anything to him, nothing had changed for her. She would continue to fight in the only way open to her to rid herself of what she knew to be a once-in-a-lifetime love that lay like a heavy yoke upon her. With even steps, she walked past him into his study and went to stand looking into the fire burning on the hearth there. Behind her he closed the door after him and they were alone together.

5

"Why?" Nicolas demanded harshly. "Why should you of all people become what I can only term an industrial spy?"

She swung round to face him. He was only a few feet from her, his expression constrained, his mouth set in an uncompromising line, and so much anger in his eyes that she almost flinched. "I didn't think of it as spying. All I wanted was to see how you had adapted your building to take the height of the Jacquard looms."

"You could have asked me to show you."

She was defensive. "I was in no position to ask favours. How could I? We are now rivals in business but, more than that, I refused to sell you raw silk when you needed it."

He gestured impatiently. "Strange as it may seem to you, in spite of my being a Devaux, I bore you no grudge over it. I know my enemies and did not consider you to be one of them. Quite the reverse." His fist slammed down on the desk beside him. "Now it seems I was mistaken! It appears you are in the same category as your brother, with nothing but enmity towards me."

"You must think whatever you like." She was hurt by what he had said—his accusation like a whiplash. "I admit I was in the wrong by coming here today, but in some ways it was an adventure I found hard to resist."

He took a step towards her as if he wanted to shake her in his rage over her actions. " 'Adventure' is not the word I would have chosen for using a trick to get my designer to show you our most secret design."

Then she comprehended what lay behind this whole interview. "Did he say that I tricked him?"

"I sent for him to ask if anything out of the ordinary had occurred today. At first he did not recall anything until he mentioned, quite casually, that a new girl in the mill had wanted to learn the process of transferring a design to a draft."

"And that's all I wanted to know! Nothing more. If I had been able to spare the time to go to Paris I could have had it all explained to me there, but it's impossible for me to leave Lyons at the present time. This was a chance not to be missed. Naturally your designer saw no harm in showing me the process since there is no secret about it and he did not hide the design itself from me, or take another for the demonstration, simply because it never occurred to him that an ordinary mill girl would understand the significance of the imperial bee."

"But you did!"

"Immediately. But that is as far as it will ever go with me. I won't pretend that I'm not aiming as high for Roche silk, but I want to do it fairly. How else could I hold my head up in the silk world? I know that such tricks are played. The feud between your family and mine is proof that there's nothing new about it, whoever was in the right or wrong at that time. I also know that in negotiating circles there are many who use every crisis in the silk trade, large or small, to lower the wages of weavers, spinners and dyers alike. That is not my way. Neither would I take an unfair advantage over a competitor through information I had gained inadvertently." She turned away from him again, her nerves close to the snapping point. "If you are going to send for the police, please do it now. I'll not deny being a trespasser, but I'll refute until my dying day all charges of industrial espionage. In that I'm innocent, whether you believe me or not."

Silence followed her statement, broken only by the crackle of flames on the hearth. Then he gave a sigh and she heard some papers rustle as he shoved them aside to rest his weight on the edge of his desk. "Now that you know how I've fitted in the Jacquard looms, do you intend to do the same?"

She hardly dared to hope that all was to be well after all. "Yes, if I'm not sent to prison."

"I'll not lay charges." He still sounded grim. "Please be seated. You must put my lack of manners down to my being thoroughly out of temper with you."

She moved with relief to take a chair, having been afraid that her knees might buckle at any moment. Putting her palms together, she linked her fingers in her lap, her upturned face and her hands in a pool of soft lamplight. "If you mean what you say, I'm thankful for it."

"I mean it." He studied her from where he sat propped against the desk's edge. "As a matter of fact, I welcome you as a rival in the silk trade. It would have been too easy driving that thick-headed brother of yours into bankruptcy."

She bridled. "I thought you said once that the feud held no importance for you any longer."

"It doesn't as far as you and I are concerned. Our personal differences have their roots in the present and not in the past. I happen not to like your brother's business methods, apart from anything else. I hear you have been through the affairs of Maison Roche like the proverbial new broom and have changed almost everything in the running of them."

She stiffened warily. "How could you know anything about that?"

He saw how close he had come to gauging the situation correctly. Gamblers like Henri Roche were always short of money, and Dominique had been notoriously tight-fisted. "I've heard all I need to know from general talk. Your name is on everyone's lips as a new force to contend with in Lyons. At the same time it's also said that your brother is not settling his gambling debts as promptly as he did in your father's time."

"I never listen to gossip," she said abruptly.

"I'm not speaking of gossip but of facts. Like you, I make it my business to get them right." He folded his arms. "A word of warning about installing Jacquard looms. Prepare your way with the weavers first, or else you're likely to have a riot on your hands."

"The situation here appears to have settled down."

"Mine were only teething troubles. To all intents and purposes, this was a new business with new methods because the old mill had been closed for such a long time. With you it would be different. When long-established mill-owners start to introduce this revolutionary mechanism, as eventually they will, whether they know it yet or not, there'll be trouble on a much wider scale. If you care to take my advice, you'll wait until other well-known Lyons silk names make the same move. Then the weavers will be facing a concerted effort, and those too short-sighted among them for their own good will be outflanked almost from the start."

She stood up. "I don't want to wait. I liked what I saw of the Jacquard loom on the day of the demonstration."

He raised his eyebrows. "You were there, were you? I never knew that."

"I also admired your rescue of Monsieur Jacquard."

He dismissed her praise with a sweep of his hand. "He is an old friend of my father's, and I served in the *chasseurs à cheval* with his son, Charles, who was killed at Cambrai. The Jacquards had to flee Lyons during the siege as we did through false accusations. Their home was burnt down. At least this place escaped that fate."

"Do you ever see Monsieur Jacquard these days?"

"Quite frequently. He has been here to see his looms in action."

"He dared to return?"

"As it happens, he is not without friends in the city."

"I should like to meet him next time if it could be arranged."

"It shall be done."

She could sense how swiftly the atmosphere was changing between them. Until now a degree of hostility had kept all else at bay, aggravated by the pain that she knew she had caused him until the matter of her presence in the mill had been cleared up. She had been hurt by his attitude in her turn. Now their yearning for each other was coming to the fore again, unabated by time or by others of strong personality in their lives. He had moved his hands to grip the edge of the desk on either side of him, almost as though he thought they might reach for her by their own volition. She felt her insides melt at the image of being held by him. It was time to leave. "I must go now."

He led her through the house to the front door. As they reached it, he asked if she was being met, not intending to let her walk unescorted. When she nodded, he opened the door for her, then barred her way with his arm, still holding the latch. "We're two of a kind," he said intently. "I look forward to competing with you for whatever commissions the Mobilier Impérial gives out in the future."

Suddenly she wondered if his reasons were the same as her own in a need for rivalry. "I shall welcome the competition." Then she was unable to resist asking him a question that had been uppermost in her mind since he had sent for her. "How did you know it was I in the winders' section this afternoon?"

Instantly she regretted having asked him, hardly able to bear the tenderness that swept into his eyes or the ache of longing that she saw there, for it was a visible expression of all that was barricaded up within herself. He brought his face nearer hers.

"Surely you don't have to ask me that? I would know you any-where."

She saw he was going to kiss her and she was powerless to move, exulting in the prospect, her lips moist and slightly apart, her lids lowering as his mouth came closer. Then a step on the stairs shattered the moment into shards and Suzanne Marache's voice cut through to them.

"La! There you are, Nicolas. I'm waiting to dine and the food is getting cold."

Mundane, domestic details to complete the destruction like the grinding under a heel, reminding the two by the door that each had an existence away from the other, with its own responsibilities, entanglements and obligations. His arm fell away from the door and Gabrielle darted through it, escaping into the evening air, the return of sanity like a physical shock. Hurrying blindly along, she did not see Gaston until he blocked her path.

"Are you all right, madame? I was just about to knock on the door and find out what was happening."

So if it had not been Suzanne Marache as an intruder, it would have been Gaston. It was often the fate of those who tried to take that to which they had no claim. This observation did not lessen the hollowness she felt at being deprived of the kiss that Nicolas would have given her. For a matter of seconds, or a minute, or a little longer, and she would have known his mouth again on her own. Maybe it was as well that it had never happened, for this time it might have set off a chain reaction that would have been impossible to stop.

She tried to take consolation from this conclusion. It brought no comfort. That night she lay awake, unable to stop wondering how it would have been. In the morning she was back at work in her office with renewed energy, taking the only course of escape from hopeless dreams that was open to her.

When she heard, not long afterwards, that Suzanne Marache had returned to Paris, she told herself that it was of no significance. Nicolas would soon take somebody else into his life. No doubt one day he would marry. Even when that day came he would be no farther from her than he was already, for Émile would always stand between them.

Henri received with dismayed disbelief the news that she intended to install Jacquard looms for the weaving of Roche silk. "You're out of your mind! The weavers would never tolerate them. You saw that for yourself. In any case, their houses aren't built to accommodate the height of those looms."

"I've considered every point you could possibly raise and I'm going

ahead. There's an old convent that was abandoned when the Revolutionary Convention outlawed Christianity, and as the nuns have been re-
established elsewhere it has remained state property. I've offered a fair
price and have every reason to believe that it will be mine."

"You would turn it into a mill?" He could scarcely believe what he
had heard, appalled by the risk she was taking and seeing his whole
future in jeopardy. This new development could not have come at a
worse time for him. He was in a considerable amount of personal debt,
and Yvonne seemed unable to curb her constant spending. Before his
father's death her extravagances had never troubled him unduly, for she
was a handsome woman and he liked to see her expensively clothed; it
had been the same with any gaming misfortunes, for there were always
ways and means to make up the difference in a cash loss behind Dominique's back. Unfortunately everything had changed under Gabrielle's
direction, and extra funds were no longer easy to come by. His salary
should have been more than adequate, for she was generous there, and
he had not had the expense of moving out of the family home and setting up his own residence, with all the luxurious appointments and
furnishings that Yvonne would have demanded. Nevertheless, he missed
the secret bonuses that had come his way and had been considering
means by which to compensate this flaw. Now Gabrielle was putting
her whole livelihood and his at stake.

She had misunderstood his reaction to her turning the convent into
a mill. "Everything of religious significance was removed from it and
destroyed during the attempted destruction of Lyons when it became a
prison for the condemned. The Church has no objection to its being
used to give honest work to craftsmen, especially since the nuns themselves used to weave there. The arched ceilings are ideal for the Jacquard
looms."

He glared at her belligerently. "I'll not let you do this. I'll query it
with the lawyers. You are going far beyond your rights."

"Calm yourself," she advised. "The lawyers are with me and, apart
from anything else, the property is a good investment. The looms have
been ordered and will be delivered as soon as the purchase has gone
through."

"I'll oppose you all the way!"

Her face grew stern. "Then you'll be the loser, Henri. I will have
co-operation from you or else it is pointless for you to remain on the
board."

He sprang to his feet, thrusting back his chair, and shook a finger at
her. "If ever I needed proof that Father was senile when he made his
will, this is it! You'll be the ruin of this business!"

"I think not." She rose to her feet with dignity and faced him across the table. "This has never been a better time for silk, in spite of present difficulties. We are privileged to be living at a time when Lyons silks are rising to a peak of sumptuousness never before seen under the encouragement of the Mobilier Impérial. Whether it is woven on old looms or new ones, there'll be no difference in the magnificence of them. Now that we have it in our power to take the new methods and speed up production, it would be dilatory not to seize the chance. Boldness in business never goes amiss."

He snorted derisively. "But foolhardiness does."

She had had enough. "Are you with me or against me? Make your choice."

His decision was what she expected. After spluttering in exasperation, he gave a reluctant nod. "I can see I must stay with you for your own good."

Left on her own, she thought how her life was turning into a series of battles. She had Henri to contend with every day in Lyons, his criticism unceasing, and whenever she was at home Émile always tried to persuade her more persistently than at any time before to go into Lyons no more than once a week.

"I'm not being unreasonable," he said patiently. "I miss you, my dear. It's lonely in the house when you're not here. Last week I slept five nights out of seven on my own again. I can think of no other husband who would tolerate this neglect."

She had not managed to get home that week, the first time in two months that she had not broken her absence with a midweek visit to her home, and it irritated her that he should emphasise this. Yet it was all part of his campaign to turn her back into his wife, with nothing more to do than select dye colours when not engaged in domestic chores or pleasing him in their marital bed. She had given up arguing that if she spent only one day a week in Lyons she would be reduced to a puppet-head with Henri in charge, because she had soon grasped that this was exactly the situation for which he was aiming.

"Please don't feel neglected, Émile," she implored. He had taken her onto his knees where he sat in his chair and she had her hands linked behind his neck. Always when she was home she demonstrated the very deep affection she had for him, and they had times of happiness together, which had the effect of making it harder for him to let her leave again.

"I love you, Gabrielle," he said gently, taking her chin between his finger and thumb. "If I did not, it would be a different matter. Why—"

She interrupted him, wishing she could have given him back the words he wanted to hear. "Why am I not like other wives?"

He gave a laugh. "God forbid! I wouldn't have you any different, even if you have a business brain in your head more suited to a man than a woman." His gaze on her softened. "I was about to say, why is it, I wonder, that you have not yet given me a child?"

She turned her head away to hide the panic in her eyes. The time when she had wanted children was in abeyance. Later she would have two or three if Nature relented and allowed her fulfilment. Above all, she wanted a son to inherit Maison Roche after her. It was as much for the son yet to be conceived as for herself that ambition drove her on.

"The time will come," she said huskily. "I'm sure of it."

"I believe the same. Your body is too perfect for there to be the flaw of barrenness in you." He pulled down the sleeve on her dress, causing the low-cut neckline to expose her breast, and he leaned forward to press his lips to it.

Later, lying in his arms as he slept beside her in their tent-like bed, she pondered her failure to conceive. Always after their love-making she felt that something indefinable had eluded her, some inner sanctum had been unbreached, some spark left unignited. It was as if the pleasure she experienced could have been increased a thousandfold if only the key could be discovered. She did not think that if it was it would lead to conception, for rape devoid of anything but pain could do that, but she did wonder if in her case it was linked to love. Maybe if her fondness for Émile could develop a little more, just to tip the scales to love, she would come into the experience and conception would follow. Then reason took over, causing her anguish. How could she ever hope to love Émile when another man kept her heart from him?

When Gabrielle approached a number of her weavers about working the new looms, she asked only that they should try them out first. She did not ask the older men, for they were set in their ways and wanted to retain the independence of working the hours of their own choice within their own homes with their families to assist them. Those coming in to the Roche workshops, where groups of four looms were in use under the same roof, were suspicious and dubious until two or three among them thought the size and airiness of the convent would give them better working conditions than their present cramped quarters, and they in turn influenced the rest into an agreement to the move. On the day the final papers were signed and the convent became hers, she still did not have a full complement of weavers for the number of looms about to be installed.

She supervised the positioning of the looms herself, having worked out exactly where they should be erected for maximum space and ease of access. While the hammering and banging and heaving were taking place, she was told that three men were waiting to see her. She supposed it would be a deputation of weavers, for she had received threats and warnings, some of which had taken the shape of rocks hurled through the new mill's windows, and this would be a final appeal not to follow the example of the Devaux mill in bringing down the old traditions.

They were waiting for her in the entrance hall outside her new office. As she had expected, they were weavers, clad in soft-crowned peaked caps, the baggy-sleeved shirts, the jerkins of leather or cloth and the full-cut breeches common to their trade. She judged their ages to be between thirty and thirty-five, their spokesman the eldest of the trio.

"*Bon jour*, madame. We have heard there are vacancies for weavers here and we are in need of work."

"Where have you worked before?" she asked. She learned that they had been at a mill which had recently laid off workers. It was common knowledge that the owner was in financial difficulties, a not unusual occurrence in the silk world. "I want no disharmony in this mill. If any of you object to the Jacquard loom I tell you to leave now." Not one of them moved. It was true that those desperate for work put bread before anything else. The fact that these men were prepared for change meant that they would soon adapt and appreciate the advantages of the new technique. "Very well. Several looms are already set up. Come and demonstrate your skills."

She took them all on. It still left four looms vacant, but she was convinced she would soon get weavers for them. Henri, who would have preferred to see the mill at half strength for the time being, thinking it was total folly to take more hands onto the payroll until the looms proved themselves, continued to deluge her with his own gloom and depression, until finally she forbade him to come near her when she was working except for matters of vital importance. He had also objected to the best of the specially commissioned designs being given completely to the new mill and not shared out among the home weavers. But Gabrielle wanted to build up her mill's reputation from the start, to make it a name to be reckoned with among the great silk mills of Lyons, to know that it was entirely her own enterprise.

For the first few days after work started a police watch was kept on the building in case there should be disturbances similar to those that had taken place at the Devaux mill. When nothing occurred to disrupt the peace the police were withdrawn to other duties.

The working hours were from six in the morning until six in the evening, in common with other mills and factories, and on Saturdays work ended at noon. On the Saturday afternoon at the end of the first full working week Gabrielle sat at her desk, finishing off some work before Gaston should arrive to drive her home to Émile. Nobody else was in the building, except the caretaker, who was having a final sweep-up with his broom in the entrance hall. Concentrating on her work, Gabrielle did not notice a rumble somewhere in the distance until suddenly her office door was flung open and the grey-haired caretaker stood there shaking with alarm.

"Rioters, madame! On their way here! Flee now while there is time!"

He was gone himself at a speed that she would not have deemed him capable of at any other time. Hastening round the desk, she hurried out into the hall where he had left the entrance doors open behind him. Darting to the threshold, she looked up and down the street, feeling herself quail. The rioters were advancing from both directions, armed with spikes and staves and carrying banners that might easily have been saved from the day of the public destruction of the Jacquard loom, for the slogans were similar. DOWN WITH JACQUARD! SAVE OUR LIVELIHOOD! PRESERVE OUR LOOMS!

She could have escaped by slipping across the street and disappearing down one of the alleyways, but she was not going to see everything she had worked for destroyed by a mindless mob. Withdrawing inside again, she slammed the heavy doors closed and shot the bolts home. A second pair of inner doors gave added protection. The building had been designed to keep out the outside world, and now it was about to be put to the test as never before. She ran into the first of the loom-rooms. All the windows were grilled from convent times, which should prevent entry even if the glass was smashed; for added protection she banged the interior shutters together before taking a hooked pole to do the same with those out of her reach. In the street, the roar of voices was reaching a new dimension and she guessed the mob was gathering outside. Fearful of attack at the rear of the building, she raced to check that the doors were barred and found all secure except the one leading out into what had been the nuns' herb garden, where the workers liked to sit when they ate a snack at midday. She was just in time. As she bolted the door she saw through the grille that the gate was giving way under the pressure behind it. The men burst through just before she closed the grille. Quickly she secured it.

Breathless through all the running about, she stood in the middle of the building, a hand pressed to her heaving chest, and tried to think if there was anywhere she had overlooked. It was an eerie feeling to be boxed in with the silent looms, for by closing the shutters she had excluded all the daylight except that which came through hairline chinks just lifting the darkness into a murky gloom. She was nearest the set of looms on which some of the choicest of all the designs were being woven. Moving across to one, she touched, almost with reverence, a marvellous spread of the white *gros de Tours broché*, on which golden tiger lilies, full of light and shade around the arching stamens, seemed to be growing along the length of the warp; when the beam of fabric was finished it would be seventy yards long. So much beauty out of the weavers' craft. She would let none of it be destroyed.

She started violently as a rock thudded against one of the high shutters, smashing the glass outside. It tinkled as it fell within the latticed framework until it wedged. Then there came a positive barrage, which was taken up by those in the herb garden in an orgy of destruction as window after window disintegrated. Then came a more ominous sound. It was a rhythmic thudding against the street entrance doors, which could only be coming from a battering-ram. Each thud seemed to shake the whole building.

Warily she went back to the inner doors in the entrance hall and opened the grille to peep through, much as the nuns would have done in the past when they wanted to view an admitted visitor without being seen themselves. The outer doors were creaking as they bulged. The old bolts were stout enough but time had taken its toll of the ancient timbers and she doubted if the strain could be taken much longer. She made a lightning decision as to what she should do. In her office there was a new sample freshly made up from one of Marcel's latest designs. She had brought it with her that morning after it had been delivered the previous evening by the weaver who had woven it in his own home. Spectacular, it was a blaze of sunflowers on cream satin. She ran to get it and draped it around herself hastily like a giant stole. Then she returned to the inner doors. At all costs she must be seen the moment the rioters broke in or else she might be trampled underfoot.

She slid back the bolts of the inner doors in readiness. Briefly she rested her forehead against the opened grille, allowing herself a moment's respite to summon up her courage before resuming her watch once more for the time when the entrance doors would give way. A booming at the rear of the building told her that the door to the herb garden was being similarly assaulted. She hoped it would hold out long enough so that the element of surprise she was planning for the main body in the street would not be destroyed.

With a resounding crash the entrance doors gave at last and those with the battering-ram spilled into the hall, some falling in the mêlée. It gave her the chance she'd been hoping for. Swinging wide the inner doors, she stood there with brilliant effect in a dazzle of orange, yellow and gold which was further enhanced by the sun slanting in through the smashed doors to touch her from head to feet, her chestnut hair as bright as flame.

"Weavers!" she cried out on a note of authority. "Stay where you are! I know that there's not one of you who would deliberately destroy the work of a fellow weaver. Most of you know that I learned to weave in some of your homes and loom-rooms. The work here is mine. Not woven by me any longer but by those I have employed in the long tradition of Lyons silk. Would I betray my apprenticeship of the past? Trust me as you used to trust me! I haven't changed. Let me show some of you the new life that the Jacquard loom has brought to Lyons!"

Those already inside the building were gaping at her. A couple of them did know her from the days when she'd been in and out of their homes, avid for knowledge when they themselves had been at the stage of thread-tying. The suddenness of her appearance when all had believed the mill to be deserted, the splendour of her silk draperies and her courage in standing up to them caused each man to stay where he was, making no attempt to advance further into the building. Those crammed into the doorway followed the example of the men in front but, behind them, others unable to see what was happening grew increasingly impatient at the delay and began to jostle forward.

She moved towards those standing by the fallen battering-ram, her hands held out in appeal. "Ask those outside to be patient. Give me a chance to save what I have achieved here. I even have work for those who want it."

She would have succeeded if it had been left to the ringleaders at the forefront. The excited anticipation of breaking up the hated looms in a deserted mill was tempered by the prospect of having to do it under the eyes of someone whom they all knew by sight or by name, and it was more difficult for those who knew her personally. But even as they hesitated, momentarily at a loss what to do, there came a great surge of movement from the crowd outside and those on the threshold were thrust forward helplessly. Nobody knew who threw the stone. It could have been aimed deliberately, or else it had ricocheted off the doorway, its aim for a window misplaced by the crush in the crowd. If Gabrielle had remained by the inner doors it would have missed her, but in leaving the shelter of them she had exposed herself to the ammunition still being hurled at the building from the street. It struck her at the side of her head and she went reeling back, stunned by the pain and completely dazed. As she collapsed in a tangle of the satin stole, blood staining it, she felt herself heaved to one side by someone coming from the loom-room behind and knew a sickening, desperate fear that the rioters had entered from the herb-garden door. The floor shook beneath her as the mob swarmed in from the street, shouting and yelling. Then she heard a pistol shot. It must have been fired at the ceiling, for there was a clatter of plaster descending. Out of the mists of pain she heard Nicolas's voice roar forth.

"Get out! All of you! That was only a warning. Next time I'll shoot the first man who takes another step forward!"

Gasping from the pain in her head, she managed to look up. Nicolas stood with feet apart under the archway of the inner doors, a pistol in each hand. There was nobody in the loom-room, which meant it was he who had pulled her out of danger. Somebody else must be holding the herb-garden mob at bay. She closed her eyes again and let her head sink back. There was a click as he cocked the second pistol and it was enough to hasten an immediate withdrawal of the intruders. From the street there came sounds of further confusion. She could no longer concentrate on anything.

Pain prevented speech, but she did not lose consciousness completely. Her awareness seemed to come and go, and it was a strange sensation. There was more shouting, the bang of a door somewhere, Gaston's exuberant laugh, and then Nicolas lifting her up and carrying her to the couch in the office. She wanted to ask him how he had got into the building, but it was impossible.

"Is she badly hurt?" That was Gaston, serious and concerned.

"Just knocked out. It's quite a deep cut." Nicolas was stemming the blood with a linen handkerchief. Leaving the pad in place, he drew away to remove his coat and lay it over her, warm from his body. Then again he was wiping the blood away. "Is the street cleared yet?"

Gaston went across to the window. "Yes, your men and the police have done their work. There's some fighting going on by an alleyway. I think some arrests are being made."

"Then bring the carriage to the door from wherever you left it. We must get Madame Valmont home to her sister-in-law. It's safe to move her."

She wanted to thank him for all his help, but she could only lie there, dizzy with pain. How long it took Gaston to fetch the carriage she did not know. Suddenly Nicolas was carrying her again, her head against his shoulder, and he continued to hold her cradled to him as Gaston drove them to the Rue Clémont.

At the house a manservant opened the door and Hélène's startled cry came from the hall. An explanation from Nicolas followed as, without fuss and immediately practical, Hélène led the way upstairs. They had reached the landing when Henri appeared.

"You!" he bellowed at the sight of Nicolas. "How dare you enter this house! What have you done to my sister? Another of your carriage accidents, was it? Give her to me!"

Gabrielle felt Nicolas's arms tighten about her, showing he had no intention of surrendering her to anyone else at this late stage of the proceedings. Now it was Hélène who took command.

"Out of our way, Henri! This is no time for quarrelsome nonsense. Monsieur Devaux has acted like the good Samaritan and you should be thanking him instead of shouting your head off." She thrust him aside, sweeping forward to open wide a bedchamber door, and Nicolas carried Gabrielle through.

There was a swish of bedclothes as Hélène folded them back and Gabrielle felt herself being lowered onto the bed. She moaned in protest as Hélène slipped Nicolas's coat away from her and returned it to him. The soft sound she had uttered had been the only way she was able to convey that she wanted him to stay. Somehow he must have understood that.

"I have to go," he said quietly, and she knew he was standing close by the bed, putting on his coat and looking down at her. Henri was still bellowing from the doorway. Hélène turned on him.

"Be quiet!" she ordered strictly. "Have you no thought for your poor sister's aching head?"

Gabrielle felt Nicolas take her hand into his and press it lovingly. Then he went from the room with Hélène, closing the door after them. Henri's shouting became muffled. He continued to shout after Nicolas all the way down the stairs, as if seeing him off the premises.

Émile arrived as soon as the message reached him as to what had happened. She was thankful that neither he nor anyone else expected her to talk, Hélène keeping her in the darkened room and looking after her like some guardian angel. It was from Hélène that she learned the missing details. Gaston had also been on the alert for trouble, having heard that something was planned from the contacts he had made, and as a former comrade of his old regiment was among Nicolas's mill guards, it was natural that they should agree to warn each other of any developments. Gaston, who had done his own round of inspection within the Roche mill, had decided that in the event of any emergency a small loft window could be entered from a neighbouring roof. It was by this way that he and Nicolas had got into the building, he to face the mob in the herb garden and Nicolas to take the main entrance.

Gaston was the first person Gabrielle asked to see when she was well enough to receive visitors. He was well satisfied with his achievement, having enjoyed the experience. Some of the old excitement of his soldiering days had returned briefly in the short, sharp campaign in which no lives had been lost. She thanked him profusely.

"Your foresightedness saved the mill from destruction and almost certainly saved me from being trampled to death. I'll always be grateful for your timely action in notifying Monsieur Devaux. I still don't know why he didn't call in his guards."

"That was what I had expected, madame, but being a Saturday

afternoon and the mill closed, none were on duty. In any case, nothing would have kept Monsieur Devaux from being first on the scene."

"I thank you again, Gaston. You're a good protector."

Outside her door, he glanced wryly back at it. "A good protector." The social gap between them was too wide for her to grasp that maybe it was more than a natural loyalty that made him watch over her like a hawk. He wouldn't say he loved her, because he had no time for sentimental nonsense, but she was the reason why he had delayed settling down with a wife, which was what he had expected to do at the end of his army days. When he could find a spirited woman who reminded him of her, however remotely, he would make his choice, but not before.

Leaving the house, the gold coins she had given him as a reward jingled in his pocket and his hand closed over them. He would have preferred something else in return for what he had done, but that would never be forthcoming from her.

Émile, compelled by business to return to the silk farm, came back to Lyons to fetch her as soon as she was able to travel. The doctor, who had put four stitches in her wound, had advised complete rest for at least three weeks, something that Émile was determined to extend to a longer period. All his suspicions, which had been dormant for a long time, had erupted again. Gabrielle's explanation that Devaux had shown an act of kindness and concilliation, owing to the fact that it was only her mill and his that had the new Jacquard loom, had failed to impress him.

It did not take Gabrielle long to recover completely and she became increasingly restless. Her requests for work to be sent to her went unheeded by Henri and her anxiety grew. Finally she could endure it no longer.

"I must return to Lyons tomorrow," she said to Émile. "I've been here far longer than the doctor deemed necessary and Henri has not answered any of my letters. Anything could be happening there."

"Let it." Émile took her by the shoulders, looking fondly at her. "Your brother has been obeying my instructions. I wanted nothing to disturb your return to me. Surely now that you have relinquished the responsibility for Roche silk for this length of time, you have come to realise just how good life can be for us again."

She stared at him incredulously. "You encouraged Henri to go openly against me? To usurp my authority completely?" Impatiently she threw off his clasp on her, stepping back. "That settles it. I'm leaving now. Gaston shall drive me there at once."

"I forbid you!" His whole face hardened, the skin taut over the bones.

Again she looked at him as if he had become a stranger. "Nobody can forbid the trust that was bequeathed to me."

"Maison Roche can exist without you. I can't. Your place is here with me."

"Surely you must see that our marriage is the stronger because I have come out of your shadow?" When she saw a haggard look deepen the hollows of his cheekbones, the compassion he could always arouse in her took her forward again to rest a hand on his arm. "You'll never lose me. I promise you that now as I did on our wedding day."

He clasped her to him ardently, an arm about her waist, his hand cupping her head as he kissed her with a kind of frenzy out of his own frustration at being unable to control her independence of spirit, which had attracted him to her in the first place.

Out of compromise, she did not leave until the next day. When she arrived in Lyons, Henri accepted her return without surprise and with suspiciously good grace, making it difficult to dismiss the notion that he had used her absence to his own advantage. Yet her excellent clerk was able to show her the ledgers and the accounts were impeccable, enabling her to see that nothing fraudulent had taken place. She finally came to the opinion that her brother's unnatural amiability was due to a run of luck at the gaming tables. Probably as a result, Yvonne had three new and expensive gowns and a sapphire bracelet that Gabrielle had not seen before. She also learned that some extremely lavish entertaining had taken place in her absence.

On the chest of drawers in her bedroom Gabrielle found the freshly laundered linen handkerchief that Nicolas had used to stem the blood from her wound. She put the embroidered initial on it to her lips. It was a great temptation to return the handkerchief herself, but wisdom prevailed. She wrapped it carefully in a piece of fine paper and wrote a simple note of thanks to go with it. Gaston delivered it. She did not ask him if he saw Nicolas. Already she had embarked again on what seemed the impossible task of not thinking about the man she loved.

6

It was at an exhibition of silks, drawing customers from far afield, that Gabrielle saw Nicolas again. Some months had gone past and her mill continued to thrive. There had been no commissions from the Mobilier Impérial, although other orders had been plentiful. She had not had to lay off any of her work force. This Exposition de Soie was a chance to show the greater part of Europe, as well as buyers from the Americas, that she was at the forefront of what was best to be had among the silks on display there. With Marcel she discussed which designs to show and how to arrange them to advantage. Henri, who had organised the business side of many such exhibitions in his time, proved his efficiency in the field best suited to his talents. She knew full well that his bitter resentment of her had not eased at all, but he was more amiable to her, less inclined to raise the roof whenever they were in opposition over a decision and, on occasion, almost too ready to fall in with her wishes. Often she wished she could get to the bottom of his attitude. It was noticeable that he and Yvonne were on better terms, probably because he was continuing to indulge her from the profits of the gaming table.

In the exhibition hall of a fine civic building erected since the siege an allotted space was given to each member of *La Grande Fabrique*. It was by invitation only, to display in the main centre of the hall, and those whose output was on a smaller, less significant scale were given less important space in adjoining but not less splendid rooms, all the walls being hung with silk from the local looms of Maison Camille Pernon, the chandeliers of crystal. To Gabrielle's disappointment, although she received one of the coveted invitations, the place given to her was in a far corner, away from the doorway into the main hall. When she exclaimed in indignation that Maison Roche did not have a prominent stand, Henri shrugged, a glint of malice in his eyes.

"What can you expect? Roche silk is in a woman's hands now. Think yourself lucky you have a place at all in the exposition."

Her whole face seemed to flash her defiance of both him and the organisers. "I'll see that our silk is not overlooked. I promise you that."

He observed that she had what he always termed to himself "her wilful look," something he detested. It always meant she intended to tear ahead in the face of all obstacles. Throughout her childhood and adolescence it had always meant trouble for those who opposed her. Nothing was different now. He took an enamelled snuffbox from his pocket, inhaled a pinch of the contents and blew his nose ferociously. "I wouldn't have been greatly surprised if the organisers had turned down our name and Devaux's," he told her, putting his handkerchief away.

"Why? Do they suppose we might brawl with Nicolas Devaux in public?" she enquired mockingly.

"No, although it happened often enough in the past when the Roches met the Devaux, I can tell you." He chose to ignore the incident that had taken place on her wedding day. Yvonne had advised him that same afternoon never to talk about it again. She had said, not meaning to be unkind but with excruciating tactlessness, that he had obviously made himself look ridiculous and cowardly. He had almost choked, the humiliation he had suffered made more acute by her words, and the vow he had already made that day to get even with Devaux had festered within him ever since. When the chance came for revenge, he would seize it and use it to full advantage. What he wanted most of all was to see the Devaux mill in ruins and its owner banished from Lyons again, this time forever. "Maison Camille Pernon made no secret of trying one of the Jacquard looms about the time when Devaux first set them up, but it was found to be unsatisfactory."

"Maybe it was a fault that could not be located. It's possible also that Maison Pernon faced disruption among its weavers."

"Whatever the reason, when a great silk name like Pernon is known to be dissatisfied, others heed the warning. Therefore, Gabrielle, you'll have prejudice as well as competition to face."

"You can't decry anything that comes from my Jacquard looms."

"Agreed," he admitted with a nod of his head. "You have a convert in me. I never thought the day would come when I'd say that, but it's true. What designs have you finally decided to show?"

When she told him, he glared at her in disbelief. "You can't show those. I forbid it. The exposition is giving us the opportunity to take a lot of orders and I'll not see the chance thrown away. Keep to flowers and vine branches and the rosettes and the rest of the motifs that always sell well. That's what buyers will be looking for. I know from experience."

She answered him with firmness, a hand raised against argument. "The day when anyone had the power to forbid me to do anything has gone, Henri. I thank God for it. My decision is made. Marcel did the designs months ago, as you have seen, and all the fabrics are ready. Admittedly, I didn't know then that I should be given such a poor position in the hall, particularly since you told me the Roche display stand always had a good place." She gestured purposefully. "It makes me even more determined to ensure that Roche silk never gets relegated to inferior status again."

The day before the exposition she arrived with Marcel and Henri at the civic hall amid a large number of other silk merchants and their assistants, her own following behind with the wrapped silks. Émile was also with her, not to have any part in the setting up of his own sample of raw silk, which had already been arranged, but in the hope of gaining new customers as well as renewing acquaintanceship with those with whom he was already well established. A room had been set aside for raw-silk dealers, and he parted company with Gabrielle within the entrance. She paused to look at the board showing the general plan of the exposition and saw that Devaux silk was to occupy the very place she would have chosen for herself. It gave Nicolas a definite advantage, and that in itself was stimulating. Any small victory she gained would count all the more for it. Even as she smiled to herself over this thought she saw him. Her heart did its topsy-turvy lurch before racing away in its own madness.

He had not seen her. The glimpse she had caught of him had been among the heads of others. She felt weak. It was as if the strength had gone from her wrists and knees. How was it possible to be so affected by the presence of one person, already lost to sight, in a gathering of several hundred people? Why did this extraordinary current flow out of her as if her whole body had been storing energy only to release it when he came near? One would have thought such a wild tenderness would have become overlain by cynicism and harsh reality and the pointlessness of it all. She was nearly twenty-five, with four years of marriage in her wake and no longer a girl to be tossed from one emotional crisis to another. In a perverse way she resented loving Nicolas, while at the same time she welcomed the feeling of coming alive. At moments like this she felt tuned to perfect pitch and everything about her was vivid and bright and held a clarity beyond any normal experience. Love was a drug far more potent than anything doctors prescribed or pedlars sold.

With everybody busy at the individual stands, she and Marcel were able to complete the Roche display without gathering much attention, while Henri grumbled at the lack of an extra chair and other minor inconveniences. Émile rejoined her in time to see the display before it was covered with soft, cambric dust-sheets to protect it and to keep it from general view. He admired it, but the whole matter of Roche silk was too much of a thorn in his side for him to give an unbiased opinion. He evaded the issue by simply giving her his good wishes. "*Bonne chance*, my dear. You've worked extremely hard over these many months and deserve some reward."

She had the impression he would have sided with Henri in choosing more conventional examples of her weavers' work if he had been brought into the original discussion. Before leaving the hall she went with him to see the room where samples of his raw silk hanks were arranged. Nearly all the stands in the main hall were in their cambric shrouds, a few exhibitors still adding final touches. The Devaux stand was completed and all who had been working there had left. She was not surprised that Nicolas had not sought her out. There was a tacit understanding between exhibitors not to view rival stands until the day of the exposition itself. It was the old habit of secrecy that was inherent in the silk trade, having its roots in centuries past.

In the morning Yvonne was up early with everyone else in the house, ready to accompany her husband, Gabrielle and Émile to the exposition instead of waiting to come later with Hélène. All three women had new outfits since it was important that they should be seen to be clothed in the best of Roche silk. Because it was rare for a woman to be in attendance at a trade stand, Gabrielle had given much thought to what she should wear and had chosen jade silk with a dashing hat in the latest military-influenced style of small rolled brim and a high crown trimmed with a plume placed upright in the front. Yvonne's velvet coat echoed the same influence in its braiding, and she preened a little before the looking-glass in the hall before going out to the carriage in which she and Gabrielle were to be driven to the civic hall with their respective husbands. Henri was not in a good mood. Yvonne refuted his accusations that she would be in the way by coming early to the exposition.

"I won't come near the Roche display until everybody else is there if that will please you," she said pertly, sitting back in the carriage seat beside Gabrielle. "I just want to look at all the silks being shown before the hall gets crowded. There's no point in being a member of this family if one doesn't take advantage of such an opportunity."

"Don't take a fancy to anything produced by our competitors," Henri warned her, "because it can neither be bought nor copied. Understand?"

"As if I would," she pouted playfully.

He grunted, knowing her too well. When Yvonne set her heart on something she was like a spoiled child, and although some charming dress silks had been incorporated into the base of the Roche display, he believed she would disregard them in the general reaction he expected to find in everybody attending the exposition that day. He had never been more pessimistic about the outcome of unveiling the new Roche designs to the silk trade.

Gabrielle, on the other hand, appeared quietly confident. He glanced across at her. Although his financial interests were bound up with hers in the success or failure of the venture, he could not keep at bay the knowledge that there would be a certain perverse satisfaction in seeing her fail. To the end of his days he would never be able to overcome his bitterness against her for the terms of their father's will. He had recently consulted a different lawyer, a young sharp-faced fellow new to Lyons, in the continued hope that some loophole might be found in the will, his other legal advisers having constantly disappointed him. Nothing had come to light yet, but there was always hope. Meanwhile he was developing a new sideline of his own.

"Here we are," Émile said, leaning towards the window as the civic hall came into sight. There was plenty of activity in the comings and goings. In the entrance hall they were met by Marcel, who joined Gabrielle and Henri to go to the Roche silk stand while Émile went to his allotted place at the opposite end of the exposition area. Yvonne, knowing herself to be a credit to the name of Roche with her own elegant appearance, began to saunter through the main hall, slowly studying everything that had already been unveiled from the lightweight dust-sheets.

Henri was satisfied at the stand to see that the extra chair had been provided for the table adjacent to the display where orders would be taken. He rearranged the inkpot, pens and ledgers as carefully as if moving pieces in a game of chess, before he set out the order books in a precise fashion. Leaving Gabrielle in discussion with Marcel about last-minute matters, he made a tour of the main hall to see what other exhibitors were showing. His pessimism increased and the state of his temper deteriorated. When he returned to the stand and found the dust-sheets still in place, he gave vent by bellowing at Marcel, who was on his own there.

"Come along! This is no time for lazing about. Get those covers off the goods. We're the last stand with them on."

Marcel remained leaning a shoulder against a pillar, his arms folded. "Madame Valmont wants them kept on until the last minute."

Gabrielle had gone to tour the main hall as her brother had done. It would not be long before the doors were opened at ten o'clock. Now that the displays were unveiled, the whole place was transformed. It filled her with a sense of pride that her city could have produced such beauty of fabric in every texture and colour. Jewel-colours blended with the metallic glints of lamé, and there was a whole range of pastels shading down to white, all of them marvellously patterned in lampas, damask, ciselé velvet, chenille, satin, moire and many other outputs of special weaving techniques which made silk the queen of fabrics, revered by weaver and wearer alike.

When she came to the Devaux display it was like the parting of clouds in summer when suddenly the brilliance of sun and sky show through. She wanted to applaud, to laugh with praise, to exclaim her admiration. Almost as if there had been connivance between them, Nicolas was the only exhibitor, other than herself, to take a single colour and show it in every variation. Dominating the stand was a spectacular swirl of sapphire damask, lampas on a satin ground, woven with the design of the golden bees which she had first seen on a drawing board at the Devaux mill. It was a masterpiece, setting him on a level with the most important manufacturers present. Complimenting the sapphire damask were other examples of the Devaux fabrics, each ashimmer, each showing what could be achieved on a Jacquard loom, silver and gold threads adding to the abundant splendour.

Nicolas was writing at his table. Had he taken an order already? Then she saw his pen check its flow, and in the same instant he turned his head abruptly and looked straight at her. It was as if she were drowning. He scraped back his chair and came across to her, neither able to hide the joy each was experiencing in this meeting.

"It's good to see you, Gabrielle," he said, his eyes full of smiles. "I knew you were here from the published list of exhibitors. How are you? Busy, of course."

"All the time. My congratulations on the Devaux display. It will be the sensation of the exposition."

He gave a shrug. "That remains to be seen. Do you realise that you and I are going to face the most severe criticism of our work? Quite apart from the fact that we can both be classed as newcomers in the field, neither of us having exhibited before in our own right, we are also the only manufacturers here with exhibits woven on the Jacquard loom."

"Maybe we'll persuade others to make the change through our example."

"That's what I'm hoping. Monsieur Jacquard is going to put in an appearance today. Do you still want to meet him?"

Her face shone. "Yes, I do. What a pleasure! What time will he be here?"

"I don't know yet. I'll bring him to you when he arrives. Incidentally, I haven't seen your display yet."

He went with her to a good viewpoint. According to her instructions, Marcel had watched the clock until it was a minute before the public was to be admitted and he had just removed the last dust-sheet from the stand. Fellow exhibitors in the vicinity were already glancing towards it with surprise. To her relief, Henri was reading through a price list that he had compiled and failed to see his detested enemy was near. It gave her the chance to watch Nicolas's reaction to her silks. He frowned assessingly while his eyes deepened into a twinkle that told her without a word being uttered that she had won his full approval.

He turned to her. "It's my turn to congratulate you." The amusement was still in his face and she chuckled. The joke was their own. Those who knew of the Devaux-Roche feud would be imagining that fuel had been added to the flames through the strange coincidence of their two stands being the only ones steeped in a specific main colour. They saw it as an affinity of thought. Neither knew that they were being observed by Émile, who had come across the hall with the intention of wishing his wife good luck in the last few minutes before the doors of the exposition opened. He watched them suspiciously.

Knowing Gabrielle as he did, it seemed to him that she was talking to Devaux as much with her body as with her mind, something she was probably unaware of, but to him every little gesture, sway from the waist and tilt of the head proclaimed an exceptional interest in the man to whom she was speaking. Something Devaux said caused them both to laugh together and this increased his resentment. There was something about laughter shared between a couple attracted to each other that made others feel shut out and abandoned. As a handbell was rung to announce to the exhibitors that the exposition was about to open, he saw his wife and Devaux part company, still smiling at each other, Gabrielle's face full of secrets. Émile turned away towards his own trade site. He could not trust himself to speak to her at the present moment.

For a few more seconds Gabrielle remained looking towards her display and seeing it with Nicolas's eyes. The sheen and glimmer and sparkle of her sumptuous silks seemed to radiate their own light. She had chosen *gris de lin*, a rich shade of violet, to hang as though in a stateroom, with eagles of gold in flight, the eyes like jewels, every feather as perfect as if it had been painted with a delicate brush. To the forefront, in careful array, was a profusion of silks from deepest pansy to heliotrope and lilac, as though the eagles flew above a turbulent sea flecked with the silver and gold of the designs, which in some cases deepened to crimson or shaded to rose, using motifs other than the eagle. The effect was handsome and dramatic.

Henri, no longer engaged in the study of prices, raised an inquiring eyebrow as she approached. "Well? What do you think of the opposition?"

"I think our most serious rival on the floor is Devaux."

Henri snorted. This was the first major exposition in Lyons for many years. The last one on this scale had been in 1789, shortly before France flared up in revolution and made Lyons the poorer for it. Then, as now, Devaux silk had proved to be the rival to fear. Louis Devaux had received a special award for a silken cloth of gold that would have been destined for Marie Antoinette if fate had not taken an unexpected turn. That was the only satisfaction Henri had gained from that occurrence, knowing that the prize-winning silk would never be reflected in the mirrors of Versailles.

"You've only yourself to blame if Devaux takes orders away from us. You should have listened to me." He cast a contemptuous glance at the display. Eagles. Customers wanted doves, or birds of paradise, or even peacocks, but the imperial eagle, which the Emperor used to evoke the might of ancient Rome like a mantle upon himself, had no place in the salons of the average well-to-do man's home. Henri had no objection to such trappings in their rightful place, and he prided himself on being an ardent supporter of Bonaparte from the moment the Corsican had shown that he had a taste for luxurious surroundings. No, he thought, none could question his loyalty, but that did not stop his keen annoyance that his sister should have diminished the chance of good sales by choosing an uncommercial theme.

Contrary to his gloomy expectations, the day proved to be an exceptionally good one. Both the Roche and Devaux stands drew immediate interest because of the exhibits having been woven on the Jacquard loom, and Henri was astonished when the dais by which he sat was surrounded by the first arrivals, a crush that continued almost without respite and filled his order book. By choosing the imperial eagle, which to date had scarcely appeared in silk, if at all, Gabrielle had caught the current mood of all involved in the world of *La Grande Fabrique*, for by being created in this beautiful material it became the aesthetic side of the powerful source from which Lyons could look to the future with optimism.

Since Bonaparte now ruled half of Europe through his conquests, many million people brought together under the Tricolore, the result was that a great majority of the buyers at the exposition were from these recently garnered lands. From them, Henri found his order book filling up, the reason being that the old royal or political symbols were having to be replaced throughout new areas of the French Empire by tributes to the Emperor. On both the Devaux and the Roche stands were some marvellous examples of what could be hung in redecorated and refurbished throne-rooms and rooms of state.

Unexpectedly there was a substantial order from an American. His new young nation had taken the eagle as a national emblem for its strength and power and all-seeing eye. For him it had to be a single great eagle woven in gold thread into a ground of crimson satin, free of other embellishments. He sketched it for Gabrielle to show exactly how it should be. On a personal level, he ordered a large number of dress lengths for the women in his family. *Le tissue lyonnaise* was so highly prized in the Americas that sometimes traders in other fields would take payment in silk in lieu of money. As for smuggling, it was common knowledge that many bolts of silk found their way across the Channel under cover of darkness, no matter that France and Great Britain were at war.

Hélène came to see the Roche display in the afternoon. She was surprised by what she saw but full of praise. "You and Nicolas have taken the world of *La Grande Fabrique* by storm, from what I can see," she said to Gabrielle, who was having a breathing space from the countless questions and enquiries that had been put to her throughout the day. "I spoke to him on the way to you. He presented Monsieur Jacquard to me. They're coming over to you shortly." Her attention was attracted by a movement in the crowd. "I think they're on their way now."

Nobody knew who started the clapping. Only Hélène knew that it might have been she. When she spoke to Joseph Jacquard she had warmed to him completely. This was the man whose invention would free children forever from the dreadful task of hand-drawing and mending if only other manufacturers would follow Gabrielle's and Nicolas's enlightened example. None could deny the perfection of their silk. Spontaneously she began to clap and the applause was taken up on all sides, people moving to make a path for this man whose name had been passed from one to another since his arrival at the exposition. He looked startled and shy, but as more and more people took up the applause, the gathering around him increasing as others came from all parts of the hall to see what was happening, he began to smile, nodding his appreciation of an acknowledgement he had long awaited. His birthplace of Lyons had taken him back into the fold at last.

Gabrielle stepped forward, dropping a curtsey to him as Nicolas introduced him. "It's an honour to meet you, Madame Valmont," he said to her, bowing courteously over her hand.

"This is a memorable day for Lyons, Monsieur Jacquard," she replied with great certainty. "May I be one of the first to thank you for what you have done to benefit all in the weaving industry?"

She led him through to the Roche stand. Henri, discerning that the winds of public opinion had taken a sudden change, came forward quickly to meet Jacquard as his sister brought the inventor to him. He did not see Nicolas, who had drawn back to talk to Hélène, wanting no friction of any kind to mar this moment for Gabrielle.

Jacquard spent nearly an hour at the Roche stand. Before he left he forestalled an invitation from Gabrielle by asking if he might visit her mill in the near future. More applause broke out as he moved away, and this time Hélène was not responsible, being in another part of the hall, but she heard it in the distance and smiled to herself.

Henri was extremely tired that night when he went to bed. It had been a long and exhausting day. At one point he had had cramp in his hand from writing the orders, some large and some less important, but nevertheless an almost continuous stream. He was almost asleep when Yvonne's voice spoke from somewhere above him. She liked to sleep propped against a soft heap of lace-trimmed and beribboned pillows, whereas he liked to lie flat, discarding even the bolster. His back was towards her.

"I saw something odd today, Henri."

"Not now," he muttered sleepily. Yvonne had a habit of wanting to gossip about her day's happenings after they came to bed. "Tell me about it tomorrow."

"I can't get it out of my mind."

He groaned inwardly. It had been a mistake to answer her. He should have feigned sleep. Without much hope he sought to persuade her. "Go to sleep now. It's late."

There was a pause. In relief he let himself drift towards oblivion. Her next words checked it abruptly. "Monsieur Devaux and Gabrielle are on more than friendly terms, I would say."

He remained quite still but his eyes flicked open in the darkness. "What makes you think that?"

She knew she had captured his interest. "I saw them together early today. It was before the exposition opened. They seemed completely taken with each other."

Later he believed it was at that moment he began to hate his sister. He had come close to it on the day their father's will was read and his attitude towards her had been deteriorating steadily ever since. For a long time he had it fixed in his mind that she was entirely to blame for what had happened between Devaux and him on her wedding day. If it had not been for her silly whim in wanting to pace out the drive through the weavers' quarters there would have been no need for a burst of speed to catch up on time and the accident would never have occurred. Then she had humiliated him by her intervention on his behalf when it was only Devaux's grip, choking the breath out of him, that had prevented him from throwing the fellow out of the carriage. Left winded and helpless, there had been nothing he could do. Oh, yes, all the blame was hers. Now there was this new development.

He saw no reason to doubt what Yvonne had said; he knew her to be keenly observant in such matters. The feminine circle in which she moved devoted its energies to discovering who was in love with whom, seeking out scandals and discerning who might be pregnant and whether the fathering was in question. He had learned a great deal that he would never have known otherwise by listening, all too often unwillingly, to Yvonne's gossiping chatter after the candle was snuffed. At times he was uncomfortably certain that she knew when he had had ill luck at gaming and, even more certain, that she knew about his latest mistress. It was one of her virtues that she never brought these particular issues into the open with him, which was what gave their marriage its strength. They could go their own ways without reproach from each other.

"What did you see?" he asked sharply, heaving himself over to prop his weight on one elbow.

"I probably wouldn't have noticed if it hadn't been for Émile."

"What has he got to do with it?"

"Well, I saw him staring fixedly at someone or something, and he looked so stern, his mouth set in a hard way not at all normal to him, so that I halted on my way to speak to him. He was staring at your sister and Devaux as if he had murder in his heart."

"What happened?"

"Nothing. That's the odd thing. I would have expected him to join them. After all, he's no part of the old feud. Instead he watched until they left each other and then he walked away."

"Well?"

"That's all that happened." Her tone was speculative. "I would say he was jealous of Devaux. Knowing Émile as we do, it is unlikely he would harbour that emotion without cause. He is always so calm and level-headed. Of course, it's an old saying that still waters run deep."

Henri rolled away again onto his back, looking up at the ceiling, which showed pale in the darkness, as he mulled over what his wife had said. Gabrielle had always been wilful, always gone her own way. It was the deepest insult to the name of Roche that she should show friendliness to a Devaux in public, and if there was more going on in private it was beyond endurance. Yvonne was chattering on. He no longer listened, since she had changed the subject to the meetings she had had with other people that day. He did not have to tell her not to repeat what she had told him. When it came to their own family affairs she could hold her tongue in public. It was possible that Émile was jealous of any man to whom his wife proved attractive, but considering that Devaux had rescued Gabrielle during the riot, what would have been more natural than for Émile to have joined them instead of watching them from afar? Yvonne had put her finger on something, there was no doubt of that. He would remember what she had said. It might be that the incident would hold some importance in the future. Anything he could garner against his sister was of value. Turning onto his side, he slept almost at once. When he began to snore, Yvonne stopped what she was saying in the middle of a sentence and sighed.

Gabrielle stood on the doorstep of her mill to welcome Joseph Jacquard when he arrived on the stroke of eleven o'clock. After his visit she would return to the exposition for its second day, and in the meantime she was looking forward to showing the inventor the weaving that was in progress.

"It seems to me that you must have had a successful day yesterday," he said to her after they had greeted each other. "I heard talk of Roche silk on all sides."

"I think we took more than our fair share of orders, I must admit," she said happily. "If it had not been for the speed of your mechanism I would never have managed to complete everything I wanted to show on time."

"I appreciate the compliment. Don't let work stop for me now."

"That's what I told my weavers. I was sure you would want to see everything in action."

Together they entered the workshop. Joseph paused on the threshold. It was a poignant moment for him. Nothing could compare with hearing the sweet *bistonclaque* sound of his mechanism in a Lyons mill.

He thought of all who had had faith in him and his invention, from Bonaparte himself to the young woman at his side, and he was grateful to every one of them.

As he began his tour the weavers, with their own special courtesy, bowed to him as he went past or stilled their shuttles when he stopped to speak to them. Afterwards, Gabrielle served him hot chocolate in her office. There was a silver dish of marrons glacés and bon-bons à la Bonaparte. Inevitably Nicolas's name came into the conversation.

"I'm pleased to see that the feud between the Roches and the Devaux is at an end," Joseph said to her. "There were times when both families were torn apart by it."

"I'm afraid it still exists between my brother and Nicolas. Neither can endure the sight of the other."

"It must be extremely difficult for you."

"It is," she admitted. "I suppose you remember the feud at its height."

"I certainly recall how Louis Devaux and your father cut each other whenever circumstances brought them to the same gathering. Louis was my good friend, but I cannot deny that he was a hot-tempered man. There were mischief-makers who would make a point of asking the two of them to a public event in order to watch for fireworks, which did occur sometimes. I've been told it was the same with their fathers before them."

"I've never been able to pin-point exactly how it all started. My father said once that it was over a matter of raw silk, as far as he knew. Could you enlighten me?"

"Nobody can be sure of the facts. I have discussed it with Nicolas, and as far as it can be discovered the original quarrel came about during 1701, which is on record as being a bad year for the mulberry crop, when raw silk was hard to come by. Apparently the Roches managed to get a shipment at great cost from a foreign source, probably from the Far East. When it was within sight of Lyons it was seized by armed robbers and disappeared. Before long the Devaux looms were in full swing, while the rest of Lyons was almost at a standstill. The Roches accused the Devaux of stealing, and that is when everything blew up between them." He put aside his cup and declined her offer of another bon-bon.

"I suppose the full truth will never be known."

"Not after so many years. It's possible that the Devaux had managed to get their own supply of raw silk from an overlooked source, which was what they claimed. The whole situation was made worse, if that were possible, by Maison Roche losing a valued commission from the Garde-Meuble through the theft of that urgently needed yarn." He let out a long-drawn breath. "It depresses me to know that your brother and Nicolas are still involved in the feud. Has there ever been the threat of a duel between them?"

• "Once. I averted that through persuasion. Nicolas showed great magnanimity."

"Then I hope you will continue that same effort to put the feud to rest once and for all. At least you and Nicolas are competing on good terms for commissions from the Mobilier Impérial, and I know there's no danger of history repeating itself there." He rose stiffly from his chair. "Now I mustn't delay you any longer. You'll be wanting to get back to the exposition again. I thank you for your hospitality and look forward to meeting you again in the not too distant future."

During the days that followed, until the exposition closed, Gabrielle saw Nicolas many times, mostly at a distance. Whenever they did get a chance to speak, whatever they said to each other bore no relationship to the silent communication between them. She knew he was waiting for her, certain that the day would come when she would forget the bonds that held her. It gave danger and excitement to these encounters, but the aftermath was always sadness and a struggle to face again the reality of life.

On the last day of the exposition, when it seemed the flood of orders had finally ebbed, there was a sudden return of the Spanish buyers still in Lyons. News had come that the Emperor had made his brother Joseph king of Spain. Once more the imperial eagle in silk was in demand, this time for the throne-room in Madrid.

One morning, when the first orders were being put into production, Gabrielle took time to go to the Place des Célestins. She was crossing it on foot, the day being fine and dry, when unexpectedly someone caught her up and held a bunch of crimson roses in front of her, making a scented barrier to bar her way. She halted in surprise and laughed when Nicolas stepped in front of her.

"It's you!"

He was enjoying her happy astonishment. "Accept my tribute for brightening my day beyond measure."

She laughed again, taking the roses from him, guessing he had bought them on impulse from one of the stalls. "These are lovely. How kind and how gallant. You really surprised me. I hadn't noticed you. Where were you?"

"By the harness-makers. I could see you were deep in thought. I probably have the same expression when I'm wondering if all is going well at the mill in my absence."

"There are always problems that present a challenge, as you know. At least neither you nor I lack work for our weavers."

He became more serious. "You did well at the exposition. Your display was very fine."

"Now we have only to wait and see who the Mobilier Impérial is going to honour with orders." Her whole stance was one of confidence, chin slightly tilted, her shoulders back. She did not expect to have eliminated Devaux silk, but she was hopeful of matching whatever orders came his way. It was vitally important to her. She had to battle with him as an equal in the field.

"I think we shall find ourselves running neck and neck."

"Do you still have the same *maître ouvrier?*" She made a little grimace, remembering the man's brusque attitude towards her.

"He's still there, but I recently appointed a manager, Michel Piat, who was with me in Paris before I sold up there."

"Why didn't he come with you when you first moved back to Lyons?"

"Domestic reasons. His wife was sick and he didn't want to move her from her family and friends. Sadly, the poor woman died last month. I'm afraid we all knew it was only a matter of time. He is glad to have a change of scene in which to put his life together again."

"So this gives you more freedom?"

"I'm able to travel on business again for longer intervals than before, knowing that everything will carry on as if I were there. Where were you going when I stopped you as I did?"

"To the Théâtre des Célestins." She indicated the building with the classical porch a few yards from where they stood. "I'm going to pick up tickets for tonight's performance. It's a play that Hélène wants to see and I encourage her to go out as much as possible."

"Have you time to take coffee with me first?"

She hesitated only briefly, not through pressure of time but through the habit of always being wary in his presence, always afraid of herself. "I think so. That would be welcome. I was extra early at the mill this morning."

There was a choice of cafés, as there was in almost any part of Lyons. They sat at a table outside one under a bower of foliage, dappled by sunlight and shade. The café-owner's daughter sat by an upstairs window, playing the flute for her own entertainment and that of anyone who cared to listen, the notes clear and sweet like a bird's song. The coffee came almost at once, it being a quiet hour and few people about. With only one other customer, well out of earshot, they were able to talk freely. Uppermost in her mind was a recent development in the feud created by Henri. To her dismay and anger he had uttered some scandalous abuse against Devaux silk at a silk merchants' meeting at the Hôtel de Ville that Nicolas had not attended, being out of Lyons at the time. For a few days it had been the talk of the city.

"I must apologise for Henri's latest offence. Sometimes I think hatred has made my brother insane. You are remarkably patient."

"He has received a letter of warning from my lawyers. I'm only patient for your sake. That's good for me. It has a stabilising effect on my temper. I would have called out anyone else long ago for less than your brother has directed against me, but you asked me on your wedding day to spare him and I'll keep to that agreement. It's not my wish for any more bloodshed in this feud, even though it will have to be resolved one day. When the time comes I don't want you to be hurt in any way. That's all I care about."

A shaft of apprehension went through her. It was impossible for her not to be involved in a final confrontation between her brother and him. She wanted neither of them to be hurt, her own welfare being of the least importance to her. "At least whatever he says these days, however infuriating for you, he can't harm you. You're building up a strong name in the silk trade and you have the respect of all those in *La Grande Fabrique.*"

"I like to think so." He wanted their talk to swing away from the troubles between them while he concentrated on the sheer pleasure of being with this beautiful woman whom he loved. "Shall you and your sister-in-law be going unescorted to the play this evening? I could come with you."

She lowered her glance to the coffee steaming in the cup in front of her. "I'm afraid not. Henri and Yvonne will be with us."

"Ah." He sighed expressively. "Another time perhaps."

"Perhaps," she said uncertainly.

"Gabrielle." His tone was soft. "Look at me."

She did not obey immediately. All her instincts told her he was about to say something of vital importance that would propel their relationship forward to a stage for which she was not yet ready or, indeed, would ever be. Slowly she raised her head and met his direct gaze.

"You are the most beautiful woman I have ever known."

"I'm glad that you should think that."

"All I want is to see you, to be with you." He leaned towards her across the round table between them as he spoke, reaching out his hand to take possession of hers, drawing her fingers away from the handle of the cup on its saucer and enfolding it within his own.

"You're saying what I want to hear," she admitted quietly, "but it's not wise for either of us."

"I love you." He tightened his clasp on her hand as she tried to jerk it away as if to refute what he had said to her, and he watched her colour come and go as she covered her eyes with her free hand.

"That should never have been said," she protested shakily.

"I should have said it the moment we met. Then this whole complicated disorder of our lives would never have come about."

"I have told you before that nothing could have altered the outcome of that day. The pattern of my life was already set." Her heart was palpitating wildly. This development between them might not be kept at bay if she did not summon up and hang onto all her will-power.

"Do you love Émile Valmont?"

She dropped her hand away from her face and her lustrous eyes were large with pain. "He loves me."

Unconsciously he again increased his clasp on the fingers he held. "I repeat my question."

"I've given you my answer. It covers everything."

"Even divorce?"

It came as a shock to hear the word spoken aloud. In all honesty she could not deny to herself that there had been times when she had dared to think how it might be to regain her freedom, but she had suppressed these rogue thoughts, refusing to bring them out into the open. Now Nicolas had done so. Somehow she found the voice to reply to him. "Even divorce," she repeated desperately.

He eased the pressure on her hand and caressed it. She could see he was not angry, only more resolved, the loving look in his eyes unshaken. "I want you forever, Gabrielle. I've never wanted you for anything less." Drawing her fingers up to his lips, he pressed a kiss against them before he let them go.

She was never to know if she might have spoken then of her love for him. A couple had come to sit at a nearby table and the moment was gone. The waiter came to pour fresh coffee before attending to the new arrivals, and there was no longer any chance to talk privately. They got up to leave, she taking up the roses, which had been lying on a chair. He went with her to the entrance of the theatre. There she selected one of the roses and held it out to him. The simple, eloquent gesture said all she was unable to voice. They shared a smile as he took it, breaking off the stem to slide it into a buttonhole in the revers of his coat. Then she entered the foyer of the theatre.

7

Gabrielle suffered an unexpected setback with the Spanish order she had received at the exposition. While the silk was being put into production, the Spaniards rose up against French rule, changing from ally to enemy overnight and creating a new war for France to fight. The silk was despatched after the Emperor himself entered the field and had won four battles, but it never reached its destination, being plundered and destroyed by Spanish guerrillas en route.

Facing up to this loss, Gabrielle encountered another disappointment. The order for imperial hangings, which she had hoped to gain from the Mobilier Impérial after her display at the exposition, went to the Devaux mill. She accepted the news in silence while Henri ranted and raved over it until she could endure his tirade no longer.

"Be quiet, for mercy's sake, Henri!" she exclaimed fiercely. She was sitting at her desk, her hands clenched together in front of her. "There are other chances. We've yet to hear who is to make the campaign tent for the Emperor."

In many ways this was the most coveted commission, since it was of a personal nature. Bonaparte, with his complex tastes, which veered between the austere and the luxurious, wanted a tent lined with Lyons silk for use in the field. All the main Lyons manufacturers had submitted designs. Gabrielle believed that Marcel's design must outshine the rest. It incorporated a lion and a lamb for the interior hangings, which surely symbolised the Emperor's aim for the future, a peaceful Europe under the French flag.

"We have a good design," Henri answered, halting his pacing across the office floor, "but so long as you are sitting in that chair everything will continue to swing against us." He held up a hand as if to stem all argument. "Admittedly you did well at the exposition. You were something of a novelty and our silks were magnificent enough to sell themselves. But remember I was there taking orders. It's possible that many customers believed I was still in control. When I tried to get commissions from the Mobilier Impérial in Paris for you, I played down your position in my favour. At that time it was not generally realised you were more than a figurehead. I'm convinced now they were already informed." He thumped a fist into the palm of his hand. "*La Grande Fabrique* has no place for a woman. We shall go on losing out on the top commissions until you accept that you're a hindrance to the business."

She jerked up her head. "I won't give in to prejudice. Everybody has to face it at some time in their lives. Look at Jacquard. Now his looms are being installed in several mills in Lyons. It is a breakthrough at last. Where there isn't space, floors are being lowered and ceilings raised. I'll win through too."

Henri straightened up, letting his hands fall to his sides, his face thunderous. "If we get the commission for the tent I'll continue to back you. But if we lose it I'll demand your resignation. I warn you that I'm not prepared to see Devaux skim away the cream from us for the rest of our days. Think about it!" He turned away and slammed out of the room.

Setting her elbows on the desk, she raised her clenched hands to press them against her mouth, aware that she was trembling. There was nothing Henri could do to dislodge her and he could demand her resignation indefinitely without the least chance that she would do what he wanted, but there were other issues at stake. She saw every victory that Nicolas achieved as an undermining of her own emotional security. Unless she could be his equal in the silk world, how could she continue to find the strength to master her love for him and control her own life?

Even when they did not see each other for months she knew that his thoughts were with her. It was a torment that never released her, and at the present moment she was in despair. She came close to a sense of panic, as if at last she had reached the quicksands and it had nothing to do with the mill or Henri. Packing up work for the day, she left early to go home to Émile.

All the way from Lyons to the village she made a silent plea to her husband. "Help me, Émile. Please realise the danger our marriage is facing and help me. Nicolas is drawing me to him. I don't know how long I can fight my love for him."

Émile was not at home. She learned that he had gone unexpectedly on business to Avignon. As it was not a time of the week when normally she went home, there was no reason why he should have notified her of his absence. All too often now their individual interests separated them. For the first time she felt no wish to return to Lyons and surprised Gaston next morning by delaying the time of her departure until midday. Usually she left not long after dawn.

She spent the morning in the flower garden, removing the faded blooms from the roses and gathering a basketful of fresh flowers for the rooms. Finally she strolled through the woods as if to gather the tranquillity of the surroundings to the old house into herself.

It was during this trip home that Gaston first began to suspect that a watch was being kept on Gabrielle's movements. His sharp brain soon deduced the instigator, but he kept his conclusions to himself and said nothing to anyone. At the present time he knew her routine well enough, for he drove her everywhere unless she was in the company of her husband or her brother, when sometimes another coachman on the staff would drive them. If at any time she should change the pattern of her days he would be instantly alert to protect her from a new source of danger as yet unknown to her. In the meantime there was nothing to worry about.

A few weeks later Henri was preparing to go out for the evening with Yvonne when a servant came to tell him that a prowler had been sighted sneaking out of the stable-yard gates and had been overcome by a couple of grooms and the gardener.

"Has he stolen anything?" Henri asked as his valet gave his neckcloth a tweak in a final touch to his appearance.

"No, sir. He's not ill dressed and had a horse of his own waiting in the shadows by the wall outside. He swears he came to keep an assignation with a maidservant he had met and mistook the address."

"Hmm. A likely story. Where is he now?"

"In the scullery under guard."

"Is Madame Valmont at home?"

"No, sir. She left with Madame Hélène to dine with friends just before the citizen's arrest was made."

"Well, I don't want them or my wife alarmed by this incident. Tell the rest of the staff there is to be no gossiping about it to the ladies until I have told them myself. Now I'll take a look at this rogue and then you shall go for the police."

It was rare for Henri to go below stairs. The last time had been during the siege of '73, when he and the rest of the family had had to leave the house by the back way. Kitchen staff whom he could not remember ever seeing before, probably because they never emerged from these lower regions into the upper part of the house, stood in their setting of scrubbed tables and flagged floors and gleaming copper pans to watch him go through to the scullery. There the intruder, a middle-aged, ferret-faced fellow, was seated in a chair, his arms bound at the wrists behind him. In the lamplight he and Henri regarded each other.

"Well, well," Henri remarked. "So it's Monsieur Brouchier. This is a surprise." He flicked a hand in the man's direction, addressing the servant who had led him there. "Release him and bring him to my study. This is a matter I want to investigate before I decide whether or not to hand him over to the authorities."

In his study he turned as Brouchier entered. The man accepted his invitation to be seated, thanking him for having had him released. "It was a nasty moment for me," he confessed. "I pride myself on never being nabbed."

Henri poured himself a glass of wine and sat down with it in his hand. "Ah, you're not out of the woods yet; I want to know what tricks you are up to. Is my wife having me followed?" It was hard to believe that Yvonne would trouble herself these days, but he could think of no other reason that would have brought this fellow to the house. Years ago he had employed Brouchier himself to keep watch on a mistress he suspected of being untrue, and now fate had caused their paths to cross again.

Brouchier gave a rusty laugh, shaking his head. "Your wife hasn't engaged me. Oh, no! I'd be obliged if you would leave the questioning there, monsieur. I am a man of honour and can't betray my clients' names or their business with me."

Henri gave a humourless smile. "You heard what I said in the scullery. I can have you taken in charge for trespassing with intent to rob." He pointed a finger at him from the hand that cupped the wineglass. "You'll tell me everything I want to know. Your talk of honour means nothing to you when your liberty is at stake, and you know it. Speak!"

Brouchier shifted his position uncomfortably in the chair, jerking his head obsequiously, and cleared his throat. "I suppose there's no harm in telling you, particularly as it is all in the family, so to say. I know I can trust you as a gentleman not to disclose whatever I tell you."

"Get on with it." Henri's interest was thoroughly aroused.

"Monsieur Valmont, your brother-in-law, has engaged me to keep a watch on his wife."

"What?" Henri sat forward with astonishment. "Who's the man?" It was an involuntary question, the answer coming to him even as Brouchier replied: "Nicolas Devaux."

Henri stayed leaning forward as though transfixed. So Yvonne had been right. Gabrielle and Devaux. "What evidence have you gathered?" he demanded hoarsely.

"Nothing of any real significance so far. They met one day quite a while ago in the Place des Célestins. He gave her roses and they went to a café afterwards, where they sat outside. There was no attempt at concealment although they were obviously on intimate terms. Since then there have been no meetings that I've been able to discover, and I assure you I have watched your sister like a hawk."

"Maybe there's nothing after all."

"Monsieur Valmont has yet to be convinced. As it happens, Devaux is among the guests at the dinner party your sister and sister-in-law are attending this evening. I was about to follow their carriage when I was overpowered in the stable yard. In saying I had an assignation with a maidservant, I was telling the truth in one way. The girl is on the servants' grapevine that links the homes of prominent citizens in Lyons, including yours. It brings in many useful titbits of information, including guest-lists."

Shifting his weight back in his chair, Henri took a swig of wine and regarded his visitor grimly. "I'll not keep you from your work any longer on one condition."

"Which is?"

"You'll be a double informant. Anything you have to tell Monsieur Valmont must also be told to me."

Brouchier stood up. "I dare say that can be arranged, seeing that you're a former client, and I'm always willing to oblige a gentleman who was generous to me."

Henri took the hint. "You'll be rewarded." He swung his half-emptied wineglass dismissively. "Now get out of here."

For a while Henri sat on alone in the room, his lower lip stuck out meditatively. It seemed he had an ally in Émile against Devaux. He felt as though he were gathering forces in readiness for attack. In the meantime he had an evening ahead of him with his wife. He left the study before she could start screaming that they would be late.

Gabrielle had not known that Nicolas would be at the dinner party, any more than she had known he was at the Place des Célestins the morning they had met. She had barely been received by her host and hostess when she saw him coming across the room towards her. He had been in conversation when he saw her appear in the doorway and felt himself go pale with desire. They had glimpsed each other only twice since the talk they had shared at the café. Once at a performance of Mourguet's puppets which, with the chief puppet, Guignol, almost always clad in weaver's garb, had taken Lyons by storm; he had been sitting only a few rows behind her. He had stared at the back of her beautiful long neck until she turned her head without the least surprise to meet his eyes in one single poignant glance before looking away again. Her husband was at her side and she had avoided all further chance of contact between them.

The second time was through a milliner's window. She had entered the shop before he could reach her. Although he waited, convinced she knew he was outside, she did not emerge. Too late he found there was a second exit, to the neighbouring street, and she had left by that route.

Now she was here. On her own under the same roof with him. He did not count the company present or her sister-in-law, who had already moved from her side, unwittingly leaving her waiting for him. Gabrielle had paused just inside the threshold of the elegant salon upon seeing him. Her luxuriant hair caught bright tints from the candle-glow, framing her lovely face, which was a little thinner than before. She was in white silk, gold embroidery giving weight to the hem and bordering the low décolletage. Her throat and bosom were bare of jewellery, but filigreed gold ear-rings hung from her pretty ears, exposed by her fashionable coiffure. She outshone every woman present.

When he reached her it was as if this unexpected sight of each other after two abortive encounters had made them more vulnerable than ever before. She was completely captivated by his presence, lost before the evening had hardly begun. He pressed the fingers of her hand lovingly.

"The gods are being good to me this evening."

She sighed in soft wonderment that he should be there. "Who would have expected anyone in Lyons to invite a Devaux and a Roche to the same table?"

"It's only because our hostess is a newcomer to the city. I knew her in Paris, which is how I came to be invited. Not being in the silk trade, she knows nothing yet about local intrigues and disputes."

"How fortunate for us," she whispered conspiratorially, thoroughly amused, "although out of the corner of my eye I can see we're already the focus of attention to those here who are not in the dark about the feud."

"Then we must show them that they can't believe all the gossip that goes circulating about it these days." Sharing their private joke, he led her into the gathering.

It was an intellectual assembly. The hostess had been known for her salon in Paris and she was anxious to establish the same reputation in Lyons. There were writers and artists present, musicians of note and a composer of international repute who happened to be in Lyons for a concert, as well as the Prefect of the city and several distinguished, re-established émigrés. Some people were already known to Gabrielle, and others she was interested to meet. There was one disturbing piece of news that penetrated the conversation, gossip being a necessary leavener for a successful salon. Someone from Paris had heard that the Emperor was considering a divorce from Joséphine. It was an open secret that he wanted a son and heir, something she had been unable to give him.

"At the moment the Emperor is looking over the available princesses of Europe in a search for a suitable womb," one wit quipped caustically. Gabrielle saw Hélène turn away from the speaker, not liking jokes about Bonaparte, particularly those in questionable taste. She felt Nicolas touch her arm.

"I'm in favour of some divorces and not others. Joséphine will be broken by a parting with the Emperor."

"How do you know she cares so much?"

He shrugged. "I heard a great deal about court affairs when I lived in Paris."

"I think Émile would be similarly broken if ever I took such a step." She moved away from him, accepted at once into a neighbouring conversational cluster. It occurred to her that she had probably shattered the magic of the evening; she was able to feel Nicolas watching her, momentarily out of humour through what she had said. But that was how the brake had to be applied, for his sake as well as her own.

He did not go near her for five minutes. That was as long as he could endure being away from her side. He linked fingers with her secretly as he joined the group in which she stood talking, and it was as though they had made up a lovers' quarrel, each assailed afresh by love and desire.

They were not seated together at dinner. He was on the opposite side of the table from her, distanced by candelabra, carnations in silver bowls and all the paraphernalia of a grand banquet. She thought it was as well that the seating plan had separated them. Except for that one short time, he had not been away from her. The angle at which they were placed enabled him to view her without hindrance between the lighted candles. Every time she happened to glance in his direction he met her gaze instantly, sending her silent messages that made his entranced eyes glow darkly like the wine in the glass that he raised once in a shared toast with her. His constant attention had its effect on her.

As the meal progressed from one course to another she was roused to a pitch of excitement that she scarcely knew how to control. Her whole body was aquiver with it. He was ravishing her with his eyes and with his mind. She believed that if he could have carried his desires through physically she might have died of her own responsive passion.

Hélène, who was more of a listener than a conversationalist, an observer more than a partaker, hoped she was the only one noticing the interchange between them. She had been alerted first by catching sight of such radiance in Gabrielle's face that she had looked automatically to see who was the recipient of such a sudden, sparkling glance. Her heart had sunk. "No, Gabrielle!" she had cried out inside herself. "That path is not for you. It can only lead to disaster."

Over coffee served in a salon panelled with ice-green silk, Nicolas found Hélène eager to talk to him and monopolise his company. He thought her charming and was pleased to get to know Gabrielle's sister-in-law, but when everybody was asked to take seats for the musical interlude, he reached Gabrielle in time to sit beside her. Hélène, feeling that she had saved gossip by keeping him away from Gabrielle for a little while, had already taken a chair where she could enjoy the music without being distracted by any glances or whispers they might ex-change. Too much force emanated from them for her not to feel disquiet on her own behalf. With the sensitivity of any young widow deprived of a loving husband, there were times when the attraction between others stirred an almost unbearable longing in her for the joys that were no longer hers. She felt no envy, only the pain of her own loss. Nobody could ever take Jules's place and she wanted no other man. A second marriage would never be for her.

To Gabrielle the music heightened her awareness of Nicolas's near-ness as if she were conscious of every breath he drew. The fervour of their love passed between them like something tangible, and when he happened to brush her wrist with his finger tips an ecstatic shiver went through her. When they rose to their feet to applaud the composer as he played the final note of his own concerto, they did not disperse with everyone else afterwards into groups again but remained facing each other.

"Meet me tomorrow," he implored quietly. "At the café in the Place des Célestins. There's so much more to be said."

She could not have refused him. It would have been sheer naïveté to argue to herself that there was no harm in meeting just to talk. From that moment she accepted the fact that after this evening they had to see each other again soon. "I will be there," she promised.

When the evening came to a close they said good night to each other amid the other departing guests. On the drive home Hélène chatted about what a success it had been for a hostess new to Lyons. Gabrielle answered automatically with a "yes" or a "no," gazing dreamily out of the window at the passing street. Eventually Hélène fell silent. She was deeply concerned. It was easy to tell that the attraction between Gabrielle and Nicolas had reached a dangerous stage and she was powerless to do anything about it.

In the morning the news broke throughout Lyons that the Devaux mill had received the Emperor's personal commission for the new campaign tent. There was not a silk merchant who had not hoped for the order, for when it was completed it would open the way to an avalanche of commissions from a satisfied Emperor noted for rewarding those who pleased him well. For Gabrielle it was a shock on two counts. Once again Nicolas had gained on her through his own well-deserved success, and at the same time it awakened her to how near she had come to a cliff's edge. Nothing symbolised the advance he had made on her emotionally than his capturing of this sought-after commission.

At the time arranged for their meeting she arrived at the Place des Célestins in a barouche driven by Gaston. While he waited she crossed to the café on foot. Nicolas was at the table where they had sat before and he stood up to meet her, able to see at once by her face that once again a gulf had come between them.

"I can't stay," she said with a half-shake of her head. "I just came to give you my warmest congratulations on your latest commission."

"Thank you. Please sit down for a few minutes."

If she sat there she would be lost again. There was too much love in his eyes and in his voice. "No, I must go. There's one thing I want to ask you. Did you know last night that you had the commission?"

"I knew a week ago."

"Why didn't you tell me when you had the chance?"

"You know why. I love you, Gabrielle. I don't want to lose you, and yesterday evening we came so close that I wanted nothing to come between us. I was going to tell you this morning when the opportunity was right and I felt we had reached a point where you could accept that outside influences no longer divided us."

It was hard to withstand such words. "All Lyons knew before me."

"I doubt that. I had told Piat he could release the news to the weavers this morning. There the information would have remained in the loom-rooms until after this hour of meeting you, but it happened that one of the boys was sent on an errand and spread the news as he went. For myself, I consider it to be a sad day for France that the Emperor should need a campaign tent more than ever at this present time." He

was referring to Austria's new declaration of war and the British landing in Portugal to drive out a French invasion of Portuguese territory
and to give aid to Spain, which had become their ally in its struggle to
rid itself of Bonaparte's rule. "I should have preferred to weave silken
banners to celebrate peace throughout the Empire."

"Will that day ever come?"

His expression was grave. "I have doubts. I never thought I should
question the Emperor's actions. Now there are times when I find myself
wondering if power has gone to his head."

"Perhaps your tent will play a part in securing that peace."

"It's my most earnest hope."

She took a pace away from him. "Farewell, Nicolas. I hope to see
the tent when it is finished. I'm sure it will be a handsome sight."

She hurried back to the barouche. Gaston, driving her away, no
longer had the least doubt in his mind that she was being trailed. Now,
at least, he had an idea why. Even from a distance he had been able to
see that the meeting at the café had been no ordinary encounter, and her
face when she returned was pale with distress.

All day Gabrielle expected Henri to arrive at the mill in a raging
temper over the lost commission, but he failed to appear. Instead, he met
her in the hall when she arrived home at the Rue Clémont. He appeared
calm and in charge of himself, although there was a truculent set to his
features, his stance bull-like.

"You've heard, of course," he said to her.

She nodded. "It just shows me that Devaux silk still has the edge on
Roche products. I intend to counteract that eventually."

"Indeed? Come into the salon. Émile's here."

She was not unduly surprised. Over recent weeks Émile had taken
to coming without notice to Lyons, sometimes to spend time with her,
at others to accompany her home to the village when it was the close of a
working week. She should have felt pleasure in these unannounced arrivals, certain that they were well meant, but at times they had a suffo-
cating effect, for there were all the signs that he was closing in on her
with a new wave of possessiveness.

He turned from the window when she entered the salon with her
quick, graceful step. To him she always brought the sun into a room
with her, even though today she looked wearied and even a little sad.
That was to be expected; she had received a severe blow. What was it
between her and Devaux that had outwardly all the evidence of intense
business rivalry while, at the same time, he still had reason to believe
there was something close to a love affair between them? On this bitter
thought the old restraint clamped down on him and he kissed her on the
cheek in greeting with little warmth. It was no indication of the turmoil

of resentment, suspicion, misery and jealousy that he suffered these days, never knowing any peace.

"Henri sent for me as soon as he heard the news of the lost commission this morning. It must have been a great disappointment to you."

"Henri sent for you?" She flashed a wary look from him to her brother's belligerent face. "I'm in a business world. I have to take setbacks from time to time in common with many others."

"But don't you think those setbacks are happening all too frequently now? The time has come for you to consult your conscience and ask yourself if you are fulfilling your late father's wishes. Knowing you as I do, Gabrielle, I'm sure you would be the last person to abuse the trust that was placed in you. The world of *La Grande Fabrique* has set its face against you. You must accept the fact that your being a woman will always relegate you to the background. The dreams you cherish of being a leading light in the silk trade will never be fulfilled."

She heard him out in silence, incredulous that he, who had suppressed his own wishes to give her his full and generous support after the reading of Dominique's will, had chosen to desert her utterly at this hour when she had never needed his backing more. Henri's cunning sickened her. Not trusting himself to keep his temper, nor confident of getting through to a raw nerve in her, he had drawn in Émile to present a line of attack that would be most likely to sway her into resignation. "Do you believe what you are saying, Émile?" she challenged fiercely, wanting him to refute this lack of faith in her, seizing a last chance to bring him back to her side. She knew he would answer truthfully.

"I do, my dear. You know full well that it doesn't suit me to share you with Roche silk, but I would not support your brother in this petition if I didn't think he was right for once. Accept the situation gracefully. You have done well, but not well enough. Dominique would never have wanted a Devaux to gain superiority over the name of Roche, and that is what has happened and will continue to happen unless you make Henri your deputy and retire from the public scene."

She was rendered speechless for the moment. Her brother's contrived treachery was nothing compared to this abandonment by Émile. In all their ups and downs over her persistence in maintaining her individuality, he had never once withdrawn his support from her. Now he had taken the step from which there was no going back. She saw she was completely on her own.

"I don't accept that I have failed. It's early days yet—"

"Four years," Henri interrupted bluntly. "You've had four years."

She rounded on him. "That's nothing! I have a lifetime of silk still before me. I won't give up for you or anybody else."

Émile spoke quietly. "You may have no choice in a few months' time. It might be better to start the change-over now."

She was puzzled. "I don't understand."

Émile indicated with a brief lift of his head that Henri would clarify the remark. She saw the malevolent satisfaction stamped on her brother's face. "Yvonne is *enceinte,*" he rasped. "If it is a boy I shall have a legal right to contest the will and establish my own claim to the trust." He knew Yvonne had been annoyed when she realised she was pregnant once again, but she had soon become reconciled to her condition when he told her his lawyer considered this a possible loophole and promised her the riches that would come to them through Roche silk once the business was his.

Gabrielle released a long sigh. "So that's it. I wish you a strong and healthy child, Henri, whether it be a boy or girl. As for the trust, Father willed it in faith to me and I'm going to prove that faith. In the meantime everything is as it was before we had this discussion, as far as I'm concerned. You must make up your own mind as to whether you want to continue working for me as before." She glanced again in turn at both of them. "Now I'm going upstairs to change and get ready for dinner. It's been a hard day. I need to relax."

She went straight-backed and self-possessed from the room, her head high. It was not until she was out of sight and behind the closed door of her bedchamber that she gave way to the shock that she had just received. Her whole body drooped as if all the strength had drained from her.

8

When the Devaux tent for the Emperor was finished, it went on show at the Hôtel de Ville. Gabrielle received an invitation to the first viewing. Times had been allotted to avoid a crush, and hers was for an evening hour. She assumed that Nicolas would be there to receive those considered the élite of *La Grand Fabrique*. Although other silk merchants with their prejudice against women in the trade might not wish to include her among their number, the quality of her silk could not be denied and Nicolas had drawn her into the high circle for the première viewing. She made a point of mentioning the invitation to Émile.

"I'm most interested to see this tent," she said to him over breakfast one Sunday morning. He had been particularly loving to her as he always was now after her absences in Lyons, and their relationship was the richer for it. "I want to see why the Devaux design won and mine did not."

He put down the cup of coffee he had been drinking and regarded her fondly, their previous night together much in his mind. Let her see the tent and Devaux in the midst of a crowd of silk merchants. There was no danger in that, and in any case his worries on that score were fast subsiding. Brouchier had not come up with a single scrap of further evidence against her, and in his own mind he considered that the little flutter she had experienced was well and truly past.

"I can't believe the winning design was any better than yours. However, it is right that you should view the opposition in this case. That is, if you're able to get near the exhibit. In my experience, these viewings are always crowded and uncomfortable affairs. Would you like me to go with you?"

She refrained from saying that his name was not included on the invitation. It was probably an oversight. There was no reason why he should not accompany her. He would never be denied admission. "Yes, if you would like to come," she answered readily.

That pleased him. Not the least hesitation there. "To be honest, the date isn't particularly convenient for me. I have other commitments here at the silk farm that day. You can tell me about it afterwards."

As the days dwindled down to the time of the viewing, the dispassionate air she had tried to maintain towards the event dissolved without warning into a raging torrent of wanting to see Nicolas again. She realised how foolish she had been to think it was possible to win against love. The long weeks and months of trying to suppress her emotions had had the reverse effect to that for which she had hoped. Nothing should keep her from seeing him that evening.

She had a few days close to panic when something she had eaten disagreed with her, making her feel quite ill, until she was not at all certain that she would be able to attend the viewing. Fortunately she recovered in good time and allowed herself to think once more how it would be when they met. There would probably be little exchange between them, nothing more than a few conventional words of welcome on his part and a reply on hers, all within the hearing of many people. But it would be some balm to the tormenting ache within her.

So much had happened since she had last seen him! Not long before Christmas the Emperor had divorced Joséphine and rumours about a new bride were now more rife than ever. As for the Grande Armée, that had been divided into two sections, one to defeat the Austrian threat once and for all and the other to surge forward in Spain in bloody conflict with the British, Spanish and Portuguese. Not all the news from Spain was good, and the bad weather there was adding to the misery of the troops on both sides of the conflict. Throughout Europe, unusually low temperatures had prevailed from the old year into the new, and already 1810 looked as if it might go on record for freak conditions and a spate of floods.

It was a bitter evening when Gaston drove Gabrielle through the poorly illuminated streets to the Hôtel de Ville. Beneath a fur cloak she had chosen to wear a gown of marbled silk in shades of blues, greys and greens, the sleeves tight and the shoulders puffed in the Paris mode, a pleated frill falling softly at her neck, around which she wore a string of opals set in gold with matching earrings. She was proud to show the quality of her own silk on any occasion and never more than when she knew that many critical eyes in the room would be unable to fault it.

Both she and Gaston were surprised to find no crush of carriages outside the Hôtel de Ville. "Are we early?" she asked him.

"No, right on time, as you wished, madame."

She had thought that by arriving exactly at the hour stated on the invitation she might have a few moments longer with Nicolas, and it appeared she was about to achieve this with better results than expected. It was a relief to get out of the cold air into the warmth of the building, which was close to being overheated. An attendant took her invitation card and led her along a corridor to open a door into a domed and panelled hall, leaving her there. She found herself to be the sole spectator, completely alone with the campaign tent.

Pegged out on a green carpet as if it stood on grass, the campaign tent was large, which was according to the measurements that had been stipulated, and a pleasing oval in shape. Woven in stripes of blue and white Brussels duck, the roof had a scalloped lambrequin embellished with scarlet embroidery and braided with black, reminiscent of the tents of the knights of old that had spread across the battlefields of Europe in medieval times, covering much of the same territory as that which the Emperor had drawn into his empire. Slipping off the cloak, she put it with her muff on a chair by the wall before approaching the tasselled ropes that formed a cordon around the tent. When she circled it to view it from every angle, she came to the gap left open for those privileged to step beyond the cordon. The entrance flaps of the tent were fastened back for access and she went inside.

Lit by lanterns suspended from poles supporting the canopied ceiling, it was spacious and well proportioned; it housed, with plenty of room to spare, the easily transportable folding camp bed, chairs and four tables that could be hooked together to form one unit when not packed away. One of the two campaign chests, lined with red and white duck, was open. It held maps to demonstrate one of its uses, the chains of both chests lying like gleaming necklaces, designed for fastening them to the backs of mules.

All these details she took in at a single glance from where she stood, a few feet inside the entrance, her hands clasped lightly before her at waist level. She was enthralled by the splendour of the silk hangings that lined the whole interior. The pattern of red and blue bouquets was simple and stylised against a pale grey ground, the effect as light and airy as a new morning.

Outside, in the hall, the door opened and closed again as someone entered. Anticipation had been high in her ever since she had found herself alone. Now it flared through her whole frame. Her back was to the tent's entrance and she did not turn, remaining motionless. Footsteps crossed the floor to become swallowed up on the green carpet. Nicolas's voice addressed her.

"I waited to give you a chance to form an opinion on your own. What do you think of it?"

She closed her eyes briefly on the almost unbearable joy of being near him again. How had she borne these many weeks of not seeing him, not hearing his voice and—hardest of all—trying to will him out of her life? She gave him a reply from where she stood completely still, only her pulse racing.

"It's splendid. Just as I knew it would be."

A lantern threw his shadow in front of her as he came to stand by her side. "I've missed you, Gabrielle."

Unexpected tears filled her eyes and choked her throat. The heavy burden of constantly denying all she felt had suddenly overtaken her. "I've missed you too," she admitted huskily, unable to answer in any other way.

He took her gently by the shoulders and swivelled her around slowly to face him, his hands sliding down to her narrow waist and remaining there. Speech deserted them both at what they saw in each other's eyes, the look they shared holding love and anguish and searing desire. As his arms went about her she raised both hands to hold his face, stroking his cheekbones with her thumbs as she savoured the perfection of the moment. When his embrace tightened ardently, she strained forward swiftly against him, her eyes closing, and there was so much pent-up passion in her that as his lips parted on hers she cried out in elation, the sound cut off by his love-frenzied kiss. She responded with complete abandonment, kissing as she had never kissed before, kissing him from the depth of her heart. The whole world had contracted to the encirclement of his arms, the pressure of his strong body against hers, and the spellbinding eroticism of a kiss she would remember all her days.

When finally they drew breath, she felt a century had gone by. As if in a dream, she let her head sink onto his shoulder and he cupped her breast to caress her tenderly, his lips against her shining hair.

"My darling," he whispered. "I can hardly believe I have you in my arms."

"I was sure you would be here." Her voice was soft and barely audible. "But I hadn't expected to find there would be no other visitors at this hour."

"I had to see you on your own. It was a chance not to be missed. All these months I've hoped to meet you at some gathering as we met before."

"It was deliberate," she confessed. "I went nowhere if I thought you would be there."

"Yet you came today."

"I had told you I wanted to view the campaign tent when it was finished. I never dreamed it would bring us together again like this."

"Do you regret what has happened?"

She lifted her rapturous face to his. "I should, but I can't."

He kissed her again and their swaying shadows were splayed fan-like by the lanterns across the silken hangings while their mouths sought to assuage in some measure the desire that engulfed them both. Her fingers were buried convulsively in his hair at the back of his head as if she would hold him to her forever, and he, crushing her in the curve of one arm, continued to trace the shape of her supple body through the fine silk that shielded but did not disguise.

It was an echo in the hall from some activity in another part of the building that brought Gabrielle back to reality. She pulled away from him and went to sink down onto a chair, her bowed head supported by her spread fingers.

"I think I'm going mad," she said dazedly. "I can't reason logically any more."

He went to crouch down in front of her, resting his arms across his bent knees, and tried to see into her face. "Why?" he questioned urgently. "Because we love each other and will go on loving each other until one or other of us dies?"

"Don't speak of death!" She sprang to her feet again, rigid with dread.

He straightened up to stand with her, taking her clenched hands from her sides into both his own, unfolding and fondling her fingers to relax her. "Let's speak of life, then." As someone paused in the corridor to open the door and look in at the tent before going on again, she would have snatched her hands away from him, but firmly he retained his clasp on her. "Let's talk of your future and mine and how it would be to make a fresh start together, each of us to make amends for having let the other go away on the day we both remember."

"That was nearly six years ago," she said brokenly.

"Yet nothing has changed between us, except that we need each other more than ever."

She knew it to be the truth. The love they shared had proved itself to be of unassailable strength. Unconsummated, fraught by every kind of difficulty, battered as much by themselves as anyone else, it remained to bind and torment them, so that each was only half alive without the other. How could she go on resisting this man who held her whole heart? Was there a chance that the kindness in Émile would prevail over all else if she made a direct appeal to him? If she explained? If she asked if she could remain his friend, as she had always been, while he released her from being his wife? On these thoughts tension began to ebb from her. It enabled her rich happiness in having this hour with Nicolas to come through unhampered and with it came an irrational lift of optimism.

She was no longer able to recognise, as she had a few minutes before, that love crowds out reason. On the crest of hope she drew up Nicolas's hands with her own and covered them with little kisses. She grew still only when he bent his head to place his lips on her neck in tender response to her spontaneous display of love. A tremor went through her and her lids drooped on the delicious sensation. Then her head swayed back as his lips went lower to meet the cleavage of her breasts, his fingers releasing the tiny pearl buttons that held them captive. Through the fringe of her half-closed lashes she glimpsed the silk canopy of red and blue bouquets overhead, and her fleeting thought before he distracted her anew with his sensitive exploration was that the flowers would hold a love-secret in their depths even when in the midst of war. Sensuously she sighed at the subtle lingering of his travelling kisses that were almost too pleasurable to bear. The sleeves had slipped from her shoulders and she was half naked in his embrace. Her whisper came to him in rapid, breathless little bursts.

"I love you. I belong to you. I've been yours in my heart since we first met. I've fought against my feelings until I can't fight any longer."

It was what he had long wanted to hear. "My darling, beautiful, wonderful Gabrielle," he whispered in return. "Now there are no more barriers between us."

With her eyes serene and heavy with ardour, she saw that his face was transfigured, every handsome bone in it etched sharply by his passion for her. Her lips parted for his as he took her mouth in renewed hunger and in his powerful embrace she felt swept away, split asunder, marvellously shattered and gloriously lost, her principles forgotten, the iron standards she had sought to maintain melted beyond salvage by the force of her love for this man and his for her. She could not go on living without him. He was the other half of her, as she was of him.

He had no doubt that if they had been somewhere else, without threat of intrusion, she would have surrendered to him immediately. She was as passionately eager for him as he was for her. If there had been a key in the door he would have turned it when he entered the hall, but there was none. For himself, he would have borne her down on the Emperor's bed. Then, as he drew her towards it, pliant and melting in his arms, footsteps resounded in the corridor. Alerted, she stiffened warily until they had passed by the closed door and faded out of hearing. Then, as if seeing how near he had brought her to the bed and perhaps fearing her own willingness to lie down upon it, she moved away, drawing up one sleeve. He checked her by putting both hands upon her breasts, adoring her seductive dishevelment.

"Let's leave this place," he urged her, "and go elsewhere. I want to have you to myself away from all these interruptions."

She was greatly tempted. It would be so easy, so blissful, and yet she could not do as he asked. Lovingly, she traced her finger tips over his lips as if memorising them, her face full of longing. "I wish we could. It can't be. Not until I'm free to come to you of my own accord."

"When will that be?" He was impatient, almost desperate. "We have been denied each other for so long. Too much time has been lost. I want an end to half-meetings and distant sightings of you. We are both too used to speaking our minds and being responsible for our own actions to be trapped any longer in this unbearable and sorry situation. I need you. We need each other. I shall go to Émile—"

"No!" She was desperately afraid of the consequences of a confrontation between Émile and him.

"Why not? We are living in enlightened times. There is no stigma attached to anybody in the dissolvement of a civil marriage, particularly when a terrible mistake has been made. I'm sure Émile would listen to me in a sensible manner—"

"You must not go to him!" She was adamant.

"Then how is this dilemma to be solved?"

"I don't know. At the moment I can only hope for a solution. I think I may have it. All I ask is that you allow me a little time. Then I'll come to you. Somehow I'll come to you."

"You'll do that?"

She gave him a love-smile, hypnotising him afresh with her beauty. "I will."

He did not doubt her. The hope in her was infectious, and they went on smiling between kisses as if they were already free to be together. Then reluctantly she drew away from him, putting her neckline to rights in preparation for leaving and finding that one of the little pearl buttons was missing, lost through love. She did not search the floor for it. Let it remain in the silken place in which her life and Nicolas's had taken a new and happy turn.

With his arm about her waist, they left the tent together. He helped her on with her fur cape and they faced each other in parting. "When am I going to see you again?" he asked her. "Tomorrow?"

"No. I can't say when. It depends on many things."

"If it rested with me, I wouldn't let you go from me at all."

At the door into the corridor, she rested a hand against his chest to prevent his accompanying her. "Don't come with me now and don't try to see me. That would only complicate matters. I must find my own way out of the maze to reach you. Good night, my darling."

Holding her cloak about her, she went from him. There were several people about. She looked at none of them. An attendant in the entrance hall took a lantern to show her down the steps to her carriage, where Gaston awaited her.

He helped her into her seat and then leapt back up onto the box. There would be trouble now, he thought, flicking the whip. She and Devaux had been closeted together for over an hour on their own. He had checked the time on the pocket watch she had given him when he first entered her service. The absence of other vehicles, with the exception of an occasional coming and going, had caused him to make his own casually expressed enquiries from an attendant with whom he had conversed. He hoped she would be prepared for the fireworks that would surely follow as soon as Valmont received the spy's report on her attending a viewing of the tent at a time at which nobody else had been invited.

A letter was delivered to Henri at breakfast. He recognised the handwriting and did not open it until he was alone in his office. As he broke the seal he had little hope of anything of interest and expected it to be a note from Brouchier to say that further investigation had been called off since no results had been forthcoming. Then, as he read, he saw that the situation was beginning to move at last. According to Brouchier's investigations, Gabrielle and Devaux had been behind a closed door at the Hôtel de Ville for far longer than it took to view a campaign tent. It appeared that only one invitation had been issued for that evening, and Gabrielle had received it. The times of her arrival and departure were duly recorded.

As Henri refolded the letter he wondered how Émile would react to this information. For himself, it was something to hold over until his son was born and he could present a strong case of appeal in the courts.

Yvonne's ability to carry this child, when all the other times had ended in miscarriages, had set him wondering whether she had previously found some method of ridding herself of her pregnancies. Now she had the inducement of the wealth and comfort that would be theirs to share if only Gabrielle could be dislodged from the trust. He was looking forward to having a son, quite apart from the advantage it would give him. It was worth putting up with Yvonne's cantankerous ways, her moaning over her bulging figure and loss of looks. He had promised her the earth once the boy was born, and he would see that her every whim was gratified. She had had the temerity to ask him once what he would do if she gave birth to a daughter. He had rounded on her so fiercely that she had actually quailed.

"It shall not be a girl!" he had roared. "If it is, I'll divorce you and you shall get nothing from me."

It was a harsh threat but he had meant it at the time. Getting up from his chair, he went to his office and locked the letter safely away in the desk that had been his father's, hoping more such valuable information would follow soon.

Brouchier went in person to deliver his written report to Émile, riding out of Lyons at an early hour. He was well pleased with what he carried because, like most of those in his line of work, he received an adequate retaining fee and a large bonus when the required information was produced. From today he expected his income to rise sharply and remain there. He knew the signs. Once lovers had begun to meet after a lengthy absence, they could not stay away from each other. He was not sure what kind of dénouement his client would eventually require. Valmont was such a withdrawn, dignified man, and even the act of hiring someone to do the spy work had obviously been extremely distasteful to him. Brouchier judged Valmont to be the type to take matters into his own hands when the time came. Probably pistols at dawn, which was a foolish way to settle things, in his opinion. Better to be rid of the woman concerned and find another. Over the years he had become cynical to a degree about human passions.

When he arrived at his destination he asked for Monsieur Valmont and was told he was at the silk sheds. Following directions, he took a path through the trees and happened to spot his client coming out of one of the buildings. Émile Valmont stiffened his back at the sight of him, almost as though rearing slightly away from something that was loathsome. Undeterred, Brouchier approached him but had no time to voice a greeting.

"You have something for me?"

"Yes, monsieur. It's what you've been waiting for." Brouchier took a sealed and folded paper from his pocket and put it into his client's outstretched hand.

"Stay here." Émile took the report into his office and read it through. Then he unlocked a drawer where he kept money, slipped a certain amount into a money-bag and took it out to where the spy waited. He tossed the money-bag to him. "There you are. You'll find you've been paid amply for what you have done. Your task is at an end."

Brouchier was astounded. "But this is only the beginning, monsieur. I know—"

"Get out. Get off my land. Never let me see you again."

Disgruntled, Brouchier obeyed, returning to where he had left his horse and riding away. Émile passed a shaking hand across his brow. He had planned what he should do if ever full confirmation of his fears came into his hands. Now he must put that plan into action.

After telling the clerk in the office that he would be away in Paris for four or five days, he hurried towards the house. When he entered he gave orders that a bag be packed and a fast travelling carriage be brought to the door within a quarter of an hour.

When Gabrielle came home at the week's end, Émile was still in Paris. She had been fully prepared to put the whole situation before him, hoping he would show compassion and all the understanding and gentleness of which he was capable when she asked for her freedom. Failing to find him there caused a violent reaction to set in. She found herself trembling from head to foot and spent most of the time resting on a chaise longue in her room. Émile had still not come home when she returned to Lyons, and it was to be another two weeks before she saw him again, for the following Friday Yvonne went into labour and Gabrielle and Hélène needed to be with her.

Thirty-six hours later, after a long and agonising struggle, Yvonne gave birth to a daughter. The infant was weak and lived only a few hours. Yvonne did not shed a tear, but Hélène wept for the loss of the infant's life as if the baby had been her own. Henri did not go near his wife for two days and then only after Hélène's persuasion.

"Please do as I ask, Henri," she implored. "A few comforting words from you would mean so much. She says you threatened to divorce her."

He had no intention of consoling Yvonne for what was essentially his own loss, but he had to see her sooner or later. She would be contrite and frightened of losing him, ready enough to admit that she had failed him, and he would let her humble herself for a while before he showed any sign of magnanimity. To gamble on the sex of a child was too slight a chance; he realised that now. Instead he would dispense with his lawyer, who had proved to be no more use than the rest after all, and watch out for some other means by which he could gain control of Roche silk. He refused to admit defeat. Brouchier should be retained, because there was always a possibility that through Gabrielle the means might be found to bring Devaux to a downfall. He gave an impatient sigh.

"Very well," he agreed heavily, "I'll see Yvonne. But she doesn't deserve the honour."

He ignored the way his sister-in-law drew in her breath at his hard attitude. When he entered the bedroom he was taken aback to see how ill his wife looked. She lay propped against the lace-frilled pillows with her eyes closed, bruises of exhaustion dark beneath them. Uncertainly he went to the bedside. She must have heard him approach, because before he could say anything her eyes opened, bright and hostile. "Never again. I'm not going through childbirth ever again. I nearly died through your vendetta against Gabrielle. If you're any kind of man you'll outwit her with one of your business tricks. You have enough of them up your sleeve, I should think." She half raised herself from the pillows. "Remember I'm your wife and I'll stay your wife." She wagged an irate finger at him. "I know too much about your pilfering ways for you to risk getting rid of me. Even silk merchants can go to prison for smuggling. Don't you forget that!"

She collapsed back on the pillows. He left the room without saying a word. In all the time they had been married he had never suspected how she had nosed out facts about his private business with the same skill with which she located scandals. It must have been a trump card she had saved for an emergency, perhaps originally to prevent his being filched away from her by a younger woman. She had certainly played it now with full effect. How the devil did she ever find out about his line in smuggling some of the Roche silk to England and elsewhere?

Gabrielle heard from Émile that he was home again from business in Paris. The tone of his letter was affectionate, expressing regret at having missed her. She was quiet and pensive after reading it.

"Is anything wrong?" Hélène asked her, releasing Juliette from her lap. She had been helping her daughter to dress a doll, and the child ran with it to show Gabrielle.

"See, Aunt Gabrielle! Isn't Denise pretty now?"

"She looks lovely, Juliette. I think I have some silk ribbon in the right colour for a sash. I'll fetch it for you."

Hélène spoke quickly to prevent her sister-in-law from leaving the room without answering her. "You're worried, I can tell. Is there anything I can do?"

Gabrielle gave her a serious little smile. "Not yet. The time is going to come when I'll be glad of your help, but not yet."

"Is Émile coming to Lyons to see you?"

"He will be here on Saturday. I sent a message to tell him I would not be journeying home this weekend."

She went from the room to get the ribbon, Juliette dancing along at her side. Hélène pondered over what had been said; Gabrielle's manner was quite strange. Normally she was quick and lively, whatever her frame of mind. Now it was as if she were completely weighed down by a problem that could not be solved.

Gabrielle planned to see Nicolas before Émile arrived in Lyons. She had to talk to him before she saw her husband again. She was in the process of writing a note at her office desk at the mill, asking him to meet her at the café in the Place des Célestins, when the door opened without warning and he stood there. The rush of joy she always felt at the sight of him was tempered immediately by anxiety at the serious expression on his drawn face.

"What's happened?" she asked faintly, in trepidation, rising slowly to her feet.

Without reply he closed the door and came towards her. He shook his head once as if the cause could not be told without preparation and moved to pull her into his arms, crushing her to him until she could hardly breathe during several moments of wordless embrace. Then he kissed her passionately, she responding almost with desperation, clinging to him in growing fear. When he took his mouth from hers he continued to hold her, looking down into her face as he tried to break gently the news he had to tell.

"I have to go away, Gabrielle. I have to leave Lyons."

"Tell me why!"

"Something has happened that I never expected. I've been recalled to the colours."

"Oh, no!" She was aghast.

"I've had orders to rejoin my old regiment of the *chasseurs à cheval.*"

Her knees threatened to give way and she tightened her arms about his neck. "When did you hear? Perhaps there's been a mistake."

"There's no mistake. I received my papers telling me to report for duty less than an hour ago. I came straight to you."

"How long before you have to leave?" Her lips felt stiff and immobile.

"I depart tomorrow morning for the campaign in the Iberian Peninsula."

The cry she gave was smothered as she buried her face in his shoulder. He cupped her head, pressing his cheek against her hair. "That's why I had to see you without delay. Good can come out of this posting to Spain if you agree to go with me."

She lifted herself to look at him. "Go with you?" she repeated unsurely.

"It can be done. A party of half a dozen wives will be leaving with the reinforcements. You could be with them! They'll be accommodated away from the battle line, but always within reach of their husbands during lulls in the fighting."

"But I should not be your wife."

"It would only be a matter of time before you were. Don't you see? Émile would never try to hold you once you had left with me." He kissed her cheek and tried to cheer her tragic expression with an encouraging smile. "We can be married in Spain as soon as you are free. When the war is won we shall return to Lyons and live our own lives together, making up for all the time we lost."

She thrust herself from him and half turned away, the fingers of both hands pressed to the sides of her face. "I can't go with you," she said in a choked voice.

"Is it your husband you're thinking of? There's still time for us to ride out to see him. I understand that you wouldn't wish to leave without a word."

"It's not entirely Émile."

"Then is it Roche silk and the mill? I know it's not easy for you to leave your brother in charge, but neither is it for me to hand over full responsibility to my manager in my absence. Thank God I can trust Michel Piat completely, or else there's no way of knowing what would happen. At least you can be sure that your brother will run Maison Roche competently, if mundanely, until we return."

"I'll never let Henri get his hands on the business," she declared vehemently, "not even for a little while. It was left in trust to me and I have a new responsibility towards it."

"Are you saying you would put Roche silk before me?" he exclaimed incredulously.

"I would put nothing before you if the way were clear. I tell you again, I can't go with you."

He reached out to grip her by the arm and swing her round to him again, giving her a half shake in the urgency of his demand. "I want you to be my wife as you should have been a long time ago. I have more right to claim you for my own than any other man. You're in my blood. You're the reason why I'm going to come back from this war unscathed, because I know we were meant to have years of loving and living and seeing our children grow. I love you more than any woman has been loved before. Listen to me! Don't let us throw away everything when it's been given to us to be together for the rest of our lives!"

There was not a vestige of colour in her face, her eyes stretched and glistening with suppressed tears, her mouth tremulous. She measured her words. "It's too late, my love—my only love. I have to stay here. I have to remain wife to Émile." Her voice faltered on a dry sob. "I'm going to have his child."

His hand fell away from her and he stepped back a pace as he stared at her, stunned by what he had heard. In the dreadful silence that fell between them the *bistonclaque* of the looms seemed to drum through the closed door. "Are you sure?" he asked on a sharp intake of breath.

She nodded helplessly. "There were signs before I came to the Hôtel de Ville that evening, but I had failed to recognise them. Perhaps it was some instinct inherent in most women that intervened and stayed me from going with you to another place where we could have been alone. I wanted you to make love to me. I wanted to lie in your arms all night. I cared nothing then for anyone or anything except you, and yet I couldn't do what you wished. It was only when the symptoms of early pregnancy returned that I understood why I had refused what I had wanted most in all the world."

"We've exchanged letters twice since that evening. Why didn't you give me some idea of what had happened?"

"I wanted to tell you myself." She indicated listlessly the half-written note on her desk. "When you arrived I was writing to ask you to meet me at the café in the Place des Célestins."

Without hesitation he seized her outstretched arm by the wrist before it could drift back to her side and drew her to him lovingly. "You can still come with me to Spain," he insisted, enfolding his arms about her as he looked into her eyes. "I'll arrange for you to have the best of care. Nothing exists that can come between you and me. I love you and I'll love any child that is part of you."

She had to turn her face away, unable to bear the hope she saw in his gaze. No woman could ever have heard a greater declaration of a man's total devotion. It made her heart break in its own terrible anguish. Her fate was to be loved by two men, one of whom she adored, as he did her, and the other whom she could not now desert. It would have been hard before she had known she was pregnant, simply because it would have caused so much pain, but now the choice had been taken completely from her.

"I can't go with you," she said again. "I care nothing for my own safety and would follow you anywhere if I were free, but in my present state I couldn't undertake such an expedition. The doctor I consulted for confirmation of my condition even advised against my journeying between my two homes. I may lose the baby if I take any risks. All is not quite as it should be."

He took her chin with his finger tips to bring her eyes back to his. His gaze was dark with concern for her well-being. "Are you in any personal danger?"

"Not if I rest."

Relief swept across his face. "Then after the baby is born—"

"No!" Her refusal of all she longed for came as though torn from her and she jerked herself from him. "Don't you see? Can't you understand? Whatever chance we had to be together has gone!"

He was stubborn, his mouth compressed in determination. "I won't accept that. Perhaps you have no idea how long the war in the Peninsula might drag on. You know as I do from the news-sheet reports that it's not going our way all the time. Far from it. I could be away for years. Do you hear me? *Years!* You must come to me as soon as you are fit to travel."

She did not know how to go on summoning up the strength to refuse what he asked, and in spite of all her efforts tears had begun to flow down her face. "You are forgetting Émile. He has always hoped we would have a child. Even if he gave me my freedom, he would never agree to part with his son or daughter." Her speech came jerkily. "I was virtually abandoned myself after my mother died, and through losing her I had a wretched childhood. I vowed long ago if ever I had a child of my own he or she should know only happiness in the early years. Under any circumstances, I would never expose a young child to the dangers of a war zone. I've read how many an isolated travelling party is liable to attack from Spanish guerrillas, who lurk in ambush amid the hills and mountains and forests. French women and children have been brutally slaughtered."

"Those poor creatures were the wives and women of foot soldiers who are often left to fend for themselves if they can't keep up with a march. You and the other officers' wives would be under constant armed protection."

"What protection could be given to my baby in a siege or a rout? As you said yourself, things are not going all our way in Spain. Please try to accept that what is between us no longer has a future." She clasped the back of a chair for support. "I love you. I'll always love you, but I'm going to have Émile's baby. Nothing can alter that for us now."

It was her quietness that flash-pointed his anger, for in it was a total rejection of everything for which he had hoped, an irrevocable decision that would withstand whatever he might say to her. He had not known himself capable of such a contained rage. It made his speech vibrate in his throat. "I want a promise from you that at some time you will at least visit me in Spain or wherever else I might be sent afterwards. I've desired you in mental and physical torment for too long to be denied some part of your life."

"You would only try to make me stay."

"I could make you forget you had any existence other than with me."

"Do you think I don't know that?" Her voice deepened on a note of despair. "That's why any visit would be out of the question."

"You have always withheld yourself from me!" he accused.

"Not through my own wish!" she retorted fiercely. "When Émile held me in his arms, do you suppose I didn't yearn for you in his place? At times I tried to imagine that he was you, but it was useless, because I knew there could be no comparison. With you I would have expressed all the love that was in me; with you I could have abandoned myself to passion and known true fulfilment."

"Then make me your promise!"

"I can't. I made a different kind of promise once to Émile and almost broke it through loving you. I'll make no new ones. I told you when you held me in your arms in the Emperor's tent that I would come to you when I was free. That still holds, except that I'm no longer able to see how or when, or if ever, it might be."

" 'Never' appears to be the appropriate word!" The hurt in his angry eyes was as stark as if he had been ripped apart inside. His eyes were glazed over by the agony of parting from her, and he could no longer endure what he saw as her final rejection of him. Bitterly he made a gesture of resignation, lifting his hands and letting them fall again. "This is beyond my belief. It would have been better for both of us if we had never met. Somehow even now I can't regret it. Farewell, Gabrielle."

Turning, he opened the office door and went out, letting in the noisy *bistonclaque* of the looms. It swung shut again behind him. She stood as if all power to move had gone from her, suffering shock waves of desolation and despair. Slowly her head drooped as if it had become too heavy for her neck. She remained motionless, hearing and seeing nothing, only remembering the last words spoken to her by the man she would love until the end of her days.

9

Émile arrived in Lyons earlier than expected. Henri heard his voice in the hall and went to meet him.

"Gabrielle is not home from the mill yet, Émile. Let me offer you some refreshment. A glass of wine?"

Émile declined with one of his dignified gestures that was so in keeping with his whole appearance. "Thank you, but no. I'll wait until Gabrielle is here. How is Yvonne? I can't tell you how sorry I was that you and she should suffer such a loss."

"She appreciated your letter of condolence. Yes, it was a great disappointment to us both that the infant did not survive. But come. There's no need for us to converse in the hall." Henri slapped a hand onto his back, a familiarity that Émile could have done without, for continued acquaintance with his brother-in-law had never lifted an initial dislike. "How is business with you these days?"

"I'm anticipating a good season. I only wish the political situation was more stable."

"I agree. The silk trade is like all luxury commodities in being among the first to feel the effect of any deterioration of wealth. Even a whim of fashion turning against us can have calamitous results."

Talking together, the two men strolled into the Gold Salon, one of the smaller rooms in the house, so named for the design of wheat ears that patterned the silk-panelled walls. There Henri took up a crystal decanter and poured himself a glass of wine. "Are you sure you wouldn't like to change your mind?" he enquired, letting the lip of the decanter hover over a second glass.

Again Émile refused. "What has been happening in Lyons?" he asked casually. "It's four weeks since I've seen Gabrielle and longer since I was here."

Henri's eyes gleamed with satisfaction. "Devaux has gone; I can tell you that for a start. Recalled to the colours. What do you think of it, eh?"

It seemed to Émile that his brother-in-law's tone bordered on the conspiratorial, almost as if Henri knew what good news it was to him. Fortunately there was no possibility of that. "Indeed? Has the Devaux mill closed down, then?"

"Far from it. He left a manager in charge, a Parisian by the name of Michel Piat. A capable man, I've heard, but there's no telling how things will go with Devaux so far afield."

"Where has Devaux been posted? Do you know?"

"To the Peninsula. From all reports, it's a difficult campaign. Our soldiers would have settled the Portuguese long ago if the British hadn't interfered."

"You must remember we invaded the territory of their oldest ally, Portugal," Émile remarked drily.

"Ah! And why? The Portuguese refused to obey the Emperor's command to close their ports to British trade. It was the only opening left in the Emperor's entire continental system of counter-blockade. We had to move in to take Lisbon and settle the matter."

"Portugal was neutral. It had a right to decide what it wanted to do with its own ports."

Henri looked at Émile over his glass, his eyes narrowing. "Are you talking treason? Do you not revere the Emperor?"

"I'm talking facts. As for Bonaparte, none can dispute he has conquered the whole of Europe."

"He has indeed." Henri straightened his shoulders proudly as if he had had some personal part in the achievement. "Only the British left. They'll be sorry they ever put a foot on Peninsula soil."

"In my opinion they'll not be driven out easily. I believe it will be a long war."

Henri's expression changed slyly. "That suits you, doesn't it? You have your reasons, just as I have mine, for wanting Devaux out of the way for as long as the Emperor has need of an army."

Émile answered him with icy civility, covering his uncertainty as to what direction the conversation was taking. "Why should I? The feud belongs to your family and is nothing to me, other than Gabrielle being my wife. Devaux never purchased my raw silk, so I'll not miss his custom."

"It was not his custom I was referring to." Henri was enjoying himself. He was certain he had Émile on hot coals. "I'm talking about Devaux's interest in Gabrielle—your wife and my sister. What do you say to that?"

"You have me at a loss," Émile bluffed coldly. "To my knowledge, she has had no business dealings with him."

"Again I was not dwelling on the business side of things." Henri's widening grin was malevolent. "Neither was that the reason why you set Brouchier on to her comings and goings. Am I not right?"

Émile saw that any further pretence was useless. Grimly he regarded his brother-in-law. "How did you know?"

Henri's reply was smug. "It reached my ears. Brouchier is accurate and reliable. Whatever he reported to you would be true. When he's on the trail no move of his quarry goes unobserved."

"He reported nothing incriminating," Émile gave back sharply. "Nothing. I dispensed with his services a while ago."

"So he told me. I retained him, mainly to keep an eye on Devaux. That's how I know that Devaux went to the mill to say farewell to Gabrielle a couple of days ago. It was a brief meeting. Not more than a quarter of an hour at the most. You have nothing to worry about. Brouchier managed to get into the entrance to the mill unobserved and had his ear to the door for a few minutes. According to him, they were keeping their distance from each other and did not part on good terms. He heard enough for me to be able to tell you that whatever may have been between them is over. They won't be seeing each other again."

Émile's carapace of calm was shattered completely. An ungovernable rage possessed him. "You bastard!" He lunged a blow at Henri's face and the shock of the impact ran up his arm. Almost with surprise, he saw his brother-in-law sag like a bag of grain and collapse back heavily on the floor, sending two chairs skeetering away as he knocked against them. Henri appeared equally amazed by such a totally unexpected source of attack and after a moment propped himself up on an elbow to feel his jaw gingerly.

"You made me bite my tongue," he growled thickly with the pain of it, wrath taking over from astonishment. Blood was showing at the corners of his mouth, his lips beginning to puff as though in the process of being inflated. "You could have knocked my teeth out." Wincing, he checked with an exploring finger that they were all there. "You've loosened them. I believe you've shaken the roots."

"They'll settle down in a little while." Émile, dazed by his own action, embarrassed by the ridiculous sight of his brother-in-law seated on the floor in a welter of anger and self-pity, went forward to assist him to his feet. Henri furiously warded off his helping hand and got up unaided. With both hands cupped to his jaw, he went to the door, where he paused to look back vengefully at his attacker.

"Gabrielle is the one who deserves a beating. Your wife—"

"Get out!" Émile's temper had flared again, his hands balling into fists at his sides. Henri did not delay.

In the hallway he came face to face with Hélène and Juliette coming in from a walk. Hélène exclaimed at the sight of him and ran forward. "Whatever happened to you?"

"I fell. Er—I hit my mouth on a chair."

"Come upstairs at once. You need a cold compress on your face or it will be purple with bruises in no time at all." Although short in stature compared with him, she put a maternal arm about his bulky waist and guided him towards the stairs. Juliette trotted up the flight in their wake. She had fallen over many times, but she had never ended up with a face like Uncle Henri's. He looked like one of the gargoyles on the church of Saint Nizier.

Henri received no sympathy from Yvonne, who found him having his face bathed by Hélène. "How much wine had you imbibed?" she questioned sharply. She had become quite a shrew since she had gained a hold over him.

"No more than half a glass," he replied with perfect truth. Then he added defensively: "The floor is too highly polished in the Gold Salon."

"Not for sober folk," she retorted, leaving him to Hélène's ministrations.

The unfair assumption was galling. Nevertheless it was wise not to have protested. Humiliation was high in him. He did not want too close an investigation of the incident. At least Émile was too much of a gentleman to talk about it. Closing his eyes, he welcomed the cold compress Hélène was applying to his face. She had gentle hands.

When Gabrielle arrived home a servant informed her that her husband awaited her in the Gold Salon. She discarded her outer clothing and went straight to see him. She found him standing with one foot propped against the fender as he gazed into the fire. At the sound of her entrance he glanced up and met her eyes piercingly in the large looking-glass above the mantel. She thought he appeared strained.

"So you're home, then, my dear," he greeted her reflection. "I was impatient for your coming."

"How are you?" she asked, coming to a standstill some distance from him. "I haven't seen you since before you went to Paris."

He turned to face her and rested an arm on the mantel. Normally he would have embraced her, but as she had not come forward to offer her lips or her cheek as she usually did, he chose not to make any move himself. "I'm well. What of you? You look tired to me." He could never resist the chance to imply she gave too much of her time to work.

"I suppose I'm always a little weary by the end of a working week."

"Ah, but more so this time, I suspect. Have you been sleeping?"

"Not very well."

"It would have done you good to spend a few days in the country with me instead of compelling me to come to you. I could ill afford the time at the present moment. What made you change your plans in this manner?"

She felt his sharp gaze following her every movement as she went to sit on a sofa. "He is ill at ease," she thought. His reserved manner was cracked by an underlying irritability that only came to the surface when he was under great emotional stress and felt himself at a disadvantage. It was a common enough male trait. She had seen it in her father as well as her brother. His quirk of mood and her own bleakness of spirit lay heavily on her. She let her hand brush the brocaded seat beside her in invitation. "Please sit down with me. I've something to tell you."

He studied her warily for a moment or two before he took the seat beside her. "What is it you want to talk about?" he asked her guardedly. Although not normally a gambling man, he had recently taken a gambler's chance to rid her life and his of the threat to their marriage. It had been his belief that by a bold and ruthless move he had nipped her entanglement with Devaux in the bud. Now he was no longer sure. Maybe his action had come too late. If it had, he still had legal authority over her. He would never let her go. "Well? I'm waiting."

She was looking down at the wedding ring that she was twisting around her finger. Slowly she raised her head again, her gaze straightforward and direct. "We are going to have a child, Émile. After all this time. Our own child."

He stared at her, stunned by what she had said, for it was entirely different from anything he had expected. Unconsciously he drew back from her, as if the news she had given him had exerted a physical force making it difficult for him to absorb the joyful portent of what he had heard. All tension left him. His whole expression crumpled into jubilation. "My dearest wife!" Choked by emotion, he raised his hands to take her face between them and leaned forward swiftly to kiss her ecstatically. He had no doubts that he had fathered the child within her, for the truth shone out of her. "When is it to be?"

"I've nearly six more months to go."

Involuntarily one part of his mind registered the fact that she had had no meetings with Devaux remotely near the time of conception. He also believed he knew why she had conceived after such a long time. Her absences in Lyons had acted strongly upon his desires, and this happy turn of events was the result.

"We must get you home without delay." He was enthusiastic. "I'll arrange that we leave in the morning—"

"No, Émile. That's out of the question. I have to stay here. The doctor insists I take no journeys of any kind."

"Do you imagine I would leave you in Lyons away from me for the next six months?"

"It has to be."

His immediate pleasure over the forthcoming baby was spoiled by her opposition to him. It was always the same, he thought with exasperation. She counteracted what he wanted at every turn and she had the power and money to do it. This evening there was no more patience left in him. He clapped his hands down on his knees in a restrained gesture of being at the end of his tether. "I suppose the same old reason is behind your determination to stay here as it has always been. It's Roche silk again, isn't it? You won't leave it? Allow me to tell you that bumping over cobbles in a calèche every day to and from the mill would be far more harmful than a slow and steady drive from Lyons to your rightful place with me under my roof."

She noted that whenever he was out of humour he always seemed to become tighter and neater, straighter and colder. Even his impeccably tailored coat appeared to mould itself more smoothly over his well-shaped shoulders. She longed for a little of the gentleness he could show towards her when he felt like it. His relentlessness was tiring her far more than anything she had done that day.

"I liked going daily to the mill, but that will stop now. The office here has always been the main one, since it is in the Grand Salon that I receive important customers."

"So the business is still to come before me! If you think I'll allow it to dominate our offspring, you're entirely mistaken. After the birth you may stay in Lyons if you wish. The child shall be with me."

"Nothing shall take precedence over the baby as far as I'm concerned at any time, whether in the early months or later in life," she informed him strongly, a determined air to the uptilt of her head. "I've made arrangements accordingly. I'm sure you will recall Madame Hoinville. She has been a customer of yours for some years. I dealt with her myself during your illness not long after we were married."

"Yes, I know who you mean. What about her? Has she gone bankrupt? I heard she was in difficulties."

"So did I. That's why I went to see her. It's no fault of hers that the situation arose. Another merchant has been trying to press her out because they specialised in the same lines, and he bought the property she rented over her head and has given her notice. I offered her a post as my deputy at the mill and employment for whatever workers have remained with her. Some, I regret to say, have deserted her for the new owner of her loom-rooms."

"Did she accept?"

"Gladly. She is already installed and has secured simple accommodation for herself in the same street. I'm extremely pleased with her. Already she has shouldered much of the work for me and will continue to do so. I want our child to grow up with the devotion of both of us, and for that reason I shall come home to you in the country as soon as I have recovered from childbirth." She went on to give him more details of her plans. "I intend to have a country office as well as a city one. Once the baby is weaned, I'm hoping I need travel only twice a week to Lyons. At a time of rush orders or emergencies, or even bad weather, I may have to stay overnight here at the Rue Clémont. With time I might even close the mill in the city and reopen in the country on land not far from the silk farm. It would be a better life for everyone. Whatever happens, I promise you that we and our child will know family life together."

He was greatly mollified by her assurance, knowing she never said anything unless she meant it. He was also aware she would receive better attention from her Lyons doctor than from the elderly if kindly man near the Valmont home.

Relaxing his aggressive attitude, he raised another point of difficulty. "It won't be easy for me to get to Lyons as your time advances. You know how busy I am from May onwards, when the mulberry harvest is due and the silkworms are hatching."

"I realise that. I shall write to you and keep you informed about everything. What is the forecast for the harvest in France and elsewhere in Europe this year?"

"I haven't heard yet. My own trees are in splendid condition."

She raised her eyebrows, surprised he should not be already in possession of the facts. This was the time of year when low-quality raw silk, held back for speculation should the mulberry harvest forecast be poor, was put on the market for a quick sale. Émile always tried to be among the first to unload what he had. "Isn't the selling of your surplus silk why you went to Paris? I thought it was a visit you make every year about this time."

"It was a trifle early when I was there. I'll be going back to Paris after I leave here on Monday morning."

"A trip again so soon? You dislike travelling. Surely in Parisian silk circles the word was already around? Possibly if you had made enquiries—"

"Probably. I happened to be engaged in other business."

"Whatever was that?"

If any other woman had been his wife, he could have told her not to enquire into affairs beyond her comprehension. With Gabrielle that was impossible. In any case, she was the reason for his journey, although on no account must she suspect that. He replied evasively and yet with truth. "I went to see Uncle Joseph. We discussed some important family matters."

"How was your uncle?" She knew Émile had high expectations from him. It explained why he had gone rushing off to Paris. Uncle Joseph Valmont, a retired colonel, now in the government, was a widower with no children. Émile was his favourite nephew.

"Extremely well. I had a pleasant stay with him. He sent you his most courteous greetings."

"Thank you." She remained puzzled. It seemed extraordinary to her that Émile, who was the most businesslike of men, should have failed to take advantage of being in Paris for several days, letting slip the chance of estimating the general state of the mulberry crop through his silk contacts. However lavish the hospitality heaped upon him, sobriety and good sense were too much a part of his nature for him to forget everything to do with his business. Surely only a catastrophe of some kind could have driven such an important matter from his mind.

However, apart from his initial tension when she first came into the room, a not uncommon state of affairs between them at times, there had been nothing about him or in his conversation to give any indication he had suffered some devastating blow unknown to her. Unless—? She dismissed the thought even as it came. What had been between Nicolas and her had blossomed, thrived and been denied consummation, all without his knowledge. In the end he had not been hurt. She was thankful for that. She made a quick movement with her hands as if to erase the weight of anguish that crushed her heart at any thought of Nicolas. It was hard to keep images of him at bay. He was always with her.

"I would have tried to get home earlier this evening if I had known you would be here. I was looking over patterns of the exhibits for the Leipzig trade fair at Easter."

"Who is to represent you since you're unable to go yourself?" He breathed easier now that Gabrielle had ended her close questioning.

"Henri and Marcel."

Behind his back, Émile flexed the hand that had struck her brother. His fingers felt stiff. "The more I see of Henri the less I like him. Maybe you were right after all to hold on to Maison Roche as you have done."

She was astounded. Not since the occasion when he had backed her at the reading of her father's will had she been able to look for such support from him. "I can't tell you how much it means to me to hear you say so."

He took her by the hands and drew her to her feet beside him. "My dear, you have made me the happiest man in the world today." His arms encircled her lightly as she stood with her hands folded across her chest. "If it's right for your own good to remain in Lyons for the rest of your pregnancy, so be it. All I want is for you to be safely delivered of a healthy baby. I ask for no more."

He meant every word. By comparison her stubbornness, her un-wifely flouting of his wishes, her aggravating dedication to silk and her sundry other faults, all paled before the fact of her being his and her womb holding his child. Admittedly she might have teetered before temptation, but that was over now. It was what many an older husband had had to face, especially in a marriage of convenience, and he had come out of it far better than most, with his wife's virtue nearly intact and almost no damage done. He knew her well enough to judge she would never have played a double game with him. His only fear all along had been that love for Devaux would bring her to a decision to break from the bonds of their marriage. Now that danger was past. He did not believe such a crisis would ever arise again. "You are everything to me, my dear. You and the baby that is to come. I pray we shall have a son."

She was touched that he should follow up his shift of attitude towards her business involvements with this show of tenderness. Again she was glad he had remained in ignorance of her love for Nicolas and that she had caused him no suffering. It was her only comfort. Tears were never far from her since she and Nicolas had parted. They threatened to overwhelm her at the most unlikely moments, and over and over again she had had to battle to keep them at bay. If she began to weep she might never stop. Although that was an absurd fear, it had helped to keep her feelings locked away inside her. She could barely trust herself to speak at the present moment. Briefly she rested a hand on his arm.

"That is my hope too." With effort, her voice strengthened in a need to get away before more was said. "It's time I went to change for dinner."

He stepped aside to let her pass. Her smile was shadowy and wan. She went quietly from the room. Left on his own, Émile crossed over to pour himself a glass of wine from the decanter that stood where Henri had set it down on a side table. He took a sip and held the glass thoughtfully, his mind elsewhere. All was well that ended well, or so it was said. In Paris, Uncle Joseph had welcomed his unannounced arrival with the quiet demeanour that matched his own, the warmth of welcome subdued but not less genuine or deeply felt for all that. More like his uncle than his own father, both in temperament and looks, Émile had always found Joseph to be the one person able to understand him without questioning, the only member of his family ever to approve, and not condemn, the reserve that in his childhood and early adolescence had kept him apart from others of the same age. Now here he was, over forty, and as much in need of his uncle's compliance as he had been at twenty, when he had desperately wanted an introduction to a girl of a well-to-do Parisian family whose name he could not now remember. When it had come to nothing, as everyone but himself had been able to foresee, it was Joseph who found an older woman to console and comfort him. When eventually he left Paris, he had loved her more than the girl, but it had been a sophisticated parting with no heartbreak, at least not on his side. After that he had not loved again until Gabrielle came into his range of vision.

Joseph had not probed or questioned him as to why he had come to Paris so unexpectedly, but after dinner, when with glasses of cognac the two of them had been seated opposite each other in winged chairs by the fire, mementoes and regalia from the days of Joseph's active service adorning the walls, Émile had brought up the subject of the recall of trained officers to the colours. He did not have to say very much before Joseph asked a question that showed he had fully grasped the situation.

"What is the name of this civilian who would best serve France by being back in uniform while at the same time being far away from you and yours?"

"Nicolas Devaux."

"Do you know with which regiment he served?"

"I've no idea."

"No matter. I shall be at the École Militaire tomorrow. I'll look up his records. Now what about a little more cognac, nephew?"

There was some delay in obtaining the information. The Emperor summoned Joseph and others with military experience to a series of meetings, and the visit to the École Militaire was postponed. Émile felt unable to leave Paris until he could be sure that what he wanted had been accomplished. Eventually Joseph sent for the necessary files and confirmed the matter. Strings had been pulled and influence used. A certain cavalry officer, destined for recall only at a time of national emergency, would in due course be receiving the papers that would cut him off from civilian life for a number of years.

Now, this evening, Henri had conveyed the news he had awaited. Devaux had left Lyons, once more in the service of his country. A burning log on the fire threatened to fall from the grate, and Émile gave it a thrust back with the toe of his shoe, causing it to shower sparks like a miniature salvo. It gave him no satisfaction to have interfered in the course of another man's life, but no other solution had presented itself to him. He himself had a pistol eye as keen as an eagle's, but to have called Devaux out to wound or kill him would have alienated Gabrielle's affections completely. Admittedly, Devaux might easily have wounded him, perhaps fatally, but either way Gabrielle's sympathies would have been with the man she loved most and the result would have been the same. It was that certainty more than anything else that had made him decide to remove Devaux from the scene by a more devious means.

In the Old Testament, David had used the same method to be rid of Bathsheba's husband, sending him to the forefront of the battle where his fate lay in the enemy's hands. In Émile's youth, when the principles of honour and integrity were being instilled in him, he had taken a poor view of King David's action. Now he comprehended more fully than ever before that David had been moved by the same fear of alienating the woman he loved by personal violence against the man in question. It made neither his own act of deception nor the great David's any more commendable. He half despised himself for it, and yet he would have done it all over again.

The sudden crack of the wineglass stem startled him. He had not realised how he had been clenching it under the pressure of his thoughts. Blood trickled down his wrist and into his sleeve.

At bedtime Gabrielle re-dressed his hand, for the wound had bled freely. He sat on the edge of the bed as she stood before him in her night-gown, her hair loosened and hanging down her back like a light-flecked cloud, while her careful fingers wrapped the strip of clean linen across his palm. He studied her face as she concentrated wholly on her task. Her eyes were serious and dark with their own secret troubles that she would never share with him, her lips moist and slightly parted with a vulnerable softness to them, and her skin had a new and delicate peach-bloom that came from the changes taking place in her womb. Momentarily it did not matter to him whether she loved him or not. She was his. She had not left his side. He saw that as a renewal of commitment and was curiously content.

"There," she said, trimming off the end of the linen ties with a pair of scissors. "That's done."

"And well done, too. I thank you." He caught her wrists when she would have moved away from the bedside, but at the bleak look that fell across her face he released her again, seeking to reassure her. "You must sleep now. I don't want to see you looking so tired in the morning."

She delayed a long time before she came to bed, almost as if she wanted to be certain he slept before she took her place beside him. He heard the swish and crackle of her hair under the brush as she went far past the usual number of strokes, and afterwards it was almost as though she might be just sitting and thinking over events of the present or the past while gazing unseeingly into her looking-glass.

He was dozing, lying on his side, when she folded back the covers to slide in beside him, pausing only to blow out the candle-lamp before settling down, leaving a space of a few inches between them. Out of consideration he let her think he slept already, but the evening had been a traumatic one for him too, and sleep continued to elude him. Gradually he became aware that she was crying silently, feeling a faint vibration to the bed from her smothered sobs. He raised himself up and saw with eyes adjusted to the darkness that she was lying curled away from him, her arms over her head in total dejection.

"Gabrielle," he said softly in concern, putting a hand on her shaking shoulder, "nothing in the world should make you cry like this."

A tortured sob broke from her throat with as much pain in it as if her heart had broken at the same time. He turned her towards him and gathered her into his arms like a child. Almost in a frenzy she clung to him.

"Help me, Émile! For mercy's sake, help me to go on living!"

He had never heard such tormented despair and guessed it had been building up in her over the past days. The terrible sobs racked her without respite, and her tears soaked his night-shirt across the shoulder until it struck chill against his flesh in the night air. Not once did he question her. He had made up his mind that later he would let her think he had supposed it to be a sudden dread of the actual childbirth that had caused her to give way to such an emotional outpouring. There were pregnant women who could not rid themselves of fear of the time of being brought to bed, for the hazards were great even for the healthiest and tragedies were not uncommon. Although it was completely out of character for Gabrielle to face the birth with anything but courage, he was sure she would welcome a lack of explanations when he assured her that he understood that pregnant women were prone to irrational behaviour at times. It would be an illusion between them that he must foster and maintain for her sake and his own. It was the only way they could go on together, for the truth would create an irreparable breach between them.

With every sob that tore agonisingly out of her, his loathing of Devaux grew. Any flicker of conscience he had had about what he had done vanished completely. For the first time he wanted Devaux dead. Struck from the saddle and spread-eagled with a British sword quivering in his chest. Blown to pieces by cannon-fire, with no trace remaining. Ambushed by Spanish guerrillas with a bullet to the head. He had not known that he was capable of such hatred towards another human being. It was akin to the blackness of mood that dragged him down from time to time and soured all life until he broke free of it again. The difference was that he wanted to harbour this hatred.

Long after Gabrielle slept from exhaustion, still lodged against him, he continued to hold her, his hand cupping her head, her hair lying like silk over his spread fingers.

Although afterwards he referred to that night only once, he was to remember every detail of it as vividly as did Gabrielle. For her it had been a last farewell to the love of her life. Her terrible sorrow had overcome her like a tidal wave, taking its toll, and there had been nothing she could do to hold it back. She would go on loving Nicolas to the day she died, but she had accepted at last that all was at an end between them. She wished that Émile's kindness, shown when she had never needed the support of a fellow human being more, could have sparked off a similar love for him. Unfortunately life was not like that. He would remain the dear friend to whom she had turned instinctively. Perhaps that was the kind of love that came to most people. She had been both blessed and cursed by a passion that would remain in her heart always.

Henri suffered more from his bitten tongue than from the swelling on his face. When he and Gabrielle met together for a short business discussion on Monday morning, she gave him a sympathetic glance. "Poor Henri. You shouldn't try to talk much for a day or two." She took some papers into her hand. "Before we discuss these matters, I've something to tell you."

The news of her pregnancy came as less of a shock than it would have done when he had cherished the hope of establishing some sort of legal hold on Roche silk through his unborn child. In fact, since that was now out of the question, he decided optimistically that Gabrielle's hold on the business would be eased after her confinement and he might yet discover a loophole of some kind. He could foresee being able to take advantage of business opportunities in her absence much as he had done when their father had lessened his vigilance in old age.

"You must leave as much work as possible to me," he said affably to her.

She eyed him shrewdly. "That's amiable of you, Henri, but I want you to carry on as you are now along your own line in the business."

She was not deceived by his shrug of acceptance or the casual smile attempted by his grotesquely swollen lips.

In April there was a royal wedding. The Emperor married Princess Marie-Louise of Austria. By the marriage the imperial seal was set firmly across that country, which was settling down at last after its final defeat at the battle of Wagram, whatever the feelings of the people might be. It was in France that unrest was brewing. The Emperor had his enemies among his own countrymen, and the political undercurrents were having an increasingly bad effect on the financial state of the country. Industry and every aspect of business were being affected, and Gabrielle and other silk merchants in Lyons began to fear for their markets.

Not long after she had given up going to the mill and had established a messenger service between Madame Hoinville and herself, Gaston came to see her one morning in her office. She had had a chaise longue moved in there, for her doctor had insisted she rest as much as possible throughout her pregnancy and she saw no reason why she should not combine mental activity with enforced immobility.

"I've something to show you, madame." He looked thoroughly pleased with himself. "It's in the courtyard. Could you come and see what I've found?"

"That sounds most intriguing," she said, smiling as she replaced the pen she was holding in a tray on the lady's correspondence desk-box that she had on her lap. He lifted it away from her and set it aside. She picked up her shawl as she went with him to see what he had discovered. As they came out of the house she gave a laugh of surprise. Standing in the middle of the courtyard with paintwork washed and brasswork polished was a sedan chair, its panels painted with pastoral scenes. "Wherever did you find it?" she exclaimed, opening the door to peep inside. As might be expected of anything belonging to a silk family, the seat was upholstered in rich brocade, the silver threads tarnished, but the pattern of roses undiminished and in good repair.

"In the stable loft under thick dust and an old cover. I thought you could use it whenever you want a gentle ride somewhere."

She was amused. Sedan chairs were a thing of the past. She could not remember having seen one since her childhood. The last of them had virtually vanished with the Revolution, for it had not been in the spirit of liberty that two men should be beasts of burden to another.

"Who would carry me?"

"I'll take the front of the poles and one of the grooms, a strong lad, has volunteered to take those at the rear. What do you say, madame? Is there anywhere you would like to be taken now?"

"What if either of you should stumble?" she queried, amused.

"Not with these." He looked down at his large feet with a hearty chuckle. "The groom's are no smaller. Well, madame? Where is it to be?"

She shook her head regretfully. "Nowhere today. I have to obey my doctor's orders and complete my rest period. Perhaps tomorrow I could take a little ride somewhere with his permission."

The doctor gave it. He had himself ridden in a sedan chair in his youth and knew that with two careful carriers a smooth ride was ensured. "But not to the mill," he warned sternly. "If you step inside there it would be difficult for you to leave again. Pay a few social calls. Visit your friends. I want you to concentrate on pleasant matters. That will help to keep you serene and ensure a contented baby when your time comes."

The sedan chair was waiting for her next morning, Gaston and the groom ready for the outing in their best coats. She seated herself. When the door was closed she was conscious of a slightly dusty and aromatic aroma like that of the petals of an old pot-pourri when stirred with a finger. She had expected the sedan to lurch as the men lifted it up at either end by the poles slotted along the outside. Instead it was a smooth lift, the two of them having practised at raising it together at Gaston's word of command, and she was borne comfortably out of the gates with none of the jerking or tossing that came from carriage wheels bounding over cobbled surfaces.

They met with some stares. People came to doorways to watch them go by, and a few impudent urchins came running in their wake until Gaston and the groom rested the sedan in order to drive them off.

She had chosen to go to the warehouse. Perhaps it was not what the doctor would have envisaged as the venue for her first outing in her new transport. Nevertheless, she always liked visiting the warehouse and she wanted to double-check on her remaining stocks of raw silk and to see where space was being cleared for new supplies later in the year.

All met with her satisfaction. Her alert glances went everywhere. She noticed that the linen cover of a bale was split, revealing hanks of dyed raw silk in the exotic hues of a peacock's neck. "See that this cover is replaced," she instructed the foreman in attendance there. Before leaving the bale, she drew one of the lustrous threads over her finger like a ring. She thought once again how miraculous it was that something so delicate and fine in appearance should be possessed of a breaking strength three times greater than any rod of steel measured to the same weight and length.

In another part of the warehouse she watched the despatching of some finished lengths of brocade, each rolled upon an individual wooden rod within the stout protective covers into which they had been stitched after going through the inspection room in her own house. Two women came daily to the Rue Clémont to lay the rolls in fine white paper before making them ready for despatch to the warehouse and thence far afield. The silk industry covered a wide range of workers, and all of them would suffer if it was hit by a slump. As she left the warehouse to take her seat in the sedan chair again, she realised how much she was pinning her hopes on the forthcoming Easter trade fair at Leipzig to ensure sufficient orders to keep her looms and her workers busy.

The sedan chair proved to be an invaluable mode of transport for her. It enabled her to attend public meetings of the Chamber of Commerce which she would otherwise have missed, and kept her abreast of all that was happening at first hand. One evening a vote was taken to send a delegation to the Emperor, banking on his interest in Lyons, to ask that the tariffs imposed on goods sold to Germany be lifted to aid Lyonnais silk merchants and other business men attending the forthcoming trade fair. There was intense disappointment when the Emperor rejected the request, reminding the delegation sharply that he had done much to help Lyons in the past and that it would not be fair to other cities to single them out for favours at the present time.

Émile came to the Rue Clémont for Easter. The weather was unusually warm and sunny, the sky taut and blue as warped silk. He arranged a boat trip on the river for Gabrielle, and Hélène and Juliette joined them for a picnic away from the city on a grassy bank. It helped Gabrielle to stop wondering how Henri and Marcel were progressing in Leipzig and it was a carefree day. Juliette's excitement over the whole event was infectious.

"Play hide-and-seek with me," she implored Émile when the picnic was over. Like most fatherless children, she was eager for adult male companionship. Unable to get it from Henri, who always brushed her aside, she was greatly attached to Émile, who was kindly and tolerant towards her.

"Very well," he agreed. "You and your *maman* shall hide first and I will count to ten. We'll leave your Aunt Gabrielle to rest in the shade of the trees."

Hélène did not join the game for long, finding it somewhat hectic. As she returned across the grass to where Gabrielle reclined against cushions, she fanned herself laughingly with a large leaf. Gabrielle thought how young and pretty she looked with her cheeks flushed from exertion and strands of hair awry. Not for the first time she wished her sister-in-law would dispense with her mourning black. It was time to let Jules rest and for Hélène to give her heart a chance to heal.

"Ah, that's better," Hélène said thankfully, sinking down onto a corner of the rug on which Gabrielle was lying and helping herself to some of the spare cushions. "Who would have thought it could be so warm at this time of year? It's nicer than summer. There are no insects to sting."

"I agree." After they had talked for a while, watching the glittering river flow past, a faint heat haze misting the hues of the boats that went by on both business and pleasure, Gabrielle brought up the subject of Hélène's mourning, broaching it tactfully.

Hélène heard her out, looking down at a wild flower she had plucked from the grass. She touched the small white petals with a delicate finger tip. "When I feel the time is right I shall put aside my black garments. To be frank, I don't think that will ever be. Please don't let us discuss it any more."

Gabrielle understood. It was as she had already believed. Hélène's mourning had nothing to do with any outward show of bereavement. It was her own private link with the man she still loved. It brought home to Gabrielle that she herself had no link at all with the living, breathing man who had gone from her life.

When Henri returned from Leipzig his conceit was enormous. Contrary to earlier fears, German customers failed to be deterred by the heavy duty on imported goods imposed on them by their new Emperor and vied with each other in placing their orders, eager to be handling French silk once again. All the Lyonnais silk merchants had returned with enough foreign orders between them to sustain the industry throughout any ups and downs of the home market. Gabrielle was highly relieved. Although Henri claimed all the credit for the full order-book, Marcel informed her that her beautiful silks had virtually sold themselves. The interest had been tremendous. She was able to let her earlier anxiety about the state of *La Grand Fabrique* fade away. Everything looked promising and even Émile expected one of the best mulberry harvests for years.

Then, like a warning knell at the beginning of May, there was news from Naples. A freak frost had killed the silkworms and damaged nearly all the mulberry trees. At the same time it began to rain throughout the whole of middle and southern France.

In Lyons the warm weather of Easter seemed to belong to another age. The central gutters of the streets ran like rivers and spilled over into filthy, swirling lakes when rubbish blocked the drains. Pedestrians conformed to a pattern of walking with their heads down against the continuing downpour. Now and again it did seem as if the weather might ease and briefly the clouds would thin out, only to press together again to let the rain come down worse than ever, reaching torrential proportions that kept the mulberry trees soaked and made harvesting impossible. Silkworms were hatching and there was almost nothing to meet their voracious appetites. The water-level of the Rhône and the

Saône rose ominously, and before long the Rhône valley was flooded as the river went into spate. Still the rain descended, and not only in France. Most of Europe began to suffer from the same bad weather and news came that in Turin the flooding had washed away a whole area of silk farming.

The clatter of a carriage arriving in haste took Gabrielle to her window one morning in time to see Émile fling himself from it and run up the steps into the house. She hurried to meet him, sure it must be a matter of vital importance to have brought him to the city in the middle of the week. One look at his haggard face as he shouldered off his rain-spattered coat in the hall prepared her for bad tidings.

"Let us go to the Blue Salon," she said, leading the way. As he accompanied her the gloom of his dark mood seemed to emanate from him like the dankness of the rain itself.

"It's disaster!" he exclaimed as soon as the door was closed after them. "The harvest is a total loss." He threw up his hands expressively and let them fall to his sides. "The mulberry trees have been attacked by a particularly deadly blight."

"Oh, no," she breathed in dismay. It was a catastrophe dreaded by every silk farmer. The exceptionally bad weather must have created the right conditions for it to take hold. "What will you do? Is there a chance to ship in leaves from elsewhere?"

His face was stark. "You don't understand. It is not only my trees. The blight is developing everywhere."

She sank down onto a chair, stunned by this major catastrophe. "Are you sure?"

He nodded despairingly, unable to stand still under the weight of the blow that had befallen him. The entire year was destined to be a terrible loss. Everything would have to be built up again from scratch. "The trees had been in such a marvellous condition that I thought they would withstand anything. Then I saw the first warning signs yesterday. I studied this blight in my early days and I know more about it than most. I said nothing to anyone but took my horse to ride out to other farms and down into Provence. It took me all day and all night. I examined the leaves on several silk farms by lantern light, unbeknown to the owners. Where my trees were already in the grip of the blight, the rest were showing the barely discernible signs that I recognised from my own special experience. It's only a matter of a day or two now, or even hours, before the news breaks that there'll be no mulberry harvest in France this year. I came to warn you. You must buy whatever raw silk you can lay your hands on while you have a head start. The brokers are going to have a field day. Anything left from last season will reach exorbitant prices in no time at all."

Her mind was racing. The trust would release the money she needed. She must contact her lawyers, the Banque Guerin à Lyons, disperse agents to buy on her behalf, and, not least of all, she would send Hélène across the city on a special mission. "I'll act at once!"

Springing to her feet too hastily, she swayed and almost fell. Émile darted forward to catch her in his supporting arms. "Not so fast! Remember your condition."

She took a deep breath and was in control of herself again. "I am remembering it. I'm also thinking of my weavers, their families and their unborn babies. Whatever happens, you and I will not go hungry, but if I fail to secure the raw silk I need they may starve."

The prospect haunted her as from her office during the next hour she despatched servants with written messages, aided by Henri, who was moving more quickly under this threat of financial loss to Maison Roche than he had done for anything else for a long time. The repercussions from the failure of the Tree of Gold would be devastating to Lyons. Already mulberry pickers and others hoping for seasonal work in sericulture had been unable to earn anything, so far unaware that it was not just a delay through the weather that was keeping them from the money they needed but was destined to be a far more permanent state of affairs.

Émile, who had left again, was going to lay off almost his entire silk-farm force as soon as the secret about the harvest was out. The throwsters, spinners and dyers would be the next to suffer hardship. Afterwards the entire weaving community would face lack of work. Although Maison Roche was in a position to weather the storm, not all the silk merchants would be so fortunate and bankruptcies were inevitable. It was as if the life-blood of Lyons was in danger of drying up.

At the first chance she left her office to go in search of Hélène. She found her in the kitchen, supervising the arrangements for dinner that night, guests being expected. By the pantry door, out of earshot of anyone else, Gabrielle told her what had happened and explained what she wanted her to do.

Hélène, alternately dismayed by the bad news and curious about the errand on which she was being sent, nodded briskly. "I'll leave now on foot. In that way I'll draw less notice to myself than by arriving at my destination in a Roche carriage."

"I thank you." Gabrielle embraced her. "You're the only one I could ask to do this for me. Now I must get back to my desk."

She returned to her office only minutes before her lawyers and a representative of the Banque Guerin were announced, having arrived at almost the same time in response to her urgent messages. They arranged everything to her satisfaction. Letters of credit were drawn up for her agents, who would be going out of Lyons as soon as the papers were in their hands, riding on their mission with the promise of a bonus for every bale of raw silk they were able to bring in. Henri also received the necessary authority to buy. As the lawyers and the bank representative departed, Henri came downstairs ready to leave for Genoa, where he had personal contacts and could hope for privileged treatment in ensuring supplies from the new season's harvest. Although Genoa had had plenty of rain, it had fared better than Turin and Henri expected to find it basking in sunshine when he arrived.

"Good luck, Henri," she said.

"Leave it to me," he replied complacently. "Father and I used to buy from this particular grower before you took charge and refused to use anything but French raw silk."

"You bought because it was cheaper than supplies from France in the days before Bonaparte put heavy tariffs on foreign imports to protect Lyons and give an advantage to its silk trade."

"I'm not disputing that. All I'm saying is that the silk family I'll be dealing with won't have forgotten I was once a good customer. In addition they'll be looking for a renewal of trade."

"I won't forget those who sell to us in these troubled times."

As he was driven away from the house, Henri looked forward to this return to Genoa. He had once been attracted to one of the daughters of the family he was to visit and she to him. She was now a widowed matriarch in command of the silk farm, much as his sister held sway over Roche silk. He was sure the lady in question would be willing to let him have whatever he wanted; in days gone by she had done so in a more intimate sphere.

Hélène was overtaken by his carriage and the wheels splashed her as they rolled by. She thought it unlikely that her brother-in-law, sitting back in comfort, would have sighted her, although her being out on foot would not have surprised him since she was known to enjoy walking, even in the rain. It was a strange task on which she had been sent. She could not deny she felt a little timorous about it, not knowing what kind of reception she might receive at the Devaux mill to which she was bound. If she had needed proof of Gabrielle's feelings for Nicolas Devaux, she had it now. Gabrielle had never confided in her about Nicolas's departure. She had heard of it through friends, the information dropped in casual confirmation. It explained the haunted look that showed in Gabrielle's eyes at times when her thoughts were far away.

The rumble of the looms as she drew near the mill told her that Nicolas's absence had made no difference to the pace of work going on there. She chose to go to the street door of the house to make her call and banged the heavy knocker. A maidservant answered.

"I want to see Monsieur Piat at once. Please tell him it's an urgent matter."

"Yes, madame. Your name, please."

"I will give it only to Monsieur Piat."

She had only a few minutes to wait until he came through a door which gave her a glimpse of a small courtyard and the mill beyond before he closed it after him. He was tallish, with light brown hair brindled with grey, his face thin and severe, but not unkindly, his greyish eyes honest and clear, his mouth wide, thin-lipped and incisive. She judged him to be about forty years old; his whole bearing was authoritative and purposeful. As he approached her she spoke out firmly, not wanting to be at a disadvantage by showing the nervousness she felt.

"I'm Hélène Roche, sister-in-law to Madame Gabrielle Valmont, who is acquainted with Monsieur Devaux. I have to speak to you in complete confidence."

"Please come this way, madame." He showed her into a study and pushed forward a chair for her before seating himself. "Now what did you wish to speak to me about?"

"First of all, I want your word that Monsieur Devaux will never know that I was here today at my sister-in-law's instigation."

"My employer is now Captain Devaux of the *chasseurs à cheval*. I'm entirely responsible for his interests while he is away and I can't undertake to give any such assurance until I know what it is you have to tell me."

She nodded nervously, linking her fingers tightly in her lap. "I came entirely with my sister-in-law's goodwill. She wanted me to give you warning that there will be little or no mulberry harvest in the *départements* of Rhône and Provence this year. A terrible blight has taken hold everywhere."

He frowned uncertainly. "Are you sure? How can you be?"

She told him everything that Gabrielle had explained to her. Then, fearing he might be wary through whatever he had heard about the Roche-Devaux feud, she sought to emphasise the importance of her message. "My sister-in-law doesn't want you to lose the chance of buying raw silk on Monsieur—er—Captain Devaux's behalf while there is still time. Please believe me and act now! If you don't, your looms will be silent next winter."

He looked surprised that she should think he would doubt her. "I don't disbelieve you. Fortunately the problem is less serious for the Devaux mill than it will be for others. My employer was foresighted enough to cover any contingency that might occur during his indefinite absence by buying all the raw silk he could get hold of before he left Lyons to rejoin his regiment. When he ran out of time I completed the task for him. It was a most fortuitous time to be buying, because many silk farmers were willing to let surplus stocks go at a reasonable return instead of risking their chances in speculation later. I have a year's supply of raw silk in hand."

Her sweet smile broke through, her whole expression lifting. "I'm so glad to hear that."

He smiled with her, satisfied that this strange little interview should have turned out so well. "Please thank Madame Valmont on my behalf for her concern."

Hélène hesitated and then leaned forward in appeal. "There's no reason for you now to mention anything of this visit to Captain Devaux, is there? I don't fully understand the circumstances, but I think my sister-in-law didn't want him to feel under any obligation to her. She was most insistent that he should never discover who let you know about the blight-stricken mulberry trees before it became general knowledge."

He answered at once. "I'll say nothing as there is nothing to tell. Nevertheless, I know how much he would have appreciated Madame Valmont's would-be timely action."

Hélène sank back in her chair, thankful that she had secured the promise that Gabrielle wanted. "How is he? Have you heard from him?"

"I had one letter brought by a wounded comrade-in-arms on returning home. Otherwise I don't suppose I would have received it. According to this officer, communications are extremely tenuous, and even military despatches don't always get through. Captain Devaux was well when he wrote, more concerned about the mill than about himself. He was one of over three hundred thousand men sent to reinforce the companies already in the Peninsula, and he had been in time to enter the first resurgence of fighting after the winter lull."

"Did he say where he was?"

"He had written 'Astorga' at the head of the letter and the date was March. It took four weeks to reach me."

"I hope he continues to be safe," she said fervently. Then, realising it was time she left, she stood up with neatness that was natural to her. "I mustn't take up any more of your time. I'm sure you're busy."

"It's been a pleasure to make your acquaintance." He moved to the door with her and reached in front to open it. "I've never met your husband, although I saw him at the Leipzig trade fair."

Her eyes went stark. It knifed her when someone assumed Jules was still living. "That was my brother-in-law you saw. Henri Roche. My husband died at Austerlitz."

It was then he realised that beneath the black cape her dress, shoes and gloves were all in the colour of bereavement. He was dismayed that he had forgotten there was a young widow at the Rue Clémont. Having supposed her to be Henri Roche's wife, he had been intrigued ever since she had announced the purpose of her visit that she and her sister-in-law should be conspirators in this act of warning Nicolas Devaux. His employer had talked freely of the animosity he felt towards Henri Roche and how the feud still lingered on between them. One of his last instructions before departure had been to be continually on guard against any unexpected trickery from Henri Roche.

"My condolences, madame," he said to Hélène, regarding her in a new and compassionate light. "It was thoughtless of me not to have noticed you were in mourning. I lost my beloved wife, Elyanne, not long before I came to Lyons. I'm afraid that I unwittingly caused you some distress."

His voice was deep with sympathy and she felt a sudden empathy with this man who had been through the same heart-tearing loss. "I know you didn't mean to. I'm still caught unawares at times as I'm sure you are too."

"I am indeed, although here in Lyons nobody knew her and I'm spared the crass blundering that I've just committed myself."

She gave a little shake of the head. "Please think no more about it. Do you have children, Monsieur Piat?"

"No, I haven't. It was a source of much disappointment to my wife and myself. Are you more fortunate?"

"I have a daughter, Juliette. She is five years old."

"A delightful age. She must be a great comfort to you."

"She is indeed. We have such fun together." She wanted to hear that his life was mending again. "Have you settled down in Lyons? Do you like our city?"

"Very much. I'm still exploring. Do sit down again if you can spare the time. Are you Lyonnais by birth?"

She had half expected him to ask her about the feud, but even after they had chatted for a while he did not mention it. Instead she went on to tell him about places of interest in the city and its environs that he had yet to see. The atmosphere between them became more and more relaxed. In turn he told her about his life in Paris and how he had worked there for Nicolas Devaux. This led to talk of his home and inevitably to his wife again. He spoke of how courageous she had been throughout her final illness.

"Elyanne insisted I should never wear mourning for her after the funeral was over. She wanted me to look to the future and not cling to the past. I need hardly say that doesn't mean I remember her the less."

"I realise that. She must have been an exceptional person."

"She was all that you say."

Her brows drew together in a thoughtful little frown. "I don't suppose Jules would have wanted me to wear extended mourning. Perhaps he would have told me that if I could have shared his last days with him. Yet it is a comfort to me."

"A shield, perhaps?"

He had startled her and he saw it. She had caught her breath at his perceptiveness. It was something she had wondered about herself, but this was the first time anyone had brought her face to face with the truth. In a cocoon of mourning she was isolated, protected from the outside world, immune to further emotional involvement, safe in a past love from any fresh hurt from any direction that the future might otherwise bring to her. "Perhaps," she evaded shakily. "I really don't know why I'm talking about Jules to you. My grief is something I always keep to myself."

"At times I'm too forthright. I hope I didn't speak out of turn."

She made a quick gesture of reassurance. "Not at all."

"If it is any consolation to you, I have never talked to anyone about my bereavement until today."

Her nod showed that she understood fully how the pain could be too great for speech. She spoke wonderingly. "Isn't it strange? I came here this morning to help you and instead I believe you have helped me."

"I prefer to think that we have helped each other."

The long look they exchanged seemed to come to each of them from far away. Once more she rose to leave and she gave her hand in farewell, still bewildered that this meeting should have taken such an unexpected turn. "I wish you well with the Devaux mill through times ahead, Monsieur Piat."

"Thank you, Madame Roche. I hope we shall meet again before long."

As she turned homeward, thinking deeply over all that had been said, she half expected to be met by the shouts of the news-sheet vendors. The first general announcement of the failure of the Tree of Gold harvest would come from them. As yet they were silent.

Gabrielle was not at home when Hélène returned. Gaston and the groom had conveyed her in her sedan to the mill, where she had taken Madame Hoinville into her confidence about the crisis and instructed that additional padlocks be installed and security tightened to avoid any breaking in by thieves intent on stealing stocks of raw silk, which overnight would become a highly saleable commodity.

Afterwards she had gone to the warehouse and made a similar check, alerting her man in charge to be particularly vigilant, although not telling him why. He would find out soon enough. While there, she remembered the bales of hanks she had once discovered, evidence of Henri's pilfering. Using her keys, she found they had gone. She was not surprised.

Back at the Rue Clémont, she tossed off her coat and went straight to Hélène's salon on one of the upper floors where sunshine always seemed to linger in the yellow and white décor even when the rain was splashing against the windows as it was today. Hélène had changed into a dry gown and shoes, but her hair was still damp where the rain had penetrated the hood of her cape and it clung to her head like a shining cap. A steaming pot of hot chocolate with two cups was ready on a tray.

"Come and sit down," she invited eagerly, taking up one of the cups to pour the chocolate into it. "I've much to tell you. How did everything go with you?"

"All was satisfactory." Gabrielle took the cup handed to her. "What of Nicolas? Did you hear news of him? How will it go with his mill?"

Hélène gave her all the details, noticing how her cheeks drew in and her lids lowered as she heard that Nicolas was safe and well. Learning that he had a store-room full of raw silk was obviously a tremendous relief to her.

"I wouldn't have wanted to know his looms were idle while I had yarn for mine," was the only comment she made.

In her own room, lying back on her bed with an arm under her head, Gabrielle marvelled that Nicolas should have shown such foresight in stocking his store-rooms to cover any emergency. The financial outlay would have been tremendous. It was her guess that he must have borrowed heavily and probably mortgaged his property as well. That was a great risk, too, but he must be certain of Monsieur Piat's ability to manage the mill and the whole business just as he would have done. She would have liked to meet the man. Hélène had spoken well of him.

10

In the morning the news broke. Only the Roche and Devaux houses remained detached from the turmoil of activity that ran through the city. Silk merchants bid against each other at a cutthroat level for whatever raw silk was still available. The outlook was bleak. The British blockade of all Napoleonic ports meant that little raw silk would slip in from the Far East and India. Many mill-owners and those whose livelihood depended on a few looms foresaw closure and bankruptcy. In all, twenty-three days of rain without respite had brought as great a disaster to the Lyons silk industry as had the Revolution.

For a while the talk was all of the mulberry harvest in the mountains, which always came later and might yet ease the situation. Hopes were soon dashed when a persistent fog, unrelieved by any good weather, did its own damage and the harvest was lost. There was further consternation when a quantity of Italian raw silk, expected to be released onto the market at a more reasonable starting price, disappeared without trace before leaving its country of origin. There seemed to be no end to the chain of calamities for Lyons.

Henri returned from Genoa full of smug satisfaction. He could have told his fellow Lyonnais where the Italian silk had gone if he had chosen to solve the mystery for them. With the co-operation of his Genoan contacts, it had been smuggled out as contraband to a British ship in a Sicilian port and the transaction had lined his pockets very generously. If he had brought it back to Lyons, it would have gone to the Roche looms with no personal gain for himself. But he had not returned empty-handed. In the wake of his carriage came three wagon-loads of good raw silk under armed guard. It was immediately stored away at the Roche mill out of harm's way.

Gabrielle took stock of her situation when eventually everything her agents had managed to purchase for her was gathered in. In addition to what had been bought, she had the surplus silk that Émile had been unable to off-load on the market by being too late on his second trip to Paris, something that still puzzled her. Although it was spun silk, which has less lustre than reeled silk, being made from the unreelable inner cocoon and the waste floss around it, it would be fit for much of the more mundane work and she was grateful to Émile for letting her have it when he could have sold it exorbitantly elsewhere, except that it was not in his nature to exploit other men's misfortunes. In all, she was confident of keeping her weavers in work throughout the difficult times ahead and filling all her orders from the Leipzig trade fair, many of which called for exquisite patterns and quality and were a pleasure to produce.

News of all that had been happening in Lyons did not reach Nicolas until late summer. Very little of the mail, both that despatched and that sent from France, reached its destination. Until now he had received no correspondence at all, and he considered himself extremely lucky that a letter from Michel Piat had finally come into his hands. It had been following him around and remarkably had not been lost amid other communications or destroyed en route.

In blistering sun, his uniform jacket open and his neckcloth and shirt drenched with sweat and sticking to his body, he sought some shade in which to read it. Before seating himself on a dusty rock beneath an orange tree, he glanced about to make sure there were no scorpions around. One of the hazards of this campaign was scorpion bites, which turned putrid in the scorching weather and had caused deaths among officers and men alike even when limbs had been chopped off in an attempt to save their lives. Dysentery had proved equally fatal among countless men. He had been ill with it himself but his army servant had cured him with thick rice water, which had a foul taste he would not easily forget.

Eagerly he broke the seal on the letter and read it through. It was the first communication he had received from his manager and the number six inscribed at the beginning told him that five previous letters had gone astray. Fortunately Piat had used his sense and given a brief résumé of the points of interest written before, explaining he would continue to do this in view of what he had heard about the unreliability of mail deliveries.

Nicolas compressed his lips wryly. One of the most dangerous assignments in this war was to be involved in communications. The Spanish guerrillas and partisans, familiar with every gully and crevice and mountain slope of their own terrain, were spread out over the whole country and kept a constant watch for a lone rider or any small military party that they could wipe out, often with ferocious brutality and torture. He did not condone their hatred, but he understood it. Spain was a country rich in tradition and with a long history. What more natural than that the Spanish should resent Bonaparte's uninvited rule and want their land to themselves again, free of French dominance.

As he read on, the present tribulations of *La Grand Fabrique* seemed as far away as if they were happening on another planet. Nothing was real except the horror of the war in which he was steeped. The competing for raw silk lost all importance beside the struggle to capture a town, retake lost ground or advance with the roll and beat of drums towards a well-matched enemy in yet another battle. Only one line stood out from the letter. *I hear that Madame Valmont has secured sufficient raw silk to see her looms through the dearth.* He would have preferred no mention of her name to have been made. Desire for her shot through his loins as he remembered her in his arms under the canopy of Napoleon's tent, her beautiful breasts bared to his view, the fragrance of her skin in his nostrils and her heart beating wildly under his hand.

He folded the letter slowly. There were times when he dreamed of Gabrielle. Vivid, lustful dreams that left him dazed when he awoke to find himself far from Lyons on a makeshift bed of straw in a deserted hovel or sleeping under his cloak in the open air with a foreign sun coming up to bring another death-ridden day. At times rage filled him that she should have made the choice she did, at others bitterness overtook him with a resolve to forget her completely, to wipe her from his mind as if she had never existed, neither reaction bringing him any peace. He loved her. That was the beginning and the end of it. The cruel fact was that he would never see her again, but that was how it had to be.

If he should survive this war to return to civilian life one day, he would never again live in Lyons. He would sell the Devaux mill and reside in Paris where he would make a new beginning in business. It was his intention to give Piat the first chance to buy. Many times over the past months he wished he had done so before his departure for Spain, but everything had happened with such speed and he had been convinced that Gabrielle would come away with him. As a result, his first thought had been to protect the mill against any crisis in his absence, particularly against failure of the mulberry harvest, a prospect that had haunted his family after one bad experience and had been drummed into him since childhood. Although it was many years since it had happened, by the law of averages it had been destined to occur again and now Piat's letter had confirmed the inevitable.

"Captain Devaux! Your new mount is ready."

He looked up. Lost in thought, he had paid no attention to the sound of a horse being led towards him. A sergeant stood smartly, holding the reins. He saw at once it was a fine animal with an arched neck, an intelligent head and strong flanks. It was ready with his own saddle and saddle-cloth, which was by tradition for officers in the *chasseurs à cheval* a full leopard skin. Braided in scarlet and gold with a pleated edge of silk that was the same dark green as the regimental jacket, it was fashioned so that the head of the leopard lay above the strap looped under the horse's tail. In this case it enhanced beyond measure the splendour of the new mount and he gave a grin of pleasure as he pushed the letter inside his jacket and fastened the silver buttons.

Rising to his feet, he picked up his hat with its tall red and green plume, which he had set down beside the rock, and brushed some dust from the dark fur before putting it on and adjusting the chin strap. It gave his already considerable height even more presence, but then the purpose of a uniform was to make a soldier appear taller and broader and more awesome to the enemy. This new horse was to bear the name of Warrior, the same as that of his former mount, which had been shot from under him, leaving him to fight sabre to sabre on a sickening carpet of dead and wounded, the cries and screams of the latter terrible to him since nothing could be done for them all the time a battle raged. He clapped Warrior's well-groomed neck in admiration.

"You have found me a splendid mount, Sergeant," he said with satisfaction. "Well done."

The sergeant left. Nicolas continued to clap the horse, talking encouragingly to him. "We're going to face a lot of hard fighting, my friend. But I can tell you have a stout heart. You'll not flinch before the British musket fire. We'll see each other through. Now let us get better acquainted."

He swung himself into the saddle. There was no doubt in his mind as to what had happened to Warrior's previous rider, but that was the fortune of war. He turned the horse into what had once been the main dirt-track through the hillside village where the brigade had bivouacked for the last couple of days. It had changed hands twice before, simply because it was sited on a point of vantage important to both sides. It was a poor place, as were most of the peasant villages he had seen, and not one of the hovels had escaped damage, the inhabitants having fled long since.

Nicolas glanced about him as he rode along at a leisurely pace. Smoke rose from camp-fires where scavenged fowls, wild birds and hunks of maggoty meat turned on spits over the flames, giving a greasy aroma to the air. The army had to live off the land, and when the peasants managed to put a torch to whatever they could not carry away, hunger was added to the trials of the campaign. The soldiers encouraged dogs to attach themselves to the brigade, but their lifespan was short when food became impossible to obtain. There were always men who had become fond of the animals and could not bring themselves to eat from the cook-pot.

A strong smell of soap drifted from the laundry where soldiers' wives, and those among the lower grade of camp-followers, were washing clothes for the men and themselves; a few shirt-sleeved soldiers were engaged in the same chore. Several children around the age of three and under were running about naked while their clothes were being rinsed and dried. These toddlers were among the fittest of those born on the campaign since French troops had first invaded Portugal, the survivors of many others left buried by the wayside amid the tears of the women.

Nicolas halted Warrior quickly as a little girl darted across his path in pursuit of a home-made ball of rags. She was slightly older than the rest of the children, proof that her mother had been pregnant at the start of the campaign. Although pregnant women were forbidden to accompany their husbands on active service, many disguised their condition in their determination to be with their men. Camp-followers were a brave if motley collection of females. The army depended on their co-operation in nursing the sick and wounded. Those wives promoted to *cantinière* status were entitled to wear jackets in their husbands' regimental colours and the same plume in their bonnets. At time of battle, when thick smoke from the cannon-fire rolled down over the whole field, their task was to move among the fighting men and dispense swigs of brandy from a metal cup, the spirit drawn from a keg on the hip. It cleared the mouth and throat as well as acting as a stimulant, and the *cantinières* were a welcome sight to those half choked by black powder.

Nicolas held them in high regard as did every army man with reason to appreciate their courage. Their lot, like that of every other woman on campaign, was entirely different from that of the officers' wives, who were kept far from danger zones and enjoyed a social round in Madrid and Seville and other cities considered safe.

Riding on, Nicolas was aware of being in the vicinity of one of the latrine pits. Although distanced, it stank in the heat. It was pleasant to come again into the shade of some fragrant orange trees towards the outskirts of the village where fewer people were about and there was a sense of solitude. Somewhere near the mass of tethered horses on the far side of the village a farrier's hammer rang out on an anvil of the mobile forge. It had a pastoral sound to it, if one allowed oneself to forget that military hooves were being reshod.

He reined in when he reached the sentry outposts and rested his hands on the pommel. There was always a danger of snipers if one ventured too far. Twice he had had narrow escapes when on advance reconnaissance. In his dark green jacket with the silver frogging, clinging grey deerskin breeches and high black boots, he would be an easy target against the bleached rocks. His gaze, narrowed against the glare, travelled down the parched hillside and on across the vast, heat-baked plain to the azure ripple of mountains on the horizon. Everything was still and quiet away from the hubbub of the bivouac. Tomorrow at first light the march across the shimmering plain would begin with all the misery of choking dust, restricted drinking from canteens, weaponry that absorbed the sun's heat until it burned the hands, and flies that hovered in swarms to plague men and animals alike.

The whole Peninsula was a place of beauty and terror at the present time. The magnificence of the brilliant landscapes never failed to please his eye, as did the rich hues in the variable vegetation and the gaudy extravagance of blossoms that blazed purple, pink, crimson, orange and yellow against ancient stone walls and tumbled profusely over archways, grilled windows and ornate balconies. In contrast to these vistas were the shell-wrecked cities and villages, the carnage of battlefields where the bodies sometimes stretched for miles and there were horrific scenes of vengeance and rape that he and his fellow officers had been unable to prevent on several occasions when the men had broken open casks of wine and run drunkenly amok. The stench of death was commonplace. It was rare to breathe the pure scent of flowers without the loathsome and pervading taint.

At times of reflection he found it difficult to believe he had ever been the young hothead who had joined Bonaparte's army after he and his parents fled from Lyons at the time of the siege. Then he had had a reckless, dashing attitude to soldiering, following a leader who exuded hope for the future and the promise of a great and glorious France. His love for his country was as powerful as it had ever been, but this war had changed him in many ways. It had nothing to do with his being recalled to the colours at an inopportune time, because he had always known there was a likelihood of a renewal of service; it was the nature of the war itself that had altered his whole outlook.

The truth was, he felt degraded as a human being by this campaign. It was like no other that had ever been waged, for it was not a fight between soldiers, men trained to do their duty on selected battlefields with courage and fortitude, their honour intact. In this conflict innocent civilians, men, women and children, were caught up everywhere in the conflict, frequently in the direct firing-line, simply because the whole Spanish nation had risen up against those whom they regarded as foreign oppressors.

This war had been an uncomfortable revelation to him. Bonaparte's claim that it had been necessary to invade Portugal to close the last European ports open to British trade no longer impressed him. He had come to see that it was a ploy by which Spain could be annexed at the same time. Although he accepted without reservation that Bonaparte's masterly government had restored France to greatness, all respect he had once held for his leadership had been stripped away. He saw him now as a man intoxicated by power, ready to override the wishes of whole nations to further his empire and add to his own glorification. The principles of liberty, equality and fraternity were being dragged through the mire by the very man who had once held them up like a beacon to the world.

He kept his views to himself. To have voiced them would have brought his loyalty to the Tricolore into doubt and that was unchanged. He would do whatever he had to do and more for his country in this campaign. If it brought about his death, so be it. Grim-faced and disillusioned, he rode back through the ruins of the village.

In Lyons, Gabrielle had developed backache that morning. By mid-afternoon Émile was notified by messenger that she had gone into labour and it was no false alarm. He set off at once for the city, full of trepidation now that her time had come and certain she would be thankful to have him nearby during her ordeal.

He was not prepared for what the sight of her pain-filled eyes and attempts at a smile did to him when he reached her bedside. Immediately he was overwhelmed by a sense of helplessness and inadequacy. There was nothing he could do to ease her suffering. The atmosphere of the birth-room oppressed him. Although Hélène did not make him feel unwelcome, the midwife was showing her dislike of his presence by bustling about in a most aggressive manner, making a point of getting between him and his wife. She was tying a clean but well-worn length of knotted linen to two posts at the foot of the bed, which had the appearance of some medieval preparation for torture. Gabrielle noticed the horrified expression on his face.

"It's for me to pull on when the pains get bad," she explained, her voice faltering as a pang seized her. To his eyes it looked as if her pains had already reached that stage. Somehow he managed a few encouraging words and then Hélène tapped him on the arm.

"I think you had better leave now if you don't mind," she said tactfully.

He was relieved, although he was at a loss as to how to spend the time. For a while he wandered aimlessly about the house, looking at old portraits and landscapes without the least interest, shuddering at the cries Gabrielle was unable to suppress. Henri and Yvonne went out for the evening, she with jewels sparkling in her hair and at her throat, the two of them laughing together in a shared joke as they went downstairs. He thought them callous to be so indifferent to what was happening in the house, and his distress increased with every fresh cry that burst upon his hearing. Hélène, leaving the birth-room on an errand, sighted him sitting in a neighbouring salon with his head in his hands. She paused at the doorway.

"Go for a long walk," she advised him kindly. "I find walking beneficial at times of stress. You're doing no good here either for yourself or Gabrielle."

He obeyed her, not knowing what else to do. For a time he followed the river, going over one bridge and returning by another. Once he stopped for wine at a café and then dined at a restaurant, suddenly overcome by hunger and realising he had had nothing to eat since leaving home that morning. It was almost midnight when he arrived back in the house. As he stepped into the hall a long agonised moan came from the direction of Gabrielle's room.

"Dear God!" He was ashen. "It's not over yet."

"No, monsieur." The manservant took his hat and cane from him.

"Is the doctor here?"

"He came two hours ago. Er—your gloves, monsieur?"

"Oh, yes." Émile pulled them off and handed them to him. Cold with dread, he went into the Blue Salon to sit and wait. Half an hour later Henri and Yvonne returned and went straight upstairs. He heard them speaking to Hélène and then Henri's heavy footsteps came downstairs again.

"I've been asked to tell you it will be a while yet," Henri announced brusquely as he came into the room, "but there is nothing to worry about."

"Does it always take as long as this?" Émile asked vaguely.

"Yvonne was longer. At least you can be sure of a healthy child. Gabrielle is young and strong and, to my knowledge, never had a day's illness in her life, except a few childhood ailments of no consequence." Henri glanced at the clock. "Well, I'm off to bed. You should take a nap on the sofa if you don't want to use the bedroom that's been prepared for you." He was on the point of suggesting that Émile should indulge in a hefty measure of cognac but decided against it. Last time he had offered his brother-in-law a drink there had been an unpleasant scene afterwards. It still rankled. "Good night to you."

It was the longest night Émile had ever known. The sounds of Gabrielle's torment made him weep. Even Yvonne was unable to sleep. She came downstairs in a peignoir and silken slippers.

"I've ordered some hot chocolate to be brought to us," she said, lifting the lid of a coffee-pot that had been served earlier to him and seeing it was barely touched and cold.

Although he had always considered Yvonne to be frivolous and superficial, selfishly concerned with her own well-being, he revised his opinion somewhat in the light of her coming downstairs to keep vigil with him at this dreadful time. As they drank the chocolate, which was too sweet for his astringent taste, her conversation kept away from the subject of Gabrielle's labour and helped to distract his mind to some degree from the room upstairs. After half an hour, she shattered his illusions in thinking she had come downstairs especially to keep him company.

"Chocolate always makes me sleepy," she said, disguising an enormous yawn behind a refined hand. "It's my favourite cure for insomnia. I'm going back to bed before the effects wear off and I start listening again to Henri's snores and Gabrielle's—" She broke off quickly at the change of expression in his face. "Good night, Émile. I hope there's good news in the morning."

He decided he detested her as much as her husband. "Isn't there anything you could do to help those in the birth-room?" he asked her harshly.

She blinked. "I'm no use when anyone is in pain. I'm too sensitive. Gabrielle is in good hands. You've nothing to be concerned about. Try to get some sleep yourself."

To his shame he did sleep, nodding where he sat to wake up with a start when his head dropped forward. Overhead Gabrielle screamed out in her agony and he clapped his hands over his ears to shut out the sound.

A hand shook his shoulder. Hélène was speaking to him. "Émile! Wake up!"

He opened his eyes to see the room flooded with early morning sunshine. Fear and memory sparked together in the same instant. He leapt to his feet in panic. "What has happened?"

Hélène, heavy-eyed with tiredness, was smiling at him. "You have a son. A beautiful boy with strong lungs. Gabrielle is exhausted, but she is going to recover quickly."

He was beyond words in his joy. She laughed as he embraced her, lifting her off the ground in his exuberance. Never before had she seen him so demonstrative. He set her on her feet again to hurry away upstairs to Gabrielle, taking the treads two at a time. He reached the open doorway. The doctor had already departed and the midwife was elsewhere. Gabrielle lay white and drawn with her eyes closed in the freshly made bed, her hair brushed and shining, her hands on the coverlets veiled by the pristine lace trimming of her long-sleeved night-gown. As he came into the room she turned her head and saw him. He was unshaven, his cravat untied and his expression so joyous that she smiled, lifting a hand to hold it out to him. He rushed to the bedside to take her hand in both his own and press it to his lips before sitting down on the edge of the bed to lean across and kiss her lovingly.

"My dearest wife." His voice was choked and there were tears on his cheeks. It seemed to him that all the anguish he had endured through fear of losing her, first to Roche silk and then to Devaux, had culminated in an even greater fear during the night that had passed. "If I had lost you—"

"Hush." She smoothed away the tears on his cheeks with her finger tips. "I'm here. I will always be here. Why not take a look at your son?"

He moved across to the crib and gazed at the scarlet-faced infant peacefully oblivious to the furor his coming had caused. "My cup of happiness is overflowing, my son," he said quietly.

Gabrielle, watching him, was thankful she had been instrumental in bringing him that happiness. He had endured much in his marriage to her, for he had been an innocent and unknowing party in a tragedy of emotions that neither she nor Nicolas would have wished on him. Like so many men passionately in love with a woman whose love did not match their own, Émile had believed when he married her that, with time, he would awaken an equal love in her. Instead she had been a disappointment to him in many ways. Never had she been more grateful for the fact that he did not have the slightest suspicion that the love he yearned for from her had gone to another man for the rest of her days. At least, through their newly born child, she had been given a way in which to make up to Émile for some of the heartache she had caused him in the past.

Their son was duly named André after Émile's father. Hélène was a natural choice for godmother. On the day of the baptism she surprised everyone by appearing out of deep black for the first time. Although in a half-mourning shade of grey, she looked slim and elegant and wore white gloves instead of black, which would have been customary. Gabrielle, placing her shawl-wrapped son in her sister-in-law's arms, smiled in admiration.

"You look marvellous."

Hélène, adjusting the shawl around the sleeping infant's head, glanced up. "It's in honour of your son. This is a time of new beginnings. I wanted to be part of this important day in every way."

Gabrielle and Émile kissed her on both cheeks in turn, he echoing his wife's compliment. Then Gabrielle took Juliette by the hand to lead her out with them to the waiting carriages, Hélène and the rest of the christening party following. Juliette kept looking back over her shoulder. She was enchanted by her mother's new appearance. Being an imaginative child, she could have found it easy to believe that the touch of a magic wand had made the dark, depressing clothes fade away as in a story-book.

True to her word, Gabrielle left the Rue Clémont for the country as soon as her doctor pronounced her fit to travel. One shed at the silk farm was not entirely at a standstill, owing to the recovery of a cluster of mulberry trees that had escaped the worst of the blight. Daily Émile turned away scores of workers who were known to him and whom he had previously employed full time, aware that no other employment was available to them and a hungry winter lay ahead. Second harvests did occur elsewhere, mostly on the Italian slopes, but hardly any of it came up for sale. Rumours were rife of it being shipped out to England. English silk had always presented Lyons with some competition. Now the silk-weaving mills of Macclesfield would be able to draw on foreign raw silk without the handicaps faced by their French counterparts. With the Portuguese ports still open, their silk fabrics would filter through into Europe in spite of the war. The danger was that now they might take markets that would be difficult for the Lyonnais to recapture.

As if Lyons had not suffered enough ill luck, another blow fell. The Tsar had decreed that luxury items of any kind were not to be imported into Russia because of an urgent need to preserve currency. In times of peace Russia had always been an insatiable market, and all over the city silk merchants, including Gabrielle at her country retreat, received cancellation of the Russian orders that had been taken at Leipzig. Those who had risked everything to buy raw silk to fulfil these orders found themselves still deeper in trouble.

By now Madame Hoinville had proved her excellence as a deputy even more than before. She made the journey twice a week to see Gabrielle and lay business matters before her, including new designs by Marcel for her consideration and approval. Sometimes Marcel came himself when a special order had to be discussed, and altogether Gabrielle was able to keep abreast of everything. She would have liked to keep a closer eye on Henri, who merely corresponded, sometimes on a sharp note when he did not agree with one of her decisions.

Émile had never been more content in his relationship with Gabrielle. At a time of great business worries she had given him peace of mind by making his marriage at last what he had wished it to be. His son was thriving, a healthy, bonny-cheeked baby that any father could be proud of, and he had Gabrielle settled without restlessness under his roof with nothing to threaten their lives together any more.

As a surprise after her confinement, he had equipped an office for her next to his and she had been delighted with it. The financial difficulties he was going through, his anxiety about the price of new cocoons to replace the thousands of silkworms he had lost, as well as sundry other business worries, all paled before the importance of having his wife for his own again. In his more cynical, self-analysing moments he wondered if it was his constant pursuit of her love that had kept romance alive in his attitude towards her. He was ever the suitor, ever the lover, ever the would-be conqueror. From what he had seen of married friends and acquaintances, marriage appeared to be the great dampener of sentiment and desire. For him, the sight of Gabrielle's nakedness was as fierce a joy as when he had first possessed her.

He never gave Devaux's fate a moment's thought, except to continue to hope quite ruthlessly that he would never return from the campaign. It had become apparent that Marshal Masséna had failed in his attempt to drive Wellington out of Portugal into the sea, and in the stalemate of the winter lull, when both sides in any conflict settled down to wait for the spring and passable terrain again, the two adversaries faced each other somewhere in the vicinity of Torres Vedras. If Gabrielle read every news-sheet reference to the war to try to glean something of Nicolas's squadron of the *chasseurs à cheval*, Émile never knew.

Remembering what Jules had told her in the past of winter conditions on campaign, Gabrielle could guess at the hardships of meagre rations, icy weather and overcrowded cantonments being endured by an army. Locally, and on the occasional visit she made to Lyons in the first two months of the new year of 1811, she was able to see the effect of similar miseries being suffered by those without work. It was many years since there had been such a number of beggars on the streets, skilful weavers brought down to starvation level and begging with their families in the wind and rain. Everywhere mills were closed and loom-rooms stood silent. Her own mill and the rest still in operation were besieged daily by workers hoping that the illnesses of winter had left gaps at the looms and winding wheels and even work with a broom that they might fill. In their desperate straits, they were blaming the Jacquard loom once again for being some indefinable part of their misfortune, bringing up old grievances. Security was reinforced at every working mill and warehouse to guard against riots. There were outbursts of trouble now and then where workers believed that stocks of yarn were being held back instead of being released for looms, but eventually the winter passed with little loss of life through violence. It was hunger and sickness that decimated the workless and their families.

Throughout the whole period Hélène distributed food, paid for out of her own pocket, to those with young children whom she knew to be in dire distress. She did not like having to take an armed servant with her, but it was a necessary protection against those who might attack her for what her basket contained. This upset her, for she knew that any likely assailant would be as ravenous as those families she visited, but she had to think of the children first.

Once, in falling snow, she met Michel Piat on the Pont du Change and she was as pleased to see him as he appeared to be to see her. They passed the time of day, during which she asked him if he knew how Captain Devaux was faring, but he had had no communication from him. On the second occasion, when the early spring weather was easing the cold away while doing nothing to lessen the hunger pains of those still struggling to exist, he caught up with her just as she was about to enter a house in La Croix Rousse not far from the Devaux mill.

"Madame Roche! This is an unexpected pleasure. How are you?"

She turned her head, eyebrows raised in surprise. "Monsieur Piat. I'm very well and extremely thankful that this dreadful winter is at an end. Pray God we never see such suffering in Lyons again."

"I agree. At least there is hope for everyone in the weaving community again with the much-published signs that the mulberry everywhere has recovered sufficiently to give a reasonable harvest."

"Yes, isn't it splendid? Are you still busy at the mill?"

"All the time. We at the Devaux mill had more German orders than anyone else, I believe, and only a minor amount from Russia, which means we felt the draught of the Tsar's decree less than most of the mills. How did your sister-in-law fare?"

"She lost a large number of Russian orders, but all her looms are still at full pace."

"I'm glad to hear it." He paused. "I wonder if you would care to see over the Devaux mill now that you are so near?"

She was making her last call of the day. "I should be delighted as soon as I have visited the family in this house."

"I shall await you."

He gave her a tour of the whole mill. Although she had no inherited background in silk, her father having been a doctor and her mother from a family in law, there was little she did not know about the process and organisation of the silk industry, having learned much from Dominique and from her own observations. There was also a natural feminine interest in the beauty of silk that made it close to her heart. She stopped by one loom where a particularly delicate design of wild roses was being woven into silk of dress weight, mist pink and green against a pale cream.

"That is quite the loveliest fabric I have seen for a long time," she praised. "It is a fortunate woman who will wear that. You have a talented designer here."

"We think so."

After the tour he had coffee served to them in the salon, where the panels of green and white damask with a pattern of acanthus leaves, lozenges and scrolls echoed the silk of the self-striped upholstery of the sculptured and gilded chairs, creating a charming and tranquil room. Michel Piat told Hélène how Nicolas had found the whole house totally vandalised upon his return to Lyons and how he had restored it with some of the first silks to come from his Jacquard looms. "I received a letter from him last week. It had been only a month in transit, which is remarkable. At the time of writing he was still in the winter cantonments. Now, as we have heard recently, the fighting has resumed and once more Marshal Masséna appears to be in some difficulty, this time in stemming a British advance."

"Was Captain Devaux well when he wrote?" she asked at once.

He considered how he should answer her. With any other woman he would have made an affirmative reply, shielding her from the ugly facts of war. Hélène Roche was different. She was a soldier's widow and there was no nonsense about her in spite of her petiteness and porcelain looks of ivory skin and smooth black hair. He decided it would be an insult to her intelligence not to tell her the truth.

"Captain Devaux wrote of how things were, not on any note of personal grievance, I assure you. In some ways his concern was as much for the Spanish and Portuguese peasants as for our own French troops. We have seen starvation in Lyons this winter. He has seen it there. As you know, madame, our army has to forage off the land for its food, whereas the British carry imported provisions. With the Spanish policy of laying waste anything that might sustain our men, it has been a desperate situation just trying to keep them alive. Hundreds have died. It is hard to discipline starving men and there were cases of peasants being tortured to reveal hidden food stores."

Her cheeks hollowed, but she continued to sit straight in her chair. "War is obscene, Monsieur Piat. On my first visit here I talked more openly to you than I would ever have expected. Again I'm revealing a secret to you, unsuspected even by those who know me best, when I tell you that I have never seen any glory in it. I understood my dear husband's passion for the army, his deep need to serve, and I shared totally his consuming love for France just as I do today, but the banners and drums and the splendid uniforms have always been symbols of death to me. Every time I watched him ride away I know that, even if I were lucky enough to have him home again, there would be many women less fortunate with their menfolk on both sides of the conflict, many children left fatherless. My prayers are always for peace." She looked down quickly at the empty cup and saucer she held on her lap. "I'm talking too much. May I have some more coffee, do you think?"

He saw that it was also a request that he should make no comment on what she had told him and he was even more impressed by her than he had been when she first came to warn him about the mulberry blight. There was another matter in Devaux's letter that he would have liked to discuss with her, but it was too soon. He must be patient. The way had to be prepared, both for her and for himself. He turned the conversation by commenting on the quality of coffee in general and he invited her to use the coffee-pot to pour fresh cups for both of them. Afterwards the talk flowed easily along other lines.

Two weeks later he sent her an invitation to dine, explaining that his sister Paulette and her husband Alexandre were visiting Lyons and he would like her to meet them. She accepted and enjoyed the evening. As this occasion had nothing to do with the business of the mill, the dinner-party was held in Michel's apartment on an upper floor of the house, where the furniture was simpler but well appointed. He was an excellent host, his brother-in-law witty company, and Hélène and his sister took a liking to each other immediately. She returned the hospitality with tickets to a concert, and afterwards the four of them had supper at a nearby restaurant. When she and Paulette said farewell to each other it was with a promise to correspond. Michel looked particularly pleased with this development.

On the first day of real spring sunshine, Hélène finally discarded the half-mourning she had worn since André's christening day. The miniature of Jules, which was the only likeness of him she had, remained by her bed, where it was the first thing she looked at in the morning and which she touched with loving finger tips every night before she slept. The rawness of grief had finally healed. The ache was still there, catching her unawares at times, but life was no longer a burden to her.

Her dressmaker had delivered a dozen new gowns, including three of Roche silk. Although pastel shades were still the most popular for diaphanous fabrics, stronger colours were becoming fashionable, reflecting the increased formality at the imperial court. These suited her colouring and her silk gowns were in Pompeian red, deep gold and sapphire. She planned to wear the gold one when she attended a ball to be held to celebrate the birth of a son to Napoleon and his Empress. The infant had been given the title King of Rome and there had been widespread national rejoicing. This had been marred somewhat by the more recent news that Masséna, far from destroying Wellington once and for all, had been driven back himself out of Portugal, and Almeida was the only Portuguese city still in French hands. But the general feeling was that the tide would soon turn again, and the local opinion was that nothing should be allowed to spoil the Lyons ball, which in itself was an expression of loyalty to the Emperor.

It was to close with a firework display said to be the most elaborate ever staged. Émile and Gabrielle were coming to Lyons especially for the event, leaving their bouncing nine-month-old son in the care of his devoted and reliable nursemaid. Michel invited Hélène to attend with him, but she had already promised to be with the family party and arranged to see him there. Gabrielle found it hard to be in a celebratory mood, even though she was glad that there was a Bonaparte heir at last, for she had heard that the *chasseurs à cheval* had suffered heavy casualties in the fighting.

Henri was making his own plans for the evening, which he would be attending with Yvonne, although not with Gabrielle and Émile's party of friends. By arrangement he met Brouchier in a back-street café, not wanting the spy to come to the house, and gave him instructions in low tones over the table at which they sat. A purse of gold was pushed surreptitiously across the marble surface and the spy's hand closed over it. There would be more when his task was completed.

"Leave it to me," he said to Henri.

"See that it is carried out thoroughly. I want no half-measures."

"You know me. Everything I do is done well."

Henri gave a brusque nod. Devaux's departure for the Peninsula had not lessened by an iota his resolve to wreak vengeance and wipe Devaux silk from the face of Lyons, which was why he had not called off Brouchier from continued investigations. It was a feeling he had had in his guts that the way to destroy his old enemy might come better in his absence. He wanted Devaux to know about it and not elude him through death in battle. That could come afterwards, and the sooner the better as far as he was concerned.

Now everything was falling into place. From Brouchier he had learned of the accumulated stocks of raw silk in the Devaux store-rooms, which must have mortgaged the mill to the hilt, and he also knew that at present many valuable bolts of woven silk were shortly due for delivery to German customers. What he had not expected was that the birth of an imperial heir would be instrumental in the timing of this final act of revenge. It was almost as if he and the Emperor had been waiting the same number of years to achieve a special aim.

"Good night," he said to Brouchier, chucking a coin down on the table to pay for the bottle of wine he had ordered for the spy's benefit. He left the café and disappeared into the night. Brouchier drank Henri's barely touched glass of wine before he resumed sipping his own.

The evening of the ball was mild after a sunny day, full of the scent of lilacs. Gabrielle in copper silk with a fillet in her hair and Hélène in her golden gown combined beauty and elegance when they made a head-turning entrance into the ballroom, Émile a white-gloved escort. With them came a party of friends, and they took seating in one of the gilded alcoves. As the Prefect of Lyons opened the dancing with his wife and almost everyone else prepared to follow suit, Michel came to bow to Hélène where she sat. They smiled at each other, a shared greeting in their eyes.

"My dance, I believe, Hélène."

She had promised the first dance at their last meeting when they had reached the stage of using each other's Christian names. Gradually she had become aware of approaching a crossroads in her life. As yet she was not sure which turning to take, but there was firm guidance in Michel's capable hand as he took her fingers to lead her into the steps of the dance. Her feet felt curiously light. Suddenly it was almost as though she were waltzing on air.

The ballroom was too warm in spite of opened windows, and too crowded. It had been difficult for the organisers to limit the number of tickets when so many people wanted to attend. For Gabrielle the high-light of the evening was meeting Nicolas's manager. The introductions took place when she was being returned to her seat by a partner after a polonaise, when her sister-in-law and Michel Piat came in from the terrace where they had been taking the air. She thought Hélène looked unusually flushed, the rose colour high on her delicate cheekbones. As it happened, Gabrielle's polonaise partner and Hélène were promised for the next dance together, and as they swept into a gavotte Gabrielle and Michel found themselves able to talk on their own. Inevitably the topic

was silk and the difficulties of the past winter. It brought Gabrielle to
what she had wanted to ask from the first moment.

"I trust Captain Devaux has suffered no harm on campaign." She
was conscious of holding her breath, of being on guard against giving
herself away by crying out if she should hear he had been wounded. A
while ago Hélène had mentioned hearing from this new acquaintance
that Nicolas had been enduring the hardships of winter conditions on
active service but was otherwise well. The information had been given
when they were alone and Émile was out of hearing. Gabrielle had been
thankful with her whole heart for the information, but putting aside her
love for Nicolas also meant not speaking about him even to someone as
close to her as Hélène. It would be all too easy to scream out in anguish
to a sympathetic ear that she was being slowly torn apart without him,
but that went against the loyalty to Émile that was his due. To ask about
Nicolas from his business manager was a different matter altogether.

"No harm that I know of," was the reply he gave her. He went on
to tell her of the one communication he had received, although not in
the detail he had given Hélène since the circumstances were different. "I
have sent him regular reports on the mill, and it was apparent from his
letter only one had reached him."

So this man had nothing new to relate. Anything could have happened in the interim. She heard herself saying: "How frustrating for
correspondents at home and on campaign!" On the ballroom floor the
gavotte had ended. When Gabrielle was claimed by her next partner,
Michel stood by one of the balcony pillars and watched Hélène disap-
pear and reappear in the twirling throng on the floor. He wanted to
dance with no one else, not even the beautiful Gabrielle Valmont, and
was content to wait until the supper dance when he could take Hélène's
hand again. On the terrace he had made his feelings known to her and
told her of his prospects for the future. It had not been his intention to
speak yet, but this evening there had been a special rapport between
them, almost as if she had released herself from a bond that had been
holding her back from him. For himself, a staid widower, he had never
thought to find again a woman he could truly love.

At the close of the evening, when everyone streamed out to crowd
the terraces to view the fireworks over the river, Michel was with the
Valmont party, having been drawn into it and introduced by Hélène
when she had wanted to rejoin them for the buffet supper. The only
person who made him feel unwelcome was Émile Valmont. The man
was polite enough but thoroughly distant.

"Oooo . . . ahhh!" The sound rose from the crowd as the fireworks
soared into the air to burst into multicoloured stars, lighting up the
buildings and the upturned faces far below. Applause rippled out at the

most spectacular displays. It was a skyful of silver stars, fading away
when another kind of glow was to be seen in the direction of La Croix
Rousse.

"Fire! Look, there's a fire!"

Michel was immediately uneasy. It was impossible to judge in the
lamp-twinkling darkness of the distant rising span of La Croix Rousse
where the fire was located, and he would have to get there as quickly as
possible. He turned urgently to Gabrielle.

"I came here on foot, madame. Might I have the loan of your carriage to get me to the fire? It may be nowhere near the mill, but I have to
be sure."

"Of course. I'll take you to my servant, Gaston. He will get you
there in no time at all." She edged her way through the crowd, Michel
and Hélène following her. It would have been no good sending Michel
off on his own to summon the carriage, for the coach servants had four
different waiting places at the end of the building and much time could
have been wasted.

The three of them hurried down the last steps of the terrace and ran
along the path that led to the courtyard. Normally those waiting for
their masters played cards under cover or boule by lamplight. Those
who had not stopped their games for the fireworks had done so for the
sight of the fire, all of them staring in the direction of La Croix Rousse.

"Gaston!" Gabrielle called twice to make herself heard above the
buzz of voices and the explosion of fireworks.

He heard her and broke away from the group with whom he had
been watching the rise of flames into the night. "Madame?"

"Take Monsieur Piat to the Devaux mill as fast as you can."

"Yes, madame. It's been confirmed, has it?"

"What do you mean?"

"Somebody came riding by just now and said it looked as though it
was the Devaux mill that was afire."

She was never sure why she went in the carriage with Michel. It
was not a conscious decision, simply an instinct to try to do whatever
she could for Nicolas's property. Hélène, whose immediate aim was to
be with Michel in any kind of danger, scrambled into the carriage with
her, and they were tossed about as Gaston drove the horses at a gallop
through the streets and over the bridge.

They had to alight at the head of the street, for a crowd had gathered. Michel groaned aloud at the sight that met them. The whole mill
was ablaze, with flames leaping out of the windows, black smoke billowing away over the rooftops. He plunged into the spectators to shoulder
his way through, Gabrielle and Hélène following. People gaped as the
evening finery of the new arrivals was glimpsed thrusting past, and

Hélène did not even notice when a diamond bracelet was snatched from her wrist in the crush. Gaston, who had roared after the two women to stay behind, threw himself after them and, with a chop-like blow, almost broke a thieving hand that clawed at Gabrielle's necklace clasp. Like a bear, he spread his arms out to envelop both women and used his wide body to ram a way through the crowd, since it was obvious they were determined.

They half fell into the clearing. An attempt was being made to save the Devaux residence as well as the tall houses at the far end of the mill where the occupants, some in night-clothes, had joined several chains of buckets passing from both ends of the street to the nearest public water ducts. Gabrielle rushed forward to take a place in a chain reaching into Nicolas's house, which was already on fire, the upper floors ignited by showers of sparks from the mill roof. Gaston gave a hand to those salvaging furniture and Hélène helped drag to safety some of the lighter pieces unceremoniously dumped outside in the open air. Michel had dashed through the hall to reach the door into the courtyard, hoping that something might be saved from the mill, only to find the whole interior was an inferno, and he slammed back into the house again. He made first for the silk portraits in the gallery, knowing the historical importance of the few that had survived the vandalism of an earlier time. With two marketing baskets grabbed from the kitchen, he loaded in Devaux family miniatures, silver and several small objects of value that had been bundled up once before when Nicolas and his parents had fled Lyons during the siege.

He tried to get upstairs to save some of his own possessions. There the smoke wrenched at his lungs and he fell back, almost choking. The fire had taken a strong hold and there were flames leaping in rooms downstairs as well as in the upper landings. People were shouting to him to come out. He reached the hall in time to see through open doors the beginning of the destruction of the green and white Grand Salon as flames crept up from the floor-boards and down from the ceiling to create expanding black holes in the silk panelling and blister the gilded woodwork.

He just had time to snatch up a package he had left earlier that day within the room before Gaston's big hand descended on his shoulder to thrust him, dazed and coughing, through falling sparks and burning splinters into the street. There was a crackling in his hair and Hélène hurled herself at him to smother the flames with her hands. He could hardly see her for the swelling of his red-rimmed eyes, while the pain from the smoke in his lungs made every breath he took excruciating, but he threw his arms about her in the certain knowledge that she was his for the rest of his days.

Émile had not seen Gabrielle leave the terrace with Hélène and Michel, the party having split into two sections in the surge out to see the fireworks. He saw the flames of the distant fire as had everyone else, but he knew from the direction that it was nowhere near any of Gabrielle's property and, unperturbed, continued to watch the firework display, joining in the applause when it ended. It was only when he joined up with the rest of the party, as people began to disperse, that he learned of Gabrielle and Hélène's hasty departure with Piat and the reason for it. Something seemed to snap in his head, releasing all the blackness of mind and soul that he had begun to believe might have left him forever. With it, making his agony more desperate, came fury with Gabrielle. She had dared to go running off to Devaux's mill in the middle of an important social event, deserting him, deserting their guests, and for what? He could guess easily enough. It was a sentimental whim to give support in time of trouble to the man she still cared for, no matter that he was hundreds of miles away in another country.

He was shaking with temper and had to clasp his hands behind his back, also half afraid the vibrations of his rage were distorting his mouth as he smiled with his guests going through to the front of the building where the carriages were lining up to bear everyone away. It was then he guessed Gaston would have driven Gabrielle and her companions to the site of the fire. Humiliation washed over him. She had given no thought to his waiting in vain for the family carriage while everybody else was driven away. It was lucky there were always hackney cabs lingering in the vicinity. He said good night to those of his guests still awaiting conveyance and hastened away across the forecourt in search of a cab. One came driving up quickly to outstrip the rest.

"Quick!" he instructed the cab-driver. "There's a fire in La Croix Rousse. It may be the Devaux mill. Drive me there as fast as you can."

He sat back in the stale-smelling interior and pinched the bridge of his nose between two fingers, trying to drive back the thundering despair that had come upon him. All these months he had been harbouring the illusion that he had at last won Gabrielle's love. His own happiness had prevented him from seeing until now that she had been merely steeped in the bliss of mother love and, because of that, had been more demonstrative to him, more compliant, more willing to subdue her own wishes, simply because he was the father of her child. What he wanted most from her was still another man's.

Lunging forward, he thumped a fist against the carriage wall behind the driver. "Faster! Do you hear me? Faster, I say!"

The hackney cab took him as far as it was possible to go. He leapt out, tossed the fare to the cabby and ran forward to reach the crowd being held back by the police from the burning building. He was at the south end of the fire, close to tall houses that had been ignited by the mill, which with the fire out of hand was clearly destined to be a total loss. Although he was a distance away, he could see that Devaux's house was also completely ablaze. Several bucket chains at that end had moved back to concentrate their efforts on the neighbouring building in an attempt to save it. A pump had been brought in and was having some effect. Suddenly across the clearing being used by the fire-fighters he saw Gabrielle.

She looked exhausted, standing beside Gaston at the forefront of the opposite crowd, gazing sadly up at Devaux's house as the fire consumed it. Her gown was torn and her face streaked with smoke grime, the gleam of her gold necklace an incongruous touch. He began to push his way through to get to the police line and make his way across to her, temper giving him a discourtesy that normally was alien to him. People protested as he shoved angrily against them. He was deaf to their shouts. His one aim was to get to his wife.

"Not so fast, monsieur. You can't go in front of those buildings."

Émile glared at the policeman whose outflung arm was restraining him. "Let me pass! I have to reach my wife. She's over there!" He pointed across to Gabrielle, who caught the disturbance out of the corner of her eye and looked across. "She's waiting for me. Can't you see?" With that, he thrust himself forward, ignoring the policeman's demand that he should come back, and began to run across the cleared area of the street, so much jealous rage in him that all he wanted was to strike Gabrielle down to the ground.

Seeing him approach across the water-sloshed cobbles, a dark figure illumined by the red and yellow glow of the flames, she took a step forward. He saw, almost to his disbelief, that she looked relieved and happy to see him, thankful that he had come. Then she smiled, giving a little wave in order that he should not miss her whereabouts in the confusion as fire-fighters and bucket chains alike moved hither and thither.

Her smile went right to his heart. His temper ebbed like a fast tide. Maybe he had made a mistake after all. Maybe it was not as he had feared. He knew that, in spite of the rage he had felt, he would never have raised a hand to this woman who was more to him than life itself. Then abruptly her expression changed, a look of terror stamping her face. She made a sharp move as if she would have run to him, arms outstretched, but her coachman grabbed her back. Instinct told him what was happening. The fire-fighters were scattering, running in total panic. There were screams and warning shouts mingling with a deafening roar and rushing sound announcing that the whole side of the mill was bending and cracking and disintegrating into white-hot bricks and flaring wood and searing ashes and slowly cascading sparks brighter than any firework display.

Gabrielle screamed as if she were dying herself. Gaston jerked her face into his shoulder and spared her the sight of Émile's instant but terrible death.

11

Gabrielle bore her bereavement with dignity. The funeral took place in the village near the silk farm, where he was laid to rest in the little churchyard. Two other people had been killed in the collapse of the wall and special prayers had been included in the service for them and for those whom they had left behind. Afterwards family and friends went to the Valmont house for refreshments before returning to Lyons or more local destinations.

"Are you sure you don't want me to stay on with you for a few days?" Hélène asked Gabrielle. She had been with her in the country ever since they had followed the coffin home to await burial.

Gabrielle declined her offer with an affectionate embrace. "Thank you for offering but you would hardly see me. There is such a vast amount of work for me on the silk farm, and I must catch up with all that has to be done."

"Are you quite sure?" Hélène was still uncertain.

"I'm sure."

When everyone had gone, Gabrielle went to sit for a long while by her son sleeping in his crib in the softly lamplit nursery. Her thoughts were full of Émile.

Yvonne had had to attend the funeral without Henri. She could not understand why he had taken his brother-in-law's death so hard, even allowing for the exceptionally tragic circumstances. She knew he had never liked Émile, and yet he appeared more upset than when his father had died or when the news had come of Jules's death. He had flatly refused to accompany her.

"My grief is too great," he had insisted brokenly. "I would only break down in public."

Looking at his haggard face, she could not doubt him. When she returned home she found him in a drunken state and felt a rare twinge of pity. She had never thought that her husband would have such depths of feeling in him. Nevertheless, it did not appear to take him long to throw off his sorrow and behave in his normal fashion again. He became positively exuberant when the ruins of the Devaux mill were demolished after it was feared that one of the remaining charred walls might collapse. It had finally happened as he had always wanted. There was not a Devaux loom left in Lyons and all trace of the family whom he hated had been literally swept away. She would have expected him to view the cleared site, his sense of triumph overcoming sad associations with the fire, but to the best of her knowledge, he did not go near it.

Only caution, and not sensitivity, prevented Henri from going. He was also relieved that Brouchier had not approached him for the rest of the fee for a job well done but had prudently decided to leave Lyons until all official enquiries were at an end. When the initial shock had waned, it had not taken him long to absolve himself from any responsibility for his brother-in-law's demise. It had been Émile's fault entirely for venturing into a dangerous area against which he had been warned. It was to be regretted that a simple plan had had tragic consequences, but that was how things happened sometimes. It had been a fateful chance also that several large shipments of Devaux fabrics, the bulk of the winter's output, worth many thousands of francs and destined for the Mobilier Impérial as well as for Germany, had been sent out a day earlier, thus escaping the fire, which everyone else except Henri had declared to be good news. It was being said in business circles that in view of this stroke of luck, together with insurance compensation, Nicolas Devaux should break even with whatever commitments he had made to the bank, but the prospect of his starting up again looked bleak. He might be away in the army too long to retain interest and, in any case, if he returned tomorrow the present trade difficulties facing Lyons silk were enough to deter anyone from beginning again until times were much better.

The situation between Michel and Hélène had reached a distressing stalemate. The fire had separated them. His prospects, which he had mapped out to her on the terrace during the ball, had vanished in the flames. Until he could be certain of his future once more, he felt himself to be in no position to propose marriage formally to a widow who was well to do in her own right. He wanted to give her a home of her own where they could start married life without any links with the past, except what each would hold individually as personal memories. She understood the situation and suffered her disappointment privately.

Michel believed himself to be the only one unconvinced that a fire-work had ignited the mill. Work had gone on all through that ill-fated night to ensure there were no more bodies than the two found with Émile's among the rubble. In the morning he had walked through the still smoking ruins and questioned people living in the vicinity. They had answered his questions readily and without reserve, eager, as people always are after a dramatic event, to relate their own witness. There had been some fire on the top floor, but in the loom-rooms the flames had swept through in seconds. His suspicions remained, even though a burnt-out rocket on the cobbles in a neighbouring street had been con-sidered additional evidence of the cause at the official enquiry. He re-mained convinced in his own mind that it had been a case of arson. As yet there was no way of obtaining proof.

Since Gabrielle no longer came to Lyons, Madame Hoinville re-sumed her visits to see her in her country abode. Gabrielle seemed to have become thinner and paler every time they met and Madame Hoinville found her inattentive, as if it were impossible for her to con-centrate on anything but the silk farm. At times she had to be pressed for a decision about some business matter, something that had never occurred before.

"I have much on my mind," she said once. "My late husband was in the process of starting all over again with new cocoons and the re-em-ployment of workers whom he had to lay off last year. It's of vital impor-tance to me to have everything done as he would have wished it to be."

Gabrielle had taken on Michel to assist her. He had once spent some time on a silk farm and she found him invaluable. The mulberry harvest fulfilled its promise of being all that could be expected in view of the setback it had had in the previous year, and there was no disease among the silkworms from the replacement cocoons that Émile had purchased at great cost. His finances had been left in a sorry state and she could guess at the worries he had kept to himself about how the future would go. Michel needed time off to see the lawyers on Nicolas's behalf about the mill disaster, as well as to deal with various business ends that needed to be tied up, and she agreed that he should come and go as was necessary. He went to see the Prefect of Lyons to ask that he use his influence to get a letter informing Nicolas of the fire sent with military despatches. The Prefect took the letter from him.

"I shall do what you ask since the name of Devaux holds a high place in Lyons silk and we all regret what has happened. However, whether it will get through is another matter. It is not only mail for the army that suffers from enemy interference. From what I have heard from reliable military sources, even despatches sent from the Emperor, or destined for him, are frequently lost en route through no fault of the bearers. The Spanish guerrillas are without mercy."

Michel left the Hôtel de Ville hoping for the best. Among other things he had done was to pass on the Devaux fabric orders still in hand at the time of the fire to the Maison Roche for weaving and despatching in return for a commission to be paid into Nicolas's bank. This was what any silk merchant would have gladly done for the valued work, providing they had yarn enough in the present difficult time.

Although Henri resented paying any commission in this case, he had seized on the orders with relish. He saw it as the gilt on the ginger-bread that, on top of complete destruction of the Devaux business, the last orders should pass through his hands for the Roche looms. He had very special looms in mind on which to execute them. Gabrielle's continued absence was also much in his favour. She had more or less implied in their correspondence that she had no intention of returning to Lyons for a long time to come. He hoped it would be never, and in the meantime everything was going his way at last.

Hélène was becoming increasingly concerned about Gabrielle. It was as if she had succumbed to Émile's domination as she had never done in his lifetime. The cause lay in the confession that had slipped out of her in the midst of her wild grief on the night of the fire. Hélène, holding her in comforting arms, had heard what she had already guessed.

"He was there because of me!" The tears had gushed from the beautiful eyes. "I had forgotten to send Gaston back with the carriage for him and I was thankful when he suddenly appeared at the forefront of the opposite crowd of spectators. It showed he was not displeased with me as I had feared he might be, because otherwise he would have gone back to the Rue Clémont in an ill temper and never troubled to seek me out. I saw his expression in those last seconds before he realised what was happening." Sobs overtook her again and her speech came jerkily as every word rasped in her throat. "There was only gladness in his face at the sight of me."

"Remember that," Hélène urged gently, rocking her as she would have rocked a child in distress. "Be comforted by it. Émile would never have blamed you for what happened. Do not punish yourself."

It seemed that her advice had not been heeded. It was only when Gabrielle was with André, cradling him in her arms, caring for him and sometimes singing him a lullaby in a low, sweet voice, that she relaxed, letting the tautness of spirit go from her. At these times she appeared to forget for a little while the sadness that was hollowing her eyes and drawing every bone in her face.

Two months to the day after Émile's death Gabrielle collapsed. She was in a silk shed after a week's routine round of visiting throwsters and dyers in the district when she folded up onto the stone floor without a sound. Michel was the first to reach her and he gathered her up to carry her along the path into the house. Hélène was sent for immediately. By the time she arrived Dr. Jaunet had called and left again. Hélène saw him on his second visit, when he returned to the house the same evening especially to discuss the patient's condition with her.

"Why hasn't Madame Valmont been eating?" He glared at Hélène as if she were wholly responsible.

"I knew she had little appetite these days, but I thought it would right itself in time."

"In time! Good heavens, madame. Malnutrition is more than a decline in appetite. Haven't we seen enough of starvation during the past winter without a widow in comfortable circumstances being allowed to bring herself to this state? You shall get nourishment into her now even if you have to spoon-feed her like a baby, and for the next few days that will be your task exactly."

Hélène, experienced in nursing the sick, carried out her assignment efficiently. She had an advantage in knowing what lay behind Gabrielle's collapse and she did everything possible to divert the patient's mind from the past. She encouraged a few of Gabrielle's closest friends to ride out from Lyons to call on her as soon as she was strong enough to receive them. Smartly dressed, in pretty bonnets or hats gay with flowers and ribbons, they chatted of fashion, related the latest gossip and enthused over André's growth as well as the progress and achievements of their own young children at home. Hélène had asked them to avoid the subject of the Peninsula campaign as well as anything else of a depressing nature and they gladly obliged, although at least three of them were highly intelligent women more used to talking to Gabrielle on a serious level. They were hard put to avoid any reference to a matter that was of political concern to them, which was that the Tsar was no longer showing friendship towards France.

Hélène made a specially happy occasion of André's first natal day. In the afternoon Gabrielle, wearing a cool black and white spotted muslin gown, lay on a chaise longue that had been carried out for her into the shade of the trees. André, who was unmistakably Gabrielle's son, with Émile's colouring, was put down on a rug spread out on the grass beside his mother, from where he was quick to crawl away in eager exploration until recaptured by Juliette, who was fondly patient with him.

Hélène had taken over the kitchen for two days to bake for the feast and on the party table, which was spread with a white lace cloth in the middle of the lawn, a superb croquembouche gleamed in a golden haze of spun sugar, giving off a caramel aroma that was extraordinarily appetising. Spiced cakes and rich pastries vied for space with simpler fare baked especially for André and Juliette. Originally Michel was to have been the only invited guest, but a few days before the party Gabrielle suggested that everyone in the silk sheds should be invited onto the lawn to drink a glass of champagne and share the food. Hélène took this as a sign that at last Gabrielle was fully on the road to recovery, whatever sad memories would always remain with her. When the workers arrived, streaming onto the lawn from the path through the trees, a merry atmosphere was created immediately and the whole event was a success in every way.

It was at the end of the day that Hélène told Gabrielle that she had written herself to Nicolas.

"As you know, it was not until my private betrothal to Michel after the night of the fire that I felt entitled to tell him that you and Nicolas loved each other. It was his suggestion that I write, as well as he, to let Nicolas know of your widowhood, and by that means we could try to ensure that at least one letter with the information got through to him."

Gabrielle lay quietly against her cushions. "Have you had a reply?"

"Neither of us has heard anything, but that doesn't mean he has not written. People say that military mail has a better chance of getting through than it has of coming out, because the ingoing letters frequently travel with army reinforcements. Why don't you write to him now?"

"No. Not all the time I'm in Émile's house."

"Then think of coming back to Lyons."

"No." Gabrielle was firm. "Not yet. Let's not talk about it any more."

The rest of Gabrielle's convalescence passed quickly. Contrary to Hélène's hopes, when she did begin work on a full scale it was again the silk farm that came first with her. Not once did she drive into Lyons to visit the mill or the design-room or to consult with Henri. All her efforts were concentrated on raw silk, with apparently no thought of the end product on the Roche looms.

Hélène prolonged her stay far longer than she had expected to, mainly because Gabrielle wanted her company and was reluctant for her to leave. The extended sojourn pleased Juliette, who had made friends with neighbouring children. As for Hélène herself, there was the opportunity to see Michel every day, for he had taken temporary accommodation in the village until such time as he should finish working at the silk farm. At Gabrielle's invitation, he dined with them most evenings and Juliette had become attached to him. Hélène's most joyous moments were when on her own with him, to know again the kisses of a loving mouth, to be stirred again into an awareness of being a desirable woman with long-dormant feelings aroused once more. On one of their country walks together he had made tender love to her in a meadow full of wild flowers. It had happened spontaneously, taking them both by surprise, and although it had not occurred again the experience had enriched their relationship immeasurably.

Gradually various commitments made it necessary for her to return to the Rue Clémont and she began to make preparations for departure. "Why not come back to Lyons with me for a few days?" she suggested to Gabrielle. The two of them were sitting together on the terrace in the balmy evening air, both children asleep in bed.

Gabrielle brushed a tendril of hair away from her brow with a relaxed hand. "I should like to, but I'm too busy here."

Although Hélène knew that Michel did not wish to continue working at the silk farm on a permanent basis, she felt compelled to make a point uppermost in her mind and tried to put it as tactfully as possible. "I think it would do you good to have a short vacation. Michel would manage everything in your absence. I can't believe you want to desert Maison Roche entirely."

There was a slight intake of breath from Gabrielle. "What are you talking about?" she asked, after a pause, with a contrived air of amused indulgence. "Madame Hoinville and Marcel are coming regularly to see me as they did before, and Henri keeps me up to date with his side of the business. As you know, I entertained an important customer to dinner here yesterday, and tomorrow the accountant comes with the books again. I'm as much involved in Maison Roche silk as ever I was. It's just that I have to share my time now."

"Have you considered selling the silk farm?"

"I might make that move when it becomes a viable proposition. At the present time there are no buyers for silk farms struggling to re-establish a good output after last season's catastrophe."

Hélène saw through her answer and was dismayed by it. "Am I to believe that it may be years before you return to live in your most favourite place and take up to the full the work you have always liked best?"

Gabrielle maintained her casual air as if such a prospect caused her no concern. "Yes, that is how it is." Then suddenly her reserve broke and she sprang to her feet as though propelled and went with a few swift steps to the edge of the terrace, standing to look out over the dark garden, the flower-beds showing pale in the moonglow and the black trees. "Why should I pretend with you? You are closer than any sister could have been. You were right to remind me of the part that Lyons has always played in my life. I hate it here. When Émile was alive it was different. I was fond of this old house from the moment I first saw it. Now it has become a prison to me."

Hélène was amazed. "Then why stay?"

"I must." Gabrielle continued to look away, clenching her hands together in front of her. "What you haven't realised is the effect that rejecting Nicolas's love had on me. It was like giving up breathing, a denial of life itself, and it took me to the extremities of my self-will. That in itself is a kind of breaking-point. I no longer have it in me to show such restraint again. Since my recovery from my collapse I have realised that to go back to Lyons would be to revive every association with the times he and I had together. It would return me to a devouring passion that I lack the strength to endure again without fulfilment from him. Here, in these comparatively isolated surroundings, I am Émile's widow, and Nicolas is far from me in the Peninsula." Her voice shattered in her despair. "In Lyons he would be back in my heart." She bowed her head, covering her face with her hands.

Hélène hurried to her. "Forgive me. I didn't mean to probe. I have been thoughtless and unkind."

Gabrielle raised her head and took Hélène by the arms. "Never say that. You are incapable of unkindness. I'll always be grateful for all you have done for me over these many weeks. You had to know why I can't face seeing Lyons again. I'm thankful I've told you."

On the morning Hélène left for Lyons with Juliette they were accompanied by Michel, who had business in the city. Gabrielle stood alone by the gates, having come right into the road to wave them out of sight, while Juliette wept at having to leave. As Hélène settled her daughter back onto the seat and dried the tears, she glanced across at Michel.

"When the Prefect took your letter, written to notify Nicolas of the fire, had you mentioned in it that Émile Valmont had been killed?"

"No. I said there were three fatal casualties, but the whole of the letter was taken up with matters of insurance and so forth. I listed Gabrielle's late husband in a letter I sent later by the usual channels."

"Pray God he receives it," Hélène said almost to herself.

When she arrived home at the Rue Clémont she found that Henri and Yvonne had had their quarters in the house completely redecorated and extravagantly refurbished; in addition they had annexed the Blue Salon and the adjoining Grand Salon for their own use. Important customers were to be received in future in the Gold Salon, previously little used, which through redecoration had become no less magnificent with gleaming orange-red brocade woven with sunflowers on the walls, the drapes of satin *broché* and the furniture Louis Quatorze.

"What do you think of it?" Henri asked with an expansive sweep of his arm. He had led her into it before she had a chance to reach her own rooms. Although tired and dusty from the journey, she looked about appreciatively. "There's only one thing to say. It's become a truly handsome room. The previous hangings did need replacing, and I remember when Marcel did these new designs." She frowned questioningly. "I thought Gabrielle had shelved the expense until the trade situation was better again."

"That's correct. She did."

"Then she doesn't know what you've done here?"

"I'm in charge now. I make all the decisions now that my sister has chosen to bury herself in the country." Then he added, seeing that Hélène was about to stalk away, not at all pleased with him, "Oh, there's something I have to say to you. In future, would you check your daughter from running all over the house? It disturbs Yvonne."

Hélène halted to stare at him in astonishment. "Juliette has never invaded the privacy of your apartment."

"No, but she has the freedom of everywhere else. I'd be obliged if you would keep her in your own rooms whenever she is at home. You'll notice that a few changes have been made in your absence, quite apart from the alterations in this sunflower salon. It seemed foolish for Yvonne and me not to use the whole house when it's beginning to appear unlikely that Gabrielle will ever return here on a permanent basis. Yvonne has also dispensed with the services of a few of the servants who never met with her approval, and the new housekeeper doesn't like anyone in the kitchen except the cook and the appropriate domestic staff, so you had better take warning. She's quite a tartar, but splendid in her management. Yvonne settles the menus with her daily. There's no longer any need for you to feel obliged to take some part in the running of the house."

"I never thought of it as an obligation. I looked upon this house as my home from the day I came here as a bride."

"That's as may be. As I said before, you'll find things have changed, and entirely for the better, I hasten to add."

That was a matter of opinion, Hélène thought angrily when she entered her own apartments to find that Yvonne had had several family pieces of furniture taken away to be placed elsewhere. The replacements looked as if they had been retrieved from storage in the cellar. As soon as she and Juliette had eaten the cold luncheon laid ready for them, she went along to Gabrielle's rooms. Nothing had been touched in that section. It seemed as though Henri was still wary enough of Gabrielle not to allow Yvonne to cause disruption there. Closing the door after her again, Hélène was thoughtful as she went back to her own apartment. Never had she expected to be made to feel unwelcome in this house. Her first instinct was to go. She had said long ago to Gabrielle that she would leave the Rue Clémont when she felt the right time had come, just as she had dispensed with mourning when its need had passed. Jules's fear had been that she would be imposed upon and given too much to do by Henri and Yvonne in his father's house. Instead, they had deprived her of all duties and shown her effectively they no longer wanted her under the same roof.

Unfortunately this was the one time when it was not convenient to leave the Rue Clémont. She did not want to buy or rent other accommodation when Michel's plans were still uncertain. He was applying for posts better suited to his ability than the assistance he was giving Gabrielle at the silk farm, and when he found something appropriate, whether it was in Lyons or elsewhere, they would marry and have their own home. In the meantime she must put up with the situation and try to keep Juliette out of trouble.

It proved difficult to confine the child to such a small part of the house. She was cheerful and friendly by nature and full of energy, liking best to be in the open air, even more so after the ban on her indoor freedom was imposed on her. In the aftermath of a slight infection, and bored by having to keep to her rooms, she was particularly fractious and naughty. One evening at bedtime, instead of obeying Hélène's call to come at once, she hid herself downstairs in a cupboard in Henri's office. If she had not been forbidden the area claimed by her aunt and uncle, where previously she had gone freely, she would probably never have thought of hiding there. Intelligently, she thought to herself that his sanctum would surely be the place most barred to her, and this certainly added to her satisfaction in her daring act of disobedience.

When the office door opened only minutes after she had secluded herself, her disappointment that her mother had located her already turned to fright when through a crack she saw her Uncle Henri's legs appear round the side of the desk. There was another man with him, who took the chair at the other side, and there came a clink of glasses and the gurgle of wine being poured.

Their grown-up conversation was of little interest to her. She was getting steadily more cramped and scared and wanted to be tucked up in her own bed. Finally she fell asleep.

Her mother found her there much later after a hue and cry had been raised. It was only the fact that she had slid against the door in her sleep, widening the opening, that she was spotted at all. She barely woke when she was undressed and put into her own bed, but it was a while before she could sleep properly because Uncle Henri returned from an evening out to hear she had been in his office and he was shouting at her *maman* in the salon.

"Don't dare to raise your voice to me in that manner!" Hélène stood her ground. Henri's rage was out of all proportion to the child's offence. "Was any harm done? Did she damage anything by sitting on it?"

"That's beside the point. I expressly forbade you to let your daughter invade my privacy in my house. And then you let her sneak into my office—"

"It is not your house, Henri. It's Gabrielle's property. Even your office is part of her property, although I respect your right to bar others from it, including my child."

"I want to speak to Juliette in the morning."

"You may do so in my presence as long as you give me your word you will not shout at her in the churlish manner in which you have been addressing me."

Juliette wanted to hide behind her mother's skirts when Uncle Henri came to see her after breakfast, but she knew she was too old to behave like that and bobbed a curtsey as she had been taught when about to be addressed by a grown-up person. He was smiling at her, although his eyes glinted like stones and the hand he clapped on her shoulder from the chair where he sat, was harder than it needed to be.

"Little girls must do as they are told, Juliette. There are reasons for everything and the one for you not being allowed in my office is that it is full of private business papers that belong to the Maison Roche and have to be guarded against prying eyes."

"I didn't read anything. I have my own reading books."

"I know that." The strain of being patient with her was revealed in his digging finger tips. "Conversations that take place there are also about private business matters. I wouldn't want to think that anything you heard was repeated outside these four walls."

"I don't know what you were talking about. I didn't listen. I'm sorry I was in your cupboard. May I go now?"

He relaxed his hold and patted her cheek instead. "Yes. I'm aware that you're really a good little girl at heart. You're forgiven this time but don't ever go near my office again. Is that understood?"

"Yes, Uncle Henri."

Juliette forgot the incident, except that she no longer strayed from her allotted quarters. The drier, cooler days allowed her long walks with her mother, the air full of the autumn scent of leaves and the sizzling crêpes that were fried and sold by vendors at street corners. Sewing was one of the lessons her mother taught her together with reading, writing and ciphering. Since she liked stitching least of all, she found it only moderately interesting to learn that her mother was going to take her to the Roche mill where some scraps of silk for patchwork would be collected for her. It proved to be more fun than she had expected when one of the spinners, a young girl, took charge of her, leaving her mother free to go into Madame Hoinville's office.

"Thank you for coming, Madame Roche," the woman greeted Hélène. "It was most urgent that I should see you and I was reluctant to come to the Rue Clémont."

"You do understand that I have no connection with the business?"

"Yes, of course. But you are close to Madame Valmont, I believe. She has spoken of you many times during my visits, when my reports have been dealt with and we have lunched together. I want you to do everything in your power to persuade her to return to Lyons."

Hélène sat back in her chair. "You don't realise what you are asking me. I can't interfere in my sister-in-law's way of life."

"Would you do what I ask if I told you I believe she is being swindled in her absence?"

Hélène was startled. "Whom do you accuse? Do you have proof?"

"I have no proof whatever and I hesitate to make an accusation. If Madame Valmont were here I feel sure she would discover for herself in a very short time what I believe is going on."

"Please explain."

"I think I can best illustrate what I suspect to be happening by telling you something from my youth, which I have never forgotten. For a while I worked in a dressmaking establishment. The chief dressmaker, who was in charge of everything, was arrested for fraud after it was discovered that when she visited clients to measure them in their homes, displaying an array of fabrics sent with her for their choice, she frequently made up the orders herself in her own time, using the establishment's material and pocketing the money. The clients she selected for her dishonest dealings were usually elderly or infirm and generally unlikely to contact the owners personally. They had no idea they were not dealing with the bona fide side of the business."

"But the missing fabric?"

"Therein lay her cunning. She always cut off what she needed before returning the bolts of fabric. You see, if she took six bolts out, six were always returned. Nobody checked on the amount left. As for the order itself, she would say the client had changed her mind about wanting anything or else, out of an order for three garments, she would put two through official channels and still keep one for herself."

"Surely she realised she would be found out sooner or later?"

"She was a trusted employee. The owner himself was not as businesslike as he should have been. I suppose she thought she would get away with it forever."

"I can see you are putting my sister-in-law on a parallel with that owner."

"Not because Madame Valmont is not businesslike, but because she has concentrated her interest in the silk farm to the detriment of Roche silk."

"You are also saying that valuable orders, which should be coming into this mill, are being siphoned off elsewhere. What makes you think that?"

"Some faulty brocade was returned to this mill direct from a foreign customer. There was only a minuscule flaw, but it was consistent throughout a very expensive piece. I went to compare it with a pattern that had been made up in advance of commencement with the same dyed yarns on the same looms. I was able to see at once that it had not come from here and yet it was a design exclusive to Maison Roche silk."

"How can you be sure?"

"We did only one piece in those colours. Even a layman knows that if different batches of dyed yarn are used for the same lengths there will be a difference in shade. Although in this case the colours were as close as to be almost indiscernible, I could observe the difference."

"Why don't you tell all this to Madame Valmont? You have only to show her the piece and the pattern. There is your proof."

Madame Hoinville sighed and gave a little thump on the desk in front of her with her clenched hand, indicating impatience with herself. "I'm unable to do that. The replacement brocade is being woven in the mill now. I have the pattern but not the faulty piece. It was removed without my knowledge from the shelf where it was placed. I should have locked it up."

"Do you know who took it?"

"I was told. There was no secrecy about the removal. Rejects are frequently sold off quickly. However, in this case if an enquiry should be made, I would expect to hear that the purchaser was a nameless stranger passing through Lyons to an unknown destination—gone without a trace."

"This is an extremely grave matter. I must insist that you tell my sister-in-law everything you have told me."

"I cannot, madame!" Madame Hoinville took a deep breath. "It is not for me to point the finger of suspicion at her brother without positive proof. Yes, it was Monsieur Roche who took the brocade away as soon as he heard about it being returned."

Hélène drove out of Lyons to see Gabrielle the next day. Upon arrival, she told her everything that Madame Hoinville had said. Although Gabrielle sat listening, her hands quiet in her lap, her gaze was directed sadly out of the window at the autumnal spread of the trees and she showed no trace of surprise at what was being related to her. At the end of it she turned her head to look at Hélène.

"How impossible it is to escape destiny. In spite of my attempts to retain some mental and physical peace for myself here, it seems I have to return to Lyons after all. It is not the first time Henri has pilfered from me—that was before André was born. Things are different now. I will not have my son's birthright erased through any lack of stewardship on my part. I'll be ready to leave by this evening."

Hélène helped her to pack. It was noticeable that Gabrielle was taking no mourning garments with her. All were put aside for disposal with other possessions no longer needed. By evening dust-sheets covered all the furniture, valuables had been packed for transfer to the Rue Clémont and the shutters were closed over the windows. An agent had been called in to arrange the sale of the silk farm, which Michel was to manage until it changed hands. The house was not for sale. There was always the possibility that André would like to use it for summer vacations when he was grown, with a family of his own.

At the moment of departure the servants, all of whom had been paid their wages until the end of the year and given letters of reference, filed out of the house with their belongings, some of the women weeping. Only Gabrielle's personal maid and André's nursemaid were to accompany her back to Lyons. They were already seated amid the baggage in the second-in-line carriage that was waiting in the drive, Hélène being seated in the first with André on her lap. Gaston, exhilarated to be returning to city life, long since bored with country pastimes and village wenches, whistled gleefully to himself under his breath as he waited with the reins in his hands, whip at the ready.

Gabrielle was the last to leave the house to which she had come as a bride. She stood alone in the silent hall. Even the pendulums of the clocks had been stilled.

"Farewell, dear Émile," she said softly. Then she turned and went out of the house, locking the door behind her.

When she and her little travelling party arrived at the Rue Clémont it was to find that Henri and Yvonne were holding a musical soirée in the Grand Salon. There was the sound of a quartet and a soprano in full voice.

"Don't interrupt the festivities," she said to the servant who had admitted them, letting him take her cape from her. He had expressed his pleasure at seeing her home again, being one of the staff whom Yvonne had not replaced. "Just make sure that all the baggage is unloaded as quickly as possible and inform the housekeeper of our arrival. You may bring a supper tray to my office. I shall be working there."

"Er—one moment, madame." He had checked her as she took up a lamp, already on her way. "Monsieur Roche moved from his office into yours several weeks ago."

"Indeed?" Gabrielle raised her eyebrows. "No matter. It is mine again now and that is where you will find me."

A glance into Henri's old office showed that her possessions had been removed there and were stacked as if in readiness for storage at a later date. As she opened the door into her own domain she saw he had ensconced himself in a masterly fashion with his large desk, which had once been their father's, his ornate silver inkstand with its inset sand-shaker and his leather chair. Since this office was far more spacious than his own, he had also had every one of his cupboard files brought in, as well as a tall chest of drawers.

She set to work at once, estimating she had two hours before Henri learned she had returned. The supper tray was brought in. She drank the wine as she worked and nibbled at some of the food, hardly aware of what she was eating. Again and again the files revealed nothing in the least incriminating. Everything was in perfect order, not a figure that did not balance with the accounting clerk's ledgers. Henri had always been an extremely efficient businessman and the state of his papers bore that out. If Madame Hoinville had not been thoroughly convinced that something fraudulent was going on, Gabrielle might have been tempted to believe that this time a mistake had been made. Inwardly she wished for that.

It was midnight when the company departed. Then, as she had expected, heavy footsteps came hurrying in the direction of the office. Henri burst into the room, his colour high and his eyes angry. "What the devil are you doing here?"

Putting down the silk order she had been reading, she gave him a direct look. "I'm back to stay, Henri."

He did not attempt to disguise his furious resentment. "I thought you had settled in the country. What about the silk farm?"

"That's to be sold. Whatever it fetches will be most welcome at the present time. The coffers of Maison Roche are low. I put the silk farm

together again, but it will take time to bring it anywhere near the standard that Émile had achieved before the blight. I don't have his ability
there."

"So you've come back to interfere with Maison Roche again."

"I've returned to take full control once more. You're not being very
gracious. Why are you so upset?"

"What do you expect?" He glared about the room. "All these drawers were locked. You had no right to go through any papers without
asking me."

"Then it was careless of you to have left the ring of keys in my
office."

"It's not your—" He bit off his words in time.

"Not my office? Is that what you were going to say? You need have
no fear that I looked at anything that did not deal with Roche silk, and
for that I don't have to ask anyone's permission."

"But why did you start work as soon as you arrived?" His loathing
of her return made it difficult for him to address her in an even moderately civil manner. His whole stance was belligerent. "I was told you
didn't get here until nine o'clock. If you had waited until the morning I
could have gone over everything with you."

"I've been away a long time. Much has been happening in my absence. As far as I was concerned there wasn't a moment to lose."

"Are you satisfied with what you've seen?" He looked as if he might
strike her if she should give anything but an affirmative answer.

She gestured towards what she had been reading. "Nobody could
fault these ledgers. Every cost is listed meticulously down to the replacement of a peg in a spinner's broken stool. Every detail of every order is
recorded here. However, the results are not as I would have hoped. I can
see we could have done with more orders from Leipzig than were forthcoming. Many of my weavers working in their own homes have been on
short time or have had no work at all, sometimes for several weeks at a
time."

"I made sure the mill was kept busy."

"That's beside the point. I should have been notified about the
workless. I know the circumstances. There would have been cases of
extreme hardship."

"I dare say Hélène saw to them."

"No. She would have told me if any of my weavers had been on her
list. I think you chose to forget them."

"Business is business. I put the work where it was best executed."
His colour was no less concentrated, a nerve throbbing wildly in his
temple. "How long are you going to work now? I'd like to get my desk
and the rest of my possessions back into my old office right away. The

file cupboards can stay here. They contain the records of all that was carried out in your absence and should be in the main office anyway. The same goes for that chest of drawers."

She collected up the papers in front of her. All unwittingly, in those few words he had made it clear to her that he had nothing to hide from her there. "I think I will go to bed. Surely the change-over of the furniture can wait until morning?"

"No, it shall not." He jerked a chair aside as if prepared to pull the desk out of the room unaided if need be. "Tomorrow I want to be able to begin work without any hindrance."

She left him summoning two menservants to begin the change-over between the two offices.

As she made ready for bed and sat brushing her hair, the silver-backed brush reflecting the glow of the candle-lamp, she thought about Henri and understood what a terrible blow it must have been for him to see her again. To him it meant that all his authority over Roche silk, reasserted throughout her absence, had been dashed from his grasp. His aggression towards her had been positively malevolent, curiously sinister, almost as though he were prepared to stop at nothing if some turn of events should release all the hatred of her that her return had brought about. She had never seen him in that light before. Always his blustering manner, his false bonhomie in difficult situations and his pompous airs had made it impossible ever to think he might be capable of doing her or anybody else serious physical harm. Tonight something had made him desperate. It had swept away whatever was amiable in him, as though he thought himself close to needing self-defence at all costs. It could only come from his having been near to panic at finding her there in the house, an indication that somewhere under this roof there was evidence that would incriminate him if found. Not that he had the least idea that she suspected him. It was his own guilt that had set him in a turmoil.

She put down the hairbrush and continued to follow her train of thought. There could be nothing in the official files or else he would not have been prepared to leave them in her office. Perhaps there were incriminating papers in his apartment, but it would be impossible for her to demand access there and he would be safe enough. Suppose he was destroying them at this moment, burning them up in a fireplace in his private salon?

It was impossible to think of rest with all this on her mind. Leaving the dressing-table, she took up the candle-lamp and went along the corridor until she came level with the double doors that led into Henri and Yvonne's apartment. All was quiet within. So much for that supposition. She was as far away as ever from any clue.

Not wanting to go back to her room, where sleep would never come to her in her present wide-awake state, she continued along the corridor to reach the staircase and follow its graceful sweep to the hall below. She had missed the old house and it was good to be back in it again. Passing through to reach the Grand Salon, which was still her most favourite room with its glorious panels of spreading peacocks, the hues as true as on the day they were hung there, she held her lamp high to look around her in home-coming. The atmosphere was musky with the perfumes of the women who had been at the soirée and she went across to open a window. A cool breeze from the river brought the night sounds of the city into the room and she stood looking out at the twinkling lamps. Now that she was back in Lyons, she never wanted to leave it again. Here she would wait for Nicolas's return. When they met again all the bitterness and pain of their parting would melt away as if it had never been.

She closed the window and turned back into the room. The yearning for Nicolas was upon her as she had known it would be. It had returned with force and had almost taken her breath away, from the moment she had viewed Lyons again from the heights of Fourvière when the carriage was bearing her homewards. It was almost as though her heart thought he might be there, waiting for her; that she had only to run to La Croix Rousse for his arms to be held out to her. Dreams. It might be that she had hurt him too deeply for their reunion to be without pain and recrimination. The shattered look in his eyes at their parting still haunted her. Yet, no matter how she reasoned, she could not shake the belief within her that everything would melt away before the love that neither had been able to deny. Contrary to what was being said in silk circles, she was convinced that a new Maison Devaux would rise up from the old site. Silk was in Nicolas's blood as it was in hers. Just as their love for each other was like the life-blood in their veins.

Slowly she wandered round the beautiful room, the lamplight catching a jewel-brilliance from walls and upholstery. It was here, under the waterfall chandeliers, that she had first learned from her father's will that Maison Roche was hers to hold in trust for her son. She felt shame that she had almost failed him, first through remorse over Émile's death, remorse that had brought her almost to death's door herself, and afterwards she had put her own personal feelings before her son's inheritance. That would never happen again. She was back in control and neither Henri's duplicity nor trade difficulties should stop her from ensuring that André would be proud to inherit Maison Roche when the day came.

She halted abruptly, holding the lamp she carried a little closer to her, faint warmth coming through the glass. In her thoughts of her father and Henri something had stirred in her memory. Fleetingly she pictured Dominique sitting at the desk that was now Henri's. Once in her childhood she had entered his office when he had been searching for a paper he had misplaced. He had not seen her enter. She had been sent on an errand to him for a reason she could no longer remember. He had been annoyed when he looked up and saw her standing there, and had jumped up from his desk to hustle her out of the room and close the door again. Although she had been used to being an annoyance to him, his slights always registered with her, and now the memory returned with a clue at last to what she had been seeking since her return to the Rue Clémont.

At a run she went in the direction of Henri's office. The door was locked. That was no problem. In an old house the key of one lock invariably fitted another. She had to try only two before the door opened. Putting the lamp on the desk, she sat down in the chair that had amply suited her father's bulk and equally accommodated her brother's. Pulling open the small middle drawer, she set it aside as it had been on that day long ago. Then she reached into the aperture. After a few minutes of fumbling she found the catch of the secret drawer and released it. The drawer slid forward into the lamplight, packed tight with papers methodically filed together according to contents, even the most recent neatly stacked. She began to go through them with trembling hands. Here was all the evidence she needed. It did not take her long to discover that Henri had his own mill just outside of Lyons, established not long after Maison Roche became hers. Ever since that day he had stolen sections, or entire orders, from her, and even when her weavers had been without work he had taken all he needed for himself by a method similar to that used by the dressmaker whom Madame Hoinville had told her about. The extent of his deviousness appalled her as she examined bills and receipts in Henri's own hand. It was impossible to estimate even roughly how many thousands of francs had been diverted from Maison Roche, but it was not the money that mattered to her. Her distress came from the fact that her own brother had perpetrated this despicable theft.

Suddenly the door was flung open. Henri stood there in a dressing-robe, his face congested with temper. She saw instantly that he intended to use violence.

"You prying bitch!"

He lunged for her. She sprang up and stumbled on the hem of her robe. As she reeled away to the side of the desk he caught her, seizing her by the throat and shaking her, the pressure of his hands choking her protests into gurgling sounds. He was shouting at her at the top of his voice, enraged to a point beyond any self-control. She tore at his hands but could not loosen his grip. Her arms flailed and her fingers touched the heavy silver inkstand. She managed to grab it by one of its filigreed rails and swung it upwards, sand and ink pouring from it down her arm and splashing over him until its weight defeated her and it crashed to the floor. Together they staggered about the room, her throat and lungs compressed by pain, her strength ebbing from her.

"Henri!" It was Yvonne's shriek of outrage that came from the doorway.

He released Gabrielle and she collapsed to the floor. Then he slumped down in a chair, his head lowered, and began to sob. Gabrielle was aware of Yvonne propping her forward to help her get her breath back. Then she was left with cushions behind her while Yvonne went at a run, robe and night-gown billowing about her, to fetch Hélène, whose apartment was too distant for her to have heard Henri's raucous bellowing during his attack on Gabrielle. Two of the servants, who had been disturbed, appeared from their quarters by way of the kitchen area. Hélène, hastily aroused, paused on her way to the office and made a shooing gesture towards them with her hands as if the sight of them in their night-clothes gave them the look of children.

"There's nothing amiss," she assured them inaccurately. "Go back to bed. Sleep well." In the office she rushed straight to kneel by Gabrielle. Supporting her with an arm, she refreshed her by wiping her face with a clean handkerchief soaked from the bottle of lavender water she had snatched up to bring downstairs with her. There was ink on Gabrielle's hair and down her robe and night-gown, and the whole floor was gritty with sand. Yvonne poured a small cognac from the decanter Henri always kept in his office and Hélène took it from her to hold to Gabrielle's lips. "Give a large measure to Henri," she instructed. "I think he needs it."

Henri emptied his glass at a gulp and returned it to his wife for a refill. She obliged with an expression of disgust on her face.

"What's all this about?" she demanded shrilly. "Why were you trying to strangle Gabrielle? Has she found out about your thieving tricks at last?"

He glanced at her with a hangdog air and looked away again. The brandy had settled his immediate reaction to the violence he had used on his sister. He heaved a telling sigh. "Yes, Gabrielle has discovered I have a little sideline."

"You fool! You must have realised she would find out sooner or later. I guessed what was going on almost from the start."

He reared up his head, more relaxed in the familiar situation of quarrelling with his wife. "The family business should have been mine and I had every right to get out of it whatever I could."

"You could have broken away from Maison Roche and started your own fabric house if you had wanted to do it. You had no need to steal from her."

He jerked himself out of the chair, still too near the end of his tether to tolerate anything more from any source, and hurled his glass away from him in emphasis, causing it to smash into smithereens. "With your damned extravagant way, what chance did I ever have to invest on a large scale?" he roared. "You've been a millstone of debts around my neck for years!"

"So I'm to blame?" She set her arms akimbo and waggled her head from side to side in mockery of him. "What of your gambling? You never were a winner! That's why your father never left you Maison Roche in the first place!"

He hit her with his fist. Then he went on hitting her as if a second bout of madness had overtaken him. Yvonne screamed as he beat her down to the floor. Hélène left Gabrielle to try to intervene, but he thrust her from him with a shout.

"Keep out of this. No one shall interfere with a man's right to chastise his wife!"

Gabrielle swayed to her feet to try to reach the bell-pull to summon help, fearful that murder was about to come near for the second time that night. Before she could stretch out her hand to it, Henri stopped his onslaught as abruptly as he had begun. He stood over Yvonne, who lay whimpering, curled up in the corner to which he had driven her, blood pouring from a cut lip, one eye closing from a vicious blow he had dealt her and her arms crossed over her bruised breasts, which he had punched most cruelly.

"I've finished with you!" he bellowed. "You have no hold over me now. Let one of your lovers keep you from now on. Oh, yes, you're not the only one who found out secrets." A sneering note had come briefly into his voice before it took force again. "You'll get out of my sight and out of this house tonight!"

He swung about to charge bull-like for the door and pulled it open. Gabrielle, ignoring Hélène's warning cry, stepped in front of him and rested a hand on either side of the door jamb, as much for physical support as to bar his way.

"It's you who must leave tonight, Henri. In spite of discovering your swindling, I would still have given you a few days to pack whatever belongs to you. Now you must go and your belongings shall follow you. I always knew you were a bully and a coward, but I never thought you would go to the lengths I've experienced and witnessed here."

He did not attempt to throw her out of his way, which Hélène had feared. Realisation of what the outcome was to be of all that had hap-

pened seemed to dawn on him for the first time. "You can't turn me out
of my home," he blustered. "I was born here."

"It was your home and would have been to the end of your days if
you hadn't chosen to do what you did. This is André's house now. I only
hold it in trust for him as I do Maison Roche, and nobody in the world is
going to harm his interests, not even my own brother."

Henri became curiously subdued. He seemed unable to accept what
he had heard, an incredulous expression registering on his face. Then
incongruously, in view of the setting and the circumstances, he adopted
a contrite manner.

"You're extremely upset and you have every right to be. I apologise
for letting my temper run away with me and causing you distress and
harm. I can see my hands marked your throat, but I'll remind you that
it's the first time I've ever used any violence against you. Never once
when you were a child did I ever slap you, and you were irritating
enough at times. I was seriously provoked at finding you at my secret
drawer. Father confided its location to me as his eldest child and he
believed, as I did, that nobody else knew about it." He raised his hands
in a conciliatory gesture. "I'm willing to make amends for what you
discovered there. After all, as you have just said, we are brother and
sister, and it is easier to settle a rift within the family than it is between
strangers. In future my looms will be at your disposal. You may take
them over in lieu of my debts to you. I know they will be no more than
the proverbial drop in the ocean perhaps, but it is my gesture of goodwill."

She was sickened by him. "Keep your looms. I want nothing to do
with them or anything that is yours. Now go, Henri. Go and never
come back to the Rue Clémont." Her arms dropped to her sides and she
leaned back against the wall to let him pass.

He stared at her, seeing that this last throw had been in vain. His
lips drew back over his teeth in a grimace of vengeance. "Damn you and
your high and mighty ways. I always pitied Émile for having you for his
wife. He had you trailed. Did you know that? During the time when
you and Devaux were meeting secretly there was a spy on your tail
wherever you went. It's my guess Émile went to his grave not knowing
whether or not he had fathered your son!"

Gabrielle, already ashen from her ordeal at his hands, pressed herself against the wall as if to stay herself from falling. "Go, Henri," she
repeated with colourless lips. "Go!"

With a self-congratulatory snort at what he had done to her, he
strode from the office, his slippered footsteps slapping away upstairs.
Gabrielle, her eyes dilated by shock, turned her head to look wordlessly
at Hélène, who had risen from attending to Yvonne to stand statue-like,

struck into horrified immobility by the words of cruelty Henri had directed towards his own sister. The only sound in the room was Yvonne's continued whimpers of pain. Gabrielle opened her mouth twice in an attempt to speak, but her jaw was jerking and her voice seemed to have gone in the shock of what had been disclosed.

12

Gabrielle received an important visitor in the Grand Salon. She stood near the ornate fireplace where flames crackled cheerfully, elegant in her gown of tangerine silk, a gold brooch at her throat. Monsieur Morard of the Mobilier Impérial, a distinguished-looking man with grey hair, entered the room as he was announced and came across to bow over her hand.

"I'm honoured, Madame Valmont. I have been an admirer of Roche fabrics ever since I first saw your display at the Lyons exposition."

"I'm delighted to hear that. Please sit down. Allow me to offer you some refreshment."

When the preliminaries were over he began to explain the exact nature of his visit. "The Emperor has decided that the palace of Versailles, which has been little used since the Revolution, when its fine rooms were wrecked and its contents stolen or destroyed, is to be completely refurbished throughout and restored to even greater glory than it knew in the past. We of the Mobilier Impérial are interested in the possibility of commissioning silks from you for several of the important salons."

She flushed with excitement. It was far more than she had dared to hope for when she first received word that this man would be coming to see her. She had thought that, since the palaces used by the Emperor had been restored and refurbished over the past decade, all she could hope for was a small commission, perhaps the rehanging of a room where newish silks had faded, or a replacement of upholstery brocade. The palace of Versailles had been isolated and ignored as if it were a monument to the decadence of the past, and it had not once crossed her mind that the commission would be on such a grand scale. Then suddenly her pleasure was dimmed.

"Am I to receive this commission because Maison Devaux is no longer in operation?" It seemed a terrible thing to her to gain an advantage through Nicolas's misfortune.

"Not at all," he hastened to assure her. "There are many rooms in Versailles. We are also commissioning from Maisons Chuard et Cie and Grands Frères and two or three other leading silk houses in Lyons. If the Maison Devaux had not been burnt down it would have received its share. The Emperor is giving Lyons its chance to outshine anything it has ever produced before to make this palace the most magnificent the world has ever seen."

"I shall be proud to take my part in such an enterprise."

"Splendid. Now please show me a selection of your new designs that will be exclusive to Versailles and we shall discuss what is required. As you know, every tiny detail of the décor down to the most exact shade of even the smallest cushion is decided by the Mobilier Impérial. Nothing is allowed to encroach on the creation of a truly beautiful and tasteful room. Whatever colour patterns you are given must be matched exactly."

Since she had had ample notification of his coming, she had a wide selection of cartoons to show him, exquisite designs from Marcel's pens and paints, several incorporating the imperial bee and other motifs symbolic of the Empire. He picked out a number to take away with him to put before the committee for a final selection.

"You should not have long to wait," he said as he was leaving. "The Emperor is most anxious there should be the least possible delay with everything now that he has finally decided on the complete restoration of Versailles."

As his carriage took him away she gave a little laugh of sheer exuberance and hugged her arms in the thrill of what was happening at last. Hurrying upstairs, she went in search of Hélène to tell her the news. It was in keeping with the whole atmosphere of the house now that Henri and Yvonne had gone after the terrible events of the night of her return.

Henri, doubtless afraid Gabrielle would summon Gaston and the servants to evict him, had left in the early hours of the morning. Hélène had insisted that Yvonne stay until her injuries were at least partially healed. Gabrielle, realising that Yvonne's sudden appearance in the office had probably saved her life, agreed, but she was thankful when a letter from Henri was delivered ten days later. Yvonne did not disclose the contents but rose from her bed, packed her belongings, ordered a cab and left the house.

"Is she really going to join him?" Gabrielle asked in surprise.

Hélène shrugged. "She has little money and probably they are so accustomed to their quarrelsome way of life that she cannot imagine any other existence. Under any circumstances, I doubt Henri will dare attack her with such violence again."

Now, once again, Juliette played wherever she wished, André toddling about after her whenever he could. She was like a sister to him, and Hélène was a second mother, always in charge until Gabrielle came home to spend time with him and to put him to bed. He was progressing steadily in this cocoon of love and attention, could express himself in a few words and was given to a fine display of temper if he could not get his own way. Fortunately Hélène could be strict at times. It was she who had made life bearable for Gabrielle again after Henri's terrible disclosure.

"Never let your brother's evil words taint your memories of Émile," she had said when it became possible to talk more calmly the next day. "I remember, when André was born, Émile came straight to me after leaving the birth-room to thank me for what I had done in helping to bring about the safe delivery. I have never seen a man so happy. There was not the least doubt in his mind, then or later, as to whether André was his child. He said to me on more than one occasion, 'I can see my father in my son.'"

Gabrielle knew she would be eternally grateful fo Hélène, who was incapable of any kind of fabrication, for this reassurance. As for the rest of it, she was forced to accept that there was every likelihood that Émile had heard or seen something to cause him concern. Knowing how afraid he had always been of losing her, it was possible he had taken steps that were normally out of character. It haunted her that he should have guessed what she had tried most to hide from him, and as yet she could find no consolation in remembering how content he had been during their last months together.

She opened the door into Hélène's salon with a flourish and found her writing at her escritoire. "Tra-la-la! It's happened!"

Hélène put down her pen and swivelled round on her chair to clap her hands. "The Mobilier Impérial has commissioned a room! Congratulations! How wonderful! Where? Fontainebleau? Saint Cloud? Compiègne?"

"You'll never guess!" Gabrielle swept herself down at an angle onto a sofa, catching up one of its cushions to hug it to herself in her excitement. "Not one room or two, but several! Roche silk is to hang at Versailles!" She related all the details and then said how her fears that she had gained at Nicolas's expense had proved groundless. "That mattered to me more than anything," she confessed soberly in a switch of mood.

"I'm sure it did."

Gabrielle let her head drop onto the back of the sofa as she looked ceilingwards, her gaze far away. "Even if Nicolas is still embittered over our parting, I know he would be pleased about this commission I've received." Her voice throbbed. "I live for his return, Hélène. Being back in Lyons has done everything to me that I knew it would. There are times when I think I'll go mad not being able to see him or feel his arms around me. Although the past is still with me, and always will be, I'm looking to the future, not only for myself, with my longing for Nicolas, but for my son and for Maison Roche and for all the weavers and the rest of the workers who depend on me."

"Have you written to him yet?"

"No. I do not dare."

"What do you mean?"

Gabrielle stirred to prop an elbow against the upholstery as she faced Hélène. "If I wrote and received no reply, I would have no way of knowing if he had written to me or if I had hurt him too much for him to become reconciled by a letter. That would be a worse torment for me. When we see each other again all will be well. I'm sure of it. Eventually he will get leave. That's what I'm waiting for. That will be the time when the break between us will be mended and we'll be able to start afresh." Her face suffused with hope and confidence. "I know Nicolas is going to come through his campaign in the Peninsula. I feel it in the marrow of my bones. I like to think my love is a shield for him against the danger there."

Hélène was moved by this uninhibited declaration of love. In spite of her devouring passion, this strong young woman had lost no dignity, no quality of independence, and what she felt for the man she loved was the richer for it. "I pray that it is, Gabrielle," she said sincerely.

That same week the silk farm was sold at a higher price than Gabrielle had hoped to get. It seemed that she was on a crest that nothing could quell. Michel returned to Lyons and she offered him the post of manager of Maison Roche, something she had decided to do immediately after Henri's ignominious departure.

"I'm honoured to accept," he said enthusiastically. "I have served one great silk house in Lyons and now I am to serve another."

He went without delay to tell Hélène of his new appointment. She was giving Juliette a reading lesson and dropped the book in her excitement as she rose to give both hands into his outstretched clasp.

"That's splendid news!" she exclaimed.

"It means I won't have to move away from Lyons, which was what I had anticipated, with the problems of the Lyonnais silk industry still unresolved. It means we can look to the future now."

"I'm so glad! I know Nicolas will understand that the burning down of his silk house finished everything there for you."

Juliette, who had been swinging her legs idly, spoke up simply out of memory stirred. "Uncle Henri paid a man to start the fire." Then, bewildered, she saw how both adults turned simultaneously to stare fixedly at her. Suddenly she was afraid of the change of atmosphere and burst into noisy sobs.

Hélène flew to her. "Hush, darling. Don't cry. Are you sure you know what you said?"

Juliette pressed her face against her mother's neck, trying to hide from this totally unexpected trouble that had overtaken her. "I heard when I was in the cupboard in his office. What have I done wrong, *Maman?*"

"Nothing! Nothing at all. Let me dry your eyes. It's just that it is upsetting to hear anything about that dreadful fire. We shall forget it now and never speak of it again. Would you like one of those special bon-bons in the silver dish in the salon? Run along then and help yourself."

On their own, Michel took Hélène into his arms, his expression as grave as hers. "The mystery as to the cause of the fire is solved. I suspected arson from the start."

"We must guard this secret from Gabrielle for the rest of our lives. She must never know that her own brother caused her husband's death."

He kissed her gently. "We shall share that bond as we will share everything else, my love. Now that my career is assured, we can set a marriage date as soon as we have found a house that you like."

She hesitated only a second or so before putting a suggestion to him that, for many reasons, had been well thought out. "Let us live here in this house for a while before we get our own home. It is a help to Gabrielle to know that André is in my charge when she is busy, and when these orders come in from the Mobilier Impérial you and she will not have a minute to spare for several weeks before everything is in hand." Smiling lovingly at him, she linked her fingers behind his neck. "In any case I don't want to wait for house-buying before we marry. Let it be soon."

"Tomorrow?" he teased, no longer averse to the Rue Clémont on a temporary basis, with only Gabrielle and her child in the house. He could never have lived in close proximity to Henri Roche.

"The day after," she said, not teasing.

Following the civil ceremony, the religious marriage took place at the church of Saint Nizier. Only a few close friends were present and the bride wore a gown of Devaux silk. Michel had rescued the length in a package in the midst of the fire. It was the cream silk with the pale pink roses that she had admired on her visit to the Devaux looms. He had had a piece put aside for her, knowing even then that she was the woman he wanted to make his wife, and he had given it to her at their betrothal. To Gabrielle, seeing the beautiful shimmer of the gown in the setting of solemn stone and mighty arches, it was like a banner being kept flying for a silk house that would rise again.

The bride and groom left for a short honeymoon in Antibes on the Mediterranean coast. It was a fishing village on a sheltered bay where they could be sure of privacy and enjoy the warm sun that lingered there in late autumn. During their absence Gabrielle heard from the Mobilier Impérial. Monsieur Morard had been correct in promising that it would not be long before she was notified. Breaking the seal eagerly, she read that she was commissioned to produce the fabrics for eight rooms, which included two salons in the *appartements des princes,* three more for the *appartements d'honneur,* a *cabinet de repos* for the Empress Marie-Louise as well as a bedchamber and one other for the King of Rome, who was not much older than André. Listed last of all was a study for the Emperor himself. This marvellous commission encompassed wall hangings, door curtains, drapes, upholstery fabrics, cushions and bed drapery. Alone in her office, Gabrielle twirled around with the letter like a very young girl, unable to take her eyes from it. Her looms would gleam with wefts and warps of imperial colours and glitter with silver and gold *filé* and *frisé* to bring Maison Roche to the notice of the world and keep every one of her best weavers busy for two or three years to come.

By the time Michel and Hélène returned she was already getting samples of dyes together. There would be severe tests given to a new indigo dye invented by a Lyons man, which she wanted to use but had to ensure would not fade. Michel took up his work as effortlessly as if he had been with Maison Roche for years, and it was not long before she realised how much more Henri could have done to assist her if he had had the good of the business truly at heart. Michel lightened burdens from her on all sides, leaving her only the special tasks that were hers. Suddenly she had more time to spend with André without feeling she should have stayed at her desk after everyone else had gone home. It was an added bonus that Madame Hoinville liked Michel and worked well with him.

When Michel was at the mill one morning a letter was brought to him that had been addressed to his former lodgings. It was from Paris, and after reading it through he put it into his pocket. Later that morning, returning to the Rue Clémont where he now had Henri's office, he went in search of his wife and gave her the letter to read.

"I thought it best that you should break the news to Gabrielle," he said.

She nodded sadly. "I'll do it now."

When she made to return the letter to him, he folded it back into her hand. "Keep it. Gabrielle may wish to read it for herself after she has heard what you have to tell her."

They went downstairs together. In the hall they went separate ways, he to his office, she to the design-room where Gabrielle sat perched on a high stool beside Marcel with a cartoon on the slope of the drawing-desk in front of them. Hélène waited until Gabrielle, catching sight of the letter in her hand through the glass door, brought the discussion to an end and came out to her, able to tell by her expression it was a serious matter.

"Let's go to the Blue Salon," Hélène said, turning to lead the way.

"Wait!" Gabrielle put out a restraining hand, her voice low and hoarse with dread. "Is Nicolas dead?"

Hélène was dismayed by the query. "No! Neither is he wounded."

Gabrielle pressed the fingers of both hands over her mouth in a reaction of relief, gulping deep in her throat. Hélène put an arm about her waist and together they went to the salon and sat down on chairs by the fire. Gabrielle was shivering, her back wand-straight. "It's still bad news, isn't it?"

"I'm afraid so."

"Say what it is."

Hélène's expression was sympathetic. She attempted to ease what she had to say. "Michel heard from Nicolas today. One thing is certain. Although the letter about the fire that the Prefect forwarded got through, mine telling of your widowhood never reached him and neither did Michel's letter that listed the names of those killed on the night of the fire."

"How do you know that?"

"Two reasons. The first is that in the last paragraph Nicolas sends his compliments to Monsieur and Madame Valmont, which was obviously the only way he had of letting you know he had not forgotten you."

The sad immobility of Gabrielle's face did not change, although she looked away briefly as if her feelings were almost too much for her. "And the second reason?"

"He has put the site of the Maison Devaux up for sale and written that he never intends to return to Lyons."

Gabrielle's response was immediate and totally incredulous. "That's impossible! He would never do that!"

"I happen to know it has been in his mind for some time. During the ball to celebrate the birth of the King of Rome, Michel confided to me that Nicolas had written to offer to sell out Maison Devaux to him if he was interested."

"I don't know how to believe this." Gabrielle put her finger tips to her temples.

"I understood right away it showed how much you meant to him. He could not face coming back to Lyons where inevitably your path and his would cross at times, however distantly. You were another man's wife and had made your choice. There was no hope for him and he had to make a new beginning to his life just as you had done."

"What decision did Michel make?" Gabrielle still spoke on a note of disbelief that came from her unwillingness to accept what she was hearing and not because she doubted the truth of it.

"Naturally he was eager to accept the offer. It was a chance in a million. Nicolas was prepared to let him have it at a price far less than it would have fetched on the open market and had promised to help him secure financial backing."

"Then the fire changed everything." Gabrielle gave a bemused shake of her head. "Why didn't you tell me before now of what had been considered?"

"Because, as you say, the fire was a turning-point for all of us. There was no longer anything to stop Nicolas from returning to Lyons. So much happened at that time, and afterwards, that in a way I forgot that the sale of Maison Devaux had ever been a possibility."

"Where was this letter to Michel sent from?"

Hélène had known that this question would come and must be answered. "From Paris. Nicolas had been granted a short leave."

Gabrielle's face was stark. "He was there and I didn't know!"

"None of us knew until today. He had seen his lawyers and his bankers, never having changed his connections from the time he lived there, and the fire insurance for his Lyons property was settled to his satisfaction." Hélène handed the letter over to Gabrielle. "You will see that he has given Michel first refusal of the site if he should be interested. If not, the lawyers will put it on the market next month."

After reading the letter through, Gabrielle let it sink to her lap. "By now he will be two days' journey on the way back to winter cantonments at Ciudad Rodrigo." She spoke almost inaudibly. "If peace should be restored tomorrow there would be nothing to stop him going anywhere in the world and I might never find him again."

Hélène briskly dismissed this statement with an optimistic air that was not easy to summon up. "The campaign in the Peninsula is far from over, which gives us the time we need. Somehow we must find a way to get a message through to him." She tapped a forefinger thoughtfully against her chin. "I wonder if the Prefect could be persuaded again? Or is there someone else we might ask?"

Gabrielle was busy with her own thoughts. The time for letters and messages and waiting was over. She shot a glance at Hélène. "Would you look after André for me while I went away? I could never leave him with anyone else."

Hélène thought she had guessed what lay behind the request. "You don't have to ask me. I love taking care of him, you know that. Are you going to Paris to ask Émile's uncle to do something on your behalf? It did cross my mind, but he was so hostile and unsympathetic towards you at the funeral that I dismissed the idea immediately."

"I could never ask Uncle Joseph for anything. It was clear from his attitude that day that he held me responsible for Émile's being at the scene of the fire."

"Are you sure that was why?" Hélène's brows drew together. "I talked to him and thought otherwise, but it is of no consequence. Where are you going then?"

A change had taken place in Gabrielle's whole bearing, an eager determination in her expression. "To Nicolas! I promised him once that if ever I were free I would go to him. That time has come."

"You can't!" Hélène threw up her hands in dismay. "No woman can travel alone into a field of war."

"I'll not be alone. Gaston will come with me, I know. He's an old war-horse himself and I'm sure he'll leap at the chance." Seeing her sister-in-law could not accept the step she had decided to take, she began to outline a plan. "I should be able to get to Ciudad Rodrigo by Christmas. I know where it is on the map, having studied it whenever any news from the campaign has reached the news-sheets. There is a fortress there that is a stronghold guarding the northern way into Spain. Wellington will never get through. In any case there'll be no fighting at that time. The troops on both sides will be in their winter cantonments with little likelihood of breaking out until mid-February at the earliest. I should be able to have at least a week or two with Nicolas before turning homewards again. I'll be back in this house before any resumption of warfare."

Hélène was aghast. "What of the guerrillas? They do terrible things to women."

"With Gaston to protect me, I'll have nothing to fear. I've heard many of his soldiering tales, and even if he does exaggerate at times there's enough truth in his stories to show he knows how to get out of any kind of scrape. The hardest thing for me to bear will be my separation from André." There was a sudden swim of tears in her eyes that she could not keep back. "He will miss me as I shall miss him."

"Then please don't go." Hélène's voice shook in the urgency of her plea. "I beg you."

"I have to. I realise now that this is why destiny brought me back to Lyons. I'm being given a last chance to share my life with the man I love." After a moment's thought she added: "If it will make you happier I will ask Gaston to find out if any reinforcements for the army are likely to be leaving for Spain about now or, even if this is unlikely, if he would recruit a few of his old friends from his army days to travel with us as additional protection."

Hélène did not feel able to say anything more after that to dissuade her.

As Gabrielle had expected, Gaston did not hesitate when she put her request to him. Without asking the whys and wherefores, he simply wanted to know how soon she wished to start.

"As soon as possible," she replied.

"Allow me two days to make preparations, madame. There are horses to select, supplies to put together and so forth."

His first step was to make enquiries about any departure of reinforcements from the local barracks. With the Emperor's system of compulsory service, there were always batches of young men being trained for campaigning and marching off when ready. He found a sergeant whom he knew. They had once served together.

"If you move fast," he was told, "you can ride with a baggage train moving out under military escort at dawn tomorrow morning. It's bound for Salamanca, which is on the same route as the road to Ciudad Rodrigo. You'd not have many miles to go after that, and all within range of French protection. That's the only chance you'll get to ride in convoy for a long time to come. No more reinforcements are going from here to Spain. From what we hear, it will be a colder climate for future recruits."

Gaston shrugged. "The Tsar deserves to be booted off his throne.

He's flouted the Emperor's counter-blockade against the English once too often. What with him and the insurrection of the Spanish, it's no wonder there has been restlessness in parts of the Empire. It will be a good thing when both the Peninsula and Russia are under the Emperor's heel once and for all. Well, I'll be on my way. I've no time to lose."

He had already checked with Gabrielle that she knew how to travel light while ensuring she had sufficient warm clothing for the mountain passes and the snow they were certain to meet. After notifying her to be ready sooner than either of them had expected, he worked the rest of the day and into the night to ensure that nothing was forgotten or overlooked. She had given him the money to pay for everything plus a heavy purse of gold for the journey; she herself was to carry gold on her person. Swiftly he ticked off the items either put away in saddle-bags or ready for the pack-horses. A spyglass, canteens for drinking water, spare horseshoes, hammer and nails, a kettle, cooking pot, tinder-box, a knife and hatchet were all there, with enough storable food to sustain them on the journey. There was also feed for the horses, his musket, a bludgeon, pistols and rounds of ammunition as well as blankets and extra clothing. Satisfied, he snatched a few hours' sleep.

Shortly before dawn he and Gabrielle rode away down the Rue Clémont, two pack-horses in their wake. Her last action before embracing her sister-in-law in farewell had been to kiss the cheek of her sleeping son. From a window Hélène watched them go as they passed through the flickering lamplight. Unbeknown to Gabrielle, Gaston had come to her with a special request the day before.

"Do you, by any chance, happen to have one of your late husband's field uniforms, madame?" he had asked her.

She had been taken aback. "Why do you want to know?"

"I'd be grateful if you would loan it to me on Madame Valmont's behalf. He was taller but he was of slim build and it's my guess his uniform would fit her well enough. I managed to get hold of one for myself. My own was worn to rags during the time I was starving in the streets. It's possible that the occasion may arise on this journey when it would be safer for your sister-in-law to be dressed as a man or to appear to have some military authority."

Fear for Gabrielle had risen up in her again. "You expect to be in great danger at times, don't you?"

He raised an eyebrow, his mouth twisting in a wry grin. "It's a possibility. I'm trying to foresee any difficulty that might arise." Then, with gentle prompting, he added: "About the uniform?"

"Since Gabrielle's safety is involved, you shall have it. It is in a trunk stored in the attic. Come with me and you shall have it now."

It had turned her heart over when she lifted the lid and saw the grey uniform there. It was one Jules had worn for a while before promotion had called for a new uniform in celebration. For some reason it had never been disposed of, and after his death she had folded it away, feeling unable to part with anything that had been his. As she handed it over, she and Gaston exchanged a glance. In it was an unspoken agreement not to let Gabrielle know that he was prepared for dire emergencies. Straining against the window glass to catch the last glimpse of the two of them before they were lost from sight, Hélène tried to draw comfort from the knowledge that Gabrielle's safety was in capable hands.

At the barracks the heavy doors stood open to the courtyard within. Gaston reined to wait and Gabrielle followed suit. Although officially they could not look for protection from the soldiers in the event of an attack, they would automatically come under their defence.

"I can hear them now," Gaston said with a nod.

The officers on horseback, soldiers on foot and the wagons loaded with ammunition and other supplies emerged from the archway and went past with a clatter of hooves and a rumble of wheels over the cobbles. Gabrielle and Gaston fell in behind the rearguard and found they were not alone. Two men rode up to take a place beside them, one a travelling priest and the other a bereaved father hoping to locate the body of his drummer-boy son. Two companionable sutlers, both drunk, came at a reeling amble, packs of wares on their backs for sale to the army, and continued to share a bottle between them.

Hurrying up behind came the camp-followers, some of whom were prostitutes as willing to follow this batch of soldiers as any other. Among the wives was a tough loud-voiced woman, a veteran of several campaigns, who was set on catching up with her errant husband, who had marched off to Spain at an earlier date without letting her know. Gabrielle's sympathies were with the husband. The wife was quite a virago. As the sky lightened, the whole convoy passed across the wide and spacious Place de Bellecour where the grand buildings facing it on all four sides were bathed in the dawn's pale glow. On the slopes of the city rising beyond, the first rays of the wintry sun touched the tips of the tallest spires.

At night the soldiers bivouacked in the shelter of a wood, for there was a cold wind blowing. Gabrielle, wrapped in a warm blanket, slept soundly in spite of the hardness of the ground. In the morning it was chilly washing herself in a nearby stream, but she had come prepared to face discomforts.

She had chosen to travel in a warm, comfortable and thoroughly unfashionable riding habit cut straight around the hem with leggings beneath such as women wore when the weather was exceptionally cold.

Her black hat was flat and brimmed against rain, one that any country woman might have worn, and over her shoulders hung a cape that was virtually rainproof. Gaston was also practically clad in a goatskin jacket, thick breeches, a cloak fastened with cord ties that were easily released for emergency action, and a well-worn rust-red felt hat pulled down to his ears. Although there was still a rakish look to him, Gabrielle thought they might be mistaken for a farming couple, and for the purpose of their journey she had agreed to his suggestion that he address her as "wife" to discourage any of the soldiers from making overtures towards her.

It was not long before she began to feel a comradeship with everyone else on the march. This sense of closeness increased when they reached Spanish territory and the soldiers marched with muskets primed, ready for any sudden attack. The father of the dead drummer boy had to fall out when his horse went lame. The priest promised to make enquiries on his behalf, and when Gabrielle glanced back she saw them kneeling together in prayer on the icy road. The women no longer walked. They waited after each halt until the officers were riding ahead again and then climbed onto the last wagons, often having to hang on tightly to prevent themselves from being thrown off when the wheels lurched over the deeply rutted surface.

It was hard on everybody, humans and horses alike, when the mountain pass was reached. Driving snow obliterated the sight of anyone a few feet ahead, and the bitter temperature rimed the horses' nostrils with ice and threatened frostbite to those who failed to cover their noses and their ears. Again and again the wheels sank into drifts and had to be manhandled out of them. One of the sutlers lost his pack and would have lost his life over a precipice if his companion had not grabbed him in the nick of time. He gave no word of thanks, bemoaning the loss of his goods as if somehow his rescuer could have saved them too. They had not been on good terms for several days and now jealousy crept in, that one had wares to sell while the other did not.

After six days and five wretched nights the convoy passed down to lower slopes that undulated gently, and the whiteness of snow gave way to harshly frozen ground. It made travel easier, the wheels almost bouncing at times on the rock-hard surface, but it was becoming clear that the whole of northern and central Spain was in the grip of exceptionally cold weather and there was no sign of any respite.

With the exception of the veteran wife, the women had long since run out of food. Currency for them had become anything the soldiers cared to give them out of rations, and when one woman was caught stealing from a food wagon, which was keeping the soldiers meagrely fed on the long trek, the officer in charge forbade her to accompany the baggage train any more. In spite of her hysterical pleas, she was left behind with her small bundle of possessions in a village among sullen-looking peasants, a soldier being ordered to fire his musket at the ground in front of her every time she tried to escape and run forward. In the middle of the night, when all but the sentries were sleeping, she reappeared. She had been raped and robbed of everything except her under-shift, her bare feet frozen and lacerated by the rough terrain. Gabrielle, awakened by the priest, helped him to attend to her, wrapping her in a thick blanket to try to bring some warmth back into her body, Gaston taking over by massaging her limbs. When it seemed they might be succeeding in saving her life, she lapsed into a coma. The priest administered the last rites just in time.

In the morning there was no burial, the ground being too frozen for speedy digging, and any delay was hazardous in guerrilla country. The body was covered with rocks and small boulders, a cross of twigs propped upright, and after a short service the baggage train lumbered on again. Gaston, knowing how upset Gabrielle was over the whole affair, tried to give her an explanation.

"Stealing food is one of the worst crimes in the army's eyes; everybody's life depends on keeping the rations intact."

"The rule doesn't apply when our troops take what they want from the peasants," she retaliated.

"That's necessary foraging, not treasonable undermining of a fighting force."

"I've never heard anything so hypocritical before. That woman should never have been left behind."

"Maybe not. An example was being made of her. Food stocks are getting low. There isn't a man or woman with this baggage train who has any doubts about what will happen if there is any more stealing. A soldier might even be shot. I've seen it happen. At best he'll be flogged within an inch of his life."

Gabrielle shuddered and kept her gaze ahead. Hunger was everywhere in this war-torn land. She hated it when the baggage train halted at every village and hamlet and miserable farmstead for foraging parties to go with muskets to see what could be found. Being on a route that had been used ever since French troops first marched onto Spanish soil, there was almost nothing to be had. Now and again a small hidden store was uncovered by some wily soldier, or a goose found with its beak bound to keep it silent until danger was past. These small successes were always met by despairing wails from the peasant women, who stood huddled with their children at their skirts, watching their food being thrown onto one of the wagons. Gabrielle became increasingly saddened by all she saw. She was thankful that she and Gaston had no share in the cook-pots that bubbled over camp-fires when evening came.

It was after one of these forays that the guerrillas struck. One moment the convoy was passing undisturbed along a narrow road through a forest and in the next there was an explosion of musket fire from the trees on either side. Gabrielle reacted as Gaston had instructed, dismounting swiftly and running forward to bring herself and her horse within the shelter of the last wagon in the convoy. He moved faster than she would have imagined possible, taking a place with the rearguard to join in the defensive firing as if he had never left the army. The women ran to join her, throwing themselves under the wagons, one screaming in panic-stricken terror until the veteran wife gave her a hard clout across the face.

The attack was soon driven off, the soldiers bounding in pursuit until ordered back in case of a trap. A count was taken of casualties. Five soldiers had been killed and eleven wounded. The sutler who had lost his wares was another victim, having received a bullet in the head. Again no burials took place. Six mounds of rocks with crosses of twigs were left by the wayside. The wounded, bandaged and groaning, lay side by side on one of the wagons, the veteran wife in charge. The unremitting freezing temperature added to their misery in spite of their blankets, and during the next few days three more mounds of rocks were left in the wake of the baggage train.

At times Gabrielle almost wondered if she had ever lived any existence other than jogging along in the saddle behind creaking wheels and the thud of marching feet. Once they passed an old battlefield where the frozen ground had yielded up limbs and bodies that had remained unburied while the fighting swept on. The blue of French uniforms and the undyed white woollen cloth of a Spanish infantry regiment could just be discerned here and there like a macabre and unreaped harvest.

Whenever she had been exposed to a sad sight Gaston did his best to cheer her, sometimes a trifle insensitively, but she did not blame him for that, knowing he only had her well-being at heart. Campaign-hardened, he took everything in his stride and was almost obsessional about her safety at all times. He was also a man from whom virility radiated in every muscled move of his big frame and there were occasions when she felt quite threatened by him, as if her need for Nicolas had made her more vulnerable in his eyes. If she made any unguarded move she believed he would not hesitate to put fondling hands on her, and this made her watchful and wary.

Strangely, she did not fear him, confident of her power to control any situation that might arise. Neither was she repelled by his cheerful ugliness; on the contrary, she liked him exactly as he was, seeing him as her friend and mainstay, his status as a servant long since gone from her mind. Nevertheless she thought it was as well that he used the camp-followers as habitually as the soldiers, not realising that she understood the reason why he took a casual stroll after supper when they had biv-ouacked for the night or left his bed when he thought her asleep, his sighs and restlessness beforehand leaving her in no doubt as to what troubled him. To be alone with him for any length of time would have put a strain on both of them, although for entirely different reasons. It was as well that the last lap of the journey from Salamanca, where they would leave the baggage train, was not to be a long one.

Contrary to her hopes, she was not to be in Ciudad Rodrigo by Christmas. The suburbs of Salamanca were reached in the first week of the new year of 1812. While the baggage train went on towards the fortress centre of the city, Gaston took two rooms at a hostelry where they stayed overnight.

In the morning they resumed their journey, leaving one of the pack-horses behind at the hostelry in order to conserve the amount of corn and hay they had left. Gaston did not tell Gabrielle that the pack-horse had been included in the bargaining for the food he had obtained to replenish their supplies. It was likely they would be served a meat stew on their return to the hostelry.

They came within sight of Ciudad Rodrigo on the evening of January 12. Gabrielle wanted to ride on then and there to reach the fortress city, but darkness was falling and Gaston was not going to risk either an unknown road or a chance encounter with a trigger-quick sentry seeing guerrillas in every shadow. Excitement made it hard for her to sleep. She and Gaston always slept in their individual blankets close beside each other for her safety and for maximum warmth, and she was un-aware that on this night the amorous anticipation that emanated from her prevented him from sleeping too. His will-power was strained as never before in an effort not to reach for her, to keep himself from leaning over to capture her mouth with his own, or to let his hands enter her blanket to seek her warm flesh beneath her garments down to the most intimate parts of her. There had been many times when the bouquet of her skin, fresh and fragrant from a dousing of melted snow, had driven him from his blanket in the middle of the night, but camp-followers were a poor substitute for the woman he most wanted. He had returned each time to her side physically slaked but mentally unre-warded, something that had never troubled him in his life before.

It was ironic to him that they had become close friends. He had never been friends with a woman before, and basically it was not friend-ship on his part now, although he still hesitated to think of what he felt as love. He had tried to keep up the difference in status between them, but it had proved impossible in the face of their addressing each other as "husband" and "wife" respectively during the weeks they had been on the road. In education, background and cultural interests they were poles apart. Here, on their journey, everything had melted away except a joint purpose to survive, she to reach the man she loved, he to keep his promise that he would get her safely to Ciudad Rodrigo and home again.

Beside him she stirred, still sleepless. Desire for her gripped his loins beyond endurance. Why not? She was a sensual woman in a highly aroused state of expectation and well disposed towards him. Boldly his hand slid snake-like across her blanket-wrapped figure to come to rest on the firm rise of her breast. "I'm awake as you are, Gabrielle," he muttered hoarsely, breathing fast.

She did not seem to notice that he had used her Christian name for the first time. It was as if the pressure of his hand had been interpreted as an innocently misplaced signal, for she moved sharply, half raising herself to bring her face close to his.

"Did you hear that clink of metal too? It sounded nearer this time."

Instantly he was on the alert, all erotic thoughts of seduction gone, savagely aware he should never have lain hesitating; now the moment was lost. Throwing off his blanket, he knelt on one knee, listening intently. At first he could discern nothing except the whisper of a cold wind in the undergrowth and the crackle of the tree branches overhead. Then he heard it. Weaponry. A familiar sound to a soldier's ears. Nearby, armed men were moving stealthily through the darkness. He thrust one of the pistols he always kept by him into Gabrielle's hands, having instructed her how to use it at the start of the journey.

"I'm going to scout around to find out what is happening. I want to make sure that we're not in the path of whoever is only a few yards away."

He slipped between the trees. It was a moonless night but starry enough to enable eyes accustomed to the dark to pick out forms and movement. Coming to a place where the land sloped down, he saw a whole sea of men making their way towards a hill where a few lights twinkled on the top. He guessed it was a redoubt, part of the defences of Ciudad Rodrigo, and these were not guerrillas he was observing. No ragtag of clothing here, no woollen caps and unkempt hair. These were British soldiers! Here was the well-ordered, hard-disciplined advance of scarlet jackets and high-plumed shakos. They were going against all the traditions of warfare in breaking out of winter cantonments early in January to make a surprise attack on his unsuspecting countrymen. He could only suppose that Wellington had decided to take advantage of the exceptionally frozen ground when thick, squelching mud and flooding were the usual handicap to army movements at this time of year. It was impossible to estimate the strength of the force in the darkness, although it looked to him as if several hundred men were involved. In wrathful frustration he watched them go by. There was nothing he could do to warn the redoubt. If he fired a pistol he was too far away from the hill to be heard and he would only get his throat slit by a bayonet for his pains. There was Gabrielle to think of, too. Somehow he must get her away from here and out of danger.

She was relieved when he came back to her. As he had half expected, she refused point-blank to consider returning to Salamanca. "I haven't come all this way not to reach Ciudad Rodrigo now! Nicolas is there. I'm only a few miles from him. If I should miss meeting him now it might be another year before I know his whereabouts for certain again. I don't care about Wellington or the rest of the British. I'm getting to Nicolas whatever happens."

"That's what I thought you'd say," he commented phlegmatically. "Now you had better get some sleep. We can be certain the enemy won't stray in this direction. They've something else to do."

He slept as soundly as she did, both of them finally overcome by the exertion of their journeying. At dawn the attack on the redoubt started. They were both awake and making ready for the day, she pinning up her hair after its morning brush, he heating water for coffee over a camp-fire and slicing some black bread. She paused, her hands to her hair, as the staccato gunfire sounded in the distance.

"Let's hope the redoubt holds out," she said fervently.

It was approximately twenty minutes later when the silence descended again. By then they had eaten, stamped out the fire and were riding through the trees to where they could look towards the hill in the expanding daylight. He looked through his spyglass before handing it to her to view the redoubt. The surprise attack had been successful. Scarlet jackets were streaming like ants through a gateway, the smoke of musket-fire hanging mistily in the cold air.

"It's fallen," Gaston stated grimly. "The next target for attack will be Ciudad Rodrigo. All my experience in campaigning tells me to keep you away from there."

"Just try!" She flicked her whip against her horse's rump and went galloping off down the slope, her cape billowing. He followed, leading the pack-horse. If he had not been certain that the stronghold of Ciudad Rodrigo had every chance of withstanding any onslaught, he would have tied her up if needs be to get her away from the place. This city would be held at all costs. He might be able to have a hand in its defence in the same way that he had helped to fight off the guerrilla attack. Everything depended on whether he and Gabrielle could reach the city

before the British, flushed with their dawn success, headed at speed in
its direction.

They kept away from the road along which any army would come,
which meant they made slower progress than he would have wished. As
it happened, it made no difference, for they would have been too late by
any route. It was only luck that saved them from riding straight into
another British force that had come from a different direction and established itself in positions for an assault on the suburbs of the city. They
had come over a hillock and suddenly there below them was an unend-
ing sea of men and artillery, commanders riding to and fro and a general
air of imminent attack. Gabrielle, who had been poised to gallop the last
lap right to the gates of the fortress city, caused her horse to rear as she
halted him sharply in shocked disbelief.

"We can't get through there!" she exclaimed. "We must find another
way."

Keeping a safe distance from the enemy, they skirted part of the
city. Gaston could tell it was virtually encircled by that seething swarm
of men and horses, and he guessed that other redoubts had fallen earlier
to Wellington to enable him to get through with such a huge army.
Somewhere on a vantage point the Englishman would be in command,
directing all that was taking place. As a soldier, Gaston admired his
brilliant strategy in making this surprise move; as a Frenchman, he
hated his guts.

There were gaps in the assembled encirclement as he had anticipated, and one of these was where the river Agueda formed a natural
barrier. This suited his purpose as, through his spyglass, he could see
there was a French outpost placed to defend the bridge that he and
Gabrielle should be able to reach. Knowing the high tension that ran
through any defensive line at such a time, he did not want to be mistaken for a spy or a guerrilla and get shot at without ceremony. Borrow-
ing a white kerchief from Gabrielle, he tied it to his musket and held it
high as they rode forward, urging their tired horses to a canter to cover
the distance as quickly as possible. When they were within hailing distance they were ordered to halt and declare themselves.

"Gaston Garcin and Madame Valmont on an important mission to
Captain Devaux of the *chasseurs à cheval*."

"Pass, friends."

Gaston gave her a wink as they rode across the bridge into the
outskirts of the suburbs. On all sides the clustered hovels and russet-
roofed homes, the walls baked almost colourless by the heat of many
summers, were as deserted as the farmsteads. French defences were set
up everywhere, the muzzles of cannons gleaming above empty pigpens
and by closed wineshops and thrusting forward over what were vegeta-

ble patches at another time of year. They had ridden only a short way when Gaston, checking the time on his pocket-watch, saw it was exactly four-thirty. In the same moment the British assault, in a tumultuous burst of artillery fire, broke forth. It was as if thunder had rolled down to vibrate from the earth itself. The French cannons leapt in reply.

Gabrielle was thrown from her saddle as her terrified horse swerved and stumbled before gathering itself together again to bolt away with a flash of hooves. Gaston, fighting for control of his own mount as well as the pack-horse, saw her lying there and could do nothing until he was able to dismount and tie the reins securely to a tree. She was getting to her feet and dusting herself off when he reached her. To his relief she was unharmed. He rescued her hat for her, which had landed nearby, and then the next second he knocked her with him to the ground again as a howitzer shell screeched overhead to explode on contact with a nearby house, showering them with debris. Another followed and then another. The horses were wild with fright, the tree swaying under their frantic efforts to pull free.

"Get into that stable!" Gaston yelled, half pulling her to her feet and giving her a thrust in its direction. "I'll fetch the horses."

She ran to it and hurled herself down on the straw inside. Never had she heard anything like this terrible bombardment. It was as if the whole world was being battered apart. When Gaston brought the horses into the stable at a run they became quieter, soothed by the familiar odours of straw and hay, although their eyes were still wild and their ears twitched constantly. Gaston pitied them. These were not war-horses. Until the guerrilla attack they had never heard anything more alarming than a fire-bell or the crackle of fireworks. When he had given them a few reassuring claps on the neck he watered them from a barrel he had noticed in a corner, breaking a film of ice as he dipped into the bucket. Afterwards he began searching around.

"What are you looking for?" Gabrielle asked him from where she sat with her back against the wall of a stall. Dust showered down from the rafters with every boom from a nearby French cannon as well as the shuddering of the ground from exploding shells and round shot.

"A saddle for the pack-horse, but there's nothing here."

"If there had been I wouldn't have it," she retorted. "I'm not taking anything from the peasants. They have little enough."

He came and settled himself on the straw beside her. "You can ride my horse for the time being. I'll pick up a saddle somewhere in the city."

"I'm sorry I allowed myself to be thrown." She released a regretful sigh. "That hasn't happened to me since childhood."

"It couldn't be helped."

"My change of clothing went with the horse. I've only a few things left." She tapped the draw-string bag that hung from her belt. In it she kept her purse, a comb and other small closely personal items. "Some clothing of yours was in the second saddle-bag."

"Mine were not important," he lied. He had had her late brother's uniform and his own in that saddle-bag, for he had had to distribute the baggage among the horses in the best possible way. Now the uniforms were lost. To date there had been no need of them. He hoped the same state of affairs would remain. "We should be able to buy replacement garments in the city."

"How long before we're inside its gates?"

"We're still a mile or more away. How soon we get there depends on the bombardment. If it shifts from this district we might dodge along for a bit without being caught up in it again."

She thumped a frustrated fist into the straw. "I hate to be skulking here when I should be finding Nicolas. So near and yet so far. At least the cavalry won't be taking part in this exchange of fire."

He did not say that much depended on whether or not British troops gained a foothold. Another explosion rattled the stable walls and instinctively she drew closer to him. The horses whinnied nervously, stamping their hooves. For a while they listened to the din, only commenting when one explosion seemed closer than another. Suddenly he cocked an ear.

"That cannon near here has stopped firing." Springing up, he ran to the door, darted a few steps out to look around, and what he saw brought him rushing back to grab hold of the horses. "Quick! The defences in this section are withdrawing. We have to get away with them."

Gabrielle had no time to be uneasy about mounting his horse, although it was a strong brute and she would need all her strength to manage him. As Gaston set the speed at a gallop she followed closely behind and they were caught up among retreating troopers, bounding gun-carriages and yelling officers on horseback, urging everyone on. Overhead, behind and in front of them the explosions continued. She saw a whole line of soldiers go down like ninepins as a cannon-ball sped on from its landing point to scythe through them, smashing their bones as it went. The screams were agonising to hear and comrades ran to pick them up and carry them in the general flight, their mangled limbs dangling. The dreaded grape-shot was being fired too, light canisters that exploded scraps of metal and gave grievous wounds. Every man who went down was snatched up by those nearest him for, in spite of appearances, this was not a panic-stricken rout but an ordered retreat. This became totally apparent when the second line of defence was reached and gun-carriages and men turned about to take up their new positions beside those already manning it, while those carrying the wounded pushed them into waiting carts. Within seconds French cannons were again booming back at the enemy.

Slackening their pace to an easy walk for the sake of their tired horses, Gabrielle and Gaston continued on towards the city on its rocky mound. They had to wait to let some reinforcements pass at a quick march, which Gaston interpreted to himself as a sign that hand-to-hand fighting was taking place somewhere along the line. They rode on again towards the wide-open gates and, when they were near, a sentry shouted to them, "Stand clear! The cavalry is coming."

Gabrielle only strained forward in the saddle for a first glimpse, excited and eager, until Gaston reached over to seize her mount's bridle and haul her in beside him to the verge of the road. In a burst of colour and a jingling of harness a squadron of the *chasseurs à cheval*, two hundred and fifty strong, came out of the gates at a gallop, sabres drawn. They wore their Hussar-like fur hats, green and red plumes swaying back, and their fur-lined pelisses, secured by a strap across the chest, hung from their left shoulders and flew out behind them, the sleeves waving. It was a startling and magnificent sight, the flapping leopardskin saddle-cloths giving an exotic touch of Africa to the drab day. Each man's face bore the same expression of ruthless satisfaction at being released for battle, jaw set, eyes glinting. Gabrielle, who had been staring wide-eyed from the second they appeared, sighted Nicolas and screamed out his name.

"Nicolas! I'm here!"

He neither saw her nor heard her cry and galloped past within a few feet of her. Seeing him again, it was as if her whole soul had flown to him. As the rest of the squadron went thundering by she sat looking after him, reeling inwardly from love, scarcely able to accept that he had not known she was there. When the last horseman had gone past, she turned her mount to follow after him, but again Gaston seized her bridle.

"No, you don't. That's no place for you."

Her face was pale and strained. "Then I'll wait for him here."

"You'll not do that either. We'll go into the city where you can eat and rest and be refreshed for his return. He'll be back. Hand-to-hand fighting has to stop at nightfall or else a man may slay his own comrades." When she remained as she was, still staring down the road at the disappearing chasseurs, he leaned over to tug at her sleeve. "Remember what you once told me when we were talking? You said you were sure he would come through this campaign."

She turned her staring eyes on him, her mouth tremulous. "Then why do I feel so afraid for him now? I have a feeling that everything is slipping out of my control."

"It's only because you've seen a battlefield for the first time and that has unnerved you. Nothing else has changed. You and he are the same as before. Don't start having doubts about the future now. It doesn't become you. Come along. We'll find a hostelry where you can watch the gates from the window for his return."

She obeyed him, looking back over her shoulder. Inside the city it appeared that life was going on much as usual. Although it looked as if goods were in short supply, the little shops were open and people were in the wineshops and cafés. Troops were billeted everywhere, the whole of Ciudad Rodrigo a mighty garrison. Gaston judged the second line of defence to be holding, for he saw no more reinforcements going out. Although he was unable to secure a room for Gabrielle with a view of the gates, he did get one in the next street and was lucky to find one in such a congested place. It was small and dirty, with no bed-linen and straw on the bed that had every sign of being bug-infested. He summoned a maid to clear out the dirty straw, wash the bedstead and leave it dry for the blanket he spread in it.

"You'll be better off on this even if the wooden slats are hard," he said.

She turned from the window where she had been looking out. "It's getting dark," she said, her thoughts away from the room.

"I tried to get bath water for you, but there isn't a bath in the place. The maid will be bringing up a jug of hot water any minute for the bowl and I'm afraid that was the best I could do."

Wrenching her thoughts back to him, she came forward to give him a smile of gratitude. "You're good to me. Forgive me for being distrait. I appreciate everything you've done to bring me here safely." Her voice faltered. "Shouldn't Nicolas be back by now? There have been no returning chasseurs going past the end of the street."

"I'll go to the gates and make enquiries."

"Please come straight back and let me know." There was an unspoken plea in her words that he should bring Nicolas with him if it was possible.

"I will as soon as I have something to report."

Once in the street, he made his way to the gates. He could tell from the number of people waiting that it was unlikely he would hear anything yet. There were many women in the crowd, army wives and Spanish women who had married or formed liaisons with men in the defence line. The bombardment was still in force, which was a cause for concern. He would have expected it to have eased off by now.

"No news yet," was the answer that did not surprise him. While waiting he went into a shop and managed to get a pair of men's breeches that he judged would fit Gabrielle should an emergency arise. With his spare coat on her and her hat pulled down, she would pass for a boy well enough. Noticing a bolt of fine white cloth on a shelf, he decided to buy a length on her behalf.

"Cut off enough for a woman's petticoat with some extra for this and that," he told the shopkeeper, who spoke good French with a strong Spanish accent. It had been folded ready for him when a shout came from the direction of the gates, making him slam the coins into the shopkeeper's palm without further bargaining over the price. He hurried back towards the gates, thrusting his purchase into one of the large pockets in his goatskin jacket as he went.

Soldiers were clearing the street, shoving people back with brutal haste. "Make room! The army is coming in! The whole defence line is falling back! Get back there!"

Gaston drew into the shelter of a doorway to watch. The tactical retreat of an earlier hour had given way to a mass exodus from the battlefield. Through the gateway came a torrent of men, horses and gun-carriages. Mostly regiments were together, interspersed with stragglers wearing plumes, pompons or other embellishments of a different colour. A number of chasseurs rode in, some wounded in the saddle but still able to keep their seats. As far as he could see, Devaux was not among them. Although he waited some time and saw other cavalrymen, there were no more chasseurs and he decided to begin finding out what had happened. Some of the returning soldiers had shouted out in reply to questions called to them by bystanders. There had been mentions of encirclement and the British breaking through and more scraps of information that had built up a rough idea of the development of events in his mind. Hoping that one of the chasseurs he had seen had been Devaux after all, he set off to find out what he could.

For Gabrielle the hours of waiting were endless. Each time there was a step on the stairs she had looked out and been disappointed. Finally she heard a heavier tread and rushed out again. Gaston was coming up the stairs.

"Is Nicolas back?" she cried, unable to endure the suspense any longer.

He paused to look up at her. She looked fresh and beautiful as a spring morning with her hair newly washed and entwined with a narrow pink ribbon, a small piece of feminine frippery she must have been saving for this time, because he had not seen it before. She had prepared herself for her lover and he had to shatter her hopes. There was no way he could think of to soften the blow. He cleared his throat and answered her.

"Captain Devaux has been taken prisoner."

She cried out, stunned to tears, and turned away to lean forlornly against the wall as if her overwhelming despair was sapping away her strength, her face buried in the crook of her arm.

For two days the fortress artillery kept up a roaring barrage against the British and in support of a few remaining outposts. The acrid smoke from the guns drifted down over the city. As a precaution, Gaston moved Gabrielle to a safer place away from the city walls. It was a room in a derelict hovel, far worse than the first, but it was safely tucked away between buildings on a side street with an entrance to the rear that would be difficult to find by anyone not knowing it was there. Gabrielle made no complaint and they slept side by side on their blankets on the floor as they had done during the journey. The horses were left in the stable of the hostelry, there being no stabling in the new vicinity, and he went daily to feed and water them.

On the third morning a thick fog had crept in from the river Agueda during the night, completely blotting out the British lines and hiding the fortress from them. It was a day of peaceful silence for soldiers and civilians alike. Gaston, who had already become familiar with the layout of the city, continued to scout around. It was his policy in a tight corner to gain whatever knowledge might prove useful to him at a later date, and there were fewer tight corners than to be in a city besieged.

Gabrielle passed the time sewing some undergarments for herself from the fabric that Gaston had bought for her. It was as well that he had made the purchase when he did, because from the moment the gates were closed for the siege, every available commodity in the city had shot up in price. As she stitched the seams her thoughts went fondly to André, whom she would be leaving to the care of his aunt far longer than she had intended, to Hélène herself, to Maison Roche and always back to Nicolas.

"The chasseurs were encircled," Gaston had told her when she was able to take in what he was saying. "Only those towards the rear of the encounter were able to get away. You were right in your conviction that he would come through this campaign. The war is over for him. He'll be shipped to England and kept there until the Emperor makes a truce with King George III's government."

"Are you sure he was not wounded?"

"Not when he was last seen at the forefront of the fighting. If he has suffered any injury we know the British treat wounded prisoners of war well. Just as we do. The cruelties that are perpetrated on both sides in this campaign don't reach out to wounded men, except when they fall victim to the Spanish guerrillas. Be thankful for his safety."

She was trying to draw stamina from that fact and not to think that she might be old before she saw Nicolas again, or indeed whether she would ever find him. Her sanity might not be able to bear such a prospect. As for her conviction that he would come through this campaign, that had not been misplaced. What she had not realised was that it had not meant she could hope for a reunion at the same time.

When the fog lifted, it could be seen that the British had entrenched themselves dangerously near and their artillery began to take greater effect on the city. It was obvious they were not prepared to make a long siege and wanted a speedy conquest. Buildings were badly damaged by shells and round shot. Frequently fires broke out, adding to the hazards. People were killed by falling debris or buried beneath the rubble of their own houses. Looters were shot and their bodies hung up in the square as a warning to others.

On the fourth day of the siege the enemy blasted two breaches in the fortress walls, rubble cascading down into the streets below and flying high over rooftops. At seven-thirty on the evening of the fifth day, an unexpected hour when the daylight was almost gone, the British, in spite of being raked by gunfire, burst through the breaches in their hundreds. When the first wave of redcoats was crowded on the sloping rubble, a strategically placed mine of immense momentum exploded under them, killing countless numbers and lighting the whole of the shaking city in a ghastly yellowish glare. The effect on the rest of the surging force was like a spark to tinder. They came yelling and shouting and swearing their vengeance, fighting like madmen and impossible to stem. Stabbing with bayonets, firing muskets point-blank and lobbing grenades into buildings as they came, the redcoats began to sweep through the streets like a scarlet river in spate, eliminating defensive forces as they went, unchecked by their own losses.

It took them two hours to take the city and even then the killing went on, the frenzied victors smashing into wineshops, striking down anyone in their path, the screams of women resounding as they were discovered and seized. Gaston, who had been firing his musket at a defence post, was on his way back to Gabrielle. On the day of the fog he had tested his sense of direction. Now it stood him in good stead as he hastened through dark passageways that threaded through and behind buildings, barely wide enough to let two people pass each other, mostly without lamps alight owing to the timing of the British assault at an unlikely hour. In one place, at an opening into a street, he had to climb over bodies and he relieved two dead French soldiers of their coats and waistcoats, hoping there was not too much blood on the garments he had grabbed for Gabrielle. For himself he did not care.

Drunken redcoats were raiding a wineshop in the street outside the hovel where he had left Gabrielle but, with the entrance being to the rear from the small alleyway, he was able to enter without the risk of being seen. Upstairs he found her pressed against the wall, watching fearfully through the window the carousing in the street below, the whole room illuminated by a burning house nearby. At the sight of him she sprang forward in relief, her features gaunt from all she had witnessed.

"You're safe! I was so afraid. They've been dragging out the women! Even old women and young girls. They pulled a baby from a mother's arms and hurled it aside like a doll." She pressed the back of her hand against her violently quivering mouth. He did not pause to answer her, throwing her the jacket and waistcoat.

"Put these on!" He darted to his saddle-bag and pulled out the breeches he had bought for her. "These too! And hurry!" Turning his back to give her privacy, he yanked off his goatskin jacket and thrust an arm into the sleeve of the uniform. It felt soggy and he knew why. Behind him she gave a moan. Swinging about, he saw that she had not moved but stood frozen with horror. She had caught the garments with both hands and now she was staring at her left palm, seeing it was wet with blood. He cursed his luck that he had not been able to discern in the darkness that her coat was as stained as his. He had to break through her shock and he bellowed at her: "Put it on! If you don't, it'll be your blood next and mine. As you've seen, the redcoats are on a rampage. Anybody in their path is being slaughtered and you know what's happening to the women. There's a blood-bath in this city tonight!"

She pulled herself together and nodded. "I'll put it on."

He turned his back again and continued talking to her. "Our only chance of getting out of this mess with our lives is to be in uniform, although even dead French soldiers are being bayoneted to make sure no life is left in them. It will take the British officers time to restore order. When there's carnage like there is in Ciudad Rodrigo tonight, they'll be in danger of their own lives in the general drunkenness of the troops. Probably it won't be until dawn before they restore discipline again. In the meantime they'll be doing their best to save lives by taking prisoners themselves and herding them into a place where they can ensure some protection. My guess is that it will be the main barracks and that's where I'm taking you. If I'm wrong, we'll try another."

"How do you know all this?"

"Because what is happening is nothing new. I've seen French soldiers behave exactly the same. I've been part of that madness at the moment of conquest. I'm not proud of it, but I admit to it. Don't ask me why it happens. I don't know. Are you ready?"

"Yes."

He turned. She was chalk-white. The breeches fitted her and she had buttoned them at the knees and tucked them into her riding boots. The waistcoat was loose enough to disguise her figure and the blue cutaway coat would pass on her, although blood darkened it all down the right side. It was her stony gaze that told him that by his own words he had driven a wedge between them. She was never going to be able to forget what he had told her, never going to succeed in disassociating the man who had become her friend from the rampaging, raping soldier he had been and who stood before her in all but mood in a corporal's blood-stained coat.

"Get your hat on," he ordered brusquely. "Whatever happens, leave everything to me. And keep your mouth shut. If a British officer should question you, be too dazed to manage a reply. That's normal with the young. I've seen drummer boys struck dumb by shock for several hours sometimes and you look young enough in those clothes to be classed with them. Now let's go. Keep close."

They crept from the building. There was no one in the alleyway and he led her to the nearest passage. She had to hold on to his coat-tails in some places where the passage became a tunnel and everything was pitch black. It was a gruesome route. Rats scuttled out of their path and every time there was an opening into the street she glimpsed gutters running with blood and bodies slumped and sprawled grotesquely at the moment of death. Shouts and drunken singing and always the screams of women echoed and re-echoed against the stone walls on either side and from the filthy cobbles underfoot. He brought her to the east wall of the barracks and left her there in terrifying solitude while he scouted ahead. In minutes he was back.

"The barrack yard is full of captured French soldiers. We'll wait until another batch is being brought in and then we'll fall in with them. You'll not let the British officers know you're a woman until discipline is restored, and then it will be safe for us to leave the city and start out on our journey home. I've only to show them my game leg at the same time to prove that I'm no longer a regular soldier and then they'll not keep me a prisoner of war with the rest."

In that second she made her resolve. She would remain a prisoner of war and be shipped to England. Then she would reveal her identity and be set free to find Nicolas. Suddenly hope was high in her again. A new phase of her life was about to begin.

13

Nicolas did not see the fall of Ciudad Rodrigo, although he was to hear about it at a later date. The day after his capture he and the rest of the prisoners of war taken at the same time were marched away on a trek to a coastal port. He and his fellow officers were treated with the customary respect by their captors and given horses to ride. Other ranks of the chasseurs had to make it on foot, much to their resentment and disgust.

It had been hard for Nicolas to part with Warrior, who had borne him through some terrible fighting since he had first acquired him, always with the extraordinary courage common to war-horses, but he had had no choice in the matter. Warrior had been annexed by a British major of the Dragoons, who knew a fine horse when he saw one. On his last sight of his mount the leopard saddle-cloth had been pulled off and thrown to the ground while the resaddling took place with another in

the Dragoons' regimental colours. It had grieved him to see that Warrior's splendid tail had already been cut short in the British military
fashion that gave no consideration to a horse's inability to flick away the
persecuting flies when the warm weather returned.

The march to the port of embarkation took two days. He and his
fellow officers talked little to each other, too sunk in gloom at being
wrenched away from the campaign to face untold months, or even
years, in captivity, and he had plenty of time to think over the battle that
had been lost on the first day of the assault. The odd thing was that, as
he had ridden out of the fortress gates towards the smoke and din that
lay ahead, he had had a curious sensation of being called back. It was
nothing that he had heard or could pin-point, and he was only able to
put it down to a premonition, something that was normally quite alien
to him. Strangely, Gabrielle had come into his mind, vividly and poi-
gnantly, with the same blow to the heart that missing her did to him
whenever he allowed his thoughts to go in her direction.

Minutes later there had been no time to think of anything else
except slicing and cutting a way through a surge of redcoats, musket fire
and rifle bullets whizzing past his head. Then there had been the coming
to grips with his British counterparts on horseback, the swing and hiss
and thrust of sabre into flesh and bones, the clang of blade meeting
blade, the spattering of blood and always the dreadful noise of battle, the
grunts and shouts of effort, the groaning of the wounded and the whin-
nying and snorting of the horses. It was only when he glimpsed fellow
chasseurs beginning to tip from the saddle through a fresh attack coming from the rear that he realised they had been cut off and surrounded.
They fought desperately but their losses were enormous. When he himself was surrounded on all sides, muskets pointing at his chest, he saw
that at least half the squadron had been wiped out and many of the
survivors were badly wounded. This was the reason why no more than
fifty-five chasseurs were making their way into captivity. The wounded,
left behind, had all been dealt with by British surgeons, brought in from
the field by carrying parties, and in spite of the swift medical attention
Nicolas feared that many would not live through the next few days.

Oporto was the point of embarkation. It had been sacked by his
own countrymen three years before when Portugal was first invaded,
and the damaged buildings bore witness to that event and its recapture
by the British. There was a warship in the harbour and a second vessel
was sailing in with troop reinforcements when the prisoners of war
reached the quay. During the journey their numbers had been increased
as detachments of captured Frenchmen fell into the march with them,
having been taken by the British when minor towns and garrisons and
outposts had been overrun during the advance to Ciudad Rodrigo. From

what was being said, Badajoz and Salamanca would be Wellington's next targets.

The officers were rowed out to the warship and were accommodated in crowded quarters with a hammock each. The men, ferried out afterwards, were directed down to the orlop deck below the water-line. Nicolas went down into the bowels of the ship to see how they were faring and was horrified by the cramped conditions and inadequate sanitation, the air there already fetid. When he complained to the captain he was informed brusquely in excruciating French that more captives would be put down there before the ship sailed.

"Troopships are always crammed," the captain said. "We can allow even less room for prisoners of war."

Within the week a further long column of captured Frenchmen appeared on the quayside. The majority had been taken after the fall of Ciudad Rodrigo and were a bedraggled-looking lot with a variety of headgear, for the cold winds did not allow for bare heads and many had lost their shakos or helmets, according to their regiment, in the battle. With his officer's privilege to move freely about the ship, Nicolas was on deck to watch the embarkation of this new crowd of prisoners. Again the officers were ferried ahead of the men to the warship or took the gangway of the sister ship, which lay alongside the quay. When the officer boatloads came aboard they were surrounded, as Nicolas and the rest wanted to hear the latest news. During this time the last space in the hold was taken up by new arrivals and the hatch closed down.

Nicolas wandered back to rest his arms on the gunwale while he watched the ribbon of prisoners still going aboard the sister ship. Without exception they appeared tired from the long march. A large fellow, who limped badly, leaned for support up the gangway on the shoulder of a youth in a black hat that would have been better suited to a country woman than a drummer boy, if that was what he was. It was impossible to tell from such a distance.

Both ships sailed with the morning tide. It was destined to be a rough voyage. In the Bay of Biscay the vessels lost sight of each other in a howling gale, but they regained visual contact not far from Land's End when the sun showed itself above the south coast of England, which went sliding by like a green ribbon under the February sky. Beyond the horizon to the starboard side, France lay tantalisingly out of sight. Nicolas was not alone among his comrades to stand looking in its direction, assailed by homesickness. The warship was bound for Portsmouth, but those on the sister ship might glimpse their own land when they sailed past the white cliffs of Dover en route for the Port of London.

Nicolas was on deck again when the two ships parted company, the warship sailing into the Solent and leaving her sister ship to continue

along the Channel. All on deck waved to one another in a final farewell
until the sails of each vessel were lost from sight.

Portsmouth was a large and busy naval town full of sailors and
seafaring folk. It was said to be impossible to walk a mile in any direction from the docks without passing a hundred taverns, and there
seemed no reason to doubt it. For three weeks Nicolas and his fellow
officers from the warship lived cheek by jowl in a barracks while registration and consideration for parole took place. He was among those to
whom it was granted after being warned it would be rescinded immediately if the rules were broken. They were put on their honour in any
case, as officers and gentlemen, not to try to escape, and to go against
this code would be to sully their oath of allegiance to their own country
and bring disgrace to the name of France. In the past this same bond of
unbroken word meant that officers on both sides of warring nations of
integrity could be repatriated and trusted to live at home and not re-
enter the conflict. Now that Bonaparte had completely changed the
rules of warfare, dispensing with the old courtesies, the chances of repatriation were slight. Although the British were aware that since the
Revolution not all French officers were gentlemen born, they kept to
their own traditions and gave them the benefit of trust.

Nicolas was thankful for this when he stepped out of the barracks
to make the best of his parole. He, and those similarly privileged, were
now able to take whatever accommodation they could afford in any city,
town or village to their liking on the strict condition that they did not
change their address without permission, kept to the curfew allotted to
officers on parole and reported twice a week to the government agent in
their district, who would give them the pay due according to their rank.

In contrast to the treatment of officers, the men were closely confined. It had always been the custom for any civilised country to finance
the food and clothing of its nationals held prisoner of war on enemy
terrain, but Bonaparte had chosen to ignore this commitment and was
leaving them all to their fate. As their uniforms wore out or if they were
already in tatters from the battlefields, the British issued them with
bright yellow suits and scarlet waistcoats, the better to sight them in any
escape. They were allowed out only to work in the fields, gather in
harvests, dig ditches, clean drains, build walls, houses and other properties, including new prisons, such as Dartmoor prison, which had been
newly completed in Devonshire to house the ever increasing number of
prisoners of war flooding into British ports.

There had been captive Frenchmen in England since France's declaration of war after the guillotine beheading of Louis XVI, and for
many the Peace of Amiens in 1802 had been of too short a duration to
allow them all to be returned home. As well as the soldiers being held,

there were sailors taken after great sea victories, privateer and merchant seamen. Nicolas learned from a reliable source that upwards of a hundred thousand Frenchmen, their allies and their mercenaries, were incarcerated in England, and that number did not include the shiploads arriving as a result of Wellington's successful advance in the Peninsula. It was not surprising that the British had had to turn the hulks of old warships and whatever other archaic vessels were available at docksides into prisons, and these were dreadful places for those unfortunate enough to be put there.

Nicolas did not intend to remain in Portsmouth, although it suited him to be there for the time being. He took a room in a private house where he received bed and board that were adequate, and on the day he moved in he took delivery of the civilian clothes he had ordered from a visiting tailor during his sojourn in the barracks. There had been two fittings for each coat, one cinnamon brown and the other dove grey. He was well pleased with the results. His uniform was sponged clean and repaired before he packed it down in a travelling box that he had purchased for his belongings. After making some enquiries he found a retired governess willing to teach him English, and he studied with her from nine until three o'clock for six days of every week. On the voyage to England he had made plans. Totally disillusioned with Bonaparte, who according to all reports was on the brink of a great attack on Russia, dragging France into further bloodshed, he had made up his mind to spend his time in captivity usefully. The thought of idling hours away each day was abhorrent to him, and he believed he had found a way to overcome the problem.

At the end of three months he wrote a letter in excellent English to an address in Macclesfield. There was an English silk merchant of that town named Josiah Barnett, who had been sent as a young man to Lyons to see for himself how the French silk industry worked and had stayed at the Devaux home. Nicolas could not remember that visit, being only three years old at the time, but he met Josiah Barnett during the Peace of Amiens when once again the silk merchant had visited Louis Devaux, accompanied that time by his wife. There had been generous invitations to visit the Barnett home at Macclesfield, which Nicolas had not thought of accepting until he found himself on a ship bound for England. Now he wrote to Josiah, not asking to stay at his home but to enquire if there was any chance of employment at Barnett Mill and explaining how he came to be in Portsmouth. There was no guarantee of a reply. Feelings against Bonaparte ran high and there was always the chance that Josiah Barnett no longer wanted to acknowledge a French acquaintance.

Almost by return post he received an agreeable letter. It stated briefly that the door of the Barnett home was always open to a Devaux.

As for employment, that could be discussed. If Nicolas's spoken English matched up to the fluency of his letter, then it was possible that some arrangement might be made.

"What do you think?" he asked his grey-haired teacher.

She, secretly enchanted by his accent since his first words in English, smiled her prim little smile at him across the verandah table on which she had served him tea and where they sat in the warm June afternoon. "Go to Macclesfield. Your English is good and it is improving every day. You deserve any post that is offered to you and more."

"I thank you, Miss Pomfret." He reached out to take up her thin, age-spotted hand and put it to his lips. "You have been a kind and patient teacher."

She knew how much she was going to miss their lessons. Her retirement was never going to be the same again.

He was given official permission to reside in Macclesfield. Before leaving Portsmouth he went to say goodbye to the men who had served under him, not knowing when, if ever, he would see any of them again. They were housed in Porchester Castle, which lay within the vicinity of the port and had become a prison for five thousand prisoners of war. The castle was not as crammed as the warship's orlop deck had been and there was a courtyard for exercise, sports and other pastimes, but it was still excessively overcrowded and depression and gloom prevailed, often with outbursts of fighting among the inmates or attacks on the guards. Both these offences received harsh punishment, as did any other misdemeanour that went against the iron rules. He had to bribe a couple of guards to gain admittance for a brief quarter of an hour.

His chasseurs, who had been proud men in the saddle, were restless and hot-headed, unable as yet to adjust to their surroundings. Those prisoners who had been there a long time had become resigned and learned to turn whatever spare time they had to their own profit. It had become common practice in all prisoner-of-war centres for these men to save bones from their meals, boil and bleach them white, and then to carve ship models of intricate and delicate detail, miniature spinning-wheels and other working models, such as dancers and marching soldiers, chess-pieces, toys, fans, watch-stands, toothpicks and tiny cradles on rockers complete with sleeping infants; from straw they plaited hats and bonnets, slippers and sandals and created straw marquetry on trinket boxes, fire-screens, snuff-boxes, tea-caddies, silk holders and other such articles. At every prison they were allowed to sell their wares to the public on allotted days. Nicolas, after handing out the tobacco he had brought with him to his chasseurs and parting from them, found himself pestered to buy some of the handmade products on his way back to the iron-studded gates. A veteran prisoner, more persistent than the rest, kept up a constant barrage of salesmanship right up to the last moment.

"If you don't want a galleon or a schooner or a clipper, what about a figurehead, monsieur? That's a novelty I'm noted for. You won't find none better."

It was thrust in front of him even as the guard began to pull on the handle of the gate. The bone figurehead was not more than eight inches in length, pale as ivory and marvellously carved, portraying the head and shoulders of a beautiful woman, her hair curling back as though in the sea wind, her draperies swathed about the swell of her breasts. Uncannily, she held the look of Gabrielle. Fascinated, he took it into his hands.

"How much?" he asked.

Back in his quarters, he wrapped it carefully in a white kerchief and packed it with the rest of his belongings in his valise. It was as near a likeness to her as he would ever get. He accepted that it had been folly to purchase it when his continual aim was to try to forget her, not to deliberately seek a reminder. She still haunted his dreams and his desires. He was coming to the conclusion that, since time was doing nothing to eradicate his passion for her, he would have to find some other means to drive her from his heart and from his mind.

On the morning he left Portsmouth on the stage-coach for Macclesfield, the news-sheets were announcing that Bonaparte had crossed the river Niemen and was advancing with the Grande Armée into Russia. Nicolas sighed to himself as he took his seat in the coach. He could not shake off the conviction that it was a black day for his beloved France.

The journey to Macclesfield took two days. As the coach lumbered out of Portsmouth to pass through five shires to reach his destination in Cheshire, he took a keen interest in all he saw. It never failed to surprise him that a strip of sea as narrow as the English Channel could make this country so entirely different from his own in scenery, architecture, politics, customs, food and drinking habits. It was no wonder that the British and the French had never seen eye to eye and old enmities had smouldered over the centuries, erupting on opposite sides in any war in which both countries were involved. He felt totally alien in this land that was, figuratively speaking, only a stone's throw from his own. Frustrated at being a captive, still filled with anger that he had allowed it to happen, albeit death had been the only alternative, he hoped that work in Barnett Mill would be hard and exacting, filling what would otherwise be a degrading vacuum in his life.

Macclesfield was reached in the evening. It was a brick-built town with sloping streets that wound like textured ribbons out into quiet rural areas. It was as if the countryside had refused to be completely

banished when the silk button industry began to take over the community in the eighteenth century and continued with silk manufacture to
expand the town gradually. He put up at a tavern, ate a hearty supper of
roast beef, new potatoes with mint, peas and carrots, followed by a rich
bread pudding, all of which was washed down with a tankard of good
ale.

In the morning, which was balmy and full of birdsong, the sky a
pale English blue, he set out for Barnett Mill. On the way he was met by
the clatter of looms coming from the weavers' homes. These were three-
storeyed terrace houses, the wide, square-paned windows on the top
floors showing that, unlike the weavers of Lyons, the families lived and
slept on the ground and middle floors with the looms located in the
garret rooms above. It was a sweet sound to hear again after the vile
crescendo of many months of war, even though it was the thwack-
thwack and not the *bistonclaque* of the loom that he preferred. Jacquard
had not had the chance to make his mark yet this far afield, but the war
would end one day.

For the first time since his capture Nicolas began to feel more at
ease. Here among all that was familiar to him in the silk world he might
find it possible to adjust and settle into a new life that would see him
through until his return to his homeland.

Barnett Mill was a brick building from the previous century, of no
particular architectural merit except for a well-proportioned portico,
the weaving windows reflecting squares of bright sunshine on three
floors. There were two other mills in the vicinity which appeared to
have been built about the same time, and a full orchestra of looms could
be heard at this point. He entered the lobby of Barnett Mill to find
himself facing glass-panelled doors leading into the loom-room on the
ground floor with an office to his right. Even as he reached out towards
it, the door from within opened and he found himself face to face with a
fair-haired young woman, small-boned and slender in a muslin dress of a
pinkish colour and a straw hat tied under her chin with ribbons. Her
strongly defined arched eyebrows, accentuated by her pale complexion,
arched still higher at the suddenness of seeing him, and the laughter of
surprise gurgled from her.

"You must be Captain Devaux! I know you from my father's description. I'm Jessica Barnett." Her laughing smile had lit her quite
unremarkable features to a liveliness that in her case was more attractive
than prettiness. It was lodged as if permanently in the depth of her grey-
blue eyes, giving them a sparkle that was decidedly impish.

He had forgotten that Josiah Barnett had a daughter, an only child
as he recalled hearing now, and he responded with a grin. Her merri-

ment was akin to the sunniness of the day and the lightening of his spirits on his way to the mill. "I'm honoured, Miss Barnett."

"I bid you welcome to Macclesfield and to Barnett Mill."

"That is most kind of you."

"I'll take you to my father right away. I know he's on his own because I've just come from spending a few minutes with him on the way to the market. Have you just arrived?"

As he answered her question and several more that she shot at him, she led him through an outer office where a clerk was writing at a high desk and there were some framed silk buttons on the wall, through another door straight into Josiah Barnett's office.

"Look who I've found, Papa!"

Josiah, a grey-haired, rotund man, was seated at a cylinder-topped desk placed against the wall in an untidy setting, a glass partition giving a direct view into the ground-floor workroom with a door beside that led into it. He sprang to his feet and greeted Nicolas heartily.

"My dear sir! How splendid to see you again."

He was just as Nicolas remembered him, amiable and ruddy-faced, although as was to be expected he had aged in the interim and he seemed to have a more serious demeanour about him than at their last meeting, almost as though he had been through some sort of crisis. Knowing the vagaries of the silk world, Nicolas guessed he had had more than a fair share of business worries, particularly as Bonaparte's counter-blockade had caused a general slump in trade over the years.

"This reunion is my pleasure, sir."

"I wish most sincerely it had not been war between our two countries that was instrumental in bringing you to Barnett Mill."

"I echo those sentiments."

"Take a chair. Sit down, do," Josiah invited, resuming his seat. "That's right. I think this calls for a little celebration." He beamed at his daughter. "Pour a glass of madeira for each of us, my dear." Then, returning his attention to Nicolas, he leaned forward eagerly. "Tell me, how is Monsieur Devaux? I trust he is well. I suppose it is some time since you had direct contact with him."

"I regret having to tell you my father died eight years ago."

Josiah looked shocked and then shook his head sadly. "I'm deeply sorry to hear that. He was a good man and always a kind friend to me. I want you to understand that the war has not changed my appreciation of times past."

"That was my hope when I wrote to you."

"I'm more than glad that you did. I bear no personal animosity towards France or any of your countrymen—with one diabolical exception." He looked quite fierce just at the thought of Bonaparte. Jessica tapped him on the shoulder.

"Papa! It was agreed that when Captain Devaux came there should be no talk of the war. It is discourteous to him in present circumstances."

He relaxed and nodded, smiling up at her and clapping his hand affectionately over hers for a moment. "You're right, my dear. It shall not be mentioned again." He raised his glass of madeira. "This is a time of celebration when once more a Barnett and a Devaux can be together under the same roof and not an occasion for recriminations of a national basis on either side. After the wine I shall take our new arrival around the mill and show him the work that is going on there."

"We dine at six-thirty," Jessica told Nicolas from the chair where she perched herself. "It is a later hour than is fashionable in London, but that is how it has to be when my father will not leave the mill before the workers."

"It's impossible to stop the habits of a lifetime at my age," Josiah admitted. "I was raised to open the mill and to lock it at night as my father did before me and my grandfather before him."

Jessica decided to refill their glasses, serving the wine first to Nicolas. "It wasn't such an exacting business in their day as it is in ours, Papa."

"Don't you believe it," he replied. "Competition was just as hard. They made buttons then, as you know, Nicolas. Very fine silk buttons that were sold throughout the country and abroad as well. Macclesfield's first water-powered silk mill was built in 1743 and my grandfather built the second a year later. Silk tapes and garters were also produced, and with the introduction of broadloom weaving in my father's time the mill changed to the manufacture of silk handkerchiefs, shawls and fancy silks suitable for dresses and waistcoats and so forth. Those are still our chief products."

Jessica was departing. "I'll see you later then, Captain Devaux."

He rose to his feet. "Call me Nicolas, please."

She paused in the doorway, looking back at him with a twinkling glance, and the sunshine coming through the window in the room beyond gave an aura to her, shining through the primrose fairness of her hair. "I may allow you to call me Jessica."

He chuckled. "How soon will you reach a decision?"

"Perhaps this evening. After we have dined." Her skirt swirled out of the door and it closed after her.

Amused, he sat down again to resume talking to her father. She struck him as a person with an enormous capacity for happiness, and the atmosphere she had created around her seemed to linger on in the dusty office like confetti after a carnival.

He enjoyed the tour of the mill. The upper floors were taken up by looms, weavers busy at their craft. On the ground floor throwsters were doubling raw silk into thicker yarn just as he had seen so often in France.

"In the past," Josiah told him, "most of the yarn thrown here went to the Spitalfields weavers in London, but now we need the bulk of it ourselves. Some of our raw silk, which you see in those opened bales, is from Turkey and the rest is still shipped in from the Far East by the East India Company as it was in the beginning of the industry here."

After a look into the design-room, Josiah led Nicolas back into the office. There he explained that he had long needed an extra right hand to relieve him of some of his work. "I have a nephew in the woollen industry, who will take over from me when I retire. I like him. He's a good fellow, but he's young and needs experience elsewhere before he comes here into silk. That is why your letter seemed like providence to me. I know your background. I've seen the silks that you and your father produced. I believe that with your skill and knowledge you can fill a gap for me. So I'm willing to give you a try if what you have seen interests you enough for you to commit the rest of your time in England, however long or short it may be, to the good of Barnett Mill. I dare say I sound blunt to you with your French manners, but that's my way. What do you say?"

"I accept gladly."

"Good." They shook hands solemnly. "I suggest we spend the rest of the day in my office while I explain different aspects of the business to you."

"I agree."

"There's one thing more. About your accommodation. Which tavern did you stay at last night? I'll send a boy to transport your baggage to my house. My wife, who wants you to stay too, has prepared a pleasant room for you and I'm sure you will be comfortable in it."

Nicolas declined politely. "I have no doubt of that, yet I can't accept your offer of accommodation. I don't want you to consider me ungracious, but if we are to have a business relationship there are bound to be differences of opinion at times, and I wouldn't want to be the cause of any disharmony in your home."

Josiah refused to be dissuaded. "When I lived in your father's house in Lyons we had differences at work, mainly because I was a know-it-all as young men often are. I must have tried Louis's patience sorely at times, but once we closed the door on the mill for the day any trouble was never mentioned until we were back again there next morning."

"Nevertheless, I must refuse."

Josiah looked uncomfortable and ran a hand over his thinning hair. "I'm afraid you have no choice. I have no wish to bring up the subject of the war between our two countries, but that is why you are here and your officer's parole would be a fragile affair if there was any bending of the rules. It is not usual for officers to work during their captivity as you wish to do. I dare say you are one of half a dozen at the most. When I received your letter I approached the government authorities about it and was informed that, provided you resided in my house and worked solely in my mill in a capacity fitting to your rank, they were agreeable. If you were not working you could live where you liked. Before you came I signed for full responsibility. There was no other way."

Nicolas's face darkened. He seethed inside. It was no fault of Josiah's that this present situation had arisen, but it was a terrible thing to be constantly subject to a foreign captor's rules, particularly in this case. "What if we don't agree or find we can't work together?"

"I can't foresee such a contingency. If it should come about, you would be free to leave and your parole would revert to its original form."

There was nothing for it but to accept with good grace. The war would not last forever and neither would his captivity. He gave Josiah a formal little bow. "Then I accept the kind hospitality of you and your wife."

That evening he and Josiah walked home together, for the Barnett house was not far from the mill, located in a residential quarter and set amid trees and a flower garden with a kitchen garden hidden by a brick wall beyond a barrier of apple and cherry trees. There was no sign of Jessica when they arrived. Phoebe, Josiah's wife, met them and welcomed Nicolas warmly into their home as if there had never been such a man as Bonaparte who might yet attempt to threaten England's shores once again when the war with Russia was over.

"We have spoken so often of the Devaux family in this house," she said happily. "I am delighted to see you again and it is wonderful for us to have the chance to do a little for you in return for all the hospitality Josiah and I received in your father's home."

Nicolas had only a slight memory of Phoebe, for during the time the Barnetts were in Paris she had been fully occupied with shopping and sightseeing while her husband discussed business matters with Louis and himself.

Now Nicolas found himself liking her just as he liked her husband and her daughter. He thought the Barnetts a charming family. Phoebe was pleasantly overweight, having kept a curvaceous figure, and her hair, which must once have been as fair as Jessica's, had faded to a platinum shade that enhanced a face that bore traces of having been a prettier version of her daughter's at the same age. The brightness of her eyes belied the matron's cap and sober-styled clothes that convention demanded. Nicolas had the impression that there was still much of the lively young girl locked up in the middle-aged body, and he remembered the old adage about studying the mother for faults before marrying the daughter. Why such a thought should have crossed his mind he did not know, but he retained the idea that Jessica would never become dull or stifled by the passing of years if she continued to resemble her mother.

Phoebe led the way upstairs, chattering as she went. His baggage had come and was in his room. Was there any English food he did not particularly like to eat? She did not think she could persuade the cook to try to prepare anything French, but if there was something he yearned to have she would do her best to see that it was served to him. He assured her that she had no need to concern herself and he would enjoy whatever was put before him.

When she left him on his own he looked about him. As Josiah had promised, it was a comfortable, spacious room with a four-poster hung with green silk and a bureau where he could write in privacy, as well as bookshelves on which some volumes in French had been thoughtfully placed.

He went to the open window and looked out to find he had a view of the rose garden. Jessica was there, clipping off the best blooms and laying them in a shallow basket hooked on her arm. He almost called out to her but decided against it, remembering with amusement the half promise she had made him about her name. In any other woman, such coquetry might have been brash or clumsy, but the sheer enjoyment of life within her had made it a tantalising lure. He saw through the game, and she knew he had, but that did not lessen the pleasure of it for both of them. Resting his weight on the wooden sill, he leaned back against the frame and continued to watch her. The last rose she took was a white one and she removed the thorns before tucking it into her bodice. She had almost no cleavage, being small-breasted, but she was prettily shaped and he smiled to himself in appreciation. As she left the garden she passed along the path right under his window and was still unaware that he was there.

When he came down to dinner he found the Barnetts in their drawing-room. Everything about the house reflected the taste and life-style of a well-to-do middle-class couple who cherished the good pieces of furniture handed down to them and had gathered solid additions of their own to make an unpretentious and comfortable home. No silk wall hangings here, strong brocade on the sofas and chairs with nothing delicate in texture or hue to soil easily. The windows had folded-back shutters with no drapes in the fashion of an earlier time. The fragrance of freshly cut roses filled the air. Josiah was sporting a red rosebud in his lapel.

"Come and join us, Nicolas," he invited with a sweep of his arm. "As this is to be your first dinner in our home, Jessica has picked a rose for each of us."

Phoebe indicated a peach rose in her brooch, smiling and nodding at him. Jessica herself had a yellow one pinned in the lace of her neckline and matching the ribbons in her hair. For him she had brought the white rose without thorns. She picked it up from the table where it lay and came across to give him one of her quick, dazzling smiles before she concentrated on slipping the flower into his lapel. He watched her under his lids. Her fingers were trembling slightly. When she glanced up before stepping back away from him he caught the depth of the look she gave the rose before it was lost in the twinkling glance conjured up by her musical laugh.

"There! Now you're as fine as the rest of us."

Raising his lapel with one hand, he bent his head to inhale the sweet scent. "This English rose has been well cared for during its wait for me, I can tell." He had the satisfaction of seeing her avert her face to address her mother on some pretext, as if for the moment she sensed what he had witnessed and did not dare to risk whatever lay in his eyes.

During a walk in the flower garden after dinner, a thick shawl about her shoulders at her mother's insistence in spite of the warmth of the evening air, she showed him a more serious side to her character after he had drawn out of her an enthusiasm for music and for books, many French authors being familiar to her in translation, and her special interest in the Elizabethan period, for she had inherited from her grandmother a workbox from the sixteenth century covered with the needlework of that time. He found her easy to talk to, more intelligent than she had chosen to reveal to him at first. They ended their stroll with his answering her questions about what it had been like to grow up at a time of unrest and revolution, something far from her comprehension, living as she did in a land of law and order with its established wealth, prosperous middle class, and growing industrial power.

"Have you reached your momentous decision as to how I may address you?" he enquired on a more light-hearted note as they were about to re-enter the house.

Immediately her face became full of fun and she tilted her head provocatively at him. "What would you call me?"

"Jessica will do, I think," he mocked gently.

"I'll allow it, because nobody else has ever made my name sound French before!" With a laugh she ran indoors ahead of him. Grinning at her good-natured jibe at his accent, he followed her.

It was the start of a curiously sensual battle between them of laughter and teasing and little jokes that drew them together as well as keeping them apart, for their repartee veiled the unspoken knowledge they shared, which was that she had been violently attracted to him from their first meeting. As the weeks and months went by he enjoyed her cheerful company more and more, for it was often exactly what he needed. It was as if she flickered sunshine through the house and had the innate ability to brighten his darkest days. Yet their physical contact remained the first evening when she had put the rose into his lapel.

His work at the mill went well. The designs were too conventional and unimaginative for his taste, but he found the designer willing enough to launch out into fresh fields at his instigation. As an experiment, some shawls went out in a new design and met with immediate success, resulting in large orders for repeats. After that Josiah gave Nicolas a free hand, able to see that he was introducing a touch of French elegance that had been completely lacking before. The fabric designs also became more French and in a matter of months business had increased tremendously.

During this time Nicolas read the news-sheets avidly, following the retreat of the Russians before Bonaparte's advance. Then there came the astounding news that when Bonaparte reached Moscow it was only to find it had been evacuated. There was no one left with whom to negotiate peace terms and the city was afire. The Grande Armée was being forced to withdraw in the merciless weather of a Russian winter through a countryside left empty of food. It did not need much imagination to picture how it would be.

Jessica came into the drawing-room one December evening when he sat alone, staring into the fire. The news-sheet he had been reading lay where he had let it fall to the floor. "What is wrong?" she asked anxiously, hurrying across to drop to her knees in front of him, looking up into his haggard face, which was etched with disillusionment and despair.

"The Emperor has deserted the Grande Armée." His voice, always beautiful to her with its French intonation, sounded strangely stretched and tired. "He is back in Paris and has left thousands and thousands of men to freeze to death in the Russian snows. To me it is another sacrifice of lives to his pride. The Peninsula showed me to what length he was prepared to go in his lust for power. Through him thousands more of my countrymen are rotting in overcrowded prisons or stinking hulks, many of them dying of privation, guilty of no crime, ordinary men who were drawn from their homes and families to serve a madman." On the last word he thumped a shaking fist in emphasis upon his knee.

"My dear Nicolas." She saw that his eyes were agleam with restrained tears and it tore at her heart to see him in such distress.

He returned his bleak gaze to the dancing flames and seemed to be speaking his thoughts aloud. "I'm never going back to France. My country is dearer to me than I could ever express, but Bonaparte is no emperor of mine. I will not live again under his rule."

"When peace comes you will want to go home, whatever you may think now." It was a time she dreaded for her own sake—never to see him again.

He shook his head wearily. "There is nothing for me there. All I ever wanted from life was in Lyons. The woman I loved, my work and my interests, my silk house and my home. Everything is gone. In future England shall be my home even though my allegiance is to France. That can never change."

She reached out a hand to him. He took it, folded it between both of his own, but continued to keep his gaze towards the fire and was far away from her.

That night she went to his room. He was lying sleepless on his side when he heard his door creak. Turning over, he sat up with a rustle of sheets and saw her clearly in a patch of moonlight. She crossed the room soundlessly on bare feet, her lawn night-gown diaphanous and wafting against her nipples, hips and limbs. He had never seen her hair loosened before; it hung down about her shoulders like a silvery cloud. When she reached the bedside she released the ribbons at her neck and the filmy garment floated down to the floor about her feet. Without a word, he held back the bedcovers for her and she threw herself in beside him as if suddenly released of all restraint. As he seized her, it was she who spoke, the words tumbling from her in a wild torrent as she buried her fingers in his hair and pressed herself against him.

"I wanted to be in your arms the moment I saw you. At times it was all I could do not to shriek out my love for you and I had to rush from the room to clap my hands over my mouth. Whenever I go near you it is to try to breathe the air you have breathed. I have been here in your room to touch the books you read, the pillow on which you sleep, and at times when there has been nobody else in the house, I have taken off my clothes and lain naked in your bed. I—"

He smothered her with a kiss such as she had never received before and her response was rapturous. Delirious with joy, she was totally uninhibited in the caresses that they shared, a woman possessed of a boundless sensuality who had been constrained by convention long past the age when she could have married. There was nothing she would not have done for his pleasure, but he was too highly roused to test her. As he had anticipated, she was wholly virgin when he took her, plunging home in an onslaught of his own passion, but she was equal to him, her body writhing ecstatically beneath his. If he had not covered her mouth with his own she would have awakened the entire household.

14

It had not been Gabrielle's intention that Gaston should accompany her into captivity. Sitting against the wall in the barrack yard of Ciudad Rodrigo, she had bluntly turned aside all the arguments as to why she should not take such a foolhardy step, their conversation conducted in mutters on his part and whispers on hers to avoid being overheard by any of the dazed and exhausted captives lying on the cobbles around them. When he failed to sway her, he stated he would come with her. She was aghast.

"No! I forbid it. You must get the horses and go back to France. I want to go to England alone. I would not have a minute's peace if you should risk permanent incarceration because of me." She had enough to bear in adjusting to an extended separation from her child without this further harassment.

"There's no fear of that happening. As I told you before, I have only to show them my game leg."

She felt more trapped by his persistence than by the whole situation. "I beg you. Don't come with me."

"I made a promise that I'd see you safely back in Lyons. You can't ask me to go against that vow. I may not be a gentleman born, but I have a soldier's pride in keeping my word. Now get some sleep. You need it."

She thought she would never sleep, but she was worn out by the events of the harrowing night and her lids closed almost at once. In the morning she was awakened by shouted orders, to find the sky clouded by thick smoke from the still burning buildings.

The British officers, grey-faced from lack of sleep themselves, were in command once again, the drunken rabble of the night before conforming once more into a disciplined army. Under the barking of sergeants, soldiers were shambling into line. The wounded were being cared for and buckets of water thrown over comrades still lying senseless in the gutters. Gabrielle, needing to relieve herself, followed Gaston and a swarm of men into the latrines. Dysentery was such a common condition that nobody then, or later, took any notice when she squatted every time, her coat-tails a shield, and although she saw much that she would have wished to avoid, she continued to escape detection.

They were marched out of the city that afternoon, a long column of blue-coated Frenchmen, and one disguised Frenchwoman, with a red-coat escort. Gaston had advised her to keep her gaze ahead and look neither to the left nor the right, and even though she obeyed him it was impossible to avoid some of the terrible sights that were evidence of the bestial outbreak of the night before. Once they were out into the countryside with the whole of the battle area left behind, the cold winter air became clear of the stench of death and smoke, sharp and frosty in the nostrils, and sweetly clean. That evening, when they halted for the night, some thieving guards in charge of their section began making everyone turn out their pockets while they helped themselves to money and anything of value that took their fancy. Those captives who swore they had nothing were forcibly searched. Gabrielle's draw-string purse was suspended by a cord around her neck and hung down between her breasts. When one of the guards reached her she put up a hand to snatch it free and toss it to him, but he thought she was making a defensive action and struck down her arm with a blow that made her gasp with pain.

"What have you got then, boy?" He wrenched open her coat and dived his hand into the inside pocket, giving a grunt of satisfaction as he brought out a few coins and a leather pouch of tobacco. Giving her a push back into line, he moved on to his next captive. Revolted by the state of her uniform, it had not occurred to her to examine the contents of the pockets and she exchanged a look of intense relief with Gaston, who had been powerless to help her. His gold had remained undetected, for he had surrendered a looted Spanish crucifix on a silver chain, which he had discovered beforehand in his pockets, together with some money and a watch of inferior quality that had belonged to the dead soldier.

His game leg was troubling him already, and the next day it became increasingly painful. By the time they reached Oporto he could barely hobble along and leaned heavily on Gabrielle for support. She had no way of knowing if Nicolas was on either of the two vessels in the harbour, or if he had been shipped out earlier; she thought the latter was probably the case as his capture had preceded hers by several days. She found she was filled with an extraordinary patience now that she knew it was simply a matter of time before she was reunited with him.

Her inner contentment sustained her when she saw what she would have to endure on board ship. The men were packed together closer than on any slave-ship, with no room to lie down, and because they were below water level the only light came from fitful lanterns swinging overhead, which gave a horrendous flicker to the crowded scene. For Gaston, in agony with his leg, it was particularly difficult, for he had to sit with it stretched out straight before him, and it was frequently knocked or kicked accidentally and sometimes squashed when a man fell across it in sleep or when helpless in a bout of seasickness from which most suffered the moment the ship put to sea.

Gabrielle, more queasy from the stench than from the rolling of the vessel, had decided she must wait twenty-four hours before revealing the truth to the authorities. She had to be sure the ship would not be putting back into port for any reason, for she could not risk being set ashore. After a night filled with groans and retchings and snoring, sailors appeared with baskets of bread and cheese and several huge tankards of drinking water that were passed around and constantly refilled, for most were thirsty. At eleven o'clock the ship's surgeon, immaculate in his blue and white naval uniform with brass buttons and gold braid, came to attend to those ill with anything other than seasickness and check that no wounds were festering. He was a hawkish-looking man in his mid-forties, and by the thoroughness of his questions to several of the men, Gabrielle guessed he would be constantly on the watch for contagious fevers, which were always dreaded aboard ship.

"Now's your chance," Gaston muttered to her. "Good luck."

They exchanged an encouraging clasp of hands before she left her place, finding footholds between the men to reach the companionway and wait by it. An armed sailor, who had accompanied the surgeon, eyed her suspiciously but did not drive her away. When the surgeon came to remount the companionway, she stepped into his path and spoke in a low voice that only he could hear.

"Doctor! I am a woman and should not be here."

He narrowed his eyes at her. She looked like a begrimed boy in her filthy uniform. Experience had taught him that there were always some who would concoct any manner of story to get out of this vile place even for a matter of minutes. He answered her in perfect French. "Open your shirt."

Her reaction was immediate. "Not here!" she exclaimed, outraged.

He was convinced. "Follow me."

In his cabin she gave him her name as she took off the hat she had worn night and day, to comb her hair with her fingers. When he told her again to open her shirt, she obeyed briefly. As she refastened it and rebuttoned her army waistcoat he invited her to sit down and asked whether she was a *cantinière* or just a soldier's wife.

"Neither. Nor am I a camp-follower."

"I did not think you were, Madame Valmont. I spent some time in France in my youth and your voice tells me you're a woman of some position in life. I'm interested to know how you came to be here. My guess is that you are following a lover. Am I right?"

"You are," she admitted. "I suppose it has happened before."

"I know of no woman who has come into captivity to follow or be with her man, simply because the only outcome is separation. With our own men there have been many cases of wives smuggled aboard in a canvas sack when a regiment is off on active service for several years, and mostly the officers in charge let them be. If they are that courageous, they are not likely to be a liability to the troops. Now what is the name of the prisoner of war you are following?"

"Captain Nicolas Devaux of the *chasseurs à cheval*. Might he be on this ship? I fear it's too much to hope for, because he was taken into captivity before me."

"There are none of that regiment in this ship. I did hear that a number of chasseurs captured before the fall of Ciudad Rodrigo boarded the warship in the harbour a few days ago." He was able to tell by the rush of joy to her face that he had given her good news. "How far have you come?"

"From Lyons." Buoyed up by what she had learned, she told him the whole story of the journey, only leaving out the personal details that had caused her to set out in the first place.

"If your companion, Gaston, is in such pain, why was I not informed before? I had two wounded prisoners put in the sick bay as soon as they came aboard."

"Gaston wouldn't allow it. He said it would only lead to questions as to why he, an invalided soldier, should be on board. It was for my sake that he did not take the risk. Is it possible for him to be brought out of that awful place now?"

He sat back in his chair, putting the finger tips of both hands together, and looked grave. "That is out of the question. Your friend has put himself in an exceptionally awkward position. He has marched with the French Army and is wearing uniform and is a prisoner of war. For him to declare himself a civilian masquerading as a soldier is to put himself under suspicion of being a spy."

She was agitated. "No! That's not possible. I've told you the truth."

"I don't doubt it. You strike me as a woman of integrity, but you may have been deceived."

"But I explained what happened! It was my decision to go to England and he came along only to protect me."

"Do you expect me to believe that a servant, such as you say he is, would deliberately sacrifice his freedom to protect his mistress in what must have struck him as a totally foolish whim? In my opinion, he either foresaw a chance to serve his country in another way or else he is more than devoted to you."

She drew back in her chair and turned her stricken face away from the surgeon's piercing gaze. It was true. She had realised soon after leaving Lyons that it was more than loyalty that had brought Gaston on this long and dreadful journey with her. Had they remained at home in their mistress and servant relationship, it would probably never have come to light, but being in close proximity over an unbroken period had made it impossible for him to hide totally that inner glow that always showed in the eyes of a man in love when he looked upon the face of the woman concerned. She had sensed the raging desire in him sometimes when they had lain under the stars and, on the night he had placed his hand over her breast, she had been saved from a confrontation by the unusual sound she had heard beyond the nearby trees. The terrible thing was that she would have preferred to come into captivity without his protection. She had no longer wanted him to be with her, because from the moment he had stood blood-stained in the room of that hovel in Ciudad Rodrigo, bathed in the sinister glow of the burning city, and confessed to rape and pillage on earlier occasions, a dreadful aversion had crept into her. Although she had forced it to the back of her mind, trying to remember only how he had saved her life that night, the warmth and pleasure she had felt in their friendship had gone from her beyond recall.

"Gaston is no spy," she said tonelessly. "He is in love with me."

The surgeon sighed as if she had disappointed him. She understood why. With worldly cynicism, he found it impossible to believe she had not indulged Gaston with some enticements along the way for her own selfish purpose. He was blaming her entirely for Gaston's precarious situation and his sympathy for her in her quest had completely gone. There was a marked difference in his voice when he spoke again, a tinge of dislike sharpening his words.

"I shall look at the fellow's leg when I make my round of the ship tomorrow morning. If I diagnose it as an injury that would have inva-lided him out of the army he must face the charge of being a spy."

She reeled a little as she stood up, owing to the movement of the ship, and she clutched the surgeon's table for support. "Let me go down to the orlop deck again to tell Gaston what is happening."

The surgeon was fierce. "Nothing you want is of any consequence to me! You seem to forget you are an enemy non-combatant and will come under the rules that apply. I shall arrange for some hot water to be brought here and you will wash yourself from head to toe because there must be no risk of infection being brought to the upper decks. There are two officers' wives on board, one English and the other Portuguese, and I am sure they will be charitable enough to find some suitable garments for you. As soon as you have discarded your uniform, such as it is, put it outside the door to be thrown overboard. When you are ready you will report to the officer in command for registration."

He left her alone in the cabin. It was impossible to pace about with the roll of the ship and she returned to the chair, drumming a fist on it in frustration and despair that Gaston should be facing imprisonment for years or charges as a spy, two terrible alternatives—dependent on the surgeon's diagnosis. If only she could have had a chance to prepare him for what was in the wind.

Two sailors brought the hot water and a stand with a bowl that swivelled with the movement of the ship to save spillage. The rough towel that was provided enabled her to dry her hair quite thoroughly and when bathing herself she changed the water three times to ensure that the last trace of travel and imprisonment on the orlop deck had gone from her body. Glowing from the massage of the towel, she put on the clothes provided. The donors had been generous. Fine undergar-ments and a slightly large olive-green woollen gown with long sleeves were completed by a thick woollen shawl for extra warmth. Although she had had to jettison her hairbrush as being too bulky on the night of donning uniform, she had managed to conceal the pouch at her waist that contained her comb, pins and other more personal items wholly necessary to a woman. She spent time combing and arranging her hair, but she did it automatically, concentrating on how she might bribe someone to take a message to Gaston.

She soon realised there was to be no chance of communication.

Registration was completed quickly, for much on the form, such as rank or number of wounds received, did not apply to her, although "Where captured and When" did, while a description of her came under "Visage," "Eyes," "Height" and "Age."

After it was over, she was escorted straight to a tiny cabin with no daylight where the two wives lay on narrow bunks, one above the other, each recovering from a bout of seasickness. While a sailor hung up a hammock for her almost at floor level to ease the task of getting in and out, then doubling it over to suspend both clews on the same hook to leave the cabin space clear until she should need it, she introduced herself and thanked the women for the clothes they had given her. The Englishwoman gave her a glare of dislike.

"I do not speak French!" she said in English, flouncing over in the bunk and turning her back rudely. There was a different reception from the very young Portuguese woman on the top bunk, who propped herself on one elbow, her rich black hair tumbling down about her shoulders, and regarded Gabrielle with magnificent long-lashed eyes in a sickness-drawn face. She seemed no more than sixteen years of age.

"I'm Isabella Harding, and it's Mrs. Moncrieffe in the bunk below. I sent you the clothes. You look nice in that colour." She spoke in fluent French. As the sailor left the cabin she reached out a hand to Gabrielle. "Please help me down. I'm nervous about falling and"—her voice dropped to a whisper—"that creature will do nothing to help me. You see, her husband is a colonel and mine is only a lieutenant. She thinks she should have the cabin to herself."

There was a ladder with a few rungs at the end of the bunk and as Isabella moved to put a foot on one Gabrielle saw she was highly pregnant, bulky and awkward and surely not far from her time.

"Shouldn't you have had the lower bunk?" she asked her.

Isabella made a little grimace. "Dr. Rogers, the ship's surgeon, asked her to let me take it, but she refused to change." She sat down heavily on one of two wooden travelling chests set against the wall.

"What made you decide to have your baby in England?" Gabrielle took a seat beside her on the second chest, thinking that such a young girl would have been better off in the midst of her own family at such a time. "Is your husband on the ship?"

"No, my dear Edward is on his way with the Duke of Wellington to Badajoz. Now that the British are advancing with such speed I could no longer follow him, and in any case he wanted me to have our baby at his home in the county of Berkshire. My own home was destroyed and all my family killed during the French invasion of Portugal. I escaped only because I was visiting friends in Lisbon and I was still with them when I met my English husband."

Gabrielle gave a little shake of her head, moved by what she had heard. "You have suffered much through the actions of my country and yet you were the one who sent me the clothes."

Isabella shrugged. "It is men that make wars. Never women. We are innocent of their crimes."

"Where did you learn to speak French so well?"

Again she shrugged as if the accomplishment was of no importance. "I speak five languages, including English. My father was a wine merchant and buyers of many nations came to our house, particularly from Great Britain. He thought it only courteous that his family should be able to converse with them and he hired the best of teachers. We were a happy and united family."

Without warning, a sob choked her and the tears gushed up to spill into trickles down her face. She fumbled for a lacy handkerchief and tried to stem the flow. "Forgive me. Although it is nearly four years since that tragedy my grief still overtakes me at times." Another wrenching sob that she stifled down. "I miss my mother more than ever now."

"I'm sure your husband's family will receive you with kindness."

"Will they? I wish I could be sure. I'm more afraid of a hostile reception than I was even when the gunfire came close." She lowered her voice to a whisper once more as she nodded towards the occupant of the lower bunk. "*She* wouldn't welcome anyone, as you saw for yourself."

"I could hardly expect her to welcome me since I am French and therefore her enemy."

"I'm afraid that's true. She's an educated woman, so she must have some French. She just refuses to use it because she loathes even the mention of France. The French are my husband's enemies in battle, but he bears them no personal hatred. During winter lulls the sentries on both sides converse, and when some British horses got loose and wandered onto the French-held terrain, they were returned with courtesy instead of being slaughtered for meat. There are many such cases of pleasantries exchanged. It is Bonaparte whom everyone on our side hates and fears. I know he is your Emperor and I hope you won't let what I have said prevent us being friends." The tears still swam in the velvety eyes that were now tinged with anxiety as if any present animosity would be unendurable.

Gabrielle, although inwardly rearing up against criticism of the Emperor from someone who was not French, a natural reaction out of loyalty and patriotism, reminded herself that it was an opinion stated but not maliciously intended. "We shall not let ourselves be divided by political issues over which we have no control," she said reassuringly.

"In the same way you must not prejudge your in-laws by that woman. I'm sure you will find Edward's parents eagerly awaiting their son's wife and their future grandchild."

Isabella blinked away her tears and appeared cheered by Gabrielle's encouragement. She wiped her eyes and blew her nose as if to show she was in command of herself again. "How do you expect to fare in England?"

"I don't know. It never occurred to me that I would be treated as a non-combatant taken in battle. I'm not even allowed to leave this cabin for the whole voyage. I had expected to be set free the moment I stepped on English soil, but it appears I'm to be kept under certain restrictions. The officer in command said that as my Emperor was failing in his obligations towards prisoners of war, including repatriation arrangements, he could give me no idea when I might return to France. Not that I want to leave until I have accomplished my purpose." She went on to tell Isabella about her search for Nicolas and how close she had come to a reunion, only to lose him again. Isabella, listening eagerly, turned her head with an impatient frown when the Englishwoman rolled over in bed and exclaimed furiously at Gabrielle.

"Mrs. Moncrieffe says you are not to sit on her travelling chest," Isabella translated angrily. "For the sake of peace and quietness, move over onto mine. You ought to know a few English words to tell her not to be impolite."

"Would you teach me?"

Isabella smiled delightedly. "With pleasure."

That night, after Gabrielle's first period of instruction, the ship hit a great storm in the Bay of Biscay. In her hammock, she fared better than the two women in the bunks, for they constantly slithered from side to side, Isabella frequently crying out in fear. Gabrielle, who had folded blankets on either side of Isabella's bunk as padding to prevent her knocking herself against the wooden guard in her pregnant state, occasionally left her hammock to stand on the edge of the lower bunk and hold the girl's hand in comfort. There were moments when she wondered if the ship could continue to withstand the onslaught, shudders passing through it with every wave that crashed over the bows while the timbers creaked and groaned as though about to fall apart.

Gabrielle thought of Gaston and her fellow countrymen in the bowels of the vessel and could imagine the fear and misery they were enduring. When morning came there was no abating of the storm's fury. A sailor who brought food was met by groans from Isabella and Mrs. Moncrieffe. Gabrielle, who had already stowed away her hammock, took it from him and persuaded Isabella to eat a few morsels, reminding her that she owed it to the baby to take some food. Later in the morning Dr.

Rogers came to see how she was faring. He beckoned Gabrielle to follow him out of the cabin afterwards, and as she held onto the ropes strung along the walls for support, he spoke first of Isabella.

"I've told her she is more advanced than she realised. She may go into labour at any time. This storm is going to delay our arrival in England by several days. We've been swept off course and there is no sign of any lessening of the gale. Would you know how to help with a delivery?"

"I attended the births of both my sister-in-laws' babies and I have a son of my own."

"Have you? Then I shall count on you being at hand for the minor matters when the hour comes."

"Yes, of course. What of Gaston?" she enquired anxiously. "Have you seen him?"

"I've seen him. My diagnosis is that it is an old wound aggravated by recent active service. He is a prisoner of war."

She stared after him as he walked away. How could a medical man of his experience make such a mistake? There could be only one explanation. He had believed her account and for that reason had chosen to spare Gaston the charge of spying, which brought the death penalty in any country at war. It was a merciful act and yet by it Gaston was condemned to a terrible future. Somehow she would have to work for his release and her own. It was a complication she could never have foreseen.

The storm lasted another two days. Even as the wind began to ease and the ship settled to less violent conflict with the waves, Isabella gave a cry that had a different note in it. Gabrielle, who by now had been given permission at the surgeon's instigation to leave the cabin to fetch food and drink from the galley for the two helpless women, put down the supper she had just collected and went at once to the surgeon's cabin to notify him that the labour had begun. Isabella was carried on a litter by two sailors to his cabin, where there was more room, and placed in his bunk. He gave Gabrielle one of his aprons and she tied it about her before rolling up her sleeves.

"It will be several hours yet," he said to her. "Do what you can to comfort Mrs. Harding. She's extremely frightened and nervous after that storm. I will leave you with her and I shall look in now and again until it is nearer the time."

She sat by the bunk and did all she could to help Isabella through the labour, bathing her forehead, talking soothingly to her and holding her hand, trying not to wince when her own was gripped in the fierceness of pain.

At dawn, when the sea lapped yellow and gold, Isabella gave birth to a daughter and when the infant was placed in her arms she sighed with happiness. "I shall name her Luisa after my mother."

She and the baby were taken back to the shared cabin later that morning. This time Mrs. Moncrieffe was compelled to surrender the lower bunk by the surgeon's order and was thoroughly ill-tempered about it. Fortunately, with the better weather, she was out of the cabin all day and Gabrielle was spared her constant, bristling hatred, which had not abated even during the storm when she had taken food and drink from her. During the rest of the voyage Gabrielle learned to say in English everything that could praise a beautiful baby girl, since that was Isabella's favourite topic. It was both pain and pleasure for Gabrielle to hold and bathe the baby, memories of André tugging at her heart-strings. There was a bad day when Mrs. Moncrieffe, who must have strained her ears on the first day to catch all that Gabrielle had told Isabella about Nicolas, came into the cabin especially to break some news.

In order not to be deprived of any pleasure in making her an-nouncement, she spoke for the first time in tolerable French. "The war-ship is putting into the Solent for Portsmouth. She is not coming on to the Port of London with us."

Gabrielle shot a dismayed glance at Isabella. They did not discuss this new development until they were on their own again. "It seems I must get to Portsmouth as soon as I can." It was hard for her to keep her voice steady. "Everything is becoming extremely complicated."

"But you'll find Nicolas. I know you will."

It was not until the ship was sailing up the Thames that Isabella ceased being wrapped up in bliss about the baby and began to worry about the imminent meeting with her husband's parents. By the time the ship docked she was almost panic-stricken, wanting to know if she looked all right, whether this bonnet or that suited her best, and did she need a touch of carmine on her cheeks to ease her pallor? All the time Mrs. Moncrieffe, packing last-minute things, tut-tutted and sighed pointedly at what she considered to be hysterical nonsense. A knock came on the door and a sailor stood there.

"Mrs. Harding. A lady and gentleman are waiting for you on the dockside. Shall I take your baggage now?"

Isabella threw her arms about Gabrielle in a hugging embrace. "I'll never forget your kindness to me. I did leave my address, didn't I?"

"Yes, it's on your bunk. Don't worry. Everyone will love you and Luisa."

Gabrielle carried the baby at Isabella's side for as far as she was allowed to go, a guard moving a hand warningly. They kissed each other's cheeks once more. Isabella, white-lipped with anxiety, took Luisa into her arms.

"Write to me as soon as you can, Gabrielle," she urged. Then she disappeared into wintry sunshine. Mrs. Moncrieffe, coming from the cabin, swept past Gabrielle without a word of farewell. As she left the ship she dropped a screwed-up ball of paper into the gap of water between ship and shore. She saw it as her own personal victory in the fight against Bonaparte. In the cabin, Gabrielle was searching high and low for the address she knew she had seen. It was only after the search proved fruitless that she remembered Mrs. Moncrieffe had been left alone there. She felt like a reed being blown this way and that by current misfortunes, but nothing was going to break her. Nothing!

A customs officer came to take her in charge. He told her his name was Woodbury and was able to make her understand that he and his wife were to be her custodians until such time as she should be granted parole. She collected up her bundle, which contained two more dresses that Isabella had insisted on giving her and which needed only small alterations to fit well, plus a change of undergarments, all wrapped up in the shawl that had been part of the first generous donation. With a crimson cape about her shoulders, another of Isabella's gifts, she followed the man to the deck and had her first sight of the Port of London. The fresh air and the bright daylight dazzled her after the gloom of the cabin. The Thames was busy with ships, a forest of masts at the dockside as far as the eye could see. She had hoped she might catch a glimpse of Gaston, but the customs officer shepherded her away before the disembarking of the prisoners began. He hurried her briskly along the dockside and they passed a new customs house being built by prisoners, some in remnants of their uniforms, others in the yellow suits and scarlet waistcoats of their prison garb, all much soiled by their work.

Then farther on she saw the first of a line of warship hulks that housed many thousands of prisoners of war and the sight struck a chill into her, sharper than the crisp February day. In their heyday these vessels would have been a stirring sight in ochre and red with gilded embellishments, and in full sail would have had the look of floating lilies across the high seas. Now everything from the rigging to the figureheads had been stripped away and they had been tarred a dismal black, each with a slattered gallery built around for patrolling guards.

On the cleared areas where the masts had been, wooden structures had been built to house those in command. With the weighty guns removed, the orlop decks of each hulk were above water level and iron grilles had been set into scuttles cut for air and across the empty gunports. The scrapyard would have been a clean end for these once mighty ships; instead their degradation echoed that of the unfortunate prisoners

that they housed. Gabrielle saw a few hands wave to her through the
bars at different deck levels and she would have waved back to her
countrymen if Mr. Woodbury had not stopped her with a "No!" that
rang in her eardrums.

The Woodburys' home was near the old customs house. It was
small, neatly furnished and clean. Mrs. Woodbury, a plain, well-mean-
ing little woman, appeared nervous at having a Frenchwoman of some
style under her roof. But when Gabrielle smiled and greeted her in
English, as taught by Isabella, the ice was broken. Even Mr. Woodbury's
strict countenance showed satisfaction when Gabrielle produced a gold
piece for her keep and she guessed they had been expecting to give her
bed and board on a meagre allowance paid to them by the authorities.
She had a small bedroom under the eaves and would have been served
meals on her own in the parlour if she had not made it clear she wished
to eat in the kitchen with them.

"I want to learn English," she said, again as she had been taught.

Mrs. Woodbury was charmed. "So you shall, ma'am. I'll 'elp yer."

Mr. Woodbury had more sense. "No, wife. Use yer loaf. She don't
want to talk like you and me. There's that young apprentice over at
Hadley's warehouse. He talks well and would be glad to earn a few
bob."

So Gabrielle was served her meals in the parlour and every evening
after his work was finished the apprentice, Oliver Burns, whose father
owned the warehouse and was making him work himself up the hard
way, gave her lessons. He was twenty years old, brash and confident and
smiling. She found their lessons fun. Mrs. Woodbury sometimes raised
her eyebrows significantly at her husband from where she sat opposite
him by the kitchen fire when laughter rang out from the parlour. She
could never associate learning with merriment, but then she had never
had much of either.

During the day Gabrielle studied. She was not allowed to go beyond the garden gate and would sometimes lean over it to gaze down the
cobbled street towards the river. It was possible to glimpse one of the
hulks and she wondered if Gaston might be on it. Through Oliver, who
always had a fund of information about what was going on in the area,
she learned that all the prisoners from her ship were lodged in the hulks
along these wharves and she asked him if he would try to find out where
Gaston was.

"That shouldn't be difficult," he boasted cheerily. "I have contacts.
The prisoners sometimes shift heavy bales for us. As soon as you get
your parole you can go to the Sunday market. That's when the prisoners
are allowed to come onto land to sell whatever they have made."

Her letters requesting parole remained unacknowledged. Nobody in authority came near her. She supposed a female non-combatant was of such little importance that no one was interested in her case. As March warmed into spring and April daffodils gave way to lilac, she took the English books she used for her studies outside to a wooden seat in the flower garden at the front of the Woodburys' house.

Local people had come to know her and conversed over the gate or spoke a greeting when they went by. It all helped with her growing command of their language. By now she knew in which hulk Gaston was housed and had given Oliver money to bribe a working prisoner into passing a note on to him. A reply had come back, a few words written on a filthy scrap of paper.

Am well, but troubled by my leg. No use sending food as you suggested. It would never reach me. Too much hunger. We will meet at the market when you get your parole. Gaston.

She asked Oliver about the hunger mentioned. "Don't the prisoners get enough to eat?"

"There are good portions per man, but the prisoners themselves have a golden rule that all food shall be divided equally among them, which means that those on punishment of bread and water still get a share, although their crimes have reduced the rations. The most hungry of the lot are the compulsive gamblers, those who gamble away everything from their clothes to their share of the food. They are the ones who perish quickly. On a winter's day I've seen them working barefoot and in a breech-clout, nothing more." He saw how she shuddered with pity for them.

One afternoon at the end of June a government agent came to see her. When they were settled in the parlour he gave her the news she had long awaited. "You have been considered for parole, Mrs. Valmont."

"At last!" She breathed with relief. "I wrote many letters of appeal."

"Did you? They appear to have been overlooked. Perhaps they went to the wrong department. Your name only came to my notice after an enquiry about you from a gentleman."

"A French officer?" she questioned eagerly, wondering if miraculously Nicolas had heard she was in England.

"No, an Englishman."

"What was his name?" She was puzzled as to who he might be.

"I can't recall. It was some weeks ago."

"Did he leave an address?"

He regarded her sympathetically, understanding how much a contact meant to those in captivity. Once during naval service he had been a prisoner of war for a short while before returning home to civilian life.

Only those who had experienced the ordeal could fully comprehend what it meant. Being confined to a house and garden must have been as hard on this woman in its own way. "No, he did not. There was no point, since as far as I knew you were not in my district, otherwise I should have given him your address without hesitation after he had shown me his credentials. Now let us get down to business. I shall first read you the conditions of your parole and give you official warning as to the consequences of breaking the rules."

She listened, nodded and duly signed the declaration that she would abide by all that was set down there. He then paid her the first allowance due to her, explaining that non-combatants in British hands were paid on the same scale as army and navy lieutenants. She was glad of the money, for the funds she had brought from Lyons were low and would soon have run out altogether.

"I should like to apply for a change of address," she said after putting the money away in her draw-string purse, a new one of velvet having replaced the old one she had had on her journey. "I want to go to Portsmouth as soon as possible."

"For what purpose?"

"I have reason to believe that someone I know is there, and I should like to meet him again."

The agent gave a nod. "I've no objection. I'll give you a written permit now. Be sure to report to the government agent in Portsmouth with your new address on the day you arrive. Now I'll bid you good day." On his way out of the house he paused and looked back at her. "I believe I recall the name of the gentleman that eluded me. Harding. Yes, that was it."

As she closed the door after him, she smiled to herself. It must have been Isabella's father, or perhaps a brother-in-law, who had been sent to look for her. Dear Isabella. It was disappointing to have missed making contact with her again. Yet somehow it remained a comfort of sorts to know she had a friend in England even though they were still out of touch. For herself, reunion with Nicolas had come one step nearer. She ran upstairs to put on a hat as if she had wings on her feet. Downstairs again and the thrill of opening the gate to go out into the street. She went to see Oliver at the warehouse. He greeted her jubilantly with applause.

"You've been paroled! Congratulations!"

"Just ten minutes ago!" she exclaimed excitedly. "Please get a message to Gaston that I'll be at the prisoners' market on Sunday afternoon."

She was at the wharf early. Already people were gathering to buy from the prisoners, each hulk having its individual display under the watchful eyes of armed military guards, fixed bayonets gleaming. Now and again there was a pungent, odorous whiff that was quite nauseous. Although most prisoners had spruced themselves up for their Sunday appearance, they could not rid their clothes of the prison stench. She had heard that the guards held their breath and released catches at arms' length when they opened the shutters over the grilles in the mornings.

As she walked along, she caught glimpses of exquisite objects made out of bone and straw before she sighted Gaston. He was leaning on a crutch by an upended barrel on which he had arranged a variety of small paper boats in bright colours. It caught at her emotions to see this big man in his prison suit, normally happiest with horses and in the open air, reduced to making these simple playthings, his big hands incapable of the intricate work done by others. His weight had fallen away, his eyes were sunken as if he was never without pain and he had an unhealthy prison pallor owing to his being prevented by his game leg from taking part in any outdoor work. Children and parents were buying from him, his wares cheap enough to suit the lowest pocket. Suddenly he caught sight of her and a broad grin of pleasure spread across his emaciated face. Immediately all the aversion she had felt towards him melted away as if it had never been. She realised it had been bound up with the shock of that terrible night of carnage and it had taken time for her to recover.

"How are you, Gaston?" she asked, coming to the barrel and picking up one of the boats. If she could have clasped his hand in a renewal of their friendship, she would have done it, but Oliver had warned her that women were forbidden company to the prisoners, adding to their misery, and she must make herself appear to be just a customer. "Is your leg very bad?"

He tossed off the enquiry with a shrug. "It's getting better all the time," he lied cheerfully. "I'm glad you gained your parole. I've been waiting to see you. Have you any trace of Captain Devaux yet?"

"None. Do you need money?"

"No. I still have enough left from our journey. It's been useful. It enabled me to get a canvas cradle instead of a hammock, which gives my leg a good rest. I can buy tobacco and soap and anything else I want. I only make these"—he gestured towards the little boats which he was selling as he talked, taking a coin and letting the customer choose—"to give me a chance to get outside on Sundays. Now I can look forward to seeing you, too, madame." He had taken up their old relationship as mistress and servant as if he felt more comfortable in the role.

"It may be awhile before I can come here again. I'm sorry that it has to be, but I'm going to Portsmouth tomorrow. It was there that the warship, which sailed with our ship from Oporto, landed its prisoners. I hope to find Nicolas among those on parole."

"I wish you luck, madame. You deserve it. You have had some hard deals."

Her cheeks hollowed, her eyes full of distress. "How can you speak of my misfortunes when you are the one who is suffering most?"

He gave a wry half grin. "It's my own fault I'm here. You are in no way to blame for my circumstances. I knew you didn't want me to accompany you. I turned you from me with a terrible confession you ought never to have heard."

"I have forgotten it now."

"No, madame. You may have forgiven me, but it will always be there between us. When there is peace and I have escorted you back to Lyons, I'll go my own way once again. I'll try to find work with horses in the south where the weather will be kinder to my aches and pains."

"Don't talk of partings yet," she burst out unhappily. "I've had too many in my life to think of another now."

"I just wanted you to know." He slewed his eyes towards a guard who had begun to stroll suspiciously towards them. "I think we've been talking too long. Take a paper toy and appear to pay me."

"I will pay you." She opened the draw-strings of her velvet purse.

"No, madame." He picked up a boat in Tricolore colours. "This is a gift from me to André. Keep it for him."

She wept as she went back along the wharf, folding the little boat in its creases to preserve it until the day when she could put it into her son's hands.

To take the stage to Portsmouth she had to go into the heart of London. On the way she glimpsed the Tower, the magnificent dome of St. Paul's Cathedral, the ancient beauty of Westminster Hall and the somewhat ramshackle old buildings of the House of Parliament, which looked ready for rebuilding. With a new leather valise stowed away on the coach, she took her seat. As the lumbering vehicle rolled forward amid shouts and the clatter of hooves on the cobbled tavern yard, fresh hope was high in her.

In Portsmouth she reported to the appropriate government agent and when he had finished writing down her new address she asked with suppressed eagerness if he could tell her the whereabouts of Nicolas, giving him all the information she had to go on. He sat back in his chair, a small-eyed, balding man with a sarcastic twist to his thin-lipped mouth, and he flicked the quill of his pen to and fro against his palm.

"I hope, Mrs. Valmont, you are not going to tell me that you are this officer's sister. You would be surprised at how many sisters your countrymen have when they move away from this city without leaving an address for the ladies with whom they have been dallying."

She had flushed, for his tone was insulting. "I'm not his sister."

"Well, you're not his wife either, since your surname doesn't tally."

"I was acquainted with Captain Devaux in my home town of Lyons. I have no reason to suppose he is not in Portsmouth. He had never been to England before he was brought here as a prisoner of war and so he would not have a preference for any particular part of the country. All I'm asking is to have it confirmed that he is on parole and that I might be given some idea of where to find him."

He leaned forward leisurely to replace the pen in its holder and shook his head on an exaggerated sigh. "You speak excellent English for a Frenchwoman, but you don't appear to understand what I am saying. Unless it is a case of genuine kinship I am not allowed to divulge any details about prisoners of war in this city or anywhere else for that matter."

"The government agent in London would have given my address, if he had had it, to an Englishman who enquired after me."

He wagged a finger. "You are a female non-combatant and therein lies the difference."

She swallowed her pride. "Is there nothing you can give me as a guide-line? It is vitally important that I find Captain Devaux again."

He looked deliberately in the direction of her waistline, although the fashionable fullness of her high-bosomed muslin dress shielded it from his smirking gaze. "Yes, I've heard that reason put forward before now, too. Ah, well. These things happen." Straightening up in his chair, he put her papers briskly into a drawer, his attitude sharpening authoritatively. "This interview is at an end. Report to me in two weeks' time and continue to do so as the terms of your parole have stated."

There began for her a search of the city that went on for weeks. It entailed finding officers on parole, none of whom were able to help her, not having been in Nicolas's regiment, and waiting endless hours outside several agents' offices in the hope of sighting him reporting there. She had come to the conclusion that he must have left Portsmouth long since when, unexpectedly, she had a lead. She heard that some chasseurs, previously imprisoned at Porchester Castle, were at Chichester in the neighouring county of Sussex. Immediately she made a request to her agent for permission to move.

"You've been only three months in Portsmouth," he grumbled. "You're supposed to choose a place you like and settle in it, not make a grand tour of your time here." But he did sign the necessary paper and she left his office clutching it, thankful not to be seeing him again.

Chichester was an ancient city dating back to Roman times. The stage stopped at the Dolphin tavern opposite the great cathedral and she took a room there. Her window looked out on the market cross, set like a magnificent stone crown at the centre of the city, and she could see over the street to the treetops in the grounds of the bishop's palace, bright as an altar cloth in their autumn tints.

The landlord of the tavern, who like most landlords knew everything that was going on over a wide area, was able to tell her where she would find prisoners working. They were building houses of Sussex flint, he told her, and showing fine craftsmanship in the doing of it. This time she hired a pony and gig to drive herself around the countryside, for it was cheaper and more convenient. Gradually she came to know many of the prettiest villages in that area, the thatched roofs coming down over small-paned windows and laced through by thick black beams as old as time.

Although it was autumn, late roses lingered on in sheltered places, a trifle spindly and putting forth a shyer colour than in summertime, but still uplifting to see. Some of the flint houses were being built on farmsteads, replacing older buildings that had stood for two or three centuries or more, and on a sunny day the flints winked amber and indigo and silvery grey, supporting peaked roofs and windows that were large enough to let in plenty of that same sunshine.

It took her quite a time to find the chasseurs, for there were many working parties in the area. When she did, they were concentrated on one site, building a barn as well as a house at a place called Trumley near Lavant, their yellow garb easily sighted from a distance away. She bribed a guard to let her go near the actual building work and called out through cupped hands, guessing the guards would not understand what she said in French: *"Chasseurs à cheval! Liberté! Égalité! Fraternité!"*

As she had expected, every one of the prisoners registered astonishment at hearing a fellow countrywoman in their midst. In spite of the guards' shouts, they shinned down ladders, ceased sawing or mixing mortar and carrying flints and bricks to cluster around her. "Where are you from, ma'amselle?" "What are you doing here?" "Have you come to work with us?"

She laughed at the jokes they made, being as happy to be with them as they were to see a Frenchwoman again. She asked them if they remembered Captain Nicolas Devaux. They all answered they did before the guards arrived at a run to shove them away with musket butts and shout at her to leave.

"Do you know where he is?" she implored. "I couldn't trace him in Portsmouth."

"He came to say adieu to us not long before we were transferred to Sussex."

"Where did he go?"

"Somewhere north, ma'amselle," one man volunteered. "That's all I know."

They were being dispersed and she cried out her appeal with out-flung arms. "Can nobody tell me more than that?" Their regretful shrugs and expressive shakes of the head told her they would have given her the information if they had known. She nodded her thanks, unable to speak for disappointment, and watched them return to work, most looking back over their shoulders at her where she stood, personifying the women they were missing in their own lives—sweethearts, wives and the girls of the village they would have tumbled and maybe married if there had not been a war.

"Get out of 'ere, you French bitch!" One of the guards was making threatening gestures, another was pointing a rifle at her, for sharpshoot-ers were always present when prisoners were on a site. She turned and walked with her head in the air out of the field. When she was seated in the gig she called out once more, loudly and in defiance: "*Vive l'Empereur! Vive la France!*"

A rifle shot rang over her head. She did not flinch as she drove away, refusing to be intimidated. The echoing shouts of the prisoners that followed her gave an exhilarating Gallic sound to the quiet English air.

That night she lay awake, staring up at the canopy above her bed. She had failed. After all the months of searching and heartache she was no nearer finding Nicolas than she had been when she first landed. She could think of no other path to follow. It was as if she were in a black abyss with no outlet. Her longing for her son, which was ever with her, added to her deep despair.

She moved to a smaller room at the back of the Dolphin tavern, one she felt better able to afford over an indefinite period. When enough time had elapsed she would apply to return to the Woodburys' home in London, where at least she would be near Gaston and see him every Sunday. She wrote to him regularly and although she had had a reply once in Portsmouth, written in his uneven, barely literate hand, she had heard nothing since.

It was close to Christmas when she returned to the Dolphin one afternoon from a walk. A visitor was waiting to see her. He was a distin-guished-looking man of average height, his wavy brown hair grey at the temples, a clever, sharply honed face with keen and alert blue eyes; his mouth, severe in repose, was charming in a smile. He addressed her in the hallway.

"Good day to you, Madame Valmont. The landlord told me to expect you and there can be no mistake. I knew you from Isabella's description. I am Andrew Harding, at your service."

"Such a pleasure, Mr. Harding!" The sadness that had been lodged in her eyes since her last great disappointment was lifted at this marvellous surprise. "I can hardly believe this is happening. How is Isabella? And Luisa? And how did you find me? Oh, there's so much I want to ask."

"I've ordered dinner to be served to us in the private dining-room where we can talk undisturbed."

At the table he told her that Isabella had become increasingly worried by not hearing from her, convinced that she had written the address incorrectly or some calamity had occurred. Whereas the girl might have settled down happily enough, for she had been warmly welcomed by them both, and his wife loved her already as the daughter they had never had, the anxiety about Gabrielle had added to a natural reaction of homesickness, reducing her to tears at times.

"I heard you were trying to find me. My name had been overlooked in the files for quite a while."

"That was what I discovered. You were not on any list of noncombatants that I could find. However, I was certain that sooner or later you would come to light and when I investigated again, more recently, I was given your address in London. There I was told you had gone to Portsmouth three months before, and when I arrived in that city it was only to find I had to travel on to Chichester."

"You speak as if you have access to government records."

"I do. I am the Member of Parliament for the Berkshire borough of Twyford and an adviser on defence to the Prime Minister."

"I had no idea. I don't believe Isabella had either before she met you, but then," she added, sharing a smile with him, "she talked of little else except her baby for most of the voyage."

"That brings me to the particular reason why I wanted to find you. My wife and I want to do something for you in return for your part in bringing our grandchild safely into the world. Isabella has continually sung your praises to us."

"Then she has exaggerated beyond all proportion, I do assure you. The ship's surgeon was extremely competent."

"But you were the one who gave her encouragement and security when she was afraid and alone, little more than a child herself. I must tell you that I know your whole story, related to me by Isabella. I can only suppose, by finding you here on your own, that you have failed to trace Captain Devaux."

"That is correct." Her breath was suddenly tight in her chest. As yet she did not dare to allow herself even a glimmer of hope that Mr. Harding might be able to locate Nicolas.

"I shall find him for you," he said with assurance. "It will take a little time for a clerk to go through all the records." He could see she was momentarily beyond speech, her eyes full. She dipped her face into her hands until she had recovered herself, then raised her head again.

"I can never thank you enough, Mr. Harding." There was a husky catch in her voice.

"There is no need for thanks. I am already in your debt. I regret having to ask you to exercise patience for a little longer after all you have been through, but the list of captives is immense. We have close on one hundred and twenty thousand prisoners of war in England now. The Duke of Wellington has been asked not to send any more for a while, but they still keep coming on every vessel that floats. He says he cannot spare soldiers for guard duty when he wants them on the battle-field. That is why it is such a problem to house your countrymen and their allies. We have had to make use of everything that is available."

"Including the hulks?"

"Ah." He gave a half-shake of his head. "I know what terrible places they are, dank and rat-ridden. At the present time they have to be used."

"You said you had heard my story from Isabella. Then you will also know of the part that my servant, Gaston, played in it, surrendering his freedom to protect me. He is in one of those hulks on the Thames. Is there any chance of his being moved to a better place? More important, is parole ever granted to the men in exceptional cases?"

"Not parole as given to officers, but men have been repatriated for special reasons, such as saving a prison guard's life or something on that scale. I'm afraid that saving yours in the manner he did would not count in any way. However, his case interests me. My solution rests with an invitation that my wife and I hope you will accept, which is to stay with us at our home until such time as I can send you in one of my own carriages to Captain Devaux's address. It will give Isabella the greatest happiness to have your company again and, as I said before, we want to do all we can for you. As for your servant, I can get his release to work for me if you can guarantee he is to be trusted and will not attempt to escape."

She was overjoyed. "He would never do that. He has sworn to escort me back to Lyons when this war ends."

"Then I'll arrange everything. We'll leave for London in the morning. My first task shall be to gain the necessary papers to take him into my charge." He took up his wineglass. "I give you a toast. To reunions!"

"To reunions," she echoed, her face radiant.

With regard to Gaston, her patience had to be tried three times.

Firstly there was the journey to London, and afterwards the wait at the
Houses of Parliament while Mr. Harding's clerks secured the papers he
needed for Gaston and for her. Then, perhaps tired himself from the
long drive that day, he insisted that nothing more be done until morning. She slept that night in a luxurious room at his Mayfair house and
awoke to see a few flakes of snow drifting down past the window.

In spite of the delicious breakfast served, she could not eat anything
in her eagerness to get to the hulk. It was an interminable time for her
while Mr. Harding read a number of letters before finally donning his
cape-collared overcoat and tall beaver hat.

On the wharf he told her to wait in the carriage while he went
aboard. She watched in suspense for Gaston to appear. When finally
there was some activity, she saw to her dismay that Gaston was being
carried off the hulk in a canvas litter borne by two soldiers, Mr. Harding
following behind. She leapt from the carriage and rushed across to the
gangway. Gaston's wasted face broke into a smile at the sight of her, but
she was staring horrified at the bloody bandages about a stump that had
once been his game leg. It had been cut off above the knee.

"What have they done to you?" she exclaimed frantically.

"The surgeon had to lop it off. All life was going from my toes and
the condition would have worsened steadily."

"Why didn't you tell me?" she cried, hurrying along beside the
stretcher to keep abreast with him.

"You had enough to worry you. Have you found him yet?"

No need to ask whom he meant. "Not yet, but very soon. Mr. Harding has promised me."

"Good. We're having a bit of luck at last, aren't we? I'm going to be
without pain and nimble once I get the peg-leg that the gentleman has
promised me."

"Oh, Gaston." She was between laughter and tears. "You are inde-
structible."

"So are you, madame. That's why you're going to win through
now."

He was carried to the Woodburys' house. Between them, Gabrielle
and Mrs. Woodbury bathed him clean of all traces of his prison life, put
him in one of Mr. Woodbury's night-shirts and made him comfortable
against the pillows. Mrs. Woodbury had bound new strips of linen about
his stump and was to nurse him until such time as he had regained his
strength and was fit to travel to Twyford. Mr. Harding arranged payment with Mrs. Woodbury for her care of the patient and left a purse of
money with Gaston for the day when he could purchase clothes in
which to attire himself. The prison garb was thrown away. When

Gabrielle kissed him on the cheek in farewell until they should meet again, he held her by the arm.

"Getting out of that hulk has made this the best day of my life so far. Yours is soon to come."

The Harding country home was of ivy-laced, plum-coloured brick, built in 1700 for one of Mr. Harding's forebears by a master builder of the Wren school, and the graceful windows were enhanced by dressings of cream stone. Isabella's face appeared at one of them as Mrs. Harding came out to welcome Gabrielle. Moments later Isabella appeared down the staircase with a shriek of delight and Gabrielle was hugged with such exuberance in the entrance hall that she was almost swept off her feet. Still in the same whirl, Isabella flung her arms about Mr. Harding.

"Thank you for finding her, dear Father-in-law!"

It amused Gabrielle that this rather staid couple, with their English attitudes and reserve, should be regarding their fly-away daughter-in-law with such enchantment. Since she now knew that Edward was their only son, she could guess how Isabella and the baby had filled a gap in their lives until such time as he should return to complete the family. Luisa, when brought to greet her, was a bonny infant, plump and contented and in the ten months since her birth her black hair had changed to the fair colour of her absent father, her eyes now as big and long-lashed and dark as her mother's.

Christmas was the happiest that Gabrielle had known for a long time. There was feasting and the waits sang carols at the door, hot punch was served, and she tasted mince pies and plum pudding for the first time. She was able to relax completely and enjoy herself because all the time she was carried along by the knowledge that Nicolas was only just beyond her reach. He was so much with her in her thoughts that it was almost as if she had only to turn her head and she would see him there.

Two days after the festivities were over, Mr. Harding opened a letter at the breakfast table, read it through and then smiled across at Gabrielle. "We have what we have been waiting for over these past days. Captain Devaux is lodging at Holly House, Paradise Lane, in Macclesfield and is employed as manager at the Barnett silk mill there."

It was Isabella who made the outburst of jubilation. Gabrielle sat silent and thankful and smiling. She was on the brink of her great day.

In a Harding carriage she journeyed to Macclesfield with every comfort from the soft velvet upholstery to a hand-warmer in her muff and a small travelling clock in a leather case that chimed the hours prettily, letting her know that the time was slipping away towards the hour of reunion. She stayed overnight on the way and in early afternoon the carriage drew up in the forecourt of Holly House. It seemed sensible to ensure he was not there before carrying on to the mill. She rang the shining brass bell-pull and a maidservant came to the door.

"Is Captain Devaux at home?" she enquired.

"No, ma'am. He's always at the mill at this hour."

"Thank you. I shall go there."

The maidservant closed the door and turned back in the direction of the kitchen. Jessica, coming downstairs, looked over the baluster at her as she passed below. "Who was that at the door?"

Looking up, her face moon-shaped, the girl answered: "A foreign lady asking for Mr. Devaux. I told her he was at the mill." The green baize door swung shut behind her. On the stairs Jessica stood with a hand pressed against her chest as if trying to still the suddenly frightened drumming of her heart.

Gabrielle arrived at the mill. Her feet did not seem to touch the ground in her excitement when she entered the hallway and the clatter of the looms made everything warm and familiar. It was as if there had been no time between this day and the last time she had seen Nicolas. She turned the handle of the outer office and went in. A clerk writing at his high desk would have left his seat, but she stayed him with a little gesture.

"Is Captain Devaux alone?"

"Yes, ma'am."

"Then you have no need to announce me."

She reached the door that had his name on it. Lifting the cape-hood from her head, she let it fall behind her and touched her hair into place with her finger tips. Then she opened the door swiftly and as swiftly closed it behind her, leaning against it. Nicolas was sitting at a roll-top desk going through some design cartoons and did not look up, although he held out a hand in her direction as if he was expecting her to be the clerk with papers for him. "You did those quickly, Briggs," he commented.

She was glad of those few seconds in which to gaze at him in profile, to absorb the sight of him into herself and not to die of joy that their reunion had come at last. He, mystified at getting no response, glanced up and saw her there. Never would she have believed that love could show itself so instantly in a man's face, filling his wondering eyes, his spreading smile, his expression and his whole being.

"Gabrielle!" He was out of his chair and had her in his arms before she could take another breath. His mouth was on hers and they kissed, wildly, ravenously, starved for each other, embracing, holding, clasping and crushing tenderly. "When did you arrive in England?" he gasped exultantly, and then kissed her again before she could answer him. Lips, breath, bodies, limbs and caressing hands blended together in the mutual expression of their love and long-denied passion.

They did not hear the door open, or know that the clerk in the outer office had been sent off on an errand out of earshot somewhere in the depths of the mill. With sight, sound and senses only for each other, they had no notion that their erotic and ecstatic kissing was being observed until a horrified hiss cut through the air like the swish of a sword's blade. Gabrielle, her back to the door, pressed her forehead into Nicolas's shoulder, laughing to herself in her happiness, sure they had surprised and startled the intruder, whoever he was, and waited for Nicolas to send him away. His loving hand cupped the back of her head protectively and his fingers stroked her shining hair, but he did not dismiss the unwelcome intruder.

"There is someone here you must meet, Gabrielle," he said to her in a low, sad voice.

She looked questioningly at him, but his gaze was directed towards the door. Turning within the circle of his arms, secure in love, her joy athrob within her, she saw a pale young woman with soft fair hair thoroughly wind-blown, leaning as if for support against the jamb of the open door, a shawl clutched untidily about her as if she had run there all the way down the long street. She glanced at Nicolas. "Yes?"

His embrace, tightening still more about her, shielded her unintentionally from any supposition that something might be seriously wrong. She was totally unprepared for what he had to say.

"This is Jessica. She is my wife. We were married on Christmas Eve."

Gabrielle stared for a long moment at Jessica while inwardly she became one entire silent scream of anguish too great to be borne. Then, as he had feared, she tilted forward in a dead faint and he swept her up in his arms before she could fall. Jessica straightened herself in the doorway and pulled the shawl closer about her, shuddering from shock. He stood there, the husband she adored, with the prostrate woman cradled in his arms, looking as though he might walk away with his beautiful burden and never return.

"Send her back wherever she came from," she urged beseechingly in a high-pitched voice she scarcely recognised as her own. Then she could not endure the starkness of his agonised face and had to turn aside, hurrying back through the outer office and out of the mill. Without reasoning, she ran back in the direction of home with the same speed with which she had left it, as if wanting to escape from the intrusion from the past that had shattered the happiness her marriage had brought her.

Her lungs tore on every gasping breath in an effort that had been forbidden her since an early sickness of the past, but she did not stop until she had hurled herself into the house and into the privacy of tears beyond the bedroom door.

At the mill, Gabrielle returned to consciousness. Nicolas was massaging her wrists where he sat facing her on the edge of the leather-upholstered bench in his office on which she was lying. She sat up at once and he put a supporting arm around her, but she stiffened away from him. As yet she did not trust herself to stand.

"How do you feel?" He peered anxiously into her face.

She avoided his eyes. "I'll be perfectly all right in a moment or two."

"How did you manage to get across the Channel?" he wanted to know. "Did you come in a smuggler's boat?"

"It's too long a tale to tell." The less said now the better. "I came because I promised you once that if ever I were free I would come to you. I admit that at the time I thought it could never be."

"Are you saying that Émile is dead?" he demanded incredulously.

She passed a hand across her brow, fighting for the strength to rise up and leave. "On the night Maison Devaux burned down. He was one of the three victims."

"So long ago! I never knew!"

She met his tormented gaze then, her own no less distraught. "I realise that."

"Oh, Gabrielle." He caught up her hand and pressed the palm to his lips and held her fingers hard when she would have drawn herself free. "I've never stopped loving you."

She was glad he made no excuses about his marriage. It showed the same affinity between them was still there. He knew she understood he had made Jessica his wife simply because he had never expected to see her again. It was all she could do not to caress his face once more, to touch his lips, but she might weaken and let him take her here on this office bench as once he would have possessed her in an emperor's tent if she had not held out against her own fiery desires. Now, exactly as it would have been then, to know the power of his passion within her own receptive body would be to destroy her entire will, for she would never be able to live without him again. Tragedy would be an inevitable consequence.

"I must go." She stood up and found her head had cleared. Mercifully her heart was still numb.

"For God's sake, not yet!" He blocked her way.

She was surprised by her own calmness. The numbness was an opiate. "There is nothing more for us. We have come to the end of all that has been between us. I wish you well with my whole heart as I have always done. This meeting mustn't be prolonged for your sake and for mine. Farewell, Nicolas!"

He seized her wrist as she reached the door, bringing her to a standstill. She did not look back at him, her whole straight-backed stance a silent rejection of any last attempt at persuasion, until he released his hold, his fingers unfolding slowly and reluctantly. His final words followed her as she went:

"You are my life and always will be."

The numbness stayed with her all the way back to Twyford. She did not break the journey overnight or rest when the horses were changed. There seemed to be no feeling in her. She imagined that if a pin were stuck into her flesh she would not know it. When she finally arrived back at the Hardings' home it was twilight and the windows glowed from the lamps within. Nobody heard her return. It gave her time to tidy herself and change out of her travelling clothes before she went downstairs again to enter the family drawing-room where Mr. and Mrs. Harding sat with Isabella by the fire having afternoon tea. Mrs. Harding, pouring from the silver teapot, saw her first and set it down in astonishment. Isabella sprang up in excitement.

"Have you brought Nicolas back with you?" Her voice trailed away, for Gabrielle had moved forward, her green gown catching the fire's sheen, her drawn face showing that something terrible had happened.

"I found him," she told them tonelessly. "He has married in Macclesfield. I met his wife. She was a bride of three weeks."

Isabella clapped a hand over her mouth, suppressing a cry. Mrs. Harding's refined features were full of compassion. Her husband went forward to lead Gabrielle to a chair by the fire. She moved as though frozen through, but it was nothing to do with lack of bodily heat. As she sat back against the cushions, Mr. Harding handed her a fresh cup of tea that his wife had poured for her.

"Drink this. You must be exhausted."

It surprised her to see there was no trembling in her hands. The cup did not rattle on its porcelain saucer. Obediently she sipped the hot brew and then addressed both her host and hostess. "May I lay claim to your hospitality a little longer?"

They replied simultaneously that she was welcome to remain with them until such time as she could return to France. That night the numbness ebbed. She never knew how she managed to live through the aftermath until morning.

As soon as Gaston was well enough he came to the Hardings' household and was in his element when allowed to work among the thoroughbred horses in the stables. At first he hobbled about with a pair of crutches, and later with a single one when fitted with his wooden leg. The chafing from the wooden cup and the leather straps keeping it in place on his stump caused him endless hours of agony. He persevered, and although his face was set almost permanently in a grimace of pain caused by every stomping step, he stubbornly refused to give himself a respite from work.

Mrs. Harding, observing Gabrielle closely, came to the conclusion that there would be nothing better for her than that she should return to France and take up her own life again.

At his wife's instigation, Mr. Harding set to work to see what could be arranged. It happened that things were changing across the other side of the Channel. Bonaparte's empire was beginning to disintegrate. The Tsar had now allied his country with Britain, Prussia, Sweden and Austria. As a result, the remnants of the Grand Armée had not only been driven from Russia but were being harried across Europe. To the west, Wellington was advancing towards the Pyrenees, the last barrier before reaching French soil. On the day that Bonaparte was soundly beaten by the Allied force in the Battle of the Nations near Leipzig, Gabrielle went running to the stables to tell Gaston some good news.

"We're going home to France! We're being repatriated! Everything has been arranged."

He embraced her in his big arms and they both shed tears together.

A few weeks later they were escorted under armed guard with seven other non-combatants and a couple of severely disabled officers down to Dover, where they were put on a fishing smack. The sails flapped and filled in the fresh wind. Gabrielle, looking back at the white cliffs of Dover, was saying farewell to Nicolas and to love itself. There would never again be anyone else for her. When the cliffs finally melted into the sea, she turned towards France, the wind tugging at her hair. She was going home. Home to Lyons and her son. Home to Maison Roche and the *bistonclaque* of her looms. After many months the blood stirred in her veins once more.

15

Gabrielle took down the silk-woven portrait of the Emperor from the wall of her office in the Rue Clémont and held it in both hands as she regarded it with mixed feelings. It should have come down at the time of his abdication last April, or when he went into exile on the island of Elba, or even on the day when the Tsar and the King of Prussia had ridden in triumphant victory into Paris. She had known his downfall was only a question of time when Wellington and his redcoats swarmed over the Pyrenees to capture Toulouse, and yet still she had hoped the Emperor would win through.

Somehow, quite indirectly, all the main events of her life had been bound up with the actions of this extraordinary man whom she had only ever seen from the heart of a cheering crowd. Through his attack on Austria, she had lost a brother and Gaston had come to Lyons to play such a part in all that took place afterwards. The imperial invasion of Portugal and Spain had taken Nicolas away from her forever.

Yet she bore the exiled Emperor no animosity. He had done what he believed right for France and given it laws and reforms that would endure and outlive the restored Bourbons no matter if they continued to reign for centuries to come. Moreover, in his time, he had helped Lyons to become once again the greatest silk centre the world had ever known and it was her personal regret that her marvellous Roche silks, commissioned for Versailles, had gone into storage with thousands of other bolts of fabrics chosen from leading Lyonnais silk houses and might never be hung in the great palace for which they had been designed. An imperial era had passed and with it had gone all the pomp and circumstance and splendour that had adhered to it.

Sadly she unfastened the back of the frame and removed the silk portrait to place it in tissue paper and put it in a drawer with other rare samples that belonged to the history of Maison Roche. Her decision to remove the portrait today had come with the news that five days ago the Emperor had escaped from Elba and landed in the Gulf of Juan in the south of France to raise a new army to advance on Paris and drive King Louis XVIII from his throne.

The last thing she wanted was to see her countrymen slain again, for she realised now that if the Emperor should succeed he would be spurred on to recapture all his lost territory with a fervour as great as, if not greater than, before. Having seen war for herself in the Peninsula, she wanted no more of it for France.

It was not as though her country were in a conquered state, which would have been a different matter. Good relations had been restored with Britain and the rest of Europe. Even Wellington had said that France had had no enemies and it was only Bonaparte who had had to be deposed. There was every sign that King Louis would be adequate and, unlike Bonaparte, he had the respect of all the reigning royal houses. Moreover, the Lyonnais had presented a petition of loyalty to him almost on the first day of his enthronement. Her country needed peace now, not more bloodshed. She herself was for liberty and all the finer principles of wise government for which the Revolution had originally been fought, and the Bourbon had sworn to uphold them. Because she could not condone the Emperor's return, knowing what the cost would be, she was now shutting the drawer on a visage that belonged to the past and not to the present.

"*Maman!*"

She turned as André came running through the office door to her, sending it crashing back in his exuberance. A boisterous five-year-old, he had just come home from a walk with his nursemaid and, as always, had sought her out immediately. Stooping to sweep him up in her arms, laughing jointly, she swung him around before hugging him to her, his round cheek cool from the March wind that had given his face such a rosy colour.

"Have you had a splendid time? Did you meet Aunt Hélène as arranged? She bought you a candy stick? La! What a lucky boy you are!"

"I'm going again tomorrow. Uncle Michel has arranged for me to start riding lessons on Juliette's pony, the little one she doesn't ride any more." He had already struggled to get down and she replaced him on his feet. It was hard for her not to mollycoddle him, and for that reason she let him spend as much time as she could with Hélène and Michel in the home they had bought within easy walking distance a few months before their happiness had been completed by the birth of a twin son and daughter.

Gabrielle knew how fatherless children needed male company in their lives. His initial shyness after her return home to Lyons had been painful to bear, for he had run from her to hide behind Hélène's skirts. Fortunately he knew her likeness from the miniature that had been Émile's, and every night during her absence Hélène had talked to him about his mother and kept the memory alive. Gradually a normal relationship was restored between them and the only sign that he remembered she had ever been away was in his need for immediate reassurance that she was in the house whenever he came home from an outing without her.

If she had to be away on business, which happened more frequently now than ever before, he was content to stay with the Piats, where her absence was not as marked as it would have been in his own home. Although Juliette, now aged ten, had outgrown him and was very occupied with her small brother and sister, besides having her own circle of girl friends, she was always good with him when he was there and took a share in reading him bedtime stories. A trip away from Lyons was in the offing now and Gabrielle decided this was as good a time as any to prepare André.

"Next week I have to go to Limousin and Auvergne to visit two large country houses where Roche silks are being hung. As you know, Maison Roche is fast becoming the silk house that people consult when they want a whole residence refurbished, and I always view the finishing stages to make sure every detail is perfect. . . ."

He understood. Some of his happiest moments were spent at the mill with his *maman*. He loved the colours and patterns of the silks he was allowed to handle, and the smell of the place was good in his nostrils, comfortable and familiar as if he had known it always. "When can I come with you to see the silks hung?" It was his usual question.

"One day when you're older," she promised as she had promised before. "You will be in charge of everything when you're a grown man."

In the remaining time before her departure she was busy every moment. She worked harder these days than she ever had before. There was much that Michel could have done for her, but Maison Roche and her son had become her whole existence. By concentrating on both she could keep at bay poignant memories that only tore her to shreds if allowed to creep through her guard. She was never without male attention. Plenty of would-be suitors were interested in an attractive, wealthy widow. Hélène had even suggested tactfully that she might think of marriage again for André's sake as well as her own, just as once Gabrielle had expressed the same idea to her.

"Never!" Gabrielle had replied with such vehemence that Hélène had never dared to mention the subject again.

Those who escorted Gabrielle to social occasions met with a barrier that kept at bay any serious physical involvement. As with most men, the unattainable became even more desirable, and several otherwise agreeable friendships ended when a determined caress and a persistent mouth threatened to awaken dormant yearnings in her that she needed to keep suppressed for the peace of both her mind and body.

As she prepared for her journey, news and further details of Bonaparte's swift approach swept in. He had made a triumphant entry in Grenoble on the seventh day after his landing on the coast. All along his route veteran soldiers of the Grande Armée were rallying to him with shouts and cheers of welcome, wearing their uniforms and waving their weapons. The old magic was still there, undiminished by months of exile, and he was rekindling France once more. The white cockades of the Bourbons were thrown to the ground and trampled underfoot as the soldiers pulled out the forbidden tricolour ribbons they had kept. They became the Emperor's men again as they had been before, falling in with the mass of officers and troops gathering in his wake.

The day before Gabrielle was due to leave, she took André to the Piats' house. On the way their barouche was brought to a halt by a surging crowd. Bonaparte was entering Lyons and the Lyonnais were going wild. King Louis's brother had been sent to defend the city against the usurper, but he had had to leave when not a soldier rallied to him.

André, excited by the noise and cheering, the waving of the Tricolore and the lusty singing of the "Marseillaise," bounced up and down on the seat in his eagerness to see all that was going on. Gabrielle, feeling he was entitled to this historic moment, opened the window and held him to it as above the heads of the crowd Bonaparte came into sight. He rode proudly, clad in his grey campaign coat and black bicorn hat. Gabrielle felt herself gripped again by the mesmerising personality of this warrior leader. It was impossible to take her eyes from him until he had ridden out of sight.

"Now you have seen the Emperor," she said as she set André back on the seat. "Whatever you may hear in the future, and whatever happens, remember he did more for Lyons and for France than any other Frenchman who has ever lived."

Celebrations were still going on when she left the city next day. She missed Gaston's presence whenever she was being driven about locally, or on these longer journeys. He had kept his word about leaving her household and going south to the coast. Their parting had been emotional on both sides, for they had been through so much together.

"I'll let you have my address as soon as I'm settled somewhere," he had promised.

"Shall you be able to do that?" she had queried. "Settle, I mean? You've led such a wandering life so far, first the army and then later through all those months when we were away from France."

He had grimaced cheerfully, too much sorrow in his eyes for it to be a grin. "Every old war-horse dreams of peaceful pastures. That time has come for me. Farewell, madame. It's been an honour to serve you."

She did not let him go empty-handed. He had a good horse, a new suit of clothes and a banker's draft to give him a moderate income until the end of his days. It was a long time before she heard from him. Then it was to let her know that he had settled in the peaceful little village of Cannes, looking after the horses of a retired colonel who, even though he had lost a leg and an arm at Arcole in the service of the Emperor, could still ride well. She had written to him, but there had been no reply. Perhaps he had succeeded in cutting off the past. She did not persist with her correspondence and hoped he had found contentment for himself. There was no doubt his quiet existence, and that of the colonel, had been disrupted during the past days, for the Emperor's first bivouac after landing from Elba with the thousand loyal soldiers who had accompanied him into exile had been at the village of Cannes. Had Gaston's blood been stirred anew by the military sights and sounds after little more than fifteen months of country peace?

For herself, it was refreshing to drive this day through the undulating Limousin countryside, passing woods and quiet villages, forgetting the turmoil of political events for a while. She was accompanied by her personal maid, who knew better than to chatter unnecessarily, which meant Gabrielle was able to devote her thoughts to the visit ahead of her.

The great country mansion in which her silks had been installed was only a few miles from Limoges, and for the dining salon she had taken the colours of an exquisite porcelain dinner service that was in use on grand occasions. From the reports she had received, everything had gone well, but there were always small, unexpected difficulties to be ironed out in any important project and she found that clients had come to appreciate her consultation at certain times. If she had not had Michel on whom to rely completely in her absence, it would have been impossible to extend this service at a personal level, and it was bringing in commissioned work all the time to keep her looms and her weavers busy. War would bring everything to a halt again; probably Lyons had borne the commercial brunt of wars more than any other French city in its time.

"Are you ready for refreshment, madame?" Her maid had opened the white linen of the travelling hamper to reveal pâté, white bread, fruit and a bottle of wine.

"That looks delicious. Yes, I am. Let us eat now."

It was a simple repast. That evening she dined far more lavishly with the owners of the mansion in the beautiful room that Maison Roche had created. Wall panels of *gros de Tours* damask held on a deep rose ground a pattern of stylised bouquets that took up the crimson, emerald, cream and sapphire of the Limoges tableware. The chairs, all twenty of them, were covered in the same rose, with borders of flowers from the bouquets, the drapes at the tall windows completing the harmonious theme.

She stayed as a guest in the mansion for over four weeks, discussing many details with the *maître ouvrier* and ensuring that all her silks had been upholstered to perfection when the last deliveries were made. While there, she heard that the Emperor had received a tumultuous welcome in Paris after King Louis's hasty departure for Belgium. From the owner of the house, who had Parisian connections, she learned that throughout the Tuileries the white lily of the Bourbons had been stripped away from hangings and carpets to reveal the imperial bee once more. It seemed as if her silks would soon be taken out of storage for Versailles after all, but the pleasure it might have given her was dimmed by an ever recurring thought: what was the cost in lives going to be this time? Already the news-sheets were proclaiming the Emperor had three hundred thousand men under arms, all loyal Frenchmen, and hundreds more were volunteering for service every day.

She travelled on to the château in Auvergne where the final work was still in progress. The owners were absent, but she was given the freedom of the place and was better able to concentrate without interruption on all that had to be done.

When the last item was in place she went from room to room, upstairs and down. There were bedchambers of lapis blue with silver, white with gold, peach with cream and palest apple green with lilac, all tranquil with exquisite designs restful to the eye. In the music salon white satin *broché* carried a pattern of lyres and crowns of roses. In the Grand Salon birds of paradise blazed jewel-like from a gold ground and sofas and chairs carried the same birds in lozenges. This salon gave way in turn to anterooms where the same hues blended and changed subtly to give variety and diversion. Everything was complete. She could go home to Lyons. As always, her heart lifted.

The news was bad by the time she arrived. The city was full of mobilised troops. British and Prussian troops were massing in Belgium and a confrontation was becoming inevitable. The armies of the Austrians and the Tsar were gathering in force farther to the east; France was again surrounded by enemies.

Shaking her head over the news-sheet that gave the gist of this information, she re-entered her home after her absence. It was too late in the evening to fetch André home and she would collect him in the morning. As she had expected, a pile of letters was awaiting her attention. She would not have looked at any of them until the next day if, after she had bathed and changed, her maid had not brought one to her in the Blue Salon where she was having a light supper.

"I think you should see this one, madame. I have been told that a gentleman came six or seven times in as many days in the hope of your having returned. Yesterday he left this letter with the request that it should be given to you immediately you arrived home."

She took it with little interest, half expecting it to be from a persistent salesman of some new dye or spinning gadget, until the handwriting almost made her heart stop. It was from Nicolas. She drew in a deep breath, waiting until she was on her own again before ripping it open. He had much to tell her.

> *Jessica died of consumption six weeks ago after a long and struggling illness. I have learned since that she suffered from the condition as a child, but it was believed she had made a full recovery, being untroubled by ill health in adult life until, without warning, she suddenly succumbed to a new attack. Her courage, as well as her devotion to me, will remain in my memory always. I hope I did all that was possible to make her last months a time of contentment and I was with her when she died. From the start I had respect and a deep affection for her, and I believe she understood that she meant more to me than circumstances might have led her to suppose. Her thoughts at the end were solely concerned with my happiness. There was no selfishness in her. I am trying to tell you that I have returned to France to find you again in the hope that there might be some time left for us to spend together after the task still left for me to do.*

For a moment Gabrielle could not read on, knowing instinctively what that duty would be. "Oh, my love," she breathed tormentedly before continuing to scan the letter.

> *I had never thought I should come back to the land of my birth. I had resigned myself to living in exile, convinced I had made the right decision and not knowing that the situation would change as it has done. The enthronement of King Louis and the end of hostilities between France and Britain released me from the code of honour which had originally kept me to British shores, and as an outbreak of hostilities has yet to be declared, I have come as a free citizen back to Lyons and rejoined my regiment of the chasseurs. Never think I have become a soldier again for any other reason than a heartfelt belief that every Frenchman is needed at this time. It is for France alone that I am prepared to die if needs must. I will not see her defeated as the world intends it now. If you have any love for me left in your heart, allow me to see you once more before I leave Lyons. If this letter reaches you too late, then let me hope to find you waiting whenever I may return.*

She ran from the room, calling to her maid as she went. "My cloak! Quick! At once!" It came and she threw it about her shoulders, rushing from the house and across the square. She knew the address on the letter. It was not far away. Perhaps he had taken accommodation there in the hope he might sight her upon her return. Her shadow flew in and out of circles of light thrown down by the overhanging street lamps. A few minutes later she arrived breathless at the door of the house and hammered the knocker. It was opened by an army servant in silhouette, sconce lights glowing in the hall behind him.

"Is Captain Devaux here? I'm Madame Valmont," she exclaimed at once.

"He's out, madame, but I know where he is. I had orders to fetch him immediately if you should call at any time of the day or night."

He showed her into Nicolas's apartments on an upper floor and left her there. She crossed swiftly to the window and a few moments later saw the servant go off at a run down the street, buttoning up his jacket as he went and jamming on his shako. Regaining her breath, she loosened her cloak and let it drop across a chair. She then stayed by the window, watching and waiting, until a hired calèche approached the house at a gallop and she saw Nicolas in uniform fling himself out of it and into the house. He came pounding up the stairs. The door was thrown wide and there he was as if the time between had never been. Once again they were looking at each other as they had done long ago when a wedding carriage and a funeral cortège had clashed wheels and brought them into each other's lives. This time they were alone. This time the hour was theirs at last.

"Nicolas," she breathed, holding out her arms and swaying towards him. "Show me this is no dream."

"My own Gabrielle!" He rushed to her and crushed her hard into him, their starving mouths meeting in a rapturous kiss, frantic with love. The tears of happiness trickled from under her closed lids and she buried her fingers in his hair to hold him to her as if she might die if he should lift his head and take his lips from hers.

Lifting her up in his arms, he kicked open the intervening door that led into the bedchamber and carried her through. The bed, large and wide and downy with pillows, awaited them. She found the sensual pleasure of his undressing her almost too great to be borne, for he kissed and caressed and explored with lips and tongue and fingers every part of her that released buttons and loosened ribbons revealed to his passionately loving mouth and she abandoned herself gloriously to his worshipping.

The sight of his nakedness was magnificent to her, the gleam of muscle, the force and strength that emanated from him, and she uttered a soft cry of sheer joy as he came to her in the bed and their bodies blended together in ardent embrace. Blissfully she traced with wondering hands the shape of his passion-torn face, his shoulders, the long scoop of his spine and hard curve of his buttocks. While she stroked him in ways that were new to her, her own body responded to his caresses and kisses as if in an ecstatic home-coming.

It was loving such as she had never previously experienced. It swept her along with him and over him and under him as if the bed were a sea of waves bearing them erotically to heights and down into valleys again. The candlelight shimmered on pale limbs, tangled sheets and illumined the most intimate of kisses for their mutual joy in each other. His final powerful possession of her engulfed them both in depths of immeasurable passion and she arched convulsively in realm after realm of fulfilment such as she had never reached before.

As he still lay within her, quiet and at rest, she slowly trailed her fingers down the back of his neck and kissed his forehead lovingly. He opened his eyes and smiled lazily at her in satisfaction, shifting his weight, embracing her anew. The hour was now long past midnight.

"I love you," he murmured as if he had not said the same words already more times than either of them could remember. "Marry me today. This morning. Before noon."

She framed his head in her arms and kissed him all over his face. "Such impatience," she teased, love and laughter in her voice. "Yes, yes, yes." Then abruptly she pressed her cheek against his to hide the sudden fear in her eyes as realisation dawned. "You're going away soon, aren't you? Is it to be tomorrow?"

"It's today. Before evening."

The news tore through her. "Where are you going? Do you know?"

"Yes, I do. Let's not talk about it now." He tried to divert her by moving his lips to her breast.

She took his face between her hands, making him look at her. "Please. Tell me."

He propped himself up on his elbows, seeing she would not give in until she had heard the truth. "The Emperor has already led an advance across the border into Belgium. The Prussians have massed at Ligny and it is said that Wellington is moving troops to a place called Quatre Bras. When these armies are defeated we march into Brussels." His face relaxed into a smile. "Will you meet me there, my love?"

"I'll do more than that," she replied fervently. "I'll travel with you. This time I'll be with the wives and the rest of the camp-followers. I'm not going to lose sight of you as I did at Ciudad Rodrigo."

Her passionate declaration, which she sealed with an ardent kiss upon his mouth, stirred his strength again and he began making love to her once more. Later, much later, when the dawn was filtering through the curtains as they emerged from sleep, lying on their sides, she enclosed within the circle of his body, he muttered drowsily in her ear from the depth of the same pillow:

"What was that you said about Ciudad Rodrigo? I was captured there."

Then she told him the whole story, and he learned the extent to which her love for him had taken her. He groaned at the suffering he had inadvertently caused her and she soothed him with gentle words. As he entered the soft, early morning warmth of her, he resolved to himself that somehow he would live through whatever lay ahead and make up to her in the years to come for all she had been through.

After breakfast they went together to see the priest at a little church nearby. Nicolas had taken out the necessary papers upon his arrival in Lyons, knowing that his days in the city would be few. It was arranged that the marriage should take place at eleven-thirty after a short civil ceremony at the Hôtel de Ville. There was the question of witnesses. Gabrielle did not want to upset André by appearing at the Piats' house only to say she was leaving again, and so it was decided that Nicolas's servant and her maid should be the only witnesses.

While Nicolas went to check on final orders for departure at the barracks, she went home to pack what she would need in saddle-bags for the journey, select a horse from the stables and write a note to Hélène with a full and happy explanation. With all this on her mind she flew into the house and was halfway up the stairs when she heard a well-remembered stump of a wooden leg coming from the direction of the kitchen towards the hall. Although her viewpoint was blocked, she called out as she spun around to race down again: "Gaston! Of all people."

He looked extremely spruce in a green brass-buttoned coat. No crutch now, but a stout cane. His normally unruly hair was brushed forward in close imitation of the fashionable quiffs favoured by men of any style, and he had a gold pin in his neat cravat. There was no mistaking his exuberance at seeing her again.

"Madame! I've been trying to find out where you were."

"About to be married! I've found Nicolas again. There has been much sadness in his life and mine, but at last we are to be together. Wish me joy, Gaston! Come and be witness to our wedding. Nobody deserves to be there more than you." Then she drew back, releasing both his hands, which she had clasped, for memories had flooded into his eyes as in hers. She no longer saw any need for pretence. "Would you prefer not to be witness or has time gone by long enough for the past to be forgotten?"

He gave her a shrewd look with something close to a twinkle in it. "I doubt that can ever be, madame. I was with you too long and too closely ever to quite forget those days in the Peninsula. But I'm wed myself now. My Jeanne is a lively creature, full of spirit, and we've a child on the way."

"I'm so glad to hear that. Where is she? Have you brought her with you?"

"No, I left her safely in Cannes. She is linen maid in the colonel's house where we both reside, and soon we're to have a cottage to ourselves." As he spoke the image of his wife came into his mind and he almost smiled. She could not be less like the beautiful woman who had always been beyond his reach, except perhaps for one occasion, although whether that was wishful thinking on his part would never be known. Jeanne was an ample armful with a handsome bosom and a rollicking laugh and had been hard to win, even after he had managed to get his hand up her petticoats. She was in every way the right wife for him. An excellent cook, a splendid bed mate, and there was every reason to believe she would be a good mother. He was as content as any man could be. Any man, that is, who had once cherished in vain a foolish dream and seen it dispelled on a burning night of pillage and horror.

"That's marvellous news. Why are you here then? What has brought you to Lyons?" Then she caught her breath on what the reply might be. "Don't tell me you followed the Emperor from Cannes?"

"I did indeed. All the way to Paris."

How could he not have answered that charismatic beckoning? Some had welcomed the Emperor to Cannes with violets. He and the colonel for whom he worked had unfurled the Tricolore and what a shout the Emperor had made. "The eagle shall fly again, from every belfry along the way to the very towers of Notre Dame!"

So two loyal and retired soldiers had mounted their horses and ridden in the wake of that glorious home-coming. Unfortunately at Grasse, where the road gave way to a steep mountain track, the colonel had had to fall back, but he had urged Gaston to go on. "Don't return until you have reached Paris. The Emperor may have need of your military strength along the way. *Vive l'Empereur!*"

Gaston had witnessed all the touching demonstrations of loyalty en route and cheered with the rest when whole battalions with their officers had joined the swift march towards Paris. Then, once the capital had been reached, he had found himself on his own with nothing to do, the excitement dispelled and the Emperor installed in the Tuileries as if he had never been away. After lingering for a while, Gaston had begun the journey homewards and that was how he had arrived at the house in the Rue Clémont.

"Come with me in a few minutes to the Hôtel de Ville and then to the church," Gabrielle urged him now. "I have no time to spare. Today Nicolas leaves Lyons for Belgium and this time I'm going too. I'll never be parted from him again."

Gaston gave one of his deep chuckles. "Then it seems I couldn't have arrived at a better time. What hour do we depart?"

She raised her eyebrows at him in astonishment. "You would accompany me to war again?"

"For two reasons. First of all, it will be like old times, and secondly, I've a mind to see the Emperor win a great victory once more. What do you say?"

"I shall be glad, my good friend. So very glad."

In the church with its shining altar there was no one else present except the wedding party of the bride and groom and the witnesses. When the ceremony was over and the priest's blessing received, Nicolas and Gabrielle had to part on the church steps. He held her lovingly and kissed her. Then he clapped a hand on Gaston's shoulder.

"Look after my wife for me as you guarded her once before."

"I shall do that, Captain. You may depend on it." It was an easy promise for Gaston to make. Now he was with her again his own wife was all but forgotten, not out of heartlessness, for he loved Jeanne in his own way, but because Gabrielle's spell had been re-cast over him as strong as ever before.

The squadron left the city two hours later, preceded by the regimental band playing a stirring tune. Behind the chasseurs came the wagons and spare horses and the usual motley collection of women and children, Gabrielle and Gaston bringing up the rear of the feminine chatter.

During the ride from Lyons to the Belgian border, the squadron bivouacked at nightfall outside villages. Each time Gabrielle was able to take lodgings in an inn or farmhouse and Nicolas came to her there. They passed the hours in loving, with snatches of sleep, insatiable for each other, the past still too much with them and the future uncertain, although neither of them referred to it, living for the moments they were still able to share.

On the seventeenth of June, on Belgian soil, Gabrielle saw Nicolas's squadron join forces with the Emperor, riding a white mare, and his successful army, which had captured Charleroi and won a battle at Ligny, putting the Prussians to flight and forcing the British to retreat. Thunderstorms and torrential rain descended to soak everyone on the march on the road from Ligny, but nothing could dampen the high spirits of the troops. Once again the Emperor was proving himself invincible. Tomorrow would come a great battle with the British, who had now taken up positions under Wellington's command at Mont Saint Jean, near the village of Waterloo.

That night, when the army halted just south of Mont Saint Jean, the accommodation that Gabrielle secured was in a peasants' cottage. Overhead the unrelenting rain continued to drum on the roof and came dripping through the cracks. The glowing embers on the hearth had long since dried off their clothes, which had become sodden during the day. They were aware only of each other in the deep warmth of the feather bed.

"Since I found you again I have known the happiest hours of my life," Nicolas said tenderly to her as she lay against his shoulder within the circle of his arm. It was time to bring out into the open what he had to say to her before the battle on the morrow. He tilted her face towards his. "If I should not come back—"

"Don't!" A superstitious shiver ran down her spine and she raised herself to lean over him, pressing her finger tips against his lips. She remembered how Jules had spoken to her of death, and now Nicolas had filled her with the same dread that she had been keeping at bay.

Gently he took her wrist and drew her fingers away. "I only want to say that it is my hope that we shall have a child from these hours of loving, because then I shall live on for you, no matter what the outcome may be in the field tomorrow."

She responded fiercely, digging her fingers into his shoulders, her tousled hair hanging down either side of her contorted face to curl against his chest. "There's only one outcome that I'll tolerate! You'll come back to me. Do you hear? I'll never let it be otherwise!"

Her wild gust of passion engulfed him. He seized her by the hips, bringing her on to him, and he was lost again in loving this woman who was everything to him.

He left her at daybreak. She was sleeping and did not feel him go from the bed. Once he thought she would waken when his sabre knocked against a chair as he buckled on the strap, but she only turned slightly on the pillow and snuggled down again. He bent over her to draw back the silky strands of hair lying across her face and kissed her temple. She did not stir. Closing the door quietly behind him, he went down the rickety stairs and out into the dawn light. It had stopped raining on this Sunday morning and already there was the promise of some heat to the day, the air sweet and balmy. His army servant was waiting with his mount and he swung himself into the saddle. As he turned his horse, he saw that Gaston had come from other quarters to wait by the gate. The fellow saluted him as he rode through.

"Good luck, Captain."

Nicolas acknowledged the salute and cantered away along the leafy lane that was liquid mud from all the rain. The first sun-rays flickered through the trees, gleaming on his high boots, giving an aura to the red and green plume in his hat and stroking the rich leopardskin of the saddle-cloth spread across the croup of his black horse. Gaston watched him go with a lurch of envy. Today the Emperor was going to wipe Wellington from the field and destroy one of the most formidable bastions that stood against the full renewal of a glorious reign. It was hard not to be taking part.

Beyond the long stretch of woods, Nicolas rode into a hive of activity. Thousands of troops were astir, folding rain-sodden blankets, shivering in uniforms still damp from the previous day, and kneeling on the muddy ground to coax reluctant camp-fires back into life with whatever dry sticks could be found. From those fires already well alight there came the blended aroma of coffee, left-over soup and pungent stew, the smoke curling away into the air. Nicolas reined in. He was gripped by the familiar excitement and dread that settled in the stomach of every soldier, no matter under which flag he was fighting, before the start of any battle. From his vantage point he could see where the Emperor's campaign tent had been pitched in readiness for decisions to be made closer to the area once the British began to draw back again under onslaught. Farther away on the high ground, close to the farm of Rossomme, straw was to be laid underfoot about this present hour to provide a dry carpet for the Emperor on the water-logged ground, for it was from there he would direct the battle.

Nicolas let his gaze, narrowed against the sun's early brilliance, drift beyond the moving throng of his fellow countrymen down the slope of the ridge they covered to the shallow valley, only two and a half miles wide, where the decisive battle would be fought. It lay still and peaceful, the fields of green rye growing high and undulating in a gentle breeze with areas of lush flower-bespeckled meadowland laced across by hedges that were destined to be flattened by advancing feet and trampled under galloping hooves. Birds were singing everywhere; overhead a hawk hovered.

On the far ridge the British were also making ready for the day, their camp-fires smoking, their scarlet jackets bright as blood under the expanding morning sky. He could see a straight-backed officer riding with aides in his wake. It was probably Wellington himself. He was in no present danger from any hidden French snipers on secret reconnoitring. It was not the code of war to kill the opposing side's commander. With spies active from both armies, it was no secret that Wellington had a force of sixty-seven thousand men of various nationalities to put into the field, while the Emperor had the edge with seventy-two thousand.

Despite his experiences in the Peninsula, Nicolas did not have the least doubt of what the outcome would be of the forthcoming battle near the previously unheard-of village of Waterloo. It had nothing to do with the Emperor's few thousand more men. The morale of the army was such that a great French victory was assured and Nicolas, whose sword-arm was totally for France, would not have been anywhere else on this particular morning. What his own fate would be remained veiled to him. If he should never see another dawn, he was thankful for having spent his last night with the woman he loved and for the marvellous sight of these golden hues in the sky, unmarred by clouds, that were giving way to a swiftly rising blue. It was going to be a glorious day. Already the ground was steaming.

He rode on and reached a party of fellow officers of his squadron just as they were about to sit down at a camp-table in the open air. It was spread with a white cloth for a breakfast of cold chicken served with champagne, which had been produced from a hamper brought by an officer newly arrived. Nicolas ate well and drank moderately. It was a light-hearted repast, a shield for each man's serious thoughts. Every one of them knew that the cost of the day would be high. It was unlikely they would enjoy one another's company in a group of this size again.

When Gabrielle awoke she had been alone for more than an hour. A sense of intense loss assailed her as she stretched out a hand and felt the coolness of the bed beside her. She might have lain there a few minutes longer if there had not been the sounds of some kind of commotion in the yard outside. Slipping on a robe, she went to the window and looked out. The family of the cottage were departing, their possessions bundled up in the back of a donkey-cart. One of the children was carrying a cat and another had a dog on a piece of string. Gaston in his shirt-sleeves appeared to have helped with the loading up and now stood watching them go on their way. It was not hard to guess the reason for their hasty departure. They were afraid that artillery fire might reach their cottage or even that the battle might engulf it later in the day, a most unlikely possibility, Gabrielle thought, since the British would never be able to break through the French lines.

Others were also on the move, getting out of range while there was still time. Among the number of fleeing peasants were army women with babies, and most of them had young children hanging on to their skirts. Meeting them from the opposite direction came all kinds of military traffic, from ammunition wagons to riders on army business who always came at a gallop, splattering everyone with mud before they could even get out of the way. Yells of abuse, particularly from the women, followed them as they disappeared into the distance.

Gabrielle watched the passing cavalcade as she washed in a chipped basin from a ewer of cold water. Afterwards she took a blue cotton gown from a saddle-bag, shaking out the creases, and put it on over her petticoats, which had dried by the fire. When she came downstairs, her newly brushed hair pinned into place, Gaston looked at her and quickly looked away again, busying himself in making coffee in the fire-blackened camp-kettle he had brought along. She still had the power to arouse him unexpectedly with her beauty and the sinuous grace of her movements. Old regrets knifed him.

"I can hear the 'Marseillaise,'" she said, listening intently.

He saw she had paused in a patch of sunlight streaming through the window and there were tendrils of gold in her hair. "The Emperor will be reviewing the troops. It's customary before a great battle."

She went to sit down on a bench at the rough board-table where he had set out a breakfast for her. Freshly boiled speckled brown eggs that must have come from the peasants' hens, coarse black bread from the cottage larder, some sliced meat and a hunk of cheese. As before on her army marches in the Peninsula, she was eating food such as she would never have been able to face in the breakfast-room of her own home. She had little appetite that morning, her thoughts too full of what the day would bring, but she ate doggedly, needing to take nourishment to sustain her through what she had planned for the hours ahead.

"What time do you think the fighting will begin?" she asked, tapping an egg with a spoon.

"My guess is not for two or three hours yet." He had eaten soon after dawn, but after filling her cup with coffee he poured a cup for himself and seated himself opposite her, the table between them. "It's no use trying to do battle until the ground has had a chance to dry out. In its present state horses and men would slither about in the mud and fall in all directions, while the guns would be completely bogged down. I've seen it happen before when those in command have had no choice, or been too inexperienced to realise what would happen. The Emperor will strike when the time is right, never fear."

"What about the family whose home we are in? Did you pay them for our accommodation?"

"Captain Devaux did that. He told them we should need the rooms for another night and paid in advance."

"I'm surprised that didn't make them decide to stay. Surely they realised that he wouldn't have paid if he hadn't expected the cottage to be still standing when the battle is won."

"I said the same thing to them. They wouldn't listen. The sight of their neighbours clearing out made them panic. You'll be safe enough here."

"I'm not sitting around here for hours twiddling my thumbs," she stated emphatically. "I'm going to one of the field hospitals. I met several of the major-surgeons during a halt on the march yesterday and offered my assistance. It was accepted."

Gaston blinked slowly, although he did not take his eyes from her. "You'll need a strong stomach," he warned phlegmatically.

Her face set grimly. "After what I saw at Ciudad Rodrigo, I have the stomach for anything."

He could not argue with that.

They covered the distance on foot to where the field hospitals had been set up, the traditional black flag flying above them to denote the site to friend and foe alike. The tents had been erected at the edge of a wood where trees would give some protection against rogue shellfire, while at the same time the site was within reasonable access to the battlefield. Since it needed four to six men, and sometimes eight, to carry a wounded man from the battlefield, many officers on the eve of a vital battle gave orders that if they fell during the fighting they were to be left where they lay until the battle was over. It was Gaston's guess that Nicolas Devaux would have given that order to his men. He himself had heard it issued many times and guessed it had been the unofficial order of the day on both the British and the French sides. It would cost lives that might otherwise have been saved, but too much depended on this day's outcome for any officer of integrity to put his own life before the slightest hindrance to the victory at stake.

Gabrielle took in the scene as she and Gaston approached. The surgeons were passing the time until they should be needed, not yet in their shirt-sleeves or wearing their leather aprons, sitting about in camp-chairs, talking together, smoking their pipes, reading and dozing.

Within the tents, operating tables had been set up, the fearsome surgical instruments glinting on side tables and ready to be handed to each surgeon by the orderlies in attendance. Outside each tent, rolled blankets, which were for carrying the wounded, had been stacked high in rows like blocks of firewood ready for winter. There were also innumerable barrels of wine ranged on trestles, the opiate and strengthener for those about to face surgery; later, when there was a breathing space, it might also be used for the treatment of wounds. The orderlies, with their authority over the army women who had gathered there to help, were organising some of them in the opening of bundles of clean linen for the binding up of wounds. The rest of the women busied themselves with other tasks or sat around on fallen tree trunks or old sacks, waiting until they should be needed, some smoking pipes themselves, and they turned their heads in curiosity to watch Gabrielle and Gaston making their way across the muddy ground.

Gabrielle paused before she reached the tents and looked towards the valley where the battle would be fought. It lay framed to her view by the foliage of trees on either side of a gap in the wood. In that quiet green hollow over one hundred and forty thousand men would try to kill each other that day, Nicolas among them. What was it in the disposition of men that made them want to rise up and slay the life from each other? Away to her left she could see her countrymen waiting. As yet they were in a state of relaxation—seated, lounging about, sleeping stretched out, playing cards and swapping yarns of previous battles. To the rear, out of her sight beyond that sea of men, were the chasseurs and the rest of the cavalry as well as the reinforcements. Between the regiments, the sullen gleam of cannon showed. Making a bright show to compete with the variety of uniforms were the sharp colours of the standards, each representing the honour of a regiment; some of the bitterest fighting would take place around the standards of both sides in the field, for the capture of these symbols was always a triumph for the captors and had a morale-shattering effect on the losers.

"Come along," Gaston urged, disrupting her train of thought. She gave one glance across at the enemy lines on the distant parallel ridge before following Gaston, who was already stomping ahead; he was eager to offer whatever aid he could give to those in charge.

It turned out that there was no need for haste. The Emperor continued to take his time in letting the ground dry out. Another two hours of steadily mounting tension went by before the drums began to roll, sounding the call to arms. She knew it meant that the whole mass of troops she had seen would be moving forward into battle lines, their playing-cards pocketed, personal mementoes looked at for the last time and tucked away, the fighting ahead filling every man's mind. The surgeons, some of whom had been chatting to Gabrielle, pleased to have had the diversion of her company, began to make a move, discarding jackets, rolling up their sleeves and donning their leather aprons. Orderlies snapped shut the camp-chairs and took them out of the way. One gave Gabrielle a thick canvas apron, such as the other women were wearing, and she tied it on. Gaston had been designated the task of helping with the wounded outside as they arrived, making sure that the most seriously injured casualties had priority over the rest.

Gabrielle went to take her place with the women until she should be called into action and was proud to stand with them. They were all the wives and lovers of men in the field. Although at first some of them regarded her with suspicion, never having seen an officer's wife at the tents before, at least not until the fighting was over, her practical attitude towards what had to be done soon made them forget she was a stranger in their midst.

At exactly half an hour before noon the French cannons opened fire at the Emperor's command with a barrage of such earth-shaking force that after a while several of the women, all hardened campaigners, began to comment on its power, saying they had never heard the like of it before. Gabrielle wondered how the British could withstand such a terrible bombardment. Thick clouds of smoke from the cannonade drifted across the tree-tops and over the black flag. Word came that fierce fighting was taking place for the capture of the château of Hougoumont, an outpost of the British line, but the first casualties to come through the gap in the woods were soldiers hit by stray round shot from enemy guns, seven having been knocked from their feet by a single one of these iron balls bouncing across the ground and shattering their legs as it ploughed through them, just as Gabrielle had witnessed in the Peninsula campaign. Distressed, she watched them carried into the tents. Then one of the surgeons hailed her.

"Madame Devaux! Prepare for bandaging!"

"I'm coming, Major Arnoul!"

He had said she should be in his tent and she grabbed up her basket of clean linen to take her place there. It was her initiation. She saw it all. The orderlies tipping wine into the mouths of the groaning men on the tables, the flowing blood, the bones showing through torn flesh like ivory spillikins, and the holding down as the saws rasped through good bone to be rid of what could never be made whole again. When the time came for her to pad and bind and bandage her first patient, she and an orderly worked together, although he told her that later she would be on her own.

"It usually starts like this," he said casually. "A trickle of wounded followed by a river and then a raging torrent. You'll see."

The courage of the patient they were binding up amazed her. He had gritted his teeth, his eyes wild with pain, and yet he had managed a joke. "You gave me a fright, madame. I thought you were an angel and I was in heaven already."

She went with him when he was carried through to the tent on a litter-blanket to one of the hundreds of trestle beds set up. Before long he would be conveyed by one of the waiting wagons back down the road to France, leaving his place free for the next man. The Emperor had made many changes to the army in his time and one of the best acts, in Gabrielle's opinion, was his insistence on the greatest possible care of the wounded, whether they were his own or those of the enemy.

The French cannonade stopped as abruptly as it had begun, giving way to the drumming of the *pas de charge*. On her way to replenish her linen basket, Gabrielle paused to look down through the gap in the woods towards the valley. At first she could see nothing. The blue-grey smoke from the guns was lying like low clouds. Then, as it eddied, she caught a glimpse of wide columns of French infantry, marching shoulder to shoulder with at least one hundred and fifty men in each straight rank, flanked by cavalry and advancing with that threatening drumming across the valley towards the British ridge. From that distance they looked like set after set of a child's toy soldiers ranged rigidly in their formations as if on a parade ground. Then the smoke closed again and she hurried on to carry out her task.

When the opposing forces met, the noise of the battle resounded in musket- and rifle-fire, shouts and yells, the booming of British cannons, and the screams of men and horses alike as the killing went on. The river of wounded began to flow in through the trees. They brought extraordinary news. The columns had been beaten back by fierce resistance, causing the soldiers to fall back on each other and trample their own comrades underfoot in their retreat.

A mad charge of the Scots Greys and the Blues cavalry over the ridge and down through the fleeing French had created havoc, and although the sabres of the chasseurs and the cuirassiers had diminished the Scotsmen's numbers to a minimum, the loss of life on both sides had been horrific. Both armies were taking a brief respite to regather, although the fighting at the château was still going on. Gabrielle, sighting a chasseur with a slashed arm, hurried across to ask him if he knew and if he had seen Nicolas. He nodded, holding his arm to ease the pain, his face chalk-white.

"He had three horses shot from under him. Each time he grabbed a riderless one in the field and remounted. Don't worry, madame. He was very much alive when I last saw him and taking full toll of the enemy."

Major Arnoul's roar broke in on her. "Your place is at my table and nowhere else, Madame Devaux!"

She darted back. He was stitching up an unconscious man. It was the only method for internal damage since there was no time for lengthy investigation. "I was making enquiries about my husband," she explained hastily.

He glared at her, although he was not entirely unsympathetic. "Time enough for that when the battle is over. The wounded need you now."

The dressing of wounds was no longer done on any of the operating tables, for the space on them was too much in demand. Outside the tents a carpet of wounded was stretching out increasingly on all sides. As soon as each surgeon had completed his work the patient was lifted by orderlies onto a bandaging table and it was at one of these that Gabrielle worked. She was on her own now as the orderly had told her she would be, although one of the other women came to help her whenever she needed an extra pair of hands.

The courage of the wounded continued to hold her admiration. They wanted their smashed limbs lopped off quickly, having a fear of being patched up and gangrene setting in. They boasted of the good colour of their blood, and suffered the gouging out of bullets by a surgeon's probe, and sometimes his fingers, with a cheerful bravado that was belied by their ashen faces and grimaces of agony that they could not control. It seemed to be an unwritten law that they should be as brave under the surgeon's instruments as they had been on the battlefield, although for many whose wounds were beyond medical aid screams could not be held back and their suffering was harrowing. There were times when Gabrielle worked with tears running down her face, and over and over again she saw a surgeon stop what he was doing as a man died on his table.

As the day went on a picture of the battle continued to be built up. The British infantry and artillery had suffered heavy losses and were pressed back into a defensive position once more, the French again at a strong advantage. By late afternoon Gabrielle had lost all sense of time. She was soaked in blood from head to foot like everyone else in those gory tents, and splashes of it had dried hard on her hair. One of the women, bringing a fresh supply of linen, told her that a massive French cavalry charge was taking place. Twelve thousand horsemen led by Marshal Ney had thundered down the valley and over the British ridge. The battle was almost won. She nodded, pushed a strand of hair back out of her eyes and uttered a silent prayer for Nicolas as she continued to bind up a terrible bayonet wound that Major Arnoul had stitched up.

More good news came. Although the cavalry had been forced to charge again and again, some thought as many as twelve times, the defensive squares of the British had been diminished and the whole enemy thrown into disaster through the capture by French infantry of the farmhouse of La Haye Sainte, which was located at a vital point. What was more, a whole battalion of Germans allied to the British had been wiped out, weakening the line to breaking point. Wellington's hours were numbered. Everyone was waiting for the Emperor to deliver the final blow.

Again Gabrielle acknowledged the news and worked on. The sun was beginning to set. She looked up once after that. An orderly appeared in the entrance of the tent and shouted out what he had just heard, electrifying everybody there.

"The Emperor has sent in the Garde Impérial!"

The cream of the whole army! The Emperor's chosen men! All day they had been held in reserve. Now they would wipe out everything in their path. Gabrielle sighed with thankfulness that the end of the battle was in sight, and she exchanged a smile with the man on the table whose thigh she was dressing after the prising out of a bullet.

"So the day is ours," she said to him.

"I never doubted it would be, madame."

Lanterns were lit in the tent to aid the fading daylight. Outside the tent the wounded waiting for treatment covered every inch of the ground except where narrow paths had been left for access between the tents and the stores. Through the gap in the woods the torrent of casualties that had developed early in the afternoon was increasing all the time. It was difficult to know where to place them. Although none of the surgeons had paused in his work, some of the wounded had been waiting several hours for treatment, the groans of many unceasing. Cries for water were constant, and Gaston had joined the women going from man to man putting cups to parched lips.

All these wounded could count themselves as the fortunate ones, for lying in the valley were thousands of their comrades similarly wounded, who could not be reached in the fighting that had been waged there all day. Half hidden in the rye, sprawled in mud, almost buried under bodies, they were trampled by the running feet of the infantry and galloped over by the cavalry. Some struggled weakly to find a place out of the fray. Nicolas was among those unable to move.

He had no clear recollection of being wounded. Vague images came into his mind between the bouts of dizziness that swept him periodically into unconsciousness. At times the regimental standard seemed to flutter its brilliance against his eyes, which he had to keep closed against the searing pain in his head. Sometimes he believed he was hacking and parrying and thrusting and yelling again, protecting the standard he had seized from a dying man, but he could not be sure. Everything was muddled and confused.

Oddly he could recall the shout of an English voice. "Spare him! Such courage deserves it!" That conjured up an image of looking death full in the face in the shape of an upraised sabre. Perhaps that enemy officer's shout had saved his head being sliced from his neck. He would never know now. His life-blood was flowing out of his wounds and his strength was ebbing. At times his mind felt curiously divorced from his body as though his thoughts were suspended above the prone figure lying face downwards in the muddy carnage of dead horses and men. It was as if his body were an entity of unbearable pain on its own and from which he would be free.

Beneath him the earth began to tremble again, coinciding with one of the brief lucid spells that still came periodically. The shaking of the ground was caused by something more than the ceaseless artillery barrage and the constant roar of musketry and rifle fire that seemed to have resurged to a new climax and had been an integral part of this day. Another cavalry charge was on the way. Was it two or three times he had been ridden over where he lay? To add to his wounds, the thundering hooves had crushed his right hand and snapped his arm like a twig. Out of the corner of his eye he had glimpsed the bellies of the warhorses flashing over him, the glint of spurs and the swirling of gilt-trimmed saddle-cloths. Now they were coming again, his own countrymen to all unknowingly trample him still deeper into the mud and slime and blood of this horrific battlefield.

With effort he opened his eyes. The sky had become the rich orange of sunset. In its splendid light the horsemen were coming at full pelt and in their wake thousands of running foot-soldiers, the brass cap-plates on their bearskins flashing the sun's late brilliance as they came. Recognition dawned. It was the Garde Impérial, the Emperor's elite, finally thrown in to smash those seemingly impenetrable British lines and take the glory of the day. A twinge of something close to wry humour stirred in him. Yet what was it amiss that his pain-wearied brain was unable to define? Where was the reed-like piping of the "Marseillaise" that accompanied an advance and the beat of drums? He could not concentrate on the matter. It was taking all his effort to slowly draw up his uninjured arm to protect his head.

The charge swept over him with crashing hooves and pounding boots and shouts and yells. He did not know if he screamed out or if it had been contained within him as he was knocked this way and the other before he slipped into the sanctuary of oblivion once more.

When he parted his bruised lids again the evening had almost taken over from the deeper, last-minute hues of sunset. Everything lay in the hushed aftermath that always comes at the end of a battle when the guns are still at last, creating a quietness that overlies even the shrieks and groans of the wounded. Again what he had seen of the last charge returned to disturb and puzzle him. Gradually his mind cleared and it came to his realisation that it had not been an advance that had passed over him but a retreat. An ignominious rout. That was what had lodged in his thoughts about the direction of the mounted officers and the infantry in relation to the sunset. They had been coming south away from the British lines. The Garde Impérial had broken and fled before some final strategic attack of Wellington's that, in spite of all odds, had won the day. As if to confirm his conclusion, the sound of cheering came echoing from the British ridge.

A great yell of rage and disappointment welled up in his throat, giving him the superhuman strength to rise up to his feet with it, a swaying, half-broken figure in the sunset's blood-red glow.

"No!" he bellowed, crazed beyond reason. "*Vive la France!*"

He staggered forward and fell against an abandoned drum, his weight propelling it away from him, tassels swinging. Lying helpless, there was a fixed urge in his mind to command the army back into battle lines. A shadow fell across him. Looking up, he saw a tired, riderless horse, flecked with dried foam, caked with blood and mud, standing by. It had probably lost its horseman hours ago and had been drawn now to the sight of a man on his feet.

He knew he was past getting up again, but he lifted himself enough to loop his good hand through the stirrup and hold on. White-hot pain seared into his brain as the horse began to trot forward and he lost consciousness. His hand would have slipped free immediately if the thick gilt ornamentation on his sleeve, loosened by a tear, had not jammed securely for a considerable distance before it finally gave and he fell with a thud face downwards and lay motionless.

The evening darkened and the stars came out. He opened his eyes once and saw garlands of red and blue flowers glowing about him in the pale moonlight. It was silk. Under and around him like a rich tumbled carpet. He knew it. It was the silk his looms had woven for the Emperor's tent, which now lay on the ground, knocked over and trampled into the mud by a fleeing army. He and Gabrielle had almost come together for the first time in the midst of these garlands. Now this Devaux silk was to be his shroud.

He closed his eyes slowly, feeling his strength go. He thought he heard her voice and tried to speak her name. It only came into his mind. *Gabrielle.*

In the surgeons' tents the work went on. The lights in the tents were attracting moths, which caused fluttering shadows to dance here and there. Gabrielle, finished with one patient, turned for the next and saw Major Arnoul, his face as exhausted as hers must be, standing by her.

"You've done enough," he said quietly. "It's time for you to give in now."

Something in his expression held back the protest she would have uttered. "What has happened?" she asked fearfully.

"I think it best that you hear it from someone you have known longer than I." He indicated Gaston, who stood in the tent's entrance, waiting for her. The expression on his drawn face confirmed her fears.

Wordlessly, she removed her apron and went towards him. He put an arm around her and she looked at him searchingly. She seemed to have lost the power of speech.

"I have had it confirmed from five different sources," he told her huskily. "I wouldn't alarm you after hearing it the first time, knowing that mistakes can be made. Now I know that there's no error and it's true. Captain Devaux is dead. In the midst of one of the great cavalry charges he was badly wounded protecting the standard, and although he handed it over and went on towards the British lines, he fell almost at once from the musket fire."

She nodded starkly to show she had grasped all she had heard. Together they left the tent, his arm still about her, and walked down through the paths of wounded into the woods and along the leafy lane that took them to the peasants' cottage. The owners were still absent. He sat her down in a kitchen chair and fetched a bowl of water. Then he washed the smudges of dried blood from her face and neck as though she were a child in his care and bathed her hands and arms clean, changing the water several times. Afterwards he took the pins from her hair and sponged the dried blood from it so that it hung damp and gleaming down her back.

"Now," he said, raising her up from the chair by her elbows, "go upstairs and change out of that soiled gown while I get a fire going. The evening is turning chill."

At the foot of the stairs she paused to look back over her shoulder at him. "I'm going to find his body and take him home to Lyons. He shall not be buried in foreign soil."

Long experience had taught him to know when her mind was made up. While she changed her garments upstairs, he checked the pair of pistols in his belt and made sure he had plenty of ammunition. He knew what a battlefield was like when darkness fell. Looters from the local peasantry always moved in and many did not hesitate to murder the wounded, or fellow felons, or anyone else if contested for a purse or other valuables.

When she came downstairs she was simply and warmly dressed, a shawl about her shoulders, her hair repinned. He had found a couple of lanterns and lit them. She took one from him and together they went out into the darkness. They harnessed one of their horses to a light farm cart from the peasants' barn and drove to the place where earlier that day there had been the vast spread of men waiting to move into their battle lines. It was deserted now. Nothing remained but abandoned cannons and other weaponry, the earth so churned up by thousands of feet, it looked as though grass might never grow there again. Their horse became alarmed, scenting death, and Gaston dealt with it harshly through necessity, using the whip to force it on. The cart had to be within reasonable access when their mission was fulfilled, for neither he, with his disability, nor Gabrielle, in her state of shock and exhaustion, would be able to carry Nicolas's body far. By some trees he brought the horse to a halt and fastened it securely before he and Gabrielle set off with the lanterns on their search.

There were other lights bobbing in the distance all over the valley, some in the hands of women looking for fallen menfolk, others held by those engaged in bringing in the wounded, who were groaning and calling out in the darkness. There was no silence in the valley. It was as if the earth itself were in death throes with the eerie terrible sounds. Now and again a pistol shot rang out as a suffering horse was put out of its agony by the rescuers of the wounded.

The dead of both sides lay everywhere. Some appeared untouched, as if they were asleep or gazing at the stars, until it was seen that half their bodies were shot away by cannon fire. The lanterns' glow passed over many awful sights. Most heart-rending to Gabrielle were the pleas of the wounded for water. Gaston had had the foresight to bring four full canteens with him, and he and Gabrielle paused to give drinks to French and British alike. Some of the wounded clutched at her skirts, begging not to be left, for many of them had been robbed already and feared that the next looters to come would slit their throats for having nothing. It was terrible to leave them and to hear some break down into sobs. Whenever possible, Gaston salvaged a pistol from a dead soldier nearby and left them some protection.

There were plenty of looters in the darkness. They moved about easily, being familiar with the terrain, and scuttled away like rats when Gaston, enraged, roared at them, firing one of his own pistols in their direction. Frequently they spilled their loot from their full pockets and sacks on the way in their haste. A gold fob watch and the miniature of a young woman set in pearls came scattering into Gabrielle's path on one occasion.

The search for Nicolas went on for hours. The canteens were

empty and there was nothing left to give as they went on shining their lanterns, hoping for the sight of a chasseur's green jacket. Among the dead in a hollow they came across a *cantinière*, her spirit keg smashed but still held by its strap across her shoulder. Gaston took out his handkerchief, unfolded it and laid it across her face. No one knew better than he how courageous these women were as they darted in and out of the eddying gun-smoke with their tin cups of cognac to wet a man's whistle, always as proud of their regimental colours as the soldiers themselves, quick to cheer on and encourage at the darkest moments of battle. This woman had been pretty, too. He was inordinately saddened. Supporting himself on his cane, he stumped after Gabrielle again and their weary search for Nicolas went on.

It was dawn when they found him. The rising sun picked out a gleam of grey silk with a figure in dark green sprawled across it. A cry burst from Gabrielle's throat as she sighted him, knowing instinctively that their search was at an end.

"There!"

She ran to him, stumbling and dodging and leaping over obstacles, Gaston following as speedily as he could. Flinging herself down on her knees beside Nicolas, her tears coming at last, she drew his head gently into her lap and bent over him, rocking in her grief. "My darling. My love. My life." Then under her finger tips she felt a faint pulse beating in his neck. "Merciful God!" she breathed incredulously. Then she reared up where she knelt to throw her head back and call with such hysterical joy to Gaston that he thought for a moment she was temporarily out of her mind. "Come quickly! He is alive!"

Gaston thumped down on the knee of his good leg and dived a hand under Nicolas to reach inside his jacket and feel his heart. "Only just," he said heavily, forewarning her.

She thrust her desperate face forward, her jaw set. "I'm going to keep him alive!"

He held back his own conviction that there was no hope. "Let's make a litter of this silk then, and carry him to the cart."

Taking a knife from his belt, he cut the amount that was needed. Since Nicolas was already on the roughly shaped rectangle they had only to turn him gently onto his back to ensure that he would be as comfortable as possible. Gaston knotted each end of the fabric to make a gigantic sling, putting one loop across his own body and giving the other to Gabrielle. Then began the arduous task of hauling Nicolas to the cart. Sometimes he was dragged and at others swung wildly as they struggled and stumbled along. Getting him into the cart was eased by Gaston rounding up two looters at pistol point to help in the lifting, after which he made them run ahead of the horse to be at hand at the cottage to bear the wounded man upstairs.

As soon as he had booted them off the premises, he returned to the upper room where Nicolas lay with eyes closed on the bed as though dead already while Gabrielle cut away his uniform. Checking, he found that a pulse was still there. "I'll fetch one of the surgeons from the field hospital."

"No!" Her face bore the same resolute expression he had seen earlier. "There's nothing any one of them could do for Nicolas that you and I can't do better in the circumstances. I saw enough in those tents to know that they would cut off his poor broken hand and stitch him up with less care than I should use. In any case, they have enough to do. Get me some hot water and plenty of wine and bring me my saddle-bag —I've some clean linen in there. After that, build up the fire. He must be kept warm."

He obeyed her without question. Then he helped her with everything she did for the patient. Together they set his broken limbs with splints, even his fingers. She gouged grape-shot out of his flesh with a spoon and stitched without flinching at the gruesome task while Gaston held the lips of a sabre slash together. When all that could be done had been done, she dripped warm wine over the wounds, a process that was to continue for days. Nicolas was highly feverish, his thirst insatiable, and his delirious mumblings were frequently broken by screams of pain. Gabrielle showed no emotion. She seemed possessed to the exclusion of all else by her will that he should live. White-faced, shadows under her eyes dark as bruises, she looked to Gaston's mind as near death as the man on the bed. Yet she never slumped or showed sign of fatigue, sleeping only when he touched her on the shoulder as a reminder that it was his turn to keep vigil, and she ate whatever food he brought her without knowing what it was.

Downstairs the peasants had returned home and were resentful at finding one of the defeated French still under their roof. Gaston, given a purse by Gabrielle, changed their attitude with a handsome payment, and as a result the wife and the grandmother both prepared whatever light and nourishing concoctions that she wanted for her charge. At first it was only a spoonful trickled into his mouth. Then two or three. Gradually his fever began to subside. The day came when recognition dawned in his sunken eyes and he knew the face of the woman by his bed.

"I thought you were here," he whispered, knowing nothing of the time that had elapsed since he had sensed her with him when he lay on the silken spread of a wrecked tent.

"Yes, my darling." She leaned forward to kiss his forehead, choked with emotional relief. "It won't be long now before we'll be able to go home."

It still took a number of weeks. As soon as it was safe to move him they travelled as far as a small town just inside the French border where Gaston had rented some comfortable accommodation in advance. It was still too soon to make the long journey to Lyons. After a further period of convalesence, during which Nicolas put on weight and was able to walk again without the support of an arm, it was decided that they should cover the last lap. It was then that Gaston said goodbye, first to Nicolas, and then to Gabrielle on her own.

"You have Captain Devaux now," he said to her. "I don't suppose you'll ever need me to escort you anywhere again, but remember, if you do, I'll come at once."

Her eyes were full. "No one has ever had such a friend as I have had in you."

"I have been the privileged one." Then he took a chance, pulling her suddenly into his arms and devouring her mouth with a lusty kiss that was totally unrestrained. She did not make the least attempt to move away. Slowly he released her. "*Adieu*, Gabrielle. Don't forget me."

She gave him a long look that he was to remember all his life. "I'll never forget you, my friend. May God go with you."

He mounted his horse and waved to her as he rode away, smiling to himself. It had been a satisfactory farewell. He had not let a chance slip by as he had done on the eve of Ciudad Rodrigo. The time for pondering what that outcome might have been was over and all regrets must be put aside. It was unlikely he would ever see her again. Now he was going home.

Not long after Gaston's departure Gabrielle and Nicolas came back to Lyons by way of Fourvière. It had been her suggestion that they should see it again from her favourite viewpoint. Even though she was joyfully impatient to see her little son again, she stopped the carriage at the spot she had always liked best, alighting first to run forward and look out eagerly across the city.

"Look! How clear everything is today. See those ripples in the wake of that boat down there on the Saône."

He had followed more slowly to reach her side. Pain was still with him and would be for months, even years to come, and his right hand would never be mobile again. None of that held the importance that it would have done in the past. He had survived one of the greatest battles ever fought and could look forward to the years ahead with the woman he loved. To add zest to their living, she was going to continue to produce Maison Roche silk until her son was of an age to take over, while he himself was to build Maison Devaux up from scratch again. They would be business rivals, lovers and partners. He foresaw a tumultuous and passionate existence. Their marriage would never be dull, and if recent signs proved to be right, it would be fruitful, too.

"It's a fine sight," he agreed, putting his arm around her. As always, she responded instantly, drawing closer to him. Pointing with his cane across the river, he indicated a large plot of land that was up for sale. "That would make a good site for Maison Devaux down there on the quayside."

"I agree. There's still the question of where our new home should be." They had decided between them that the Rue Clémont house should be closed up and kept in order until André was of age. They themselves would build a new residence.

He smiled broadly, turning her to him. "I think that was settled a long time ago when you told me of marking out a place here on these slopes with a piece of Roman pottery."

"So you have always remembered that." She was deeply moved, putting her hand lovingly against his face, and he covered it with his own.

Then together they looked out again towards the mellow vista of roofs and glinting spires and lush tree-tops and gleaming water that would be theirs for the rest of their lives. She drew it into herself as though it were the air she breathed. Lyons. Her beloved city.